"Are you in trouble, lass?"

Lady Maura shook her head. "No," she said quietly.

Dugan came close enough to touch her. The top of her head barely met his shoulder, and he could not resist reaching out to feel the texture of one of her soft curls.

"A woman as lovely as you should have naught to worry about."

She frowned as she looked up at him, and he could not resist sliding his hand down to cup her jaw. Her cheek was so smooth, he ran his thumb across it as he thought about tasting her. Just one kiss, though, 'twould not be nearly enough to satisfy his burgeoning arousal.

She shivered and closed her eyes. "As lovely? As much trouble, you must mean."

"Are you trouble, Lady Maura?" he asked quietly, tipping his head down toward hers.

"Aye. Trouble to all who know me."

Duncan had an urge to discover exactly how much trouble she could bring him. And he intended to start with a kiss . . .

Romances by **Margo Maguire**

THE WARRIOR LAIRD
BRAZEN
SEDUCING THE GOVERNESS
THE ROGUE PRINCE
TAKEN BY THE LAIRD
WILD
TEMPTATION OF THE WARRIOR
A WARRIOR'S TAKING
THE PERFECT SEDUCTION
THE BRIDE HUNT

Margo Maguire

The Warrior Laird

AVON
An Imprint of HarperCollinsPublishers

AVON BOOKS
An Imprint of HarperCollins*Publishers*
10 East 53rd Street
New York, New York 10022-5299

First Avon Books mass market printing: August 2012

As always, this book is dedicated to my gang—Mike, Julia, Joe, and Michael. You guys are the best!

Acknowledgments

Many thanks to my agent, Paige Wheeler, for her quiet guidance right when I need it, and to Amanda Bergeron, my astute Avon editor, for her perceptive critiques of my work, and all her helpful suggestions.

The Warrior Laird

Prologue

Glencoe, Scotland. February 13, 1692.

It was nearly dawn, not quite time for six-year-old Dugan MacIain to crawl out of the bed he shared with his brothers. But he was awakened by his mother's urgent whisper to his father.

"Gavin, something is wrong. 'Tis just as old Sorcha said—the eerie quiet on a winter's morn."

The hair at the back of Dugan's neck prickled. The village seer and her strange utterings never failed to frighten him, though neither he nor anyone else understood them. He heard the steady breathing of his brothers, Gordon, Robert, and Lachann. He knew his infant sister, Alexandra, must still be asleep between his parents in the bed they shared, else she would be squalling and demanding to be fed.

An ominous stillness came over the croft, and Dugan sensed something in the air, though he knew not what. His father slipped soundlessly out of bed and started to pull on his clothes.

Dugan crawled over seven-year-old Gordon and crept across the one-room croft to his father.

"Da?" he whispered. "What is it?"

"Dugan, lad," he murmured. "Wake Gordon, and the two of you get yerselves and yer brothers dressed. I do'na know what it is, but yer ma is never wrong . . . I want ye ready in case . . ."

Their family slept alone in the house, unlike most of the other members of the MacIain clan. Laird Argyll's soldiers were billeted with nearly all the other families. To Dugan's young mind, they'd been staying at Glencoe for a very long time, eating Glencoe food, drinking Glencoe ale, and sleeping in homes that were already crowded.

The soldiers wandered at will among the crofts and in the glen, their coats as red as blood, their boots shining like the black obsidian handle of his father's small dagger, the *sgian dubh*.

Dugan had heard his father mutter disparagingly of the Sassenachs in their midst. His hatred and resentment of the men who would destroy their highland ways was clear to anyone who heard him, but he was as powerless as the laird to do anything about it.

Dugan woke Gordon and whispered their father's instructions. "What, Dugan?" Gordon asked, rubbing his eyes. "What is amiss?"

Dugan shook his head as he roused his younger brothers and admonished them to be silent. "Da says 'tis a game," he whispered to them. "The quietest one will win a prize."

Excitement flared in Robert's eyes, but two-year-old Lachann frowned, his expression wary. He was far cannier than any wee lad his age ought to be. His ma said he had auld eyes. "Da?"

Gavin came to his youngest son and lifted him into his arms. "Be a good lad now, Lachann, and do as yer brother says." He gave him a quick kiss on his forehead before setting him on his feet.

Wee Alexandra gave out one short cry, and Dugan's mother put her quickly to her breast to quiet her.

"Make haste, Dugan," his father whispered. He slid his sword into his belt and turned to his wife, leaning down to plant a quick kiss on her mouth and then the top of Alexandra's wee downy head. The infant was a mere eight months old, and even Dugan could see that his mother was rounding again with yet another bairn.

Gavin started for the door of the croft. "Stay here and stay quiet. I'll be back as soon as I know what's afoot."

Dugan's mother kept Alexandra in her arms as she slipped awkwardly from the bed and pulled a heavy woolen shawl about her shoulders. "Dugan, take yer sister."

Dugan did as he was told and bounced Alexandra in his arms while his mother dressed Lachann. She wrapped each of her sons in their thick woolen plaids, and let out a startled cry when the first gunshot sounded. She gathered Lachann into her arms and stood trembling as Gordon ran to the door and darted out, screaming "Da!" as the second shot rang out.

Dugan put Alexandra on the bed and followed right behind his brother. He saw Sassenach soldiers crouched everywhere, their rifles at their shoulders, shooting at will. Some of the crofts were on fire, and people were running out of them, crying out and clutching their meager blankets 'round their nightclothes.

One of the Sassenach soldiers strode out of Laird

Glencoe's croft, reloading his rifle. Dugan's father drew his sword, but yet another shot sounded and Gavin MacIain fell.

A jolt of pure horror burst through Dugan, and he stood frozen in place, watching as his father's blood stained the snow on the ground. His stomach roiled and he turned away just as Gordon made a mad dash toward their father.

"No!" Dugan screamed for Gordon to stop, but his brother did not listen, running directly into the line of fire.

"Dugan!" his mother cried out, jerking him back into the house so he could not see. She clutched at the doorjamb as shots rang out. Her face drained of color and Dugan knew the worst had happened.

"Ma!" he screamed.

His mother crumpled to the floor in a dead faint. His wee brothers were crying, and Dugan smelled smoke—not the usual kind from the fireplace, and not from outside. He looked up, and his terror increased tenfold.

Dugan dropped to his knees and started shaking his mother's shoulders. "Ma! The thatching is on fire!"

They had to get out, but even young Dugan knew they could not escape through the door. He could still hear gunfire, and was afraid they would be killed if they went that way, just like the others.

"Ma!" he cried, weeping like a wee bairn. "We've got to get out!"

He felt doom in his bones. They were going to burn, or be shot. Surely they had no chance at all unless his mother came awake and took them . . . somehow got them away.

He ran to the largest window and shoved a chair

beneath it. Climbing up, he pushed the shutters open and looked outside. No one was there. 'Twas safe. He could climb out. He could run far away from the soldiers, from the death and destruction in the village.

But he could not leave his brothers, could not leave his ma and Alexandra to burn.

He climbed down from the chair, hastened past his crying brothers to the cistern, and filled a ladle with water. He carried it carefully back to his mother, and though he knew what he was about to do was cruel, there was no time to waste. He tossed the water on her face and she sat up quickly, sputtering.

The room was filling with smoke, and there was even more gunfire than before. "Ma! The roof is afire! We must get out!"

She grabbed him and pulled him close, then took a deep, shuddering breath. "Aye. Come!"

Her tears did not abate, but she managed to pick up Alexandra and put the bairn in Dugan's arms. "Hand her to me after I've climbed out, lad. Then help Lachann and Robert onto the chair and out the window."

"Aye, Ma."

He got Lachann out first, then Robert. By the time Dugan made the climb through the window, there was no air left in the croft to breathe.

The sun was just barely up, and Dugan tried in vain to shut out the sound of screams as what remained of his family kept to the shadows and headed for the hills that ringed the glen.

Chapter 1

Braemore Keep, the Scottish Highlands.
Late March 1717.

"**E**vict us?" Dugan MacMillan drew his claymore from his belt and placed the tip at the throat of Argyll's lackey, Major Donal Ferguson. "You can take the duke's order right back to him and shove it up his arse!" he growled.

It had already been a long, hard winter, and now this. What more could the whoreson Campbells do to him, do to the MacMillan sept?

Ferguson broke a sweat, even though he had to know Dugan could not risk killing one of the duke's agents, not without bringing down the wrath of Argyll himself.

"You do not want to do this, MacMillan," the man said, boldly pushing the blade aside.

Ach, aye, he did. Dugan would have liked nothing more than to run the bastard through. But he had become laird of this clan upon the death of his beloved grandfather, the man who'd taken in him and his brothers and sister and raised them after the massacre at Glencoe. He had to think of the good of his clan. "Argyll cannot evict us from our own lands."

"Aye, he can," said the Scot who was no better than a traitor in Dugan's eyes. He was a Sassenach soldier, no different from those who'd slaughtered his father and Gordon. The same as the ones who'd forced so many MacIains into the mountains to die in the raw winter weather, including his mother and her unborn bairn. And he'd come with a full contingent of Argyll's men. If Dugan committed the slightest act of aggression, he had no doubt the soldiers would retaliate savagely. "The Duke of Argyll owns this land," Ferguson said with a smirk, "and he has decided to use it. For his own purposes."

Dugan was well armed and well trained, and he'd seen to it that his men were, too. They drilled and engaged in mock battles until their hands were blistered and their bodies bruised. But Dugan would not risk a battle here, where Argyll's men could quickly scatter and slay unsuspecting members of his clan.

He now knew the soldiers at Glencoe had been members of Argyll's regiment, and had followed orders from the Master of Stair—and other powerful noblemen who'd decided to make an example of Laird Glencoe to the rest of the highlands. Comply or die.

Dugan wanted the duke's soldiers gone before an incident like the horror he'd experienced at his childhood home could take place once again.

He stood with his legs planted solidly on the timber floor of his grandfather's massive stone keep and slid his sword back into his belt. He folded his brawny arms across his chest. "Get out,

Ferguson," he said, his tone low and lethal. "Leave Braemore now and take your men with you."

"Not until I've finished delivering my message, Laird MacMillan," Ferguson said smugly.

"You've said your piece, now go before I toss you out on your arse."

"The duke commissioned me to inform you that he will accept three thousand pounds, and no less, for these lands—"

Dugan muttered an oath of fury as he charged Ferguson, taking hold of the bastard by the throat and shoving him up against the cold stone wall of the great hall. He was angry enough to squeeze the life out of him. But killing Ferguson would only ignite something beyond his control.

"Your damned duke knows exactly what the MacMillan finances are, Ferguson," he said through gritted teeth. "Go back and tell him—" He abruptly released Ferguson, who swallowed thickly and rubbed his throat.

Good Christ. Dugan had to keep his wits in dealing with Argyll's lackey. This was no way to ensure his clan's safety, though he experienced a moment's satisfaction when he saw the fear in Ferguson's eyes. For just a moment, the man had thought Dugan would kill him with one hand.

Dugan didn't know how he would come up with the money Argyll demanded. A cattle raid would not net them enough funds, and there was no clan rich enough to borrow from. There was naught . . .

Ah, he thought, *but there might be.* 'Twas a gamble, but perhaps . . . "Tell Argyll we'll have an answer for him at month's end."

"There's no answer to give, MacMillan." Ferguson slinked away. "You'll pay the duke his money . . . or be gone by May Day."

"Ach, aye, and where will we go?" Dugan demanded.

Ferguson shrugged as though the fate of more than five hundred MacMillans was of no consequence.

Well, the MacMillan clan mattered to Dugan. He clenched his fists at his sides but remained standing in place, his mind racing as he glowered at the duke's minion. Three thousand pounds was an astronomical sum. 'Twas outrageous.

He and his three siblings had come to Braemore—to their mother's clan—twenty-five years before. His grandfather, the MacMillan laird, had taken them to his heart and raised them, each one, to be leaders of the MacMillans. Dugan had been laird since his grandfather's death a year ago. He could not fail his people now.

As soon as Ferguson said his piece, the man fled the ancient MacMillan hall with as much dignity as he could muster. Dugan barely heard the opening and closing of the thick oak door of the keep, not when all he could think of was riding to the Duke of Argyll's house at Inverness and cleaving the bastard in two. It might even be worth attending his own hanging to do it.

But he was no fool and had no intention of committing suicide. Ending his own life would accomplish naught, though the satisfaction of watching the bastard take his last breath might be well worth it. He had to come up with some way of raising the money Argyll demanded.

He clasped his hands behind his back and had

paced only a few steps before his brother Lachann stormed into the keep. "They've gone, Dugan."

Dugan braced his hands against the mantel and gazed into the peat fire. He did not need to look at his brother, for the younger man was nearly a mirror image of himself. Dark-haired and square-jawed, they were both of a size. Imposing to most, though their middle brother, Robert, towered over them.

Unfortunately, neither Dugan's size nor the heft of his claymore had meant aught to Ferguson. The bastard would have the power of the law—if not the truth—on his side.

The MacMillans were merely tenants on their lands, subject to the whims of Argyll, the man whose father had sanctioned the slaughter of the MacIains at Glencoe. An investigation of the event had gone all the way to the English Parliament, and 'twas a bitter draught to swallow, knowing that none of the actual perpetrators—Captain Campbell and Major Duncanson—had ever been seriously accused or punished. Their actions had been endorsed by the English crown itself.

In Dugan's estimation, the current Duke of Argyll was no better than his sire, nor were any of his Campbell relations.

"What did the bloody bastard want?" Lachann asked. He was restless, as usual, his body taut with pent-up energy.

"Argyll intends to evict us unless we can pay him an exorbitant rent by month's end." He looked up starkly at his brother.

Lachann frowned fiercely, his blue eyes darkening. "How much?"

"Three thousand pounds."

Lachann drew his claymore and started for the door.

"Hold, Lachann."

"And let that slimy bawbag ride unchallenged through our lands?"

"I will not give reason for another massacre, Lachann. We will figure a way out of this."

"Oh, and how do you propose to do that?" his brother demanded. "Because there's so much free land to be had hereabouts?"

"You know there's no free land."

"Aye. Everyone knows it—especially Argyll. Killing the duke and his lackeys would go a long way to easing the grief they cause us." He slid his sword back into his belt and took a seat in a chair by the fire. "What'll we do? I say we rouse the clans and attack Argyll where he sleeps."

"Lachann, think," Dugan said, turning to face his brother. "Open warfare must be our last resort. Argyll has more men and more firepower than our clan will ever have. Unless we rouse all the clans to stand with us, he will mow us down, every man, woman, and child. And you know full well there is no magistrate, laird, or judge who will condemn him."

Dugan's words seemed to shudder through his brother. As young as Lachann was when they'd fled Glencoe, Dugan knew he remembered. How could he—or any of them—forget? Only Alexandra was unaffected by the horrific memories of the morn when their family had been slaughtered, for she'd been too young to understand.

None of them would ever want to bring misfortune to their mother's people—to the clan that had taken them in as orphans and treated them as their own.

This was trouble Dugan did not need. Their cattle herds were just beginning to grow after severe losses during the uprising two years before. He'd spent years training an army of men to protect the livestock—and the clan—from raiders. After his grandfather's death, Dugan had seen to the expansion of their arable lands, which were ready for planting and should show a sizable yield at the end of summer.

He was damned if he'd allow his kin to be put off the lands they'd farmed for generations.

"We could send a party out to Skye," Lachann said, swallowing thickly, "and see if the MacDonalds will take in our clan."

Dugan shook his head and resumed his pacing as his mind raced. "They've no land to spare. Remember when we traveled to Sligachan for Fiona MacDonald's wedding?"

Of course Lachann did. He'd hoped to wed Fiona himself, but she'd chosen Cullen Macauley instead. Dugan believed Lachann had consumed more whiskey than any other guest at that wedding. And his brother was not about to trust another comely face any time soon.

"Mayhap," Lachann said. "But they're kin, after all. And when all this is sorted, we can—"

"No, Lachann. Moving in on the MacDonalds' lands is not the answer. Not even temporarily."

"Well then, what is?" His frustration was palpable, but far less than Robert's would have been. 'Twas fortunate their hotheaded brother was away. "We're not likely to find anyone to loan us three thousand pounds. We'd be hard-pressed to find someone who could lend more than a few shillings."

"We have another option." The highlands had risen up against English rule two years before with the backing and assistance of the French king, who'd sent soldiers as well as funds. 'Twas said they'd hidden a cache of gold somewhere in the highlands.

"Oh aye?" Sarcasm infused his words.

Dugan considered his words carefully. "You remember the map Grandfather gave me before he died?"

"Aye—a worthless scrap of a map," Lachann retorted.

Dugan shook his head.

"Mayhap 'twas a useless scrap of parchment a year ago. But I heard some talk when I was up at Ullapool last month . . ."

"What kind of talk?" Lachann frowned as fiercely as he'd done as a mere bairn. His skepticism was as healthy as ever. Dugan was not about to tell him he'd heard it from a Campbell.

"It seems there's a man in possession of another piece of the map."

"Where?"

"Down east of Fort William—in Kinlochleven."

"Ach, well then. That settles it!" Lachann scoffed. "We find the man, and when we look at his piece of the map, we'll surely know where our bonny King James's loyal Frenchmen hid their stash of gold. Especially if the damned thing is as well marked as Grandfather's."

Dugan narrowed his eyes. Lachann's cynicism could be worse than irritating. True enough, the map showed no place names, and only drawings of lochs and mountains, but Dugan knew there was a way to interpret it. Why else would the French have made the map? "Grandfather was sure it could be read. But only if he found the key to it."

And the former laird, Hamish MacMillan, was no fool.

"Grandfather was riddled with sickness when he died, Dugan. How can you put any stock—"

"Even before he became ill, old Hamish believed the gold could be found. The Frenchman who gave it to him said the map had been torn into quarters and if the four pieces were put together, the way to the gold would be clear."

Lachann rolled his eyes toward the heavy oak beams of the ceiling. "When did he speak to you of this?"

"Two years ago, when I came home wounded in battle during the uprising. He spoke of it often and spent many a night studying the map."

"If he believed so firmly, why did he not go looking for the other parts of the map—or the gold—himself?"

"Because he only had the one piece of the map. And he could not read any clues from it."

"Why didn't he ask the bloody Frenchman where the other parts were?"

"Lachann—"

"You believe you can find the rest of the map in Kinlochleven? And decipher the clues?"

Dugan gave a quick nod, though he was not entirely sure of it. All he knew was that he could not think of any other viable possibility for raising the kind of funds Argyll demanded. Three thousand pounds was an astronomical sum, and no cattle raid on earth would garner that much money.

"Well, then," Lachann said with resignation. "Mayhap a trip to Fort William is in order, eh?"

Chapter 2

Ilay House. Glasgow, Scotland. Early April 1717.

All was quiet in the richly appointed mansion Maura Duncanson had been forced to call home for the past two interminable years. She slipped out of bed and listened at the door for a few moments, just to be sure.

Naught. No sounds of movement could be heard.

Maura crept silently to her dressing table, took a handkerchief from a drawer, then picked up her shawl. Tossing the warm wrapper about her shoulders, she caught a quick glance of her reflection in the mirror.

Her bright red hair was its usual frantic mess, but at least she appeared calm. Far calmer than she felt after reading the callous missive her father had sent her from the family seat at Aucharnie Castle, many miles away near Edinburgh. The moment she'd been waiting for had arrived.

She was going to escape her prison and rescue her young and helpless sister.

She'd tried to leave Ilay House twice before, but had been found out before reaching the city's edge.

And Lady Ilay watched her as though she were the lowest of felons. Guards patrolled the grounds at night and made certain she did not attempt to escape again.

With one deep breath, Maura left her room and slipped down the long corridor of the mansion. Pausing at the top of the stairs, she listened again for sounds of anyone who might be up and about, which would not be surprising, given that the Duke of Argyll was in residence, visiting his brother, Lord Ilay.

She had not been invited to sup with the family that evening. The duke and Lord Ilay were her father's cousins, but Maura was a mere daughter of an earl. And an unfavored daughter, at that. There was no reason on earth for Lord and Lady Ilay to include her in their intimate family gathering.

It suited her just as well. All through her own solitary supper, Maura's mind had whirled with plans and schemes. She was not about to travel up to Cromarty as her parents had decreed, to marry the decrepit old baron they'd chosen as her husband. She would cut her own wrists before taking vows with Kildary.

And it was not only because of his age and his questionable reputation. Maura knew the old man would never allow her to bring her poor wee sister Rosie to Cromarty to live with them. And that was a requirement of any man she wed.

Not that suitors were lining up to woo her.

The opposite was true. Any mirror told Maura that she was not unattractive, but she would never become a sophisticated lady like her mother and elder sisters, not when she preferred riding to housekeeping. Not when she was more adept at hiking than keeping her hair and clothes in good order, or smiling like a perfect idiot through mind-less conversation with fops in lace cuffs and pow-dered wigs.

Maura knew her dull, two-year "visit" at Ilay House was but a thinly veiled ruse her parents had used to separate her from Rosie and remove her from the family seat at Aucharnie Castle, where she had always managed to do as she pleased. She also knew Lady Ilay had been charged with groom-ing Maura as a proper wife.

But Lady Anne had not been entirely successful. Oh, aye, Maura had learned the skills to manage a household, and deal with housekeepers, servants, and dressmakers. She'd studied household ac-counts and listened to reports given by Lord Ilay's steward until her eyes crossed.

But still, the idea of marriage to any one of Lady Anne's silly milkweed acquaintances was as distasteful as the specter of Baron Kildary as her husband. Maura knew any prospective bride-groom would expect her to give up her freedom of thought and deed.

Maura was twenty-four years old. She should have wed by now, and had children of her own, and yet she'd vehemently rejected every suitor her parents had foisted upon her, as well as the men Lady Ilay had brought 'round. Clearly, she was not meant to be any man's wife, not when her own opinions and preferences were so marked.

Hadn't she defied her own father to save Rosie after he'd given the order to leave his poor, weak, newborn bairn in the hills to die? It was two years before Lord Aucharnie had discovered that Rosie still lived. The old midwife had not told him what

Maura had done, and Maura had secretly made sure the Elliott family, who'd taken Rosie in, always had food from the castle kitchen and every other necessity to be comfortable in their croft.

But Rosie had not developed the way Deirdre Elliott's own bairns had done. She'd become pink like wee Janet, but had not grown to normal size. She did not speak until she was five years old, and even then her speech was not entirely intelligible.

But Maura loved and protected her from her callous parents and their many coldhearted siblings, and Rosie returned her love absolutely. The child grew to be pure and sweet, with a loving personality that defied logic, considering her weakness and various infirmities.

In the two years since Maura and her sister had been separated, not a day had passed that Maura did not think of poor Rosie and the callous stick of a woman her father had hired to take her away from Aucharnie. Tilda Crane was mean-spirited if not outright cruel, and Rosie did not deserve to be banished to the ends of the earth just because her parents were embarrassed by their youngest daughter's shortcomings.

Now Maura's banishment was to become complete. She'd been instructed to leave Ilay House at dawn with Lieutenant Baird, the grim officer who carried out her father's most contemptible assignments. Evictions. Arrests. Mayhap even killings.

No doubt escorting a detested daughter fell into the category of distasteful tasks. She was sure the lieutenant was displeased with his assignment, for he despised her, ever since the day he'd made advances and she'd set him down in no uncertain terms. She supposed she ought to have attempted to be more tactful with him, but Baird had crossed a line. He'd grabbed her and whirled her into his arms while his men laughed.

Maura had been incensed, though not surprised by Baird's treatment of her. For her own father showed naught but disdain in his dealings with her. How could she expect anything better from his men?

Maura cringed at the memory of Baird's rough handling and the thought of spending several days on the road with him. She had no intention of going all the way to Cromarty and yielding to a betrothal agreement—especially *this* one—made by her father without her consent. She had a plan to get away from Baird and his men and rescue Rosie from Tilda Crane. And then . . .

Well, perhaps one of their four brothers would take them in. Though she had not seen any of them in years, Maura could certainly hope at least one of them would feel sufficient responsibility toward his youngest sisters to help them.

Maura heard no voices as she took the first step down the wide staircase, but she was cautious. This was likely her last chance to get to Rosie and take her away from Tilda Crane. If she failed and was forced to wed the old baron, he would never allow her to collect her sister, who'd been exiled far away in the wild highlands at Loch Camerochlan, away from everything she knew—from the Aucharnie hills, from the Elliotts and their youngest daughter, Janet. Away from Maura.

She reached the main floor and turned the corner toward Lord Ilay's study. The floor beneath her feet creaked, and Maura stopped on her toes. She held her breath and waited, certain that someone would burst through a doorway and expose her midnight wanderings.

But no one came, so she moved on, finally reaching the study. If discovered, she had an excuse for being there, but hoped she would not need to use it. She did not relish an encounter with her father's cousin, whom she barely knew since he spent most of his time at Stirling with his mistress.

She shuddered at the thought of encountering Ilay's brother, the duke.

The study door opened soundlessly and Maura slipped inside. Her plan was to accompany her father's surly guards only as far as Fort William. Then she intended to slip away and find the road to Loch Camerochlan, which she knew was many leagues to the northwest. Once there, Maura would remove Rosie from Miss Crane's care.

With only a pale stream of moonlight from the window to guide her, Maura went straight to Lord Ilay's desk, where the money sent by her father for her allowance and expenses was kept. She'd removed small amounts of his coin over the past two years, collecting funds with the hope that one of her attempts to get away from Glasgow would finally work. So she knew a few more pounds would not be missed, not when there was well over a hundred. She would take what she needed and—

The sound of voices outside and the clop of horseshoes startled her. Maura glanced through the window and saw that it was the duke, riding alongside Lord Ilay, with several of their men following behind.

As they dismounted and turned their horses over to the grooms, Maura felt a moment's panic. If the duke and his brother were not yet abed, then there must be servants about.

All at once, she pulled open the drawer and located the strongbox at the back. Beside it was a map she'd not seen before, rolled to expose its markings. It was just what she would need—along with the money—for her foray into the highlands.

A door opened, spurring Maura to action. She tucked the map under her arm and removed the top of the money box. Hastily grabbing as many coins as possible, she wrapped them inside the handkerchief she'd brought for that purpose.

The voices and footsteps became louder, approaching the study. In a panic, Maura looked for a place to hide. She went to one of the large chairs near the fireplace and crouched down behind it, but quickly realized one of the men might sit down in it if they happened to come in. Desperate, she fled to the large bank of windows and concealed herself behind the thick velvet curtains that framed either side.

Her heart in her throat, she tucked her feet in and waited. The footsteps came closer and she heard the sound of men's voices. She prayed they would not open the door. Swallowing hard, she held her breath.

"We'll want a party of at least twenty men," she heard Argyll say, his voice low and secretive.

"It may take some time to gather them," Lord Ilay replied.

"No. I must move quickly. And make sure no one else hears of my plan, Archie," Argyll said. "We'll need men we can trust."

"Of course. Any talk of French gold hidden in

the highlands would bring out every clan in the hills."

French gold? Maura continued to hold her breath.

"I feel sure it's there . . . 'Tis only a matter of time before the damned western clans hear of it and go . . ."

Maura squeezed her eyes shut, straining to hear their muffled words. The moments dragged on, and then the men's voices receded, along with their footsteps.

It seemed hours before there was silence again, and even then, Maura didn't move. She waited another few minutes to be sure, and then stepped out from behind the draperies. She moved furtively to the door and stopped to listen, but there seemed to be no one outside.

With one deep breath, she opened the door and quickly crept away from the study and back up the stairs to her room. Her trunks had already been loaded onto the carriage in which she would ride on the morrow, but she had one small traveling bag that she would keep with her.

An interesting thought occurred to her and she unrolled the map she'd taken from Ilay's desk. 'Twas a strange document, quite obviously torn along two of its edges. There were ink markings indicating lochs and mountains, but no towns or villages were noted. And certainly no reference to any gold.

Yet what else could this be? The map had not been there the last time Maura had slipped into the study to pilfer her father's money. Argyll must have brought it.

Feeling suddenly quite tired, Maura tucked the

map into the bag along with her stolen money to be ready when she made her escape from Lieutenant Baird and the rest of her father's guards.

What she would do about Argyll's gold remained to be seen.

The village of Kinlochleven.

Dugan and his warriors dismounted and approached a filthy little hovel located in a copse of trees a good half mile outside the village. He knew Lachann still thought this was a wasted trip, but Dugan thought his brother was wrong. His grandfather believed the French had hidden a significant cache of gold somewhere in the highlands, and Dugan was determined to be the one who found it.

He was sure he was on the right track.

"Could this be it?" Lachann asked, glancing 'round the place.

"The villagers said Mackenzie lives here. That's who we want." While in Ullapool last month, Dugan had saved a fool Campbell from a bloody beating outside a tavern, and the idiot had blathered drunkenly about a man named Hector Mackenzie in Kinlochleven who had possession of a French map. 'Twas all Dugan needed to hear for his instincts to flare to life.

And it could not have pleased him more to have received his information from a hated Campbell.

Lachann knocked on the cottage door.

"Go 'way!" called a gravelly voice inside.

"We've come to trade, Mackenzie!" Dugan called.

An old, disheveled drunkard came to the door.

"Ach, aye, and what d' ye have that I might possibly want?"

"More important, Mackenzie," Dugan said as he walked past the man and into his stinking cottage, "is what you have that I want."

It took only a bit of bargaining and a handful of coins for the man to give up the map, though Dugan was disappointed to see that 'twas only another piece of the whole. And, like the scrap his grandfather had given him, there were no markings or any lettering to give him the names of the mountain ranges and glens, or the lochs and rivers.

He began to doubt the possibility of finding the gold without more information.

He ignored Lachann's disparaging glance and stepped outside with the rolled parchment in his hand. He would study the two documents together once they were away from Kinlochleven and try to determine the clues to where the gold was hidden.

"Is that it, Laird?" Kieran Cameron asked. He tipped his head toward the rolled parchment in Dugan's hand.

Dugan nodded and mounted his horse. "Aye. This is it."

"'Tis so small, Laird," said Archie MacLean, the youngest of their company. Dugan remembered the days when Archie had followed Alexandra about the village as a tiny lad, barely able to walk. And she—no more than five years old—had taken him under her wing as though he were one of her wee wounded beasties.

Now Archie was a man grown and the best shot of all the MacMillan warriors, and Alexandra was the midwife and healer of their clan. Robert had married Meg Cameron and was a father to Dugan's two young nephews. MacMillan blood ran through their veins, and he would do everything in his power to keep his people from being evicted from their ancestral lands.

He reined in any misgivings he might have about the maps.

"Is the treasure . . . Is it shown on Mackenzie's part of the map?" Conall asked.

Dugan gave a shake of his head. "I'm not sure. We'll all have a look when we're away from here and we'll find the clues we need."

Bryce Cameron rode up alongside Dugan. He'd been as skeptical as Lachann about locating the French king's gold, but Bryce was Dugan's best swordsman and was a fair shot with either rifle or bow. Dugan wanted him at his side in case of trouble during their search, and when they found the treasure.

They *had* to find gold, for there wasn't any way in the highlands to raise the kind of money Argyll demanded.

"Laird, when you were up in Ullapool and heard of Mackenzie's map," Archie asked, "was there talk of exactly where the treasure lies?"

Dugan shook his head. "No, Arch. Only about the map."

"But what if the map—"

"Let's get away from Kinlochleven," he said. "Then we'll take a look." He wanted to find a location where no one was likely to come upon them.

They rode for miles through high country in the direction of Fort William, and came upon the same wide burn and waterfall that they'd passed earlier in the day. This time, a flash of red on the far side of the water caught Dugan's eye. He came to a halt.

"Holy Lord, Dugan," Lachann said quietly. "She's too near the edge."

"Aye." 'Twas the lass's red hair that had caught his attention, but he could see that she was in immediate danger. She had backed away from the horns of a fierce ram, and there was nowhere left to go. The ram was snorting and it pawed at the ground when it wasn't moving aggressively toward her.

If she took another step back, she was going to fall into the waterfall.

Chapter 3

Maura hardly dared breathe. Her eyes darted to each side, searching frantically for an escape. And yet there was none. She did not know what to do.

Not until something whistled past her, slamming into the ram and knocking it over.

Maura fell to her knees beside it and looked across the swiftly flowing burn toward her rescuer, a burly, dark-haired highlander. He sat mounted on his horse amidst a group of rough, tartan-clad warriors, and casually slipped a long, lethal bow into his saddle behind him.

His impact on Maura was nearly as potent as the ram's. Of course Maura had seen highlanders before, but none like the one who'd just saved her from certain death. He sat taller than the others in his saddle, and his shoulders were beyond impressive. His brawn filled out a linen shirt with a kind of rough beauty that fascinated her.

He looked at her for a moment, his gaze so sharp and keen, Maura felt him touch the very essence of her.

She shivered with an acute awareness of him as he turned his horse and led the others away, leaving before Maura could summon the wits to call out her thanks or give a wave of acknowledgment.

Or merely to gaze at his wondrous visage for just another moment. Had Lady Ilay invited a specimen like this highlander to her home instead of the overdressed dandies who frequented Ilay House, Maura might have taken notice.

The highlanders rode away from the burn and out of sight, giving Maura a moment to recover from her brush with death before returning to her carriage, where she would have to face Lieutenant Baird.

She had needed a few moments away from the close confines of the carriage and the sour breath of her chaperone, Bridget Hammond. Baird had ordered her to stay close, but Maura had defied the lieutenant in front of his men. She'd insisted on being left alone to take a short walk to the waterfall, and she realized her defiance must have rankled her spiteful tyrant.

But Maura was tired to death of his condescending manner and imperious ways. She cringed at the way he tugged at one side of his pale eyebrow when he looked at her, and loathed the way his greasy head shone in the light.

She knelt in the damp grass beside the burn and pressed one hand to her breast, watching as the highlanders disappeared into the trees. Her rescuer's aim had been perfect, killing the ram instantly. She did not like to think what would have happened had he not been in exactly the right place at the moment she needed him.

She never would have made it to Loch Camerochlan to rescue Rosie. She wouldn't even have made it back to her carriage.

Maura rose to her feet and brushed off her

skirts, though she was not able to get them completely clean. She started back through the woods, and nearly collided with Lieutenant Baird.

"Watch it!" he growled.

"I could say the same to you, Lieutenant. 'Twas you who nearly knocked *me* over."

He grabbed hold of her arm, his eyes flashing a barely suppressed anger. "I'll do more than that if you defy my orders again."

A chill came over Maura as she pulled her arm away and pushed past her father's loathsome lackey. He fell into step behind her and she suddenly realized the danger she was in. Mayhap worse than when she'd faced the angry ram.

It occurred to her how very possible it would be for Lieutenant Baird to return to the carriage without her. He could tell his men that she'd fallen into the waterfall, and who would be there to gainsay him? They would take pains to recover her body, and when he returned her to Aucharnie Castle, no one would question Baird's story. Why would they?

The lieutenant had been a burr in her side since his arrival at Aucharnie Castle, but now she knew he was ever so much worse. She had been pleasant toward him at first, but he had misinterpreted her polite attitude as something altogether different.

She needed to be wary of him. He'd quickly learned of her unfavorable status at home . . . Mayhap her elimination would suit her father more than her marriage to Kildary.

"Look at yer gown!" old Bridget cried when Maura came out from the copse of trees. " 'Tis ruined!"

"Nay, Bridget," Maura retorted, turning impatiently to face the older woman, whose hearing

was as poor as her temperament. She was exactly
the kind of companion Maura expected her parents to send. One who was nearly as crotchety as
Tilda Crane, and who had not let Maura out of
her sight in the four days since they'd left Glasgow.
" 'Tis only slightly soiled. 'Twill come clean with
some scrubbing."

Bridget's scolding reminded Maura just how isolated she'd become in the two years since she and
Rosie had been sent away from Aucharnie to their
own separate prisons. Maura longed to see her
sister, wished she could think of some faster, easier
way to release the child from her confinement at
Loch Camerochlan.

If only she could trust one of her siblings to assist
her. Aiden was the least pompous of her brothers,
and the only one who might be prevailed upon. But
he had a wife now, and his own child. Besides, his
home was near Aberdeen—the opposite direction
Maura needed to go.

Her only choice was to press on with the plan
she'd concocted the night Lieutenant Baird had
turned up at Ilay House. She knew it was flawed,
but it was the only way she could think of to get
to her sister.

Lieutenant Baird mounted his horse and looked
down at her with a deep anger in his charcoal gray
eyes. Twin peaks of color had bloomed on his
cheekbones and an invisible wave of fury rolled off
the man as he straightened up in his saddle.

"Next time, you'll do as you're ordered, Lady
Maura," he said. "Men, do not allow her out of
your sight."

Her few moments without Baird or Bridget hovering over her had not been worth this new, far

more intense animosity. Fortunately, she was going to leave his arrogant presence that night, soon after they reached Fort William.

"Your mother warned me that you were headstrong," Bridget scolded in a huff, "but I had no idea!"

Maura said naught to Bridget, but went directly to the carriage. She climbed inside, having no intention of discussing the incident any further. Already her jailers were primed to watch her more closely, and that was the last thing she wanted.

She could hardly wait until they reached the garrison town and she could leave Lieutenant Baird and her overbearing companion. She'd packed good walking clothes in her overnight bag, and figured she would secrete away some of tonight's supper for later, when she struck out alone.

She had not yet had a moment by herself to look at the strange map she'd pilfered from Lord Ilay's study, not when she'd had to share a room every night with Bridget Hammond and the old woman watching over her every second. Argyll had spoken of gold the night before she'd left Ilay House, and Maura believed it was possible the map showed the location of the gold.

The thought of using Argyll's map to find it left Maura a little breathless. With the French king's treasure in her possession, she would be able to care for Rosie and herself without worries.

Maura contained her excitement at the thought of escape and glanced up at the hills 'round her. They were tall, but not insurmountable. Even so, she knew her path would not be easy once she left Baird and the others at Fort William. She was familiar with the geography of the highlands, for she'd studied Lord Ilay's conventional maps over the past two years, in case the chance to escape Ilay House ever presented itself.

Now that a serious opportunity had come along, Maura concentrated on what she remembered of Fort William and its environs. The loch was just west of the garrison and ran north, curving to the west. If she kept the loch on her left as she hiked away from the town, she would soon find herself in the highlands and on her way to Rosie at Loch Camerochlan.

But perhaps a slight detour to find the French riches would not be amiss. First, though, she had to get away from her escort.

"I have no intention of marrying Baron Kildary," Maura said to Bridget. "If only Captain Baird would take me back to Glasgow, I could write to my father and ask—"

"Your father is set on this marriage, Lady Maura," Bridget retorted sourly.

Maura crossed her arms over her chest and turned a petulant glare toward the floor of the carriage, like a spoiled adolescent. 'Twas an intentional ruse that she'd used numerous times over the course of their journey. She hoped her escort and companion would think she was merely a foolish, incompetent child, and when she disappeared, they would backtrack and look for her on the road to Glasgow.

It would garner her some much needed time to get ahead of Baird and lose herself in the mountains.

Maura knew her plan to travel to Loch Camerochlan was an ambitious one, but she could do no less for her frail sister. The two of them had been outcasts together, and Maura had vowed always to take care of her.

She'd failed her once, but would not fail her again.

" 'Twas a bonny shot, Laird," Bryce remarked as they turned their horses to head north, away from the water.

Kieran slapped Dugan on the back and grinned. "You might have crossed through the burn and spoken to the lass, Dugan. She'd likely show you her gratitude in a very—"

"Ach, aye, Laird!" Archie chimed in with enthusiasm. "Ye've missed a wondrous opportunity for a fine tumble. The lass was as fair as any I've seen."

"And leave you bloomin' idiots to find your way to Fort William without me?" In truth, Dugan could think of little but those bright eyes and full, sensuous lips that had been frozen in fear. He'd like naught more than to feel that bonny mouth upon his, but he could not afford to be distracted from his purpose.

The men laughed, clearly in need of a bit of good humor, for they all knew the dubious state of Dugan's grand plan.

At least he had a plan. Of sorts.

"We'll stop here, while we still have daylight," Dugan said. He dismounted in a dry, rocky area and pulled the two sections of the map from his traveling pack behind his saddle.

Lachann took both pieces from him and laid them out side by side on a large, flat rock. The men all gathered 'round to look.

"What do ye see, Lachann?" Archie asked.

"Blue ink, which seems to indicate lochs and rivers," Lachann replied, pointing to a large, elongated blue pool that looked to Dugan like the shape of Loch Shin, far in the north.

"What are those?" Calum pointed to the various symbols that had been drawn in black ink.

"Mountains and forests," Dugan replied. He'd studied his grandfather's portion of the map often enough to know what they meant. And it was quite clear that they were looking at the northernmost portion of the highlands.

" 'Tis not much of a map," Archie remarked.

Dugan could not deny it. Mackenzie's quarter had been torn from the whole, just like his grandfather's. But perhaps this was the part that held the all-important clue that Dugan needed to discover where the gold was hidden. The bottom edge of it fit against the top of the MacMillan map, and Dugan recognized the shapes of his own territory—Loch Maree and Skye, to the west.

"Look at that marking." Dugan pointed to an irregular pattern of black ink next to what looked like Loch Monar.

"Is it a village?" Lachann asked.

Dugan frowned. "There are no other villages marked."

"Do ye think the gold is hidden there, Laird?" Archie asked.

Dugan gave a puzzled shake of his head. He did not know what to think.

" 'Tis possible there are villages marked on the other pieces of the map," Lachann said.

"True." But they did not have any other pieces of map to compare this to.

"Do ye think the French would have hidden their gold in a village, Dugan?" Conall MacMillan asked. "Seems like they'd want it away and well hidden, where only their own men could find it."

"Aye." That's what his grandfather had believed, too.

Lachann walked away from the group. He'd never hidden his doubts about this quest. Hell, Dugan had his own doubts. But their grandfather's faith in the map and the rumors about gold had been too strong for him to ignore.

And his clan had never been in such dire need.

The MacMillans had lived at Braemore on the banks of Loch Maree for centuries, raising cattle and growing the crops they needed for sustenance. To Dugan, Braemore was the most beautiful place on earth, and not just because it had become his home after he and his siblings had fled Glencoe.

The loch was grand, as were the mountains that circled it. Dugan and his brothers and sister had been raised in the auld keep, the home where his mother had spent her childhood, before going to Glencoe and marrying Gavin of the MacIain clan. Dugan was damned if he would let it fall into Argyll's hands.

He was going to use whatever means necessary to find that gold and save his people from being dislodged from their ancestral home.

Lieutenant Alastair Baird was in a high temper by the time he reached the Speckled Trout Inn at Fort William, just ahead of the carriage and passengers in his charge. He'd had more than enough of Lord

Aucharnie's headstrong daughter, and wanted to get her off his hands in Cromarty as soon as possible.

The willful wench did not know how to obey the simplest of orders. And next time she went off on her own, he was going to see to it that she suffered more serious consequences than a bit of mud on her skirts.

It was beyond irksome to have been sent on this nursemaid mission by the earl, and Alastair hoped his father never got wind of it. 'Twas a humiliating task for the son of the illustrious General John Baird.

Alastair muttered a few disparaging words that only he could hear. Lord Aucharnie had been all set to send Major Ramsay, their idiot commander, to escort Lady Maura. But the wily bawbag had managed to talk his way out of it, as he did every other unpleasant task. The bloody fool was useless.

"Aye, old and useless," he mumbled.

Baird was the one who should have stayed behind and trained with the rest of Aucharnie's troops while Ramsay played road nanny to Maura Duncanson. Somehow, Ramsay always managed to have the earl's ear, and it had gotten so far past annoying, Baird had begun to dream of smothering the old man in his sleep. The bastard was an absolute incompetent in everything but empty talk—as if the bloody bastard's useless blatherskite ever had any value.

Baird stood in front of the inn and observed as Corporal Higgins assisted Maura from the carriage and walked to the inn beside her. He remembered a time when he'd thought he wanted the red-haired wench for himself. 'Twas when he first arrived at

Aucharnie, nearly six years before, when she was just a girl of eighteen. He felt sure he'd heard his father's voice telling him to take his chance with her, to go after the earl's disfavored daughter. She was young enough still to be a biddable lass, but she'd spurned him rudely, and in front of two of his men. Her actions were unforgivable.

His only satisfaction was that her father the earl must despise Maura as much as he did. To marry her off to a man like Kildary . . . Well, Baird had heard a few things about the old baron that made him a questionable candidate for marriage.

Such decisions were beyond him, but one truth had become perfectly clear. The Earl of Aucharnie did not care what happened to his daughter. And if she dared to embarrass him in front of his men again, he was going to see that she suffered a mishap from which she would not return.

While Bridget napped in the carriage, Maura's thoughts turned to the braw highlander who'd rescued her from certain death.

She'd been told to keep away from any tartanwearing Scots whose path she might cross, both in Edinburgh and in Glasgow, for they were said to be untrustworthy barbarians.

And yet this "barbarian" had saved her life. He'd not attempted to do anything untoward at all. Of course, the man had been a fair distance away. What could he possibly have done to her?

Maura's skin heated when she considered the possibilities.

He seemed to be of some other world, one without wigs and lace cuffs, where men braved the el-

ements and battled fierce foes to survive. Maura
wondered how it would feel to have the admiration
of such a man. She'd experienced his protection,
and it had felt utterly foreign to her. And utterly
wondrous.

Her knees were no longer shaky, but the rest of
her body shimmered with an intense awareness.
Of the man, she was sure. She'd never felt this
way before, had never reacted in such a physical
manner to any other man.

She yawned, deliberately abandoning her
thoughts of the highlander. He had no part in her
plans, and besides—he was long gone, and 'twas
unlikely their paths would cross again.

Maura drifted off to sleep and awoke sometime
later as the carriage slowed and came to a stop. She
had a vague recollection of her dreams, and felt her
cheeks flush at the thought of them. She had not
known that a man's touch could feel so—

She sat up straight on the seat. The highlander
had *not* touched her. Nor had any other man. She
looked up to see Bridget Hammond frowning at her.

"What did I do now, Miss Hammond?" Maura
asked in spite of the raw sensations that shuddered
through her when she thought of the liberties she'd
allowed the highlander. In her dream.

The old woman merely raised her brows and
frowned.

Every detail of the tartan-clad warrior was
etched upon her memory, from his disheveled black
hair to the plaid that draped his body from waist
to knees. Surely he was laird of some great highland clan. Maura sighed, then covered the sound
with a small cough so that Bridget would have no
cause to question her.

The carriage stopped and as one of the soldiers opened the door and took Maura's arm, she gathered her wits and glanced 'round at the area about the inn. She wanted to get her bearings so she would know exactly which streets would lead her away from the inn. Perhaps she and Bridget could take a walk later.

Lieutenant Baird came out of the inn and approached her as he smoothed down his thick, pale blond mustache—the only hair he possessed above his neck, other than light, wispy eyebrows. "I have some bad news," he said, blinking his eyes rapidly in a way that Maura found unnerving. "Or rather, inconvenient news."

She frowned. "What is it, Lieutenant?"

"The inn is full. I'm afraid Miss Hammond will have to share quarters below stairs with one or two of the servants."

Bridget huffed behind her. "We'll just put in a pallet—"

"No," Baird said. "The only room left to let is barely large enough for one narrow bed."

Maura did not show her delight at this news, for if she did, Baird might suspect something. No doubt he'd been warned by her father that she might not be a cooperative traveler, for Lord Aucharnie had to know that marriage to Kildary would not sit well with her.

However, Maura had not caused any delays or difficulties whatsoever during their journey from Glasgow, with the exception of her foray into the woods that afternoon.

Maura decided the incident at the waterfall was just an odd mishap, and if she was careful, nothing of the sort would occur again. Her walks in the hills and fields 'round Edinburgh and Glasgow had been completely without risk—especially since she always had an escort when she left Ilay House— but now she knew she would need to be far more watchful when she set out for Loch Camerochlan.

"I believe I shall manage alone for one night, Bridget," she said.

"Come along then, Lady Maura," said Lieutenant Baird, his tone and manner deceptively polite.

She could mimic his feigned respect. She gave him a demure nod and walked to the building with Bridget bringing up the rear. They entered the inn and Maura stopped just inside, taking stock of the place.

"My lady, welcome," said the innkeeper.

Baird had obviously told the man she was the daughter of a nobleman, and he was far more impressed than he ought to be with the forsaken daughter of the Earl of Aucharnie. The proprietor attempted to draw Maura toward the stairs, but she had another idea. She needed to put her plan into action.

"Your room is this way, my lady," said the man. "But I must offer my apologies for—"

"Hold, good sir," Maura said to the innkeeper. "I am quite sure the room will do. But I wish to visit your kitchen."

Her request raised his brows. "My lady?"

"I do apologize, but I am hungry," she said in a light tone, making sure not even to glance in Lieutenant Baird's direction, for he was far too canny. "Quite famished, in fact."

Bridget took hold of Maura's arm and made an attempt to draw her toward the staircase. "Lady Maura—"

Maura pulled her arm away. "Do not presume to maul me, Miss Hammond," she said firmly, but keeping what might pass for a pleasant tone.

Bridget must have heard the steel in her voice because she released Maura's arm. While Baird walked ahead, Maura glanced up at the innkeeper and used the little bit of rank she possessed to intimidate him. She started moving in Baird's wake, toward the back of the inn. "Shall we?"

"Well, aye. W-we can find somethin' for ye."

The main floor consisted of a sitting room on one side of the main staircase and a taproom on the other. A very proper-looking lady and gentleman were alone in the sitting room, but the taproom was full, and Maura's step faltered as they walked past. The brawny highlander she'd dreamed of stood at the bar with his companions, while several other guests—clearly more civilized travelers—sat at the tables in the room, enjoying an early supper.

Ignoring Bridget's objections to her quest, Maura could not take her eyes from the hero who'd saved her with one well-placed arrow at the waterfall. His black hair was pulled into a queue at his nape, and his eyes were the clear, light blue of a mountain loch. The sleeves of his linen shirt were rolled to the elbows, baring muscular forearms with a roping of thick veins. His tartan was a vibrant, deep red plaid, ending just at his knees, and Maura saw that his powerful lower legs were laced into rough leather coverings.

He was different from anyone she'd ever known. Maura was certain he was not a barbarian as her father had always characterized the colorful highlanders.

This man had shown more chivalry than any

member of Maura's family, saving her from certain death when he was under no obligation to assist her, and with no promise of a reward. He was a big and bold warrior, and had acted on gallant instinct. Maura wondered if his honor would prevent him from rejecting a child like Rosie for her shortcomings.

If only her father had chosen this kind of man as her husband . . .

Her wanton dreams came back to her, and she felt her skin flame once again. She doubted that the passionate embraces she'd dreamed of ever occurred in reality. Surely no man's arms could cause her blood to sizzle the way his had done.

But she would not mind the opportunity to disprove her doubts.

As she stood staring, the warrior turned to speak to one of his companions and caught sight of her. Maura's heart stopped for a moment when his eyes met hers and she saw recognition dawn in their pale blue depths.

He set down his mug and started toward her.

Chapter 4

"This way, my lady," said the innkeeper, jarring Maura's attention from the highlander.

The moment of recognition passed, and if the man had actually intended to approach her, the innkeeper's interruption kept him away. She and Bridget followed the proprietor to the back of the inn to the busy kitchen. Two industrious serving maids were arranging food-laden plates on trays while a cook stood at the fire, lifting a huge roast from a spit.

"Have we any cheese in the larder, Donald?" the innkeeper asked.

Maura pondered whether the highlander would have spoken to her if the innkeeper hadn't come for her at that very moment. She wondered about his voice and whether his English was tinged with the Gaelic sounds of the highlands.

She realized she longed to hear it.

"Aye," the cook replied to the innkeeper, "but ye'll get it yerself since we've a full house and I've got me hands full."

While Maura's host collected bread and cheese and put them onto a plate, she turned her attention to what really mattered. There was a dark passageway behind the kitchen, but no servants' stairway. She saw a door in an outer corridor that might lead outside, but did not open it to check. Lieutenant Baird had come into the kitchen with them, and if he noticed her interest, he would surely assign one of his men to keep watch over her during the night.

The men had been fairly vigilant during their travels thus far, but relaxed, since Maura had been careful to be compliant for the most part. She hoped they would not suspect she had any plan but to travel with them all the way to Cromarty, in spite of all her pleas to be returned to Glasgow.

"My lady," said the innkeeper, "I would be happy to carry a meal up to your room if—"

"Thank you, kind sir," Maura replied, surprising him by taking the plate from him and going back toward the public room. "But I've been confined inside my carriage for three days and I need . . ." She glanced pointedly at a scowling Lieutenant Baird. "The taproom suits me well."

She left Bridget to settle into her room and went back to the main rooms of the inn.

"Lady Maura," the lieutenant said as she stopped at the crowded taproom. "I would caution you not to—"

"Do you see all the other ladies here, Lieutenant? Surely there is no reason why I cannot join them."

"This is unwise, my lady."

His tone grated upon her nerves, so Maura decided to ignore him. She took advantage of the few moments she could breathe without Bridget Hammond's company, and sat down at a table not far from the highlanders. Her heart gave a great sigh at the pure savage power emanating from the man who'd been the focus of her attention. He and his companions seemed to be in some disagreement, and Maura strained to hear their voices.

One of them mentioned gold and a map, but he was quickly hushed by the leader.

Almost before Maura had a chance to connect the highlander's words with those spoken by the Duke of Argyll and his brother, Lieutenant Baird came to stand between her and the highlander warriors. Baird leaned forward, laying his hand flat on her table and making no attempt to mask his displeasure as she looked up at him.

Maura used her haughtiest tone to put him in his place. "I would take a glass of ale, Lieutenant Baird . . . if you would be so kind . . ."

She wanted the observant lieutenant away for just a moment, so she could look her fill at the bold highlander whose low voice caused an undeniable flip in the pit of her stomach.

She took a deep breath and admonished herself to pay attention to the matter at hand, which was escaping Lieutenant Baird and his men.

Still, she could not help but wonder if the warrior's mention of gold could be connected to Argyll's warning that once the highlanders heard of it—

"I thought you were famished, Lady Maura," Lieutenant Baird said in a blatantly sarcastic tone when he returned and placed her cup of ale on the table. Maura looked at her plate and realized she hadn't yet taken a bite.

"I was waiting for my ale, Lieutenant," she retorted. "My mouth was too dry to eat." Aye, dry from gawking at the highlander.

Maura took a sip of ale and considered the possibility that the highlanders had yet another portion of the same map she had taken from Ilay's desk. Hers had been torn from some larger part, she was sure. What she would not give for a look at the warrior's map.

Baird hovered near Maura's table, so close that she had trouble gathering her thoughts. "My lady, I implore you to make haste." He framed it as a request, bur Maura knew it was an order.

The lieutenant was annoyed with her, but that was nothing unusual. She ignored him and tucked into the bread and cheese while she perused the room. Now she knew most of the layout of the main floor, and exactly where to look for the food she intended to take when she left the inn.

For she had to leave that night, without fail, whether or not the highlanders had part of her map. Argyll had spoken of recruiting twenty men, and as soon as he did so, he was sure to look in his brother's desk for his map. If not before.

Maura did not have much time before he realized who must have taken it and came after her. The sooner she got away, the better.

For the first time since she'd begun her journey to Cromarty, Maura had a room to herself, which gave her a perfect opportunity to study her map and see if she could determine exactly where the gold was hidden. If she could find it before Argyll, she and Rosie wouldn't have to rely upon the largesse of any of their brothers, for 'twas unlikely any of them—even Aiden—would defy their father's wishes and take them in. Her righteous sisters would be even worse.

She refused to think how improbable it was that she would be able to track down the gold before

Argyll. Or at all. If there was even the slightest possibility of getting herself and Rosie away from the tyrants who dictated their—

"Lieutenant, a word." It was Corporal Higgins, one of Baird's men, who'd come up behind the lieutenant.

"Stay here," Baird ordered Maura, eyeing the highlanders with mistrust.

"Of course, Lieutenant." What did he think the Scotsmen would do? Abduct her from a crowded tavern? She almost laughed at the very idea. Lord Aucharnie would pay no ransom for her. On the contrary, he would welcome the disappearance of his problematic daughter, for he had six very successful ones, not to mention four strapping sons.

If Maura vanished, so would her frequent letters imploring her parents to relent and reunite her with Rosie. Gone would be the constant reminder that he'd condemned his youngest child to death at her birth, then abandoned her when he learned she still lived.

Maura resumed her surreptitious observation of the highlanders as Baird and his man stepped a few paces away and carried on an earnest conversation.

She heard the rich masculine tones of the warriors' voices and noted the deep connection they shared. 'Twas the same kind of bond she shared with Rosie— unbreakable—for they only had each other.

The lass was even more beautiful in close quarters. And Dugan would not mind getting even closer. The opportunity came when she dropped something to the floor.

Dugan left his brother and the others at the bar

and stepped over to her table, bending to retrieve
the handkerchief she'd dropped. Purposely, if he
was not mistaken. She intrigued him, and his fas-
cination grew in pace with his arousal.

"Madam . . ." He handed the delicate cloth to
her. And when he looked into her eyes that were the
clear, deep green of his beautiful Braemore glen, he
felt his breath catch and his knees wobble. 'Twas
pure lust, and it was invigorating. He'd become so
accustomed to duty and worry that he'd forgotten the sheer, unadulterated pleasure of desiring a
beautiful woman.

"Thank you, sir," she said quietly, "or is it
Laird?" Her rosy lips parted slightly and she drew
her lower lip slowly through her teeth. Dugan reacted with a full-blown arousal. His cock twitched
to life even though it seemed she had no idea how
sensuous the gesture was.

He wanted to taste those lips, wanted to spar
with her tongue and teeth. Ach, aye—he would
love to feel those soft curves against his body.

"Aye," he managed to reply. "Laird Dugan Mac-
Millan."

"And I must thank you, too, for . . . earlier."

"'Twas my very great pleasure to aid you."
He would have taken her hand in his, just for the
wonder of feeling her skin against his own. But
he would not compromise her any further in this
public place.

"Are you very far from home, Laird MacMillan?" Her voice was the soft trickle of a burn over
mossy pebbles.

"Aye. A fairly good piece."

"Is it business that brings you to Fort William?"
she asked.

He nodded, taking note of the rapid pulse at her throat. What he would not give to touch his mouth to that spot, to taste the spicy tang of her skin. Her face was devoid of freckles, but for a tiny mole at the outside corner of her eye, which he found unusual for a red-haired lass. A silky lock of her hair curled at her nape, and he resisted the urge to wrap it 'round his finger.

"And you?" he asked, reining in his lust. 'Twas clear she was not some tavern trollop who would welcome his advances. And yet she'd been all alone earlier at the burn.

The English officer he'd seen earlier came to the lady's table and stood rigidly facing him. When the man spoke, his harsh tone indicated his willingness to engage in an unpleasant confrontation, here and now. Dugan put his hand on his claymore, ready for anything the damned bleater might try.

"Is there something I can do for you, highlander?"

"I happened to drop something, Lieutenant, and the gentleman merely handed it to me," Maura said hurriedly. She did not want to cause any problems for Laird MacMillan. The man had thoroughly charmed her. Her heart and lungs still quivered impossibly, just from his proximity, and her skin radiated a heated awareness.

He was ruggedly handsome and entirely self-assured, and Maura did not think Baird stood a chance against him. But she did not care to see any blood shed because of her tiny flirtation.

She knew 'twas wholly improper to engage in conversation with a stranger, but she had not been

able to resist speaking to the man who had saved
her life. She needed to thank him for killing the
ram with his clean shot. And to be truthful, she'd
wanted—no, *needed*—to see if he shared the same
astonishing attraction she felt.

"Then you can just go on your way, *Sandy*,"
Lieutenant Baird said, using the shortened form
of the ubiquitous Scottish name Alexander. Its use
dismissed the laird as rudely as possible without
insulting him overtly.

"Aye, I could if I were ready, Lieutenant Napper."

Maura nearly laughed aloud at the highlander's
retort, an insulting reference to Lieutenant Baird's
bare scalp.

Laird MacMillan turned to her. "All is well,
then, miss?" he asked. "You do not need me to
remove this rough character from your presence?"

"Now see here, man!" A torturous vein pulsed
at Baird's temple. "Lady Maura—"

"That is enough, Lieutenant Baird." Maura did
not trust herself to look up at the highlander for
fear of betraying her mirth . . . or her interest. Lieutenant Baird need not be alerted to the notice she'd
taken of the man who'd rescued her, or her amusement at his expense. There was no good reason to
foment the natural animosity between the highlander and her English escort.

"Yes," she replied to the highlander with a slight
nod. "The lieutenant and I have a mission."

Laird MacMillan bowed elegantly. "Then I will
leave you in his dubious care." He looked at Baird
as he would at the lowest creature on earth.

Baird started to say something more, but seemed
to think better of it. Instead, he glared back at
MacMillan as the highlander returned to the bar.

Then he sat down across from Maura, glowering.

"Is there a problem, Lieutenant?" Maura asked, still distracted. She could hardly believe she'd had the nerve to begin a flirtation with the highland laird by dropping her handkerchief. But she did not regret it, not in the least.

"Only that I leave you for half a moment and return to find you in the arms of that filthy red shanks."

"In the arms—!" Maura closed her mouth rather than dignifying the man's accusation with a response. Besides, it would not do to become involved in a row with the lieutenant now, not when she wanted him feeling relaxed and complacent enough for her to escape. "You misunderstood, Lieutenant. That's all," she managed to say. Soon she would be away from her odious escort and all his men. "What did Corporal Higgins say?"

Baird wiped his brow, and the movement of his hand against his smooth skin grated on Maura. But she ignored it, needing to know what issue had called him away. "There is a question of space for my men here at the inn," he explained.

Maura frowned with feigned concern. "And . . . did the innkeeper find rooms for them?"

"Only one. For me. My men will stay at the fort tonight," he replied, and Maura felt relieved. She did not want to trip over a member of her escort as she sneaked out of the inn after dark.

"Oh. That's very good, then, is it not?"

He gave her a sour look, which she ignored.

"I believe I'll take a walk through town after I finish here, Lieutenant Baird. Perhaps Bridget will accompany me, or would you rather assign one of your men?"

Dugan could not believe the comely lass was in the company of English soldiers. He should have known a pampered beauty like *Lady Maura* would be the wife or daughter of some high and mighty lowland lord. Who else would be dressed in such fine cloth? Not that she was the least bit ostentatious. Her cloak was black and her unadorned gown was a dark green that gave her eyes the richness of deep summer.

He'd fallen for her flirtatious ploy. What a bloody neep he was. He should have noticed her military escort, but he and the lads had been in deep discussion about their plans for the morrow. He would have to be more vigilant, especially while they remained in this garrison town. He had no interest in having any sort of confrontation with her escort.

His eyes wandered back to Lady Maura, and even though she was a *lady*, and in the company of a royalist officer, Dugan could not forget her womanly scent or the dimples that creased her cheeks when she smiled.

He would enjoy doing more than just passing the time of day with her. 'Twas far too easy to imagine the sweet bounty of feminine skin hidden beneath her traveling gown, and how soft it would feel in his hands. He grew hard thinking about grazing her full lower lip with his teeth while he brought the tips of her breasts to hardened peaks. He would—

"Did she invite ye to her room then, Laird?" Archie asked in a low tone.

"Shut your trap, MacLean," he snapped, far too aware of the heated flesh beneath his plaid. "We need to decide on the direction we'll take on the morrow."

Baird sent Higgins with Lady Maura on her walk about town. He did not think he could abide spending any more time than was absolutely necessary with the woman, especially not after seeing her making eyes at the filthy highlander.

Was that not just like her—to find favor with a cursed Jacobite? He spit on the ground as he walked toward the garrison to check in with the commanding officer there.

Maura had been quite clear about her distaste for her chosen bridegroom. Not that Baird blamed her, but she'd received her father's orders. It was not up to her to question—or defy—the earl. He most certainly was not going to take her back to Glasgow, no matter how desperately or how often she entreated him.

Maura was the most intractable female he'd ever met. He would not bet against her refusing to wed Kildary when she arrived on the church steps for their nuptials. 'Twould be the one way to guarantee that the old baron would have naught to do with her when Aucharnie tried to make reparation.

Baird wondered what kind of pact Aucharnie had made with Kildary. 'Twas likely that a great deal of money was involved. But whose? Did Aucharnie pay a handsome dowry to be rid of his troublesome offspring? Or had Kildary paid the earl a generous bride price for a young, fertile wife?

Of course, Lord Aucharnie had not shared any information with him. But he hoped his success in this mission would prompt Lord Aucharnie finally to recommend his promotion. He deserved a captaincy, by God. Everyone knew it.

His posting at Aucharnie Castle was supposed to have been a boon to his career. His father, General John Baird, had promised as much when he'd recommended Alastair for transfer to Aucharnie from a tiny outpost west of Aberdeen. The general had told him to bide his time, and when Alastair was ready, he would be transferred.

But Aucharnie was hardly any better than the outpost.

" 'Tis Ramsay who is in Lord Aucharnie's confidence," Baird muttered as though his father could hear.

Early in his tenure at Aucharnie, he'd taken matters into his own hands and set his sights upon the earl's daughter. For surely the son-in-law of an earl would possess significant prestige and authority. 'Twas the perfect way to bypass Ramsay's influence.

Alastair's ears burned at the memory of Maura's humiliating rejection. She'd toyed with him for months, leading him on until he'd been in a fever to possess her. The lass wandered about the estate at all hours with no escort but her stunted cripple of a sister. 'Twas only right that he rein her in and rid her of the wee red-thatched troll that was so attached to her.

But the bitch had spurned him at the last while two of his subordinates looked on. Her behavior toward him was utterly unforgivable, and Baird had every intention of seeing that the earl's daughter got what she deserved—marriage to the old lecher in Cromarty. Either that . . . or perhaps 'twould be more satisfactory if she met with a convenient "accident" if she defied him again.

They had at least two more days on the road before they reached Cromarty, and Baird was not familiar with the territory ahead of them. According to his map, there would be no inn where they could spend the intervening night. They would have to sleep in some cold, dank crofter's cottage if he found one along the way.

The more he thought of it, an accident was far more appealing than having to complete the rest of his journey to Cromarty with the higher-than-mighty Maura and her crotchety old companion. Next time Maura decided to take a walk among the craggy cliffs of the highlands, he intended to give his permission. Gladly.

Then he would follow her and show her the error of her ways—while he took his pleasure of her sinfully enticing body—and then discard her like the proud piece of rubbish she was.

Chapter 5

Taking his ale in the shadow of a British fort chafed at Dugan. The town was crawling with lowlanders, as well as Campbells who were loyal to the English king and responsible for the slaughter of his family.

Dugan would never forget what had happened at Glencoe all those years ago. Murder under trust was the most heinous of crimes, and Captain Robert Campbell of Glenlyon had been hideously guilty of it.

He tamped down the bile that always came to his throat when he thought of his family's horrible fate. He knew who was responsible, from Major Robert Duncanson, who had ordered Campbell to put everyone under seventy to the sword, to the Duke of Argyll, whose men had shot down his father and Gordon in cold blood. *A child!* They'd murdered a mere child because of the fecking king's wish to make an example of a highland clan.

Dugan swallowed his ale in one long gulp. He could not think of his parents and Gordon now, not when the risk of eviction was very real and more menacing than any disaster the MacMillans had faced in the past twenty-five years.

He had to decide what to do about finding the French gold. If they could not decipher some marking or clue on the two parts of the map in his possession, he was unsure what to do next. Travel up to the western isles and rouse the MacDonalds in his cause?

The thought of war repulsed him. He'd battled for Prince James during the uprising two years before, and been sorely wounded in the process. Dugan had healed, but the MacDonald septs had lost too many men in '15, and Dugan knew the western clans were still licking their wounds.

He'd already ruled out a cattle raid, for 'twould yield too little profit, and besides, he did not care to rouse any of the clans against him. If the maps were no good, he might not be able to avoid war, and he would need every highland clan to stand with him.

He looked 'round the crowded taproom. He had not been able to secure even one room for himself and his men to share, but the innkeeper had given them leave to sleep in the large sitting room on the opposite side of the stairs. They'd been sleeping out of doors during their travels away from Braemore, and were grateful to be out of the cold for the one night, with a tidy peat fire to warm them. They were to take over the room after all the guests had retired, and planned to be away at dawn.

But it meant they couldn't really examine their two sections of the map again until everyone— even the servants—had retired and the inn was quiet. By then, Dugan was sure Bryce and Conall would be stretched out in a couple of chairs with their mouths hanging open and snoring to raise the dead.

Dugan was weary as well, but thoughts of the lass who'd left the inn a while ago . . .

No, 'twould be thoughts of the map that kept him awake. He had to have missed the marking that showed the location of the gold. Perhaps he ought to leave it to Lachann to figure it out, for his brother was the canny one. Dugan's strength was in defense and decisiveness, the main reasons his grandfather had chosen Dugan to succeed him as laird.

'Twas unfortunate that he'd not been decisive when it came time to marry. If he had wed sooner, mayhap he would not find his thoughts quite so tangled up with the beautiful Lady Maura. Auld Hamish MacMillan had been after Dugan to woo and wed Artis MacLean several years ago. But back then Dugan had not felt ready to take a wife. He was fully occupied with training his men and seeing to the fortifications at Braemore. And then the old man had died and Dugan's responsibilities to the clan had piled up even more, one after the other.

Artis was a comely lass, and had shown some shy interest in him. Mayhap Dugan had been a dolt to let her slip through his fingers, but she'd been painfully quiet and far too timid for him. No, he did not want a shrew, either, but a wife he did not have to fear would faint away if he raised his voice.

Someone more like Lady Maura, who had set Lieutenant Baird in his place firmly and without hesitation. And 'twould be no hardship to take her to his bed every night.

Dugan took note when the red-haired lady returned to the inn with her soldier escort. She did not seem pleased with his company, and it occurred to Dugan that she might be a prisoner of sorts.

He discarded the notion as soon as it entered

his brain. The woman could not possibly be a prisoner, else she would not have been allowed to walk alone near the waterfall that afternoon. One of the soldiers would have accompanied her.

No, she traveled with them willingly.

Dugan tamped down his disappointment when the twitchy, bald lieutenant came to escort Lady Maura to a chamber at the top of the stairs. 'Twas the last he would see of her, for he intended to leave at first light.

He kept his eyes on her as the soldier opened her door and stood aside. Instead of entering the room, Maura turned to look down the stairs, catching Dugan's gaze. Her eyes were wildly alluring in spite of her connection to the royalist soldiers.

Dugan decided he would not hold her allegiance against her if she happened to favor him with a smile.

Her cheeks flushed bright with color, and then she did flash him a brilliant smile before ducking into the room. Her escort closed the door behind her and took his own leave.

What Dugan would not give to follow her, to join her in that room, where he would loosen her hair from its coils and let the bonny, silken mass stream down her back. A few kisses and he would begin to undress her, uncovering pale, smooth skin inch by inch . . .

"Ach," he muttered. Until he settled his outrageous debt to Argyll, there would be no room in his life for distractions. He put Lady Maura from his mind, finished his ale, and looked at his men. He knew they were tired. Even Dugan felt the burn of fatigue behind his eyes. They'd been riding for days, away from the familiarity and comforts of home, and the result of their travels so far was dubious at best.

"I still think we ought to go raiding," Lachann remarked, breaking into Dugan's thoughts. "Clan Chattan is not far away and 'tis said they have hundreds of cattle. Mayhap even thousands. We could drive them south and then sell them in the lowlands."

"Lachann, not even a thousand head of cattle would cover Argyll's demands," Dugan said bluntly.

"But the map isn't—"

"We don't yet know what it is or is not," Dugan said. "We'll look at it again later, when all is quiet. And then mayhap one of us will see the clue we need."

Archie stepped back from the bar. "My eyes are burnin', Laird. Can it wait until the morn?"

"Aye, mine as well," Kieran said with a yawn. "I'm not sure I'm up to any map readin' tonight."

They spent another hour or so at the bar, waiting for the sitting room to clear out. When they were finally alone, Dugan's companions wrapped themselves in their plaids and stretched out wherever they found adequate space. Lachann made a trip outside while Dugan took out the maps and spread them out on a low table. He pulled a lamp close, but before sitting down with Lachann, he saw a fetching feminine figure slip down the stairs and out the door.

The inn was shrouded in darkness, so Dugan wasn't certain who had gone out, but he had a suspicion. 'Twas the bonny Lady Maura, the thoughts of whom he had not been able to eliminate completely from his mind.

He followed her scent and was rewarded when he stepped into the shadowy veranda of the inn.

"You've abandoned your escort, Lady Maura?"

She whirled to face him, and in the soft light of the moon, Dugan saw that her expression was troubled. Her distress touched him deeply and he put aside his own difficulties for the moment.

"Are you in trouble, lass?" he asked, recalling the obvious animosity between the lady and her escort. He felt a perverse satisfaction in it.

Lady Maura shook her head. "No," she said quietly. "I'm . . ."

Dugan came close enough to touch her. The top of her head barely met his shoulder, and he could not resist reaching out to feel the texture of one of her soft curls. "You are what, Lady Maura?"

"I-I am . . ." She turned her gaze upon him, seemingly at a loss for words.

"A woman as lovely as you should have naught to worry about."

She frowned as she looked up at him, and he could not resist sliding his hand down to cup her jaw. Her cheek was so smooth, he ran his thumb across it as he thought about tasting her. Just one kiss, though 'twould not be nearly enough to satisfy his burgeoning arousal.

She shivered and closed her eyes. "As lovely? As much trouble, you must mean."

"Are you trouble, Lady Maura?" he asked quietly, tipping his head down toward hers. Aye, she was more enticing than any lass in Braemore Glen—and as unsuitable for him as any lowlander would ever be.

He felt her throat constrict beneath his hand. She was so delicate, he wanted her as he'd wanted no other. She made all his protective instincts come to the fore.

"Aye. Trouble to all who know me." He heard her tremulous sigh and knew there was a world of turmoil lurking within her breast.

Dugan had an urge to discover exactly how much trouble she could bring him. And he intended to start with a kiss. He leaned down and touched his mouth to hers. He felt her sharp intake of breath, but then she softened and her body drifted toward his.

Dugan gathered her close, fitting her wondrous curves against him. He sensed her inexperience, but deepened the kiss anyway, as raw desire shot through him.

Some part of him knew there could be naught but a kiss between them, but Dugan could not keep from drawing her tightly against him and ravishing her mouth with his lips, tongue, and teeth. She tasted of sweet highland water and smelled like heather.

He was lost. The desire to do more than just steal the most incredible kiss of his life nearly overpowered him. With a low growl, Dugan continued to plunder her mouth while he fought a savage instinct to carry her away to some private bower and gratify the primitive needs she roused in him.

He slid one hand down to her waist, and she slipped her fingers into the hair at his nape, loosening his queue. He let his hand drop lower, pulling her hips against his, making her quite sure of her effect on him.

She pressed back against him, fitting his hard length to her body in just the right place. Dugan felt glorious and powerful, all at once.

He had to be insane.

He could not do this, not with a highborn lady who was under the protection of a Sassenach guard. Rational sense slammed into him and he broke away, ending the kiss.

She made a small sound he thought must be dismay, but for what, Dugan was not sure. Dismay that the kiss was finished? Dismay that she'd allowed it? The latter, of course. A minor flirtation in the taproom was not an invitation for ravishment.

"Lady Maura—"

"'Twas my fault, Dugan MacMillan," she said with a tinge of anger in her voice, "so please do not apologize." Besides her anger, she sounded as frustrated as Dugan felt. Lowering her hands from his shoulders, she looked at him with confusion in her eyes. Or perhaps 'twas mistrust.

"Maura." He took hold of both her arms before she could run from him, and held her so that she had no choice but to look up into his eyes. He wanted her still. But he knew better, and he tamped down the arousal that continued to rage within him. "I should not have taken advantage."

"Laird Mac—"

"You are a beautiful lady who deserves a man of means who will take you to wife. Not a rogue who lost his head for a moment here in the moonlight. And so I *do* apologize, though I will ever regret the experience."

Maura closed the door behind her and leaned back against it, the sound of her heartbeats pulsing in her ears. Her little foray down the steps and outside had been for the purpose of seeing if anyone was about, to determine whether it was safe for her to leave yet.

She hadn't thought she would see the highland laird again. Or let him kiss her breathless.

Her body tingled, still. The yearning for more of MacMillan's touch, more of his masculine power persisted.

The interlude had done more than take her breath away. It had shown her what else had been absent in all the men Lady Ilay had brought 'round—raw male potency. Dugan MacMillan's touch had given rise to an excitement that charged through her nether parts like lightning. 'Twas the yearning of a woman for a man's touch.

Maura shivered even now when she remembered the slide of his hand down to her hips. The press of his body against hers had felt so intimate and so incredibly arousing, she had lost all sense of reality. She'd forgotten her purpose, failed to ascertain who was up and about.

Besides Dugan MacMillan.

But now her reckless moment was over. She had a plan to put into play and it could be delayed no longer. With Bridget tucked away downstairs, Maura had looked closely at Argyll's map and found no indication of any hidden treasure. There hadn't even been the expected notations giving the names of villages and lochs. Even worse, the map seemed to be merely a torn portion of a larger document.

It appeared to be completely useless, but Maura knew that could not possibly be. Not when it had been tucked away in Lord Ilay's desk.

She and Rosie could manage for a time with

the money she'd been pilfering from Ilay's desk for months in anticipation of her escape. 'Twas enough to get them away at least to Belfast. Or perhaps even to America, where no one would know them.

Maura could not waste any time thinking about what they would do then. She knew her money would not last forever, and Rosie was too frail to work. Somehow she would figure a way to support them. Marriage to Baron Kildary was out of the question. And asking her brother Aiden for help was a dodgy proposition at best. He was as likely to confine them in his house and send for their father as he was to give them shelter and listen to reason.

Her bag was packed and she was more than ready to start on her hike toward Loch Camerochlan. But she could not leave yet, not while the highlanders were still about.

She looked down at her map again and wondered if Laird MacMillan's map had anything to do with Argyll's gold. What if he had the missing piece?

Maura wrung her hands together. A cache of gold would solve her problems. With only a few handfuls of gold coin, she could take Rosie to America and buy a house somewhere, and their father would never find them.

But she needed to figure out where to look for the treasure before she began making grandiose plans.

Dugan took a moment to compose himself.

It had taken every bit of discipline he possessed to let Lady Maura go, and even now he was as hard as the claymore in his belt.

He did not know when he'd ever wanted a
woman more. She possessed a compelling combi-
nation of strength and vulnerability, and he found
himself wanting to protect and care for her.

After he bedded her, of course. Even now, the
desire to broach her bedchamber bedeviled him.
And yet he knew he could not. She was no strum-
pet. He'd tasted inexperience as well as passion in
her kiss.

Dugan swore under his breath. He would not
seduce an innocent. Besides, there was no time for
any sort of dalliance, especially not with a woman
who was accompanied by a troop of Sassenach soldiers.

Aye, the woman was trouble.

He finally returned to the sitting room to find
Lachann studying the map. He glanced up. "What
is it?"

"Naught." Was his state of arousal so transparent? "One of the guests stepped outside. We . . .
spoke for a few minutes, that's all."

Lachann's eyes narrowed slightly, but Dugan
sat down and turned the maps to see them better.
He found that the markings were just the same as
before. Unhelpful.

"I don't know what you can possibly be thinking, Dugan. I don't see how this bloody puzzle
helps us."

"The man who gave the scrap of map to Grandfather," Dugan said quietly, "was a dying Frenchman."

"Where? In Perth, I suppose?"

"Aye," Dugan said, scrubbing one hand across
his face. He suddenly felt exhausted. During the uprising two years before, Dugan had been wounded

protecting his grandfather from an Englishman's blade, and taken it himself. Old Hamish had gotten him home alive, though. "He said the map had been torn asunder so that only allies could band together to find it."

"'Tis ridiculous when you think of it, Dugan. Why would—"

"Look here," said Dugan.

"Where it's torn?" Lachann moved the lamp closer.

"Aye. Do you see it? A different sort of marking."

"You think this spot shows where the gold is hidden?" Lachann frowned. "I don't know. Mayhap."

"'Tis not the same kind of scratching that marks a loch or a town. It doesn't look like a mountain, either."

Lachann was silent for a moment. "If the Frenchman was right, won't we need the last pieces of the map?"

"Look. The mark is right at the juncture of the two sections. We would not have noticed it without having both."

Lachann sighed and tapped his finger on the strange mark. "But it might mean naught."

Dugan's vision blurred with fatigue. He did not want to argue with Lachann, nor did he care to ponder the maps or the possibility of gold, or the bloody Duke of Argyll any longer. He had to get some sleep, for they would ride long and hard on the morrow. "Aye. You're right."

'Twas past midnight, and Maura assumed everyone in the inn must be asleep by now. Even the highlanders.

She dressed warmly and put on her good walking shoes, then picked up her traveling bag and exited her room. It was dark in the stairway, but she made her way down to the main floor of the inn just as she'd done before. This time, there was naught but moonlight coming in through the windows.

She wondered how long it had been since she'd left Laird MacMillan. Well over an hour, she was sure.

And yet the impossible yearning Dugan had engendered with his kiss had not dissipated. If only Rosie's well-being was not at stake, Maura might—

She quickly came to her senses. Even if she had not been on her way to find Rosie, she could not possibly entertain any romantic notions about the highlander. Maura knew nothing about him, other than the deep rumble of his voice and the way his touch made her feel. But he might be a Jacobite rebel, or one of the road bandits Lieutenant Baird warned about as they traveled to Fort William.

He was certainly a rascal.

But the most impressive rascal she'd ever encountered, boldly kissing her on the veranda where anyone might have come upon them.

Maura crept toward the back kitchen, but stopped suddenly when she heard the sound of snoring to her left.

She held her breath, afraid Lieutenant Baird had decided to post a guard after all. He had not hidden his dislike of the highlanders, no doubt believing they posed some threat.

Keeping her feet where they were, she leaned forward to peer into the sitting room and heard it again. A soft snore. The fire had burned low, but she could see that the only occupants of the room were the highlanders, all wrapped in their plaids and lying on whatever surface was handy—chairs, settees, floor. All were sound asleep, even Dugan. Now she understood how he had seen her when she'd come down earlier.

She wondered why these men had come to Fort William. Surely, they did not enjoy the presence of the king's troops. Clearly, they were en route somewhere.

She clutched her traveling bag tightly in her hand and held her breath, wondering . . . It seemed impossible that the other piece of her map would be in the highlanders' possession—that it was not merely hidden somewhere in Lord Ilay's study and she'd just missed it during her midnight foray. And yet . . .

Her mind raced as she took a moment to let her eyes adjust to the faint light cast by the glowing embers in the fireplace. Laird MacMillan lay on the floor, wrapped in his tartan, his pack right beside him. She told herself that if she did not look now, she would never know.

She took a deep breath and crept silently to the spot.

MacMillan shifted in his sleep, startling her.

She held her breath and considered what to do. Did she dare untie the laces and look inside his pack? She could take just a wee peek at the map his companion had spoken of, and if it was not like hers, she would tie up the pack and leave.

But if it looked to be the other part of the document she'd taken from Argyll—

Dugan took a long, deep breath, and Maura heard him mutter something low. *Her name?*

No, of course she'd only imagined it, mayhap wishing it was true. For his embrace had shown her how a man's touch could soothe and excite, all at once. Even in her dreams, she hadn't imagined that a kiss could make her blood sizzle and her knees weak.

Of course, she'd never encountered a man like Dugan MacMillan.

The sound of a deep snore to Maura's left startled her and she realized she tarried too long. If she was going to satisfy her curiosity, she had to do it now, and do it quickly. She opened Dugan's pack and slid her hand inside. In complete silence, she watched his handsome face for any sign of awakening as she felt for a document. She quickly came upon a rolled piece of parchment at the bottom of the pack.

Drawing it out carefully, Maura did not unroll it, but held it up to the light of the fire. Her heart pounded with excitement when she realized 'twas exactly like Argyll's—tattered, with markings for lochs and mountains, but little else. Maura had no doubt its ragged edge would fit perfectly against the edge of the map in her possession.

An ominous creak sounded above her, and she knew she had to move.

Chapter 6

Maura pulled up her hood as she slipped unseen into the street. Moving quickly, she headed toward the loch and found the narrow road that bordered it. Walking north, she intended to continue until the road disappeared into the woodlands north of town. She would not lose her way if she kept to the water's edge and followed it west in the direction of the highlands.

She avoided thinking about her theft of the highlander's map and concentrated on getting away from Fort William, as far and as quickly as possible. She knew it had been wrong to take the map, but perhaps her guilt could be ameliorated by the good use she would put it to. Surely, saving her helpless sister was a justifiable reason for her thievery.

It was not the first impulsive act of her life and Maura doubted it would be her last. Her quick actions were never mindless, but always based on some innate instinct. Sometimes her deeds landed her in serious trouble, but she never regretted them—especially her rash behavior on the day Rosie was born.

Maura had been hiding in the room where her mother labored loudly and painfully with her twelfth child. From what Maura could tell, the bairn had come early, and the birth had not gone well. Rosie had been born far too tiny, her color a sickly gray. The poor bairn did not cry, and she hardly moved in the well-used crib in which the midwife had placed her. But Maura had loved her on first sight, her wee rosebud lips and perfect little fingers and toes.

Lord Aucharnie had roared his displeasure with his wife, with the midwife, and with the tiny, frail bairn. He had given orders for his child to be left alone to die. *His own child.*

Maura had no intention of allowing her father to kill her tiny sister. The midwife had made no objection when Maura had wrapped the bairn in soft wool and taken her from the castle. She'd run through the Aucharnie hills to her refuge from her father's frequent wrath—the quiet warmth of Deirdre Elliott's cottage. Deirdre's own bairn, Janet, was but a few months old, and Maura knew the woman would be able to feed her sister.

Maura's father, however, had shown his rage through the use of a stout birch switch to Maura's backside when he discovered what she'd done. By then, Rosie had reached the age of two years, though she had not thrived like the Elliott children. Lord Aucharnie was disgusted with them both—at Rosie for being so backward, and at Maura for her defiance.

The two sisters were outcasts within their own family. But at least they had each other.

Maura walked on. The night was clear and there was sufficient moonlight for her to find her way without falling into the loch. She was a strong hiker, having walked all over the hills and glens 'round Aucharnie, and with an escort after being sent to Glasgow. She'd learned from experience that it was necessary to do her hiking off the beaten path or someone would surely find her.

She pressed her tidy leather purse against her waist, reassuring herself that she had sufficient money for food and shelter during her travels, and eventually to take Rosie far away from Scotland. Once she was far enough away from Fort William, she was going to see how the highlander's map fit against Argyll's, and mayhap she would discover where to look for the treasure.

Moving along as quickly as possible, Maura soon turned west where she took note of a shadowy village in the distance on her right. She kept her head down, stayed close to the cover of the trees that lined her path, and continued on the north bank of the loch.

As practiced a hiker as she was, Maura had never before walked out in the middle of the night. The sound of the wind rustling through the trees unnerved her, and she huddled deeper within her cloak as she walked. And while she hoped that daylight would come soon, she wanted to put a good many miles between herself and the fort before Lieutenant Baird awoke and discovered she was gone.

Thinking of her odious escort, Maura quickened her pace. She would walk as long as her legs would carry her, then find a place to rest while she hid from anyone who might come searching for her.

Dugan woke from a restless sleep. 'Twas still dark, but his dream . . .

He sat up abruptly and looked about the room. All his men were still asleep. As he should be.

He rubbed the back of his neck. Something was wrong. He could feel it in his bones. He reached down below his knee and found his father's dagger, his *sgian dubh*, still secure in his stocking. 'Twas the only thing of value—

Dugan grabbed his pack and tore open the laces. He reached inside. "Where in hell is the map?"

"What?" Lachann sat up and scrubbed his hand over his face as Dugan lit the lamps. "The map?"

The other men awoke as Dugan looked in every corner, then searched under the cushions of each chair of the sitting room.

It could not be lost.

"You put it in your pack," Lachann said. "Did you wake up during the night and look at it?"

"No," Dugan growled. He'd spent the entire night dreaming of a certain russet-haired beauty. "Someone took it from my pack."

"Laird, are ye saying someone slinked in here like a wee stoat and stole it from under our noses?" Archie asked.

Aye, that was exactly what must have happened, and the thief might not have gotten far. Dugan started for the door, trying to think who might have heard Archie's mention of the map and decided to search their belongings for it.

Anyone in the taproom could have heard Archie before Dugan had quashed his loose talk. But who would have had the audacity to come into the room and dig inside his pack for it?

Dugan stepped outside and looked all 'round, but saw no one. He realized the thief might still be inside the inn, sleeping contentedly until dawn when he could leave with impunity. Dugan had no authority to call for a search of the inn or any of the guests.

He returned to the sitting room.

Lachann stood with his arms folded across his chest. "How could anyone sneak in here with all of us—"

"We all slept soundly for the first time in a fortnight," Dugan said. "They might have set fire to the place and none of us would have noticed it until our hair was on fire."

"It makes no sense, Dugan. Who knew we had pieces of the French map?"

Dugan shook his head. He did not know, but he could not just stand there doing naught but scratching his head. He turned to his men. "All of you—get your horses and take to the road. Two of you ride southward, the rest of you head north and see if you can find our thief. If he's left the inn, he couldn't have gone far. Lachann, come with me."

"What are you going to do, Dugan?"

"If anyone in this place is up and about," he said, "that could be our thief."

"You're going to listen at every door?"

"If need be." Dugan headed up the stairs and when he reached the top, noted one door that was slightly ajar. He pushed it open and saw that the room was empty.

"I thought there were no spare rooms to let," Lachann whispered.

"Damn all," Dugan muttered. 'Twas Lady Maura's room. With his own eyes, he'd seen Baird escort her to it.

The fire was out, but Dugan could see that the lady had done no more than lie on top of the bedclothes—probably so she would not become too comfortable and sleep through until morning.

The wench had decided to steal from him last night, when the taste of him was still on her lips.

"Do you think she left alone, Dugan?" Lachann asked quietly.

"I doubt it," he replied. "What highborn lady would go off in the night without a servant or two to take care of her?"

"Or an escort."

"Aye."

'Twas infuriating. To have been so taken in by a bonny face and form. He and Lachann returned to the main floor, Dugan vowing never again to be so taken in.

Had Maura and Baird concocted a quick plan together after hearing Archie's slip of the tongue? She had not seemed particularly glad of Baird's company, but mayhap he was her only choice.

Damn all! Dugan wanted to punch his fist through a wall. He could not believe he'd been so lax that he'd allowed the woman to steal away his only possibility of raising the funds he needed to keep his clan on their land.

As the sun rose, Dugan and Lachann gathered their belongings together. They heard activity in the kitchen and found the innkeeper there, along with two maids. Dugan made haste in settling his account with the man, asking him if he knew when Lady Maura's party had left the inn.

"They hav'na left, Laird." The man frowned fiercely. "At least, not that I know of. They've no' paid me fer their lodgings."

No, of course they had not settled their account, not if they—

A shrill voice and the clomping of heavy shoes on the staircase interrupted Dugan's thoughts. The old woman he had seen with Lady Maura burst into the kitchen. "She's gone!" she cried. "Gone!"

"Lady Maura, ye mean?" asked the innkeeper.

"Well, who else would I be talking about, man?" the woman demanded in a panicked but decidedly sour tone. "Where could she have gone?"

The innkeeper spoke to one of the maids. "Go out to the privy and see if the lady is there."

"I've been there, sir," the old woman countered. "Which is why I know that Lady Maura is not there *or* in her room!"

Dugan stepped forward. "What about her lieutenant?"

The old woman looked askance at Dugan for suggesting the possibility that the two were together, but turned to the innkeeper. "Rouse Lieutenant Baird, sir." Then she turned to Dugan and pointed one pale finger at him. "And you keep out of this, you . . . you . . . *highlander*!"

Dugan crossed his arms over his chest and leaned back against a large, heavy worktable. "Nay, woman. I do not think so," he said in his most intimidating tone. 'Twould take only a moment to confirm or deny Baird's absence, then Dugan intended to go after Maura. Mayhap his men had already found them.

Deep color rose upon the old woman's cheeks. She turned in a huff and followed the innkeeper out of the kitchen. Dugan returned to the sitting room and once again tore through every corner and every cushion of every piece of furniture, hoping to find the map tucked away somewhere.

He swore again, furious not only with Maura,

but with himself. He never should have assumed they were safe in the inn. He should have posted a guard last night.

Dugan caught sight of Bryce and Kieran outside, returning to the inn after their search. Lady Maura was not with them.

A moment later, he heard the sound of voices above stairs, and soon Lieutenant Baird was racing down to the ground floor. He wore only his trews and shirt, and had not even taken the time to pull on his boots. "She must be here somewhere, by God!"

If Lieutenant Napper was still there, then where was Lady Maura? Had she gone off by herself? 'Twas unthinkable.

"You there!" the lieutenant called to Dugan.

Dugan did not even pretend to listen to the man. He shouldered his pack and started out the door, determined to go after the little thief himself. But the lieutenant grabbed his arm as he passed.

"I'm speaking to you, highlander!"

Dugan pulled away and headed out the door. "You may be speaking, but I've better things to do than listen to a bloody Sassenach."

"**S**end someone to the fort for my men!" Baird ordered the innkeeper.

"What about me?" the Hammond woman whined.

"Well, what about you, woman?" *Christ almighty.* He could not *lose* Maura. At least, not unintentionally.

"What are you going to do? What shall *I* do?"

"I do not give a bloody hell what you do," he

said. He caught the innkeeper before the man went to find a messenger. "I want this building searched, top to bottom."

The innkeeper shot Baird a look of indignation. "Lieutenant Baird, I cannot rouse every patron from his bed!"

"Aye, you can and you will. Unless you'd like me to bring soldiers from the garrison to do it for you."

Goddamn it, the wench had not waited until her arrival in Cromarty to rebel against her father's wishes as Baird had assumed.

"Ach, dear heavens, where would she go? Home?" the Hammond woman whined.

Baird's mind raced. He'd known she would at least attempt to talk the baron out of marriage, and if that didn't work, *then* try something drastic. 'Twas likely she'd found someone to take her back to Glasgow. Or even to Aucharnie Castle to confront her father. Baird went to the window and watched carefully as the highlanders gathered in front of the inn, and knew she was not with them.

So where was she and with whom?

He wondered if she'd found a soldier to escort her back south. God knew there were plenty of them about Fort William, but if he laid hands on any such soldier, the man was going to suffer court-martial for his actions.

Baird climbed to his room to dress properly for a day that was likely to get worse before it got any better. This was not at all what he had in mind when he considered ridding Lord Aucharnie of his troublesome daughter.

Chapter 7

Dugan heard the English lieutenant order the innkeeper to search the inn and to send someone to the fort for his men. The old woman seemed to think the lass would return home. Considering the site where she'd nearly met her demise at the business end of the ram's horns, her home must be south.

Perfect. Dugan hoped the bald-pated lieutenant took his men away south to search for her. If she knew anything about the map and the gold, she would have set out in a northerly direction, on a path toward his treasure in the highlands.

"Laird MacMillan," the innkeeper called to him just as he was about to ride out.

"What is it, man?" Dugan asked sharply. He was barely able to contain his anger and was eager to be on his way.

"Ye did'na leave coin in me pantry, now, did ye?"

Dugan must have shown a puzzled expression, for the innkeeper went on to explain. "There's food missing, but coins on the shelf in its place."

"Nay, 'twas not us, though I'd gladly pay you for whatever provisions you can spare." Dugan knew who'd taken the inn's food. The same woman who'd stolen his map.

"**Y**e're out and about early, lass."

The rasping voice startled Maura, and she realized it had come from an old woman sitting outside a small croft at the edge of the trees, away from the beaten path. A huge wolfhound lay in the grass by her side, but sat up to attention when Maura stopped.

"Come and sit awhile," the woman said.

Maura hesitated. She'd been walking at a very good pace for at least three hours, but figured she'd covered no more than ten miles. Yet she was weary. She could use a moment's respite.

"Thank you," she said. "I wouldn't mind a drink of water. But your dog—"

"He will'na harm ye. No' without my say." She spoke softly to the beast, and it almost seemed . . . No, the huge animal had *not* nodded at the woman's words. "Come inside, then," she said to Maura.

The bent and wrinkled old woman stood and led the way into the croft, and when she turned to face Maura by the weak light of the peat fire, Maura saw that the irises of her eyes were milky white. The woman was blind.

"Ye're far from home, lass." The woman went right to a bucket next to a table and ladled some water into an earthen cup. She turned and handed it to Maura.

"How do you know that?" The big dog sat down near the fire, alert, watching her.

"I might be blind, but there's things I can see, lassie."

Maura took a drink and eyed the woman with a fair degree of caution. "What can you see?"

"I can see that ye've been travelin' awhile and yer feet are tired. Sit and rest."

"I haven't much time."

"Aye, but ye're ahead o' them and will be fer a fair piece."

The woman's words shocked Maura. "Ahead of whom?"

"Them who's after ye."

Maura sat down in shock. "Wh-what do you know of them?"

The woman touched her forehead. "What's more important is what old Sorcha knows o' *ye*, lass."

He is anger unabated, Dugan rode alongside his men and set out to follow his beautiful seductress. Ach, he could not believe the pretty little thief had beguiled him so well.

And here he thought he'd been so noble, ending their intimate encounter that never should have taken place to begin with. He should have spent the time on the veranda talking with her, finding out who she was and why she was traveling with the English soldiers. But Dugan had never felt such a hard, swift attraction to any other woman.

"Dugan, do you really think the daft woman left the inn on her own?" Lachann asked in a deprecating tone.

"She did not leave with the lieutenant," he replied, his words clipped.

"Do you suppose she had another accomplice?" Bryce asked.

Dugan sorted through his thoughts. "She couldn't have known about the gold and the map. At least, not that they were connected."

"Except that if *you* heard about the map in Ullapool," Lachann said, "*she* might have heard the rumor as well."

"But she wouldn't have had time to enlist a man to help her. Not in the short time she was here." Or would she?

Dugan spurred his horse and led them onto the northerly bridle path, nearly certain this was the way she would travel. She had the map, and it showed only the highlands.

Dugan still could not grasp how Maura had taken him in. He might have initiated their kiss, but he'd been the one completely seduced. It had been next to impossible to pull away from her, and all night he'd been tortured by dreams of her, of sharing the French king's gold with her. Christ, he was a fool.

He wondered why she'd been traveling in the company of the English soldiers, but he did not stay in town long enough to watch them ride southward to look for her.

"I'm not inclined to show the little thief any mercy, Dugan," said Lachann.

"Nay, after you saved her bloody life," said Kieran, "she should have had some respect for your property."

Aye, 'twas exactly what Dugan thought.

"Her bonny face won't keep me from running her through when we catch up to her," Lachann said, his face grave.

Dugan's throat went dry at the thought of killing her. He ought not to care, for she'd stolen from

him. Damn all, she'd taken the map while he was
dreaming of her.

He hoped Maura stayed on the bridle path and
did not go wandering into the woods on some un-
charted path, for he did not have time to chase
about the hills to look for a damned thief. He
had to find the gold and get his payment to Argyll
before the month's end.

"Which way, Dugan?" Conall asked as they
came to a split in the path.

"We'll take the westward path."

He'd lost all track of time during his restless
sleep, so he couldn't estimate how long it had been
since she'd left the inn. The fire in her room had
burned down to embers, so it was likely she had
several hours' lead. He hoped she twisted an ankle
and they would soon find her nursing the injury at
the side of the path.

"D'ye think she's on horseback, Laird?" Archie
asked.

Dugan shook his head. "She wasn't wearing
riding clothes when she arrived last night, so she
probably came in a carriage."

"There were so many grooms in the stable,
Laird, 'tis unlikely she'd have been able to steal a
horse," Conall remarked.

Lachann nodded in agreement. "But even on
foot, she could have walked a good ten miles in the
last few hours."

Or more, Dugan feared, in spite of her clothing.
She was young and fit, and even wearing a dress,
she should be able to cover two or three miles every
hour.

They were wasting precious time. The lass had
a good lead on them, no matter what her mode of

transportation, and plenty of good places to hide. They would need to keep all their wits about them if they were to find her.

And Dugan fully intended to find her.

Sorcha sat down across from Maura and reached for her hand. Maura hesitated.

"Ye're no' afeart, are ye?"

"Of course not." Maura placed her hand in the woman's dry palm. She would humor the old crone; after all, the woman had provided her some respite from the path as well as a cool drink when she needed it.

Sorcha smiled when Maura's hand slid into hers.

"What?"

"Well, if naught else, ye've a good heart, *a chiallain*."

Maura frowned. "What do you mean—if naught else?"

The crone tipped her head and gazed at her with those eerie blind eyes. "Ye need to use yer own good sense, lass. And there'll be times when ye need t' listen t' yer heart."

"I am. Well, I'm trying to." For two long years, her heart had been telling her to go to Rosie, and her good sense had given her the means to do it.

The old crone's eyes remained unfocused, but Maura somehow felt their unseeing gaze. "Ach, lass. I fear 'tis only the dust in the fields and on the wind that'll give ye what ye seek."

Dust and wind? The woman spoke nonsense. Maura was going to put the pieces of the map together in order to find her way. She started to pull her hand away, but Sorcha tightened her grip.

"Ye carry most all that ye need, lass."

Maura eyed the woman with suspicion. First, nonsense, and now . . . she wondered if Sorcha intended for her to divulge what was in her belongings . . . including her money. She used her aforementioned good sense. "Most?"

"Aye." Sorcha frowned and gave a quick shake of her head. "But yer wee prize will'na divulge its secrets, no' even to the Glencoe lad. No' unless . . ."

"Who is the Glencoe lad?" Her words made no sense to Maura, but Sorcha sat back and pressed one trembling hand to her breast.

"Ach, 'twas many a year ago. He's a great fierce warrior now."

"I do not know whom you speak of." She'd heard of terrible events happening at Glencoe, and her own family had played no small part in it. But that was years ago, before Maura was born.

Sorcha nodded absently, as though recollecting something so distant it was difficult to remember.

The crackle of the fire startled Maura. "What about a prize? M-my prize?" Did the woman refer to the maps? Maura sincerely hoped the map she'd taken from Dugan MacMillan would divulge its secrets when joined with Argyll's map.

At least the woman had not made mention of the theft. Maura still felt shame and embarrassment for taking what belonged to Laird MacMillan. But she'd had no choice. She—

" 'Twill no' show you the path t' Loch Camerochlan, my lady."

Maura's brain froze inside her skull.

She'd told no one of her plan to go to Loch Camerochlan. "What do . . . How do you know—" She shook her head. It had to be some kind of weird luck. Or perhaps when Maura had first encountered the woman she'd spoken her destination aloud. She was so weary 'twas possible she'd said it without meaning to.

But she did not think so.

Maura shivered and thought of all the wintry nights spent in the Elliott croft with Deirdre's old mother telling tales of ghosts, witches, and faeries. Maura did not believe in such things . . . much. On the contrary, she'd found that real, mortal beings were most dangerous—men like her father, who would cast out an innocent bairn to die because she was sickly.

But Maura did not know what to think now, when she was faced with the specter of a real witch. She found herself glancing 'round the small croft, looking for obvious signs of witchcraft.

She let out the breath she was holding. There was naught but the dog. "Why do you say I will not go to Loch Camerochlan?"

"I did'na say that," Sorcha retorted.

"Will you explain yourself?"

Sorcha rocked back into her chair and began to hum, and Maura decided the old woman was full of so much nonsense. She knew naught.

And yet a small part of Maura recognized that there could be otherworldly elements at work in the world. How else had Rosie survived past her birth than because of the extraordinary care taken by the Elliotts to keep her away from the powers that could harm her? Deirdre had kept Rosie from exposure to harmful moonlight when she was a wee bairn. And she'd been careful never to put a stitch of clothing on the child until she passed it through the smoke of their peat fire, to be sure no witches would ever hold sway over her.

A chill crawled up Maura's spine and she wondered if anyone had ever passed *her* clothes through the smoke of a fire. Likely not, for here she was, in company of a wizened old witch, and listening to her cryptic speech.

"There's them that would help ye, lassie," Sorcha whispered, leaning forward to take Maura's hand again, "if they do'na kill ye first."

Maura held perfectly still, tempted to discount Sorcha's words. The only help or encouragement she'd received since defying her father and saving Rosie from certain death had been from the Elliotts. Maura had spent nearly all her time at their small croft after that, taking care of her infant sister whenever Deirdre was not feeding her. Maura had been the one to raise her sister, following Deirdre's example with her own children.

Her parents had seen Rosie only a few times in the eleven years since her birth, and only by accident. The earl and countess Aucharnie were ashamed of their youngest offspring, and they did not like Maura much better. Fortunately, Deirdre Elliott had provided the motherly warmth and affection Maura and her sister had lacked from their own mother.

Sorcha was wrong. There was no one in this vicinity to help her.

But she feared her clandestine flight from the inn might have angered someone enough to kill her. Baird or the highlander? Or both?

"I see yer prize. 'Twill will be of no use to ye without an ally, *a chiallain*."

Maura shuddered. "How do you know all this, Sorcha?"

The woman closed one eye and seemed to look inward with the other. "'Tis a gift."

From where, Maura could only imagine.

She shook off the eerie sensations that had been running through her since her arrival at Sorcha's cottage. She was fatigued, but rationality returned to her.

Of course she would have allies. "Fellow travelers and crofters will likely point out the right paths for me." She spoke dismissively, more than ready to take her leave.

Sorcha rubbed her thumb over Maura's palm. "Ah, but danger follows ye."

Maura pulled her hand away. "What do you mean?"

"Ye must take care, lass."

Maura swallowed as her guilt came back to haunt her. She should never have taken the map, but she could not undo what was done. "Can you not be more specific, Sorcha?"

The lines between Sorcha's brows deepened. "I can'na . . ." She tipped her head to one side, as if listening to some unseen speaker. "Ach, nay. It can'na be. He has returned . . . ?"

"Whoever *he* is, he will not find me," Maura countered, shivering at the thought of the highland laird coming after her. She'd felt such power in the man's arms . . . Would he harm her if he found her? She certainly hoped not, for then she'd have misjudged him completely. Sorcha must mean Lieutenant Baird, for she'd always sensed a bitter malice in him. "I'll stay ahead of him, and I will most certainly hide when he comes near."

But Sorcha's words left her thoroughly shaken. It would not go well for Baird if he lost her, and Maura believed he was perfectly capable of concocting a tale for her parents . . .

With unease rising in her chest, she stood and walked out the door of the croft. She'd gone only two steps outside when she turned and faced the woman. "Th-thank you for the water, Sorcha."

Chapter 8

Dugan had been dreaming of Campbells and Duncansons for as long as he could remember. Over and over, he'd heard the report of their rifles and known they'd murdered his father and brother. He'd seen his poor mother turn blue with the cold, unable to run any farther into the mountains . . .

But Dugan's nights had never been invaded by a russet-haired beauty who softened his heart as she inflamed his body with lust.

Last night he'd been dreaming of her, of Maura, and the interlude they'd shared earlier in the evening. Even in sleep, he'd been able to feel her mouth on his, but the dream had taken it even further. Dugan had undressed her as every male instinct had urged him to do as they stood together on the veranda, baring every inch of her soft skin to his touch.

And in his dream, he had touched her everywhere.

"Bloody neep."

"What?" Lachann asked.

"Naught." Just giving himself a well-deserved scolding. "I wonder if she came this far." They'd caught up to Conall and Kieran, who'd seen no sign of her.

Clearly, something was seriously wrong with him if he was so susceptible to a pretty face. What ailed him could probably be cured by a wife—a spirited lass, one who possessed a strong backbone and would stand with him at the head of their clan.

Such a woman must exist, and Dugan intended to find her as soon as he resolved the issue of Argyll's rent. For he could not bring a wife into that perilous situation, not until he knew the MacMillans would keep their lands.

"I'd say she must have," Lachann answered. "Else Kieran or Conall would have seen her."

"I should have posted a guard last night," Dugan said.

"You cannot blame yourself, brother," Lachann retorted. "We were all exhausted last night."

"Mayhap." But a MacMillan laird should have risen above his fatigue to take better care of the map. 'Twas what any competent laird would have done.

They followed the curve of the river and passed a small town to the north. 'Twas still early, and there were only a few hearth fires burning. Dugan was fairly certain Maura had traveled this path, but they didn't see any sign of her.

Soon they passed a crooked little croft situated a few yards into the woods, but no one was about, except for a huge dog that sat in front of its door. The giant hound watched as they passed, but made no sound to alert its master of their passing, as though it understood they were no threat.

They might be no threat to the crofter, but the

redhead was going to suffer severe consequences when they found her.

"Do ye think she knows about the gold, Laird?" Archie asked.

"Without question. One of you idiots mentioned gold in the taproom last night," Lachann responded hotly. "What else was she to think when she saw the map?"

'Twas difficult for Dugan to grasp the notion of Lady Maura leaving the town alone on a search for gold that she'd heard about only in passing, with a map that had not yet yielded any clues. Women did not travel alone. They did not take to the hills on foot without wagons full of supplies, without armed men to protect them.

And they certainly did not tryst with strange men on the verandas of inns.

Clearly, Dugan had misapprehended the woman from the moment he'd set eyes upon her. And now he was paying the price.

They'd traveled a full league past the croft when Dugan signaled for his men to split up. Even though riding through the woods would slow them down, they would cover more territory, and it was possible she'd abandoned the path in order to walk under cover of the trees.

"We'll ride parallel. I'll keep to the road. Lachann, go into the woods where I can hear you if you call out. Archie, ride past Lachann, but stay within earshot. The rest of you do the same."

He hoped they didn't have to go too far before one of them stumbled upon the thieving wench.

During her journey from Glasgow, Maura had never, *ever* spoken of Rosie to anyone, for fear that someone would guess the goal she'd harbored these past two years.

She'd done all she could to cause Bridget and Baird to believe she would take a southerly path. By the time they realized their mistake, she would be so far into the highlands they would never find her.

The same was not true of the MacMillan laird. If he figured out who had stolen his map, he would be on her trail so fast she would not have time to hide. Maura did not think Dugan MacMillan would kill her, but it was imperative that she evade him. She hoped he and his men did not awaken too soon.

She regretted that the highland laird's amazing kisses could mean naught to her. They'd touched something deep inside her, awakening feelings she'd long kept buried. 'Twas more than just desire for a man's touch.

Of course she wanted a man who cared for her, one who would protect her and give her a home and children of her own. Someone who would accept Rosie into his life, without having to be asked.

But until Maura rescued her sister from Loch Camerochlan, she could not think of husbands or children of her own. And if she did not move along far more quickly, she was going to be caught by the highland laird and then . . . who knew what he would do?

The faint light of morning dawned, and Maura realized she needed to get off the narrow bridle path that skirted alongside the loch. For that was the route Laird MacMillan would take, and she would be too easily seen.

She veered into the woods, where she knew she would not be able to keep up the same quick pace, for the ground was uneven and strewn with broken timber and clumps of foliage. Twice she tripped and nearly fell to her knees before she decided 'twas time to rest.

Maura soon came upon a fallen log where she brushed off the loose bark and made it an acceptable seat. Once she was off her feet, she untied the skin of water from the handle of her bag, then reached inside and took out the cheese she'd taken from the inn.

She was anxious to see what she could learn from the map, so she took both pieces out, and quickly realized there was a third portion, rolled inside the map she'd taken from Laird MacMillan. With her heart thundering with excitement, she pieced them together in the grass.

The three sections were definitely part of a whole, and Maura could tell there was still at least one portion missing. Without any printed words on the document, she found it nearly impossible to tell what she was looking at. But then she noticed a symbol near the bottom of one of the pieces she'd taken from Dugan's pack that indicated a fortified building. Fort William, perhaps? Or Inverary Castle?

It had to be one or the other. She traced the blue ink that represented the loch to the west of the fort, and another one that flared out north. Loch Eil, she hoped.

But locating her own position did naught to help her identify Loch Camerochlan. Maura had made a point of studying a real map of Scotland at Lord Ilay's house in Glasgow, so she knew Rosie had been taken far into the northwest. But there were numerous small blue marks on the sections of map before her that indicated rivers and lochs. The only way she was going to be able to locate Camerochlan was by continuing to travel northwest and asking for directions from the people she met on her way.

If only 'twould be so easy to find the French king's gold, for there was no grand X marking any spot on the map. But Maura had time. 'Twas going to take more than a few days to make her way up to Loch Camerochlan—mayhap she would figure out the key to the map during her travels.

Maura put the pieces of the map away. Her only interest in the treasure was for Rosie's sake. If she could whisk her sister away from Tilda Crane and get them far from Scotland, her father would hold no sway over them. 'Twould be so much easier to accomplish if she had more money than the sum she carried with her.

She thought of Sorcha, but discounted her warning. The highlander wouldn't kill her for taking his map. He would merely take it back.

Wouldn't he?

She knew she should not assume so. He wore his claymore in his belt as though he would not hesitate to use it. And there was that dirk in his stocking . . .

Still, Maura could not forget the interlude on the veranda of the inn. His touch had been potent, not painful. He'd been considerate, building his seduction slowly, and Maura had done naught to stop him. She'd craved more than just his kiss. Her breasts had tingled and ached for his touch, and when she felt his intense arousal against her belly, Maura had lost all sense of decency.

But he had not. He'd pulled away.

Maura supposed a highland warrior might allow himself to enjoy a few moments' passion, especially when freely offered, but he would never ally himself with the daughter of a lowland lord. Nor would that lowland lord allow his daughter to be courted by such a man.

Maura shivered and rubbed her arms to warm them. She opened her eyes to the brightening sky and caught the sight of three unsavory men coming toward her from the deep woods, all of them on foot.

She stood abruptly, her heart pounding.

All three men were large and dirty, their expressions menacing. Maura did not know what to do. She was entirely alone, with no weapon, no way to defend herself.

"What have we here, lads?" the first one called out.

"A wee pigeon, ripe for the pluckin'," another one said with a wicked grin.

Maura realized she was going to die there, and die horribly.

Chapter 9

Maura grabbed her bag and made a run for it. She ran as fast as she could, cursing the twisting of her skirts about her legs. They slowed her immeasurably, and if she could have torn them off to get away from the filthy brigands, she'd have done it.

She began to pray for her salvation when she turned back for a quick glance and saw them gaining on her. But the rumble of galloping hooves was coming toward her through the dense woods, distracting her. She tripped and nearly fell, but suddenly Laird MacMillan was there, jumping from his horse and catching her in his arms.

He quickly shoved her behind him as he drew out his massive claymore from his sword belt.

"You'd be wise to stop where you are, lads." His voice sounded like steel.

The outlaws laughed. Maura gaped at the men, her terror in her throat. Her knees wobbled so badly she was afraid they would not support her. She tried to step back, away from Laird MacMillan, but quickly realized she was holding on to the back of his tartan. She was using him as a shield, the very man who'd come to take back the property she'd stolen from him.

He was poised to fight. His knees bent, arms spread wide, his plaid swaying against his legs as though naught was amiss. As though he was about to spar for his own amusement.

"You do not want to test me," he said. Maura let go of his tartan and watched in horror as the men surrounded them. Did he not understand what a dire predicament this was?

"Nay?" asked the tallest of the men, lunging at Dugan with his sword.

Dugan leaped away to one side, pulling Maura with him. Her ankle shrieked in pain when she took a step. "Stand away, Maura," he commanded.

But there was nowhere to go. Their attackers seemed to come from every direction all at once, two with long swords, the other from behind, wielding a short dirk.

But MacMillan turned and dodged quickly and effectively, parrying every thrust and jab. The clang of steel echoed in the woods, as did the taunts of his attackers. Maura ducked and tried to stay out of MacMillan's way and out of the reach of the men who'd come upon her.

"Ye can'na keep this up, ye wee bloody bastard!" one of them shouted.

But yes, it seemed that Dugan MacMillan, who was not wee in any way, could keep it up indefinitely. And he would have, but one of the swordsmen came for her. Maura turned to run, but her injured ankle prevented it. She lost her footing and fell to the ground.

MacMillan spun quickly and speared her assailant before Maura could look away.

Screams of rage came from the two who remained and they charged MacMillan, clearly intending to slaughter him for killing their accomplice.

He dealt with each one, seemingly all at once. And yet Maura knew it could not be possible. No one was that fast or that capable a swordsman. But when all was quiet in the woods, the three robbers lay in the grass all 'round them.

The only man standing was Dugan MacMillan, and he was coming toward her with his claymore in hand, his steely blue gaze upon her.

She swallowed hard. "Please . . ."

"Please *what*, Lady Maura? Please do not take back what you stole from me?" His voice was harsh, and for the first time, she actually feared him. He seemed exactly the kind of barbarian warrior she'd been warned of—a man who was frighteningly capable of using that sword in his hand.

Maura tried to scramble away from him, but he grabbed her ankle and pulled her to him through the grass. It was humiliating to be caught this way, with her skirts sliding up past her knees. But at least he held his claymore down at his side. He was not going to kill her.

Yet.

"'Twas only a map, Laird MacMillan," she said, despising the wobble in her voice. "And I . . ."

"You *what*?"

His plaid reached only to his knees, and from her position on the ground, Maura could not help but notice the powerful muscles and sinews of his legs. Her eyes drifted up to his broad chest when he

crossed his arms over it, then to his unshaven jaw.
He truly was a barbarian.

She had to get away from him.

"I n-need to find my way into the h-highlands."
She knew it sounded lame, but she didn't think he
would appreciate *any* reason she might give him
for taking his map.

His expression darkened and she recoiled at the
sound of his low growl. She felt the blood leave her
head as he raised his huge sword. Mayhap now he
would kill her.

Dugan sheathed his sword in his belt. The woman
made no sense, but she was as beguiling as ever.

"Your man Baird is not taking you into the
highlands?" He wanted to throttle her. But he was
not in the habit of committing violence against
women, even one who'd wronged him.

Lady Maura shoved down her skirts, depriving
him of the sight of her delectable legs. "Lieutenant
Baird is not my man," she shot back at him.

"No? Then where was he taking you?"

She looked away, unwilling to answer.

"Back to a husband, I suppose," Dugan said,
feeling some disgust at his part in cuckolding her
husband. "Let me guess—he is an unaccountable
brute and you decided to flee him." He should have
thought of that before. But last night, he did not
know she was wholly lacking in scruples.

"No!" she retorted angrily. She leaned forward
and rubbed her injured ankle through her boot.
"Well, not exactly. Not that it's any of your concern, Lieutenant Baird was taking me to Cromarty
to be married."

Dugan let out a low, bitter chuckle. "A bride-groom awaits you? 'Tis almost as bad as a husband. What do you suppose he would say about what took place on the veranda at the inn last night?"

She rose to her feet, but faltered, her ankle quite obviously injured.

Dugan did naught to assist her, but turned and gave out a loud whistle in the direction of the woods, where his men continued to search for her. Lachann would give out a whistle toward the next man who was searching, and so on, until each of the men had heard the signal and returned.

"I had no intention of going to Cromarty, Laird MacMillan." She went for her traveling bag, but Dugan reached it first.

"No, I can see that. You planned to run away, *alone*, into the highlands." Daft woman.

He grabbed her bag and when he opened it, saw his maps lying inside. Looking askance at Maura, he took out the parchments, quickly realizing there was yet another beneath it.

He let out a quiet, low whistle of surprise. "What have you here?"

She tried to get up, but her ankle would not support her. She could barely walk.

Dugan left her to her fate—and her pain. 'Twas nothing less than she deserved. He took out all three quarters of the map and crouched down, spreading out the documents on the ground. "Where did you get this?" he demanded.

She ignored him and limped awkwardly to a large, flat rock, where she took a seat. Reaching down to her boot, she unlaced it, then rubbed her ankle again.

Dugan averted his eyes from the surprisingly

sensuous movement. He was angry and intended to stay that way, and lust had no part of it now.

He pieced the three portions of the map together and found that they fit. But Maura's piece added no clearer clues than the ones she'd stolen from Dugan. Similar markings were all over it, but—

The only thing that helped was having more territory to compare with what he knew. He'd traveled through a good many parts of the highlands, so he knew it well. But he couldn't identify every forest, glen, or loch.

At least he had one more section of the whole now, even though there was nothing that marked any particular spot.

"Where did you get this map, Maura?" he demanded.

"From a desk drawer in a house in Glasgow," she replied grudgingly.

"Whose drawer?"

She shrugged and he swore under his breath. 'Twas difficult to believe this was the woman who'd given herself so completely—and so honestly—the night before. Dugan had never experienced the kind of kiss they'd shared. Had never found it so difficult to part from a woman.

Even now, as she sat rightfully accused, with the hood of her cloak down and her hair askew, she was more compelling than Artis MacLean or any other woman of his acquaintance could ever hope to be.

He took his eyes from those lips that had so bewitched him, and returned his attention to the maps. Lachann and the others would soon arrive, and Dugan wanted to have some answers for them.

Not the least of which was what to do with Lady Maura.

" 'Twas in a desk belonging to my father's cousin. I thought it would help me make my way—"

"Aye. Through the highlands. Right." Dugan took a deep, disparaging breath. "How long have you had it?" he asked her.

She looked up at him then, frowning. "I don't know what right you have to question me so, Laird MacMillan. We are not on your lands, and you have no authority here."

"I have the authority of a man whose property was stolen. By you."

She sagged slightly. "I took it just before I left Glasgow. I had no idea how little use it would be."

Damn all. "So, you stole this one, too."

She did not refute his statement, but pulled on her boot once more and began lacing it.

"So you know naught about the map . . . who made it or where the—" He stopped himself before speaking of the gold.

Maura seemed not to know the true purpose of the map. If she'd taken it thinking it would guide her through the highlands . . . Could she be unaware of the treasure?

Mayhap she was intentionally keeping her knowledge of it from him. As he was most certainly doing to her.

"I assume you had a destination in mind. Where did you intend to go?"

She weighed her words before answering, and then she gave him little to go on. "Into the northwest highlands."

"That's a great deal of territory, Lady Maura.

Exactly *where* in the northwest highlands were you going?"

She rose to her feet and faced him with her hands upon her bonny hips. "To Loch Camerochlan, if you must know, Laird MacMillan."

Her answer was baffling. "Loch Camerochlan? 'Tis well beyond any civilization you would enjoy." Not to mention only a few leagues from Braemore Glenn and his own loch.

"That may be, MacMillan, but that is where I intend to go," she snapped. "And I might ask *you* what you are doing with the other parts of my map!"

Maura knew her statement was bold. In truth, it was ridiculous. But the laird had pierced her with a look so fierce she would not give him the satisfaction of knowing he'd succeeded in intimidating her. At least he was not quite so threatening now that his sword was away.

"*Your* map! By God, woman, you're unbelievable."

She supposed she was. She'd shared impossible intimacies with him, then stolen from him only a few hours later. She wondered at her own audacity.

"Tell me of your bridegroom."

"No. Why should I?"

"Because I am curious." He did not appear curious at all, except for his interest in the maps, which he studied even as he conversed with her. "What kind of man has Lady Maura fleeing into the highlands? Mayhap he has the temerity to dislike thieves."

Maura bristled. "He is not to my liking, if you must know."

"Who is the man?"

"What difference does it make, Laird MacMillan?" she said. "I will not travel to Cromarty or anywhere else for any reason that is unacceptable to me."

He had the impudence to laugh at her. "Do you truly believe Lieutenant Baird will not find you?"

"He won't if I get right back on the path and put several more miles between me and Fort William."

MacMillan shook his head with obvious disdain for her plan. "On that ankle? How far do you think you'll get before it swells to twice its size and strands you in the middle of nowhere?"

It was a question that had worried her ever since she'd tried to take a few steps on it. But she was spared having to reply when a horseman—one of MacMillan's men—raced into the site, dismounting before his horse had even stopped.

"Dugan?" he asked, taking in the carnage all 'round him. "What the . . . ?"

MacMillan barely took his eyes from the map. "Thieves, Lachann. 'Twas necessary."

Truly, the brigands had intended them harm. But Maura had never seen so much death. She shuddered, hoping to figure some way to flee these brutal highlanders. If she just gave them her map . . .

She nearly laughed aloud. *Gave* them? Dugan MacMillan was quite capable of taking anything he wanted. She could protest all she liked, but he had the upper hand in this.

MacMillan's man barely took note of the slaughter all 'round them. 'Twas as though the sight of a massacre was nothing new. While she was grateful the highlander had ridden in to rescue her, the reality of what had just happened gave her pause. She took a deep breath and casually glanced toward the woods for a means of escape. The only town she'd seen had been several miles back, as was Sorcha's croft. Not that Sorcha could offer any protection from Laird MacMillan.

Maura clasped her hands together and calmed her nerves as she studied the two men.

Lachann was similar to Dugan in both features and build. Both were large men, and Maura decided they must be brothers. But 'twas Dugan whose kiss she could still taste. Dugan who'd saved her and protected her with his life.

'Twas a novelty to feel quite so valued, but Maura knew it wouldn't last. Most of her life she'd been either chastised or ignored by her family, and scolded for her mistakes by Lady Ilay. And Dugan MacMillan was obviously displeased with her.

"What's this?" Lachann asked, taking note of the three pieces of map, their torn edges abutted together.

"The lass had yet another part of the map," Dugan replied. "It fits our two."

Lachann tossed Maura a dour look and she recoiled, afraid to consider what they intended to do with her. The parallel between the would-be thieves and herself did not escape her.

But surely if Dugan intended to kill her, he would have done so by now. She knew it was not going to be possible to get away from these men. They had two options. They could take her back to Fort William—against her will, of course. Or take her with them.

Or a third possibility that just occurred to her. They could leave her there in the woods to make her way—wherever—on her own. Maura was afraid she would not get far on her injured ankle.

The only acceptable choice was for her to go with the highlanders. Cromarty and Baron Kildary were out of the question.

But she could not think of any reason that MacMillan would want her along. Unless she could be of some use to them.

As the rest of the MacMillan men rode into the area, Maura knew she was going to have to think of something. Soon.

Chapter 10

"What's your interest in the map, Laird?" Maura asked. "Surely you know your way 'round the highlands without it."

Dugan heard a hint of sarcasm in the woman's voice and he did not like it. "What's your purpose at Loch Camerochlan, Lady Maura?" he asked right back. "I know the loch and the area 'round it, and there is naught there but a few crofts gathered together on the hillside."

She licked her lips, and Dugan forced himself to keep his attention on her eyes. 'Twas much safer that way. "'Tis a place where I'll not be easily found."

"By whom? Your father?"

She gave a little nod and looked away. "And the baron my father would have me wed."

"Baron?" He considered what he knew of the noblemen who lived in and around Cromarty, and thought of one in particular. "Would that be Kildary of Cromarty?" Dugan felt a victory of sorts when Maura's cheeks blushed a deep scarlet.

"Kildary?" Lachann asked, frowning. "He's a wee beast, eh, Dugan?"

Maura stiffened and Dugan narrowed his eyes

as he studied her. Aye, he knew of Kildary. The man was said to be a fiend who misused his family and servants alike.

"Have you a dowry?" he asked her.

She shrugged and looked away.

"How old are you, Lady Maura?" he asked as a plan began to form in his head.

She stuck her chin up and faced him squarely. "I am twenty-four years of age, Dugan MacMillan, not that it's any concern of yours."

Aye, she had no dowry, else she would have been married well before now. She was old to be a maiden. Or, he decided, if she did have a dowry, it was unsubstantial. Either her father was a poor man, or she was out of favor with him.

Dugan therefore concluded 'twas the baron who would pay for the privilege of taking Maura to wife. He needed an heir, for his only son had died at Perth two years before, in battle against King James's forces. Dugan supposed 'twas not difficult for Kildary to find a bride when he was younger, but now the man had to be at least seventy.

In spite of Maura's thievery, Dugan felt a wave of sympathy at the thought of her being led to the old man's bed.

He called to Kieran and Calum.

"Aye, Laird," they responded, dismounting and coming to him, leading their horses.

"Ride to Cromarty," Dugan ordered, carefully watching Maura's expression. "Go to the house of Baron Kildary and tell him Laird MacMillan has his bride at Braemore. Tell him that a mere three thousand pounds will buy her back."

Maura gave out a strangled cry, but Dugan paid

her no heed. This was an opportunity he could not ignore. A fortune in French gold would be a grand find, but ransoming Lady Maura was a sure thing.

He felt as though a weight had been lifted from his shoulders. Ransoming a bride was a fine tradition in the highlands, and 'twas high time the MacMillans took part in the practice.

Oh aye, he still intended to search for the gold, and if he found it, it would be a windfall in addition to what Kildary paid him.

He mounted his horse and rode to Maura, who was still sitting on the rock, and fuming with anger, by the looks of her.

"Lachann, toss the lady up to me."

Lieutenant Baird rode to the fort and approached the commander's office. He mopped his damp brow with his sleeve when he considered how his father would react when he learned of his son's failure to transport one useless female from Glasgow to Cromarty. General Baird was nothing if not exacting, and he tolerated no disappointments from his subordinates.

His father held the respect of every officer and regiment under his command. Even King George paid heed to John Baird's counsel. For his entire life, Alastair had striven to make his father proud, anticipating and obeying his every command. He had yet to prove himself in battle—but only because the opportunity had not presented itself.

Alastair had written to the general more than once, asking to be transferred to an active regiment—specifically, to the Duke of Argyll's forces, where his father had distinguished himself many times over. But General Baird had responded by telling Alastair to be patient.

It had been a blow. And so had been his specific orders to remain at Aucharnie during the last Jacobite uprising. Alastair was to keep order at Aucharnie's holding in case of any unrest in the nearby environs. So he'd missed the action at Edinburgh when the Duke of Argyll's men had arrived and routed the rebels.

'Twas such a humiliation to stand in the public house beside the men who'd seen action. Next to those who'd christened their sabers with the blood of those damned rebels.

Soon, though. Soon Alastair would *demand* to be transferred to a regiment where he could demonstrate his worth. 'Twas past time, despite his father's advice to avoid becoming overwrought.

As though Alastair's anxiety was unfounded.

He sent for his own men while the commander of the fort assembled his regiment and called the roll. Every soldier was accounted for.

That, however, did not mean Maura Duncanson couldn't have found some other likely fool to guide her south. There were farmers and shopkeepers . . . many a young man about town who might well be pleased and flattered at the request of a comely lass like Lady Maura Duncanson.

Whoever it was would soon learn what a royal pain in the arse she was.

He wasted far too much time looking for the wench in Fort William and searching for any missing soldier who might have accompanied her. When it became clear she had neither stolen a horse nor convinced some hapless soldier to go with her,

Baird and his men set off on the southern road to look for her.

Not that she was going to be easy to find. He did not know if she was a proficient rider and had taken someone's horse—someone who had not missed it yet—or if she was on foot. He wanted to assume she traveled on foot, but he knew it was not necessarily so.

Somehow, this affair was going to end in his favor.

Chapter 11

Maura let out a sharp squeal of shock as Lachann MacMillan picked her up and chucked her onto Laird MacMillan's horse. Dugan caught her before she flopped over the other side.

'Twas horribly embarrassing to be handled so roughly and with no decorum at all. That, and the fact that her skirts were askew, showing her legs and ankles to all these rough highlanders.

At least they gave the impression of looking away as she tried to arrange herself in a more dignified position. But the laird gave her no chance to regain her pride, picking her up and placing her into the saddle in front of him.

"If you think I'll ride on this horse with you, in this way—"

"Aye, you *will* ride this way, lass."

"But 'tis so—"

He reached 'round her for the reins and in so doing, pulled her against his chest. She closed her eyes tightly and took a deep breath. "Baron Kildary will not pay any ransom for me."

He ignored her statement and turned the horse in the direction she'd been going before the incident with the thieves. The thought of them made her shudder, and she wondered again what kind of man she'd become saddled with.

He was a brute, certainly. And as bad as any thief, for he intended to wrest a ransom from Kildary in exchange for her person. Mayhap he was the one Sorcha had warned her about.

"Baron Kildary doesn't even know me."

"Then I can thank the saints for that. Else he might see fit to leave you to your fate and ignore my ransom demand."

She gave out a great huff. "I am not a thief, Laird MacMillan."

"Ach, right, lass. I'm sure of that." His tone indicated his disagreement.

"You know I have good reason for going to Loch Camerochlan." She shouldn't allow him to make her feel defensive, but he did.

He gave out a quiet snort. "We all have good reasons for what we do."

"You're saying my grounds for going to the loch are not valid." Escaping Kildary was perfectly valid, but she did not think it prudent to tell him about Rosie as well. She knew he would somehow figure a way to use that information against her.

"Nay, Lady Maura," he remarked. "'Tis not what I said at all."

"But that's what you meant." She turned to face him then, and felt the power of his gaze. Icy blue and full of disdain. Maura forgot what she was going to say.

"I generally mean exactly what I say. So do not put words into my mouth."

Her eyes were drawn to his mouth then, and she remembered how it had felt when pressed against hers. Warm and firm, yet giving. It looked hard and implacable now.

She looked away. "Where is Braemore? Is it . . . what is it?"

He shrugged. "'Tis our home, only a few days' ride from here."

She jerked her head 'round to look at him. "A few days' ride! I cannot possibly stay with you that long!"

He raised a brow at her confrontational tone. Apparently, he expected her to submit without question to his twisted demands. "Do you have an assignation at Loch Camerochlan that you cannot miss?"

"Of course not!"

"Then 'twould behoove you to be patient and see how this all plays out."

"I know exactly how it will play out." She wanted to slap the condescending expression from his face. "Your men will return from Cromarty empty-handed, but with a message from Kildary."

MacMillan laughed mirthlessly.

"The baron's message will be something along the lines of 'Do what you will with her.'"

His expression grew serious then, and Maura realized there was more than one meaning to what she'd said. Her breath caught in her throat at the sensual glint in his eyes and she considered the possibilities.

But no. She had to leave him as soon as possible and make her way to Loch Camerochlan. Now that he had all three sections of the map, Maura had no chance of finding the gold. She needed to follow her original plan to escape marriage with Kildary and rescue Rosie.

Maura wondered if her father held some sway over the baron. That made the most sense to Maura's mind, for this was the first time her parents had attempted to make a match for her. She'd been deemed intractable years ago when they learned she'd taken Rosie away on the day of her birth—not to die, but to be nurtured and raised by Deirdre Elliott.

Lord and Lady Aucharnie had all but disowned her while they lavished their attentions and efforts on their older, more successful children. Maura wanted to believe her mother was secretly glad that she'd saved Rosie, but she could never be sure. Lady Aucharnie never acted against her husband, either in word or in deed.

During the years of her youth, Maura had spent most of her time at the Elliott croft. But one day nearly two years ago, her father had sent for her. He'd ordered the despicable Lieutenant Baird to confine her to one of the towers in Aucharnie Castle while Major Ramsay and his men collected Rosie and took her away with the Crane woman.

While Lieutenant Baird had taken far too much pleasure in tossing Maura into her chamber and locking her in, poor Rosie's cries of despair tormented her.

'Twas all her father's doing. Maura had gone to her mother to plead for Rosie's return, but Lady Aucharnie had not said a word. Her face had gone pale with her lips pinched tightly together.

Within the week, Maura had been removed to Ilay House in Glasgow, in hopes that Lady Ilay could "improve" her and make her not only manageable, but marriageable. It had been months before she'd been able to discover where Rosie had been taken, and the remote loch seemed unreachable. As soon as she'd heard, Maura had made an attempt to slip away from Ilay House and make her way to Loch Camerochlan. But she'd been found out. Twice.

And ever after, she'd been forbidden to leave Lord Ilay's property without an escort. A guard, really.

Maura did not know why it was so important to her parents that she and Rosie be kept apart. If they wanted their two youngest daughters to disappear, they could have arranged it with little trouble. They could have given her all the money he'd sent to Ilay for her upkeep and insist that Maura take Rosie and move far from Aucharnie Castle and their vaunted social circle. The family never need see her or Rosie again.

Maura was determined to see that they didn't.

With some subtle signal Maura did not understand, MacMillan urged his horse into a fast trot, and gathered the reins tighter, pulling her even closer to his chest.

There was one very good reason for Dugan to ride faster—to get as far ahead of Lieutenant Baird as possible. When the man came to realize Maura had not traveled south, he would be right on their trail. But Dugan had yet another motive. To hold Maura more tightly in his arms. To breathe deeply of her warm, spicy scent and feel how incredible her soft curves fit against the hard planes of his body.

His attraction to the little thief should have abated, but it had not. She was full of mystery—betrothed to Baron Kildary, in possession of one quarter of the map, and traveling to Loch Camerochlan. She could not be more enticing.

Her hood was down, and long wisps of her hair had come loose from their bindings, catching in the stubble of his beard. Dugan fought hard against the urge to press his lips against the soft skin at her nape; to take her on a short detour from the path and lay her in the grass to—

He caught himself from taking his erotic vision too far. 'Twould only make the ride impossible when it was now just uncomfortable. Dugan had his principles. Once old Kildary paid him the ransom, he would return his bride in the same condition he'd taken her. Untouched.

Or *somewhat* untouched. He did not think that kiss on the veranda counted for much. Her fiery response had staggered him—and yet it could not have meant anything to her, for she'd taken his most valuable possession from him only a few hours afterward.

Could she be as mercenary as she seemed?

"Loch Camerochlan is a fair distance from here, Lady Maura," he said. Anything to get his mind from the lush bounty that lay so close to his hands. He knew she was lying about the loch, or at the very least, holding back something about it. Mayhap she knew the French gold had been hidden there.

"Of course it is."

"Do you think you can hide from your bridegroom up there indefinitely?"

He felt her stiffen and shift away from him, but he pulled her back against his chest and ignored the daft notion that that was where she belonged.

"Of course not," she said with a sigh. "But perhaps long enough for him to give up on me and settle on another bride."

"Why Loch Camerochlan and not some other—more comfortable—place?"

She'd denied having an assignation, and Dugan wanted to believe it. He wanted to believe her reason for choosing Camerochlan was its remoteness. But he knew there were far better places to hide. Which left only one other possible reason that she wanted to go there. The gold.

And to think Loch Camerochlan was only a matter of a few leagues from Braemore Glen. The irony of its proximity did not escape him.

Maura did not answer his question, which reinforced Dugan's suspicions. He decided to let her think he believed her only reason for trying to get to the loch was to avoid marriage to Kildary.

"'Twill be pleasant up at the loch during the summer months, but come the winter, you'll be lucky not to freeze to death."

"*What?*" she cried, whipping her head 'round to face him. His statement upset her, and he realized the brightness in her eyes was caused by the sheen of tears. "Winters are so harsh?"

"Aye," he said simply, hoping she would divulge why she cared. If she knew the gold was there, she probably knew where to look for it, too. She would not have to worry about the cold weather.

"Are they always so?" she asked earnestly.

"Of course. 'Tis the highlands, lass. There will be snow and bitter cold. There's likely snow there now."

After the massacre at Glencoe, Dugan's mother had taken him and his younger siblings into the mountains to escape the carnage. But she—and many others—had died of the cold, and hunger. The mountains had provided little shelter and they'd struggled to find food.

His priority as laird of the MacMillans had been to make sure his clan had enough food and adequate shelter to keep them through the winter months. He would not allow his people to endure any unnecessary deaths because of the elements.

And he was damned if he'd allow them to be evicted from their lands.

"But people can survive the winter in the north country." Her statement sounded more like a question. An urgent one, at that.

"Aye. With proper shelter and stores of food put by, they can—and do—survive very well."

Her body relaxed slightly.

" 'Tis a long way until winter, Maura. You surely did not plan to spend more than a month or two up there." How long did she think it would take her to find the French treasure? "Or . . . did you?"

She gave a quick shake of her head. "No. I-I did not think so."

" 'Tis a moot point now," he said harshly. "You will be going to Braemore Keep to await your betrothed."

"No. Please."

"Aye, m'lady." 'Twas the more likely way for Dugan to raise the money demanded by the Duke of Argyll, in spite of Maura's doubts about Kildary's willingness to pay.

"But if Kildary pays you the ransom . . ." She left the rest unspoken.

Dugan knew what was unsaid. If the baron paid

up, he would be compelled to turn Maura over to him—or to the men he sent for her. Honor demanded it.

He didn't want to dwell on the events that would follow payment of the ransom. "How did you choose Loch Camerochlan as your hiding place?"

"I've told you. 'Tis because Loch Camerochlan is far away and remote." She sounded as distant and bleak as the loch itself.

"Aye. For hiding in the backside of beyond, you chose well." And perhaps the French had done so, too, in concealing their treasure.

She was not exactly forthcoming with information. Dugan wanted to know more about where she'd found her piece of the map, and whether she had discovered some indication that King Louis's gold was hidden at Loch Camerochlan. But he did not care to tip his own hand, in case she was unaware of the treasure.

If, indeed, there was any treasure.

Fleeing to the northwest highlands to avoid marriage to Baron Kildary was one thing. If she located the gold, Maura would be able to evade marriage to the baron—and every other man—forever. It would give her the freedom to leave Scotland—to travel perhaps to France, where the baron would never find her.

Dugan wondered about her father. Would he pursue her if she disappeared? Dugan didn't believe the man had provided Maura with a dowry, but perhaps he needed to use her for a political alliance. Or he hoped to collect a handsome bride price. Such marriages were commonplace, so it would not be unusual for her to be used this way.

But the thought of it grated on him.

As she sagged against him, Dugan realized Maura was exhausted. He did naught to startle her, but allowed the movement of the horse to lull her to sleep in his arms. He held her close and did not let himself think about the moment he would turn her over to Baron Kildary.

Even though, at the same moment, he would collect the money that would save his clan.

Chapter 12

When Maura awoke, she found herself deep in the mountains, still in Dugan MacMillan's arms. She pretended to sleep a few moments more, just so she could enjoy the heat of his powerful body curved around hers.

'Twas so much easier to relive the pleasure of his kiss when he held her this way—she did not want it to end.

"Ah, you're awake?"

Maura sighed and straightened up, pulling away from his body. Those quiet moments of feigned sleep had been far too few. "Yes. How long did I sleep?"

"I don't know. I didn't pay much heed." His voice was lower and softer than when he'd spoken to her before. It sent a wave of warmth through her body.

"We've come a long way?"

She was facing forward, but felt his nod.

The countryside was more beautiful than anything Maura had ever seen. They rode through a high, mossy glen where the shrubs and grasses were just beginning to turn green. Mountains more imposing than any Maura could have imagined rose high up from the valley floor, and she felt as though they were the only humans on earth.

The mountain peaks were shrouded in a light mist, and Maura could feel the threat of rain in the air. She'd hoped to find friendly crofters who would allow her to spend her nights indoors while she traveled, and none would be more welcome than now, as the weather became inclement.

Dugan's men rode ahead of them, riding at a casual pace, as though they were in no hurry to reach their destination.

"Is there a place nearby where we can take shelter when the rains come?" she asked.

He shrugged, and Maura realized that a spring rainstorm meant little to him. He would keep his steady pace regardless of the weather.

Maura shivered.

"Are you cold, Maura?"

"Not very," she replied. But he did something with his plaid and she found herself wrapped in another layer of wool over her cloak.

He was an odd set of contradictions. After the incident with the thieves in the woods near Sorcha's cottage, she'd been prepared to think the worst of him. He'd mowed them down, all three of them, singlehandedly. Savagely.

And yet he was not a savage. He'd saved her life at the waterfall, only to discover that she'd stolen from him. He had every right to slay her, or at the very least punish her for her thievery. And yet he'd done naught but take care of her.

Yes, he had taken her captive in order to exact a ransom from Baron Kildary, but he had not harmed her in any way. He could have been far rougher with her than he'd been, but he'd seen to her comfort and even allowed her to sleep against his chest while he took them deep into the mountains.

Maura could not complain about that. The farther she traveled on horseback with Laird MacMillan, the faster she would arrive at Loch Camerochlan.

But what a tangled mess she was in. As captive of a man who intended to sell her to a wretched old neep of a fiancé, she would not be going to Loch Camerochlan.

She needed to get away from him. But one glance at the rugged landscape around her made it clear how unlikely that was.

What if she told him she knew of the gold? Maura wondered if he would consider working with her to find it. To be of any value to him, she would need to bluff having knowledge about its location, and she was not sure she could carry it off. At some point he would demand that she tell him exactly where she thought it was.

She sighed. Even if she managed to determine the location of the gold and they found it, the highlanders might not see fit to share the treasure with her.

"You're not planning to use the map to guide you through the highlands, are you, Dugan?" she asked.

He did not answer right away and she wondered if he was weighing his responses to her, just as she was doing. "Aye. As it happens, I am. I don't know every inch of these mountains."

She did not believe him for an instant. "So . . . you're going into unfamiliar territory?"

"Enough questions, woman," he said gruffly

and sped up to a swift canter to catch up to his men.

He was intentionally concealing something from her, but she knew what it was. He had hoped—just as she had—to use the map to find King Louis's gold.

And now Maura had to decide whether to tell him that she knew of the treasure, too.

They came to a copse of trees and stopped for a while, taking a short rest before continuing north. Not that Dugan's men needed the respite, but this was rough travel for Maura. He figured she would welcome a reprieve from the back of his horse.

While Maura limped on her injured ankle into the brush for a moment of privacy, Dugan took out the maps and studied them.

"If ye're tired o' carrying the lass in yer saddle, Laird," said Calum with a shy grin, "I'd be happy to take on the task fer ye."

Archie punched the man in the arm. "Nay, 'tis I who said it first and gave ye the idea, ye great tumshie."

Dugan ignored them as he scoured the maps for any kind of symbol that might represent treasure.

"Do you see anything useful, Dugan?" Lachann crouched down beside him.

Dugan shook his head. "I cannot fathom how anyone is meant to use the damn thing. We have three of the quarters and I still see no marking to show where the treasure is hidden."

"But now we needn't worry about it," Lachann said. "We'll be in the clear when we get the ransom for Lady Maura and pay Argyll."

"Except that Lady Maura doesn't believe Kildary will pay it."

Lachann stared at his brother in disbelief. "Ach, shite." He stood and walked to his horse. He gathered the reins in hand and mounted, then rode ahead. The others finished their small meal and followed him, leaving Dugan to wait for Maura.

Lachann had every right to be angry. If Kildary did not pay . . .

Dugan felt more frustrated than ever. His path to the money he needed seemed to escape him at every turn. He'd be so close, and then . . . He bit out a quiet curse as he turned his attention to the map and studied every detail.

There were small triangles to indicate the mountains and blue ink designating lochs. Intertwining circles showed woodlands. As much as he scoured all three pieces of the map, he saw naught to symbolize coins or riches. There was no convenient square to represent a treasure chest. He was completely thwarted.

Lachann thought they should go raiding, but Dugan knew full well that a raid would not garner the funds they needed. They had to wait until they knew whether Baron Kildary would turn up with the ransom. Then their troubles would be over and Dugan could pursue the rumor about gold at his leisure.

'Twould be good to have a wee cushion, for there was no guarantee that Argyll would not come back next year and demand yet another impossible rent. If there was gold to be had, Dugan intended to be the one to take possession of it.

He was just about to roll up the maps and stash them away when he realized he was seeing something on Maura's piece of the map he'd not noticed when he looked at it earlier. 'Twas a wee mark in green at the edge of one of the lochs. He could see how he'd overlooked the tiny dot, for it was nearly overshadowed by the blue ink of the loch. But now, the late afternoon light caught it just right. Or perhaps it was just his desperate eyes.

Bloody hell—was he seeing things?

He rubbed his eyes. No, the small green dot was still there. But what loch was it? There were so many in the northwest highlands. Could it be Loch Monar?

Dugan studied the long blue slash of a loch and the symbols all around it, and came to the conclusion he was right.

He felt Maura's presence before he even saw her, and then she stood beside him, her skirts brushing his shoulder as she looked at the maps. Dugan's mood was decidedly improved with the sighting of the green spot, but he somehow managed to resist grinning like a lad who'd just stolen his first kiss.

Maura crouched down beside him, and Dugan felt the urge to see if her kisses still had the power to arouse him, in spite of her untrustworthiness. "Why do you suppose there's naught but symbols on the maps?" she asked.

Dugan gave a shake of his head, as much to clear it of his erotic thoughts as to indicate his negative reply. "I don't know. Why do you think?"

She shrugged. "Do you see anything that might be Loch Camerochlan?"

He pointed to a long, narrow strip of blue ink, not far from the area he believed was Braemore Glen. He was no geographer, but he knew his own lands. "Here."

She did not speak for a moment, and when she did, she nearly knocked him off his heels. "You know about the French gold, don't you?" Her voice was quiet and slightly unsure.

Bloody hell.

He almost rolled up the maps to stash them out of sight, but thought better of it. There was no need to tip his hand just yet. "French gold?"

"You've heard the rumor, have you not?" she asked quietly, crouching down beside him. "That's why you need the map. Not to find your way through the highlands."

She touched her document with one finger, drawing it down the blue length of Loch Camerochlan, and Dugan felt a tightening in his groin at the thought of how her intimate touch would feel. On the most sensitive parts of his body.

"*Gesu.*"

"What?"

"What do you know of it? The gold?" he asked, gaining control of his unwieldy thoughts. He was going to turn this woman over to her intended husband, not bury himself inside her.

She shrugged, the movement of her shoulders and neck so sensual, Dugan nearly groaned aloud. "I know naught but a rumor of a cache of French gold hidden somewhere in the highlands."

The question of Loch Camerochlan returned to Dugan, and he suspected she knew more than she was saying. Was the green mark significant? "You know naught of Loch Camerochlan, then? That the gold is hidden there?"

Her brows creased. "No."

"You wouldn't be trying to mislead me, Lady Maura?"

"Not at all, Laird," she said. "I must go there whether or not there is gold to be found."

"Ach, aye. To elude Baron Kildary."

"To rescue my sister."

Maura had not meant to say so much, but Dugan's deep blue eyes kindled what she knew was a misplaced sense of trust. She had not been able to resist them.

"My sister is very young," she explained, realizing how pointless it was to hold back now. "She is unable . . . Rosie was not right at birth. My father wanted to take her away and let her die, but I just couldn't . . ."

Dugan frowned fiercely and looked as though her words made no sense to him. Maura realized they wouldn't. He did not know the kind of man her father was. And she was not explaining very well.

"Rosie managed to survive her birth, but she does not function as others do. She is frail and has difficulty walking. She can speak no more than a few words and her hearing is poor. But she is a sweet child, and she is in need."

"Why is she in need? From what—or whom—do you rescue her?" He brushed away a tear that slid down her cheek. She had not even noticed the moisture gathering in her eyes as she spoke of Rosie, and his kindness was nearly her undoing. It had been so very long since she'd cradled her wee sister in her arms.

Maura cleared her throat and blinked away her tears. "My father does not wish to see her. Ever. And so he hired a horrible stick of a woman to take her far into the highlands . . ."

"To Loch Camerochlan."

Maura nodded. "A severe winter could kill my sister, Dugan, and she has already been at the loch for two years. I must get her away from there."

Dugan rested back on his heels, letting his hand drop away from her face, quite obviously pondering her tale of woe.

But it was more than a tale. She swallowed hard and prayed Rosie had managed to survive so far.

" 'Tis a father's right to deal with his children as he will, is it not? But—"

" 'Tis a father's duty to take care of his children! All of them!"

Maura would have risen to her feet and stalked away, but Dugan grasped her arm before she could move.

"I do not disagree, Maura. 'Tis harsh to send away a bairn that needs cosseting. 'Tis murder."

She considered which of the sentiments he'd expressed was the true one, but did not know him well enough to draw a solid conclusion. "How you manage your family is no concern of mine, Laird." She tried to yank her arm away. "But I will somehow find my way to Loch Camerochlan and take my sister from the pitiless nurse my father hired to tend her."

"I have no family, Maura. None but my brothers and sister. No children. No wife."

The low, seductive tone of his voice sent a wave of acute longing through Maura. She wanted . . . Well, perhaps she wanted more than just Rosie. Perhaps there could be more to her life than the care of her sister.

Maura recognized that Laird MacMillan treated

his brother with respect and humor—the same way he treated his men. And he'd been kind to her, in spite of the wrong she'd done him.

He leaned toward her, the hand on her arm shifting to her waist. Tipping his head slightly, he touched his lips to hers.

Maura felt the sizzle immediately, coursing through her veins. He was powerful and gentle all at once, drawing her against his body as he deepened their kiss. She felt as though her body was on fire, and when the tips of her breasts touched his hard chest, an arc of pure pleasure crackled through her, centering in her womb.

Maura slipped her hands up to his shoulders, 'round to his nape, and pulled out the leather tie that held his queue in place. When she slid her fingers into his thick hair, he made a low sound that rumbled through her.

She wanted to feel him closer. It was an unconscious need to feel his skin against hers.

He shifted slightly and speared his tongue into her mouth as he eased her down to the ground. Maura's senses reeled when his hand slid up to the side of her breast, then fully cupped it.

'Twas not enough.

She arched her back and he broke the kiss, nuzzling her cheek and her neck, touching her as she yearned to be touched. He drew her nipple out to a hard peak through the fabric of her gown, and every nerve in Maura's body cried out for more.

"Ach, Maura."

His low voice rippled through her and her breath caught in her lungs. Somewhere in the back of her mind, Maura knew she should be trying to figure a way to interpret the map and take it from him. She ought to be keeping her distance, and not lying like some wanton creature beneath him.

But when he kissed her mouth again and slid his hand beneath her gown, Maura closed her eyes and yearned for more—like the wanton she must be.

Chapter 13

The first drops of rain shocked Dugan to his senses. He moved his hand away from the temptation of heaven beneath her skirts and pushed himself up onto his forearms. He knew better than to look at Maura's kiss-swollen lips, for he wanted her—wanted more than he should.

She might be the most beautiful woman he'd ever laid eyes upon, but she was his captive. A woman he was about to ransom for the price of saving his clan.

He muttered a low curse of abject frustration. *Gesu*, but life was unfair.

He took Maura's hand, and as he rose to his feet, pulled her up. "We should catch up to my men. They'll have found shelter." Perhaps. Usually, they just wrapped themselves in their warm woolen plaids and pushed on. If absolutely necessary, they laid out their fur blankets and took cover under the trees.

Dugan lifted her onto his horse and climbed up behind her, but felt no relief from the urge to pull her into his arms and ravish her fully.

'Twas impossible, he knew, and far better to join

his men before he lost his head and found yet another opportunity to kiss those captivating lips.

By all the saints, he should have taken a wife years ago. Then he would not be so tempted . . . *Ach, you're an idiot, MacMillan.* There wasn't a woman within fifty miles of Braemore who fascinated him the way Lady Maura did.

She remained silent as he kicked his heels into the gelding and began a slow trot northwest, in the wake of his brother and the others. The rain was more of a heavy mist, but Dugan covered Maura with his loose plaid, drawing her close once again.

Best not to think of those lovely curves that were nestled against him. Instead, Dugan concentrated on what must be done. For the good of his clan. The green dot on the northern shore of what *might* be Loch Monar was not enough to go on. Dugan needed to collect from Maura's bridegroom to be sure he had the money to pay Argyll.

"When Kildary comes for you . . ." he said.

He felt her sharp intake of breath. "He will not."

Oh aye, he would. The baron had his pride, and would never allow his betrothed to remain in the hands of a "barbaric" highlander. The day would come—soon—when Kildary would ride to Braemore to make the exchange. A blessed three thousand pounds for his bride.

"He'll see to it that you and your clan are deemed outlaw, whether he comes for me or not."

Dugan knew it was an empty threat. Kildary would not want it known that he was bested by a highlander. He would quietly pay the ransom and take his woman back to Cromarty.

"I will not go with him," she said.

And Dugan did not want to send her. His jaws clenched tightly together and he decided not to argue about it. 'Twas a pointless discussion, for he *would* take her to Braemore Keep. He *would* meet Kildary there, and he *would* exchange Lady Maura for the money the baron brought.

They rode in silence for a time while Dugan considered that small green marking on the map. There were so many lochs in the western highlands, he could not be positive of its location. And of course, he could not swear that it indicated the location of the treasure. Mayhap it signified something altogether different. And useless.

Maura's recounting of her sister's plight rang true, but she could be concealing crucial information. A chest of gold or even a small bag of riches would be quite useful to her in her grand plan to rescue her sister, and she'd been desperate enough to go after it alone. On foot and utterly unprepared, into the highlands that were entirely unfamiliar to her.

Was she desperate enough to deceive him regarding what she knew about it? Aye. He'd wager she'd do anything to get to her sister as well as the treasure.

"You are certain the French gold is not hidden at Loch Camerochlan?" he asked at length.

"Do you not trust me, Laird MacMillan?" she asked, turning to look into his eyes with luminous innocence.

"Why should I, Maura?"

She looked away. "I deserved that. But I want you to know I am not in the habit of stealing." She paused, perhaps weighing her words. "'Tis just that Rosie cannot stay at Loch Camerochlan any longer. She is so very small and fragile. And Tilda Crane . . . her nurse . . ." Maura shuddered.

Dugan did not know what to believe, so he concentrated on getting them up the steep, narrow path to the pass that would lead into yet another scenic glen on the way to both Braemore Keep and Loch Monar.

"How did you learn of the gold?" he asked.

She did not answer right away, and he could almost hear her mentally weighing her words. He wondered if she would give him the truth. "I overheard my father's cousin say he intended to organize some men to ride out and search for it. He said naught of its location. I didn't even know what the map was when I took it."

Bloody hell. He'd hoped there would be no other searchers to compete with. At least they didn't possess three quarters of the map as Dugan did. But he was painfully aware that the section with the green dot near what he thought was Loch Monar was the piece Maura had stolen from her cousin. If he'd already figured it out . . .

"You didn't realize it was a treasure map when you took it?"

"I only thought it would show me the way to Loch Camerochlan once I left my escort at Fort William."

"There was no writing on it, Maura."

" 'Twas dark in the room at the time, so I didn't get a good look at it . . . And I feared they would return at any minute. I did not take the time to examine it before I left."

"When did you realize I carried another part of the map?"

"I didn't really know it," she said. "I . . . I heard one of your men speak of a map . . . and gold . . ."

Damn Archie's mouth. "So you took it."

"No! I mean, yes. But I didn't intend to."

"Explain."

Her lovely throat moved tightly as she swallowed before answering. "I was curious. I wanted a quick glance at it, so I looked. But then I heard a noise and I had to get out of there. I took it without thinking."

"I should have posted a guard," Dugan muttered, chastising himself once more. He'd allowed his fatigue to make him vulnerable.

'Twould not happen again. Ever.

Maura twisted 'round to face him fully, putting her hand on his arm. "I'm sorry I took your map, Dugan. I've felt naught but guilt since then. A handful or two of gold would be very helpful once I find Rosie, but I know 'twas not right to steal from you."

Dugan found Maura's loyalty to her sister admirable, even if he could not quite forgive her for her thievery.

He found he could not take his eyes off her, for she had the most vivid coloring imaginable—her green eyes were the color of Braemore Glen and her hair was as red as burnished copper. The hand she'd placed on his arm seemed to burn through to his skin, and Dugan would have liked to find a quiet little copse and lay her down upon his plaid and finish what he'd begun a short while ago.

But he would not, not while he awaited her bridegroom to turn up with the money he needed.

"Dugan . . . you cannot give me to Lord Kildary," she said quietly, as though reading his thoughts.

Dugan had no choice, but he had the wisdom not to mention it again.

"He does not care what happens to me."

"Of course he does. He's a man, and you are his possession."

She looked up at him then, with fire in her eyes. "I am no man's possession!"

"Your father—"

"Has had little to do with me since he found I had taken Rosie away and aided her survival. I am naught to him."

Dugan did not bother to state the obvious. She was still under her father's jurisdiction. She was a woman with no resources, therefore, she had no choice but to capitulate.

Unless she knew more about the gold or the map than she was telling. If she found the treasure, she would be an incredibly wealthy woman and have all the freedom she needed.

Dugan wished he knew for certain whether that green spot on the map signified the location of the treasure, or if she was deceiving him about what she knew. "You wouldn't have gotten far in the highlands on your own," he finally said. Mayhap if he got her talking, she would divulge something of use.

"Yes, I would have."

"Maura, you couldn't get past Loch Eil without running into trouble. And as soon as Lieutenant Baird realizes you haven't traveled south, he'll be right behind you."

She stopped breathing for an instant. "He *cannot* find me. I must get to Rosie before she has to endure another winter at Loch Camerochlan. I had always planned to take her away whether or not there is any gold to be had. I-I have a bit of money . . . I will manage."

Dugan wondered if Rosie could have survived two winters if she was as frail and helpless as her sister believed. His mention of the harsh highland winter had disturbed Maura, who was as devoted to Rosie as Dugan was to his clan. But the good of the MacMillans had to take precedence over what Maura wanted.

He could not make her plight his concern, even though it went against the grain to ignore it.

Dugan had never known a woman like Maura. He wanted to touch her, wanted to kiss her until neither of them could breathe. She responded to him like dry tinder to a spark, and seemed immune to intimidation. And it only made him crave her more.

His mind raced through the possibilities. They could go directly to Loch Monar and begin the search before Kildary arrived at Bracmore. And if the green mark led him to the treasure, there would be no need to collect the baron's ransom.

"You must need money very badly to do this to me," Maura said, sounding more than a little desperate.

"Aye. My clan will be evicted from our lands unless we pay an exorbitant rent." He was desperate, too.

"What about the gold? You can—"

"If the clues on the map were slightly clearer, I might have some confidence of finding it." He was not about to tell her about the green mark.

"Dugan . . ." She frowned, deep in thought.

Dugan wondered if she had finally thought through her predicament and decided 'twould be best to admit that she knew more than she was saying. If she confirmed that the treasure could be found at Loch Monar, 'twould save them both a great deal of time and trouble.

And there would be no need to turn her over to Kildary.

"Do you believe there are witches . . ." she asked, twisting the conversation into a completely different direction. "I mean . . . do you think there are canny old women who know . . . *things* . . . that the rest of us do not?"

Dugan sighed. "The highlands are rife with tales of witches and faeries." And some of those witches were said to be able to prognosticate. Dugan remembered hearing about a seer who'd foretold the slaughter at Glencoe. In a fatal mistake, the MacIain laird had scoffed at her prediction, unwilling to believe that the soldiers they hosted in their homes would attack them. Such an act would be murder under trust.

And they called highlanders barbarians.

"What have witches to do with anything?"

"I'm not sure," Maura replied. "But I crossed paths with an old soothsayer after leaving Fort William."

"Looking to relieve you of your coin, no doubt."

"I-I suppose so." Now that she was far from the blind old woman's little croft and the huge dog that guarded her, Maura realized how silly it was even to think of her. She knew better than to believe in such nonsense.

"We need no soothsayer to tell us how long it will be before Lieutenant Baird realizes his mistake and comes after you."

Maura's pulse drummed in her ears. She had not

forgotten about her father's lackey, and knew Baird must be furious with her. Ever since his posting at Aucharnie, he'd been trying to inveigle himself into her father's good graces, and had succeeded only to the extent that the earl allowed him to carry out his more odious commands. Losing her would not go well for him.

She swallowed. *Unless he could bring back her body.*

"At least we'll be a full day ahead of him," Dugan said. "And we can hope for some bad weather."

"*This* is not bad weather?" Maura asked, relieved to have something to think about besides her ill-tempered escort.

"Ach, no. A wee mist is all this is."

She shuddered and hoped they soon found some sort of shelter. She would be satisfied with any small place where they could build up a fire and nestle themselves together against the cold and wet.

Her body throbbed with an intense awareness of Dugan's powerful thighs lying alongside her own, fueling the urge to learn whether he responded to a caress at the back of his knee just as she had done.

Maura realized now what was missing from those men Lady Ilay had invited to the house. They were bland, colorless milksops who wore too much lace on their shirts and powder on their heads. She'd had no wish to touch any of them, no desire to feel their caresses.

Why couldn't her father have come to a betrothal agreement with a man like Dugan MacMillan?

Maura answered her own question. *Because he was a highlander, just a wee formality away from being an outlaw.*

And he fully intended to turn her over to Baron

Kildary if the man turned up with the ransom money.

"I will not marry him, you know," she said. "Baron Kildary. No one can force me to exchange marriage vows with him."

Ah, but they can, Dugan thought. They had exactly the leverage they needed—Rosie. Maura's father could hold the lass's safety against Maura doing his bidding. From what he'd heard of the man, he might actually harm Rosie.

"When you find the gold and pay your rents, will you be safe from eviction?" Maura asked.

"For a time, at least," Dugan replied. "Until our landlord thinks of some other way to harass us."

He saw her brows come together in deep thought. It seemed impossible that she did not know of the difficulties faced by the highland clans. Mostly, the highlanders' problems centered 'round rich landlords who wanted to take the land held for generations by his people. Far too many lowland Scots had decided to side with them in order to line their own pockets.

"Maura, if you know anything more about the location of the gold, now would be a good time to tell me."

"Dugan, I am fully aware that you would not need to collect a ransom from Kildary if you had the French treasure. If I knew anything more about it, I would certainly tell you."

Frustration rippled through him. Of course she understood the ramifications of the useless maps. She was not a daftie. A bit impulsive, perhaps, but not a fool.

"On the night before I set out from Glasgow," she explained, "I heard only a few whispered words about gold. And I barely had a chance to look at the maps—even my portion—before I left Fort William and those bandits came after me. I know no more than you."

Her earnest tone was unmistakable, and Dugan was inclined to believe her. She was not so foolish as to think she could search the highlands and find the gold on her own. He wasn't sure that *he* could do it.

"Maura . . . If you do not wed Kildary, your father will likely come after you. Or Rosie. He'll use her as leverage against you."

Somehow, she managed to keep her voice steady. "So I must get to my sister quickly and take her someplace where he cannot find us. To Ireland, perhaps. Or America."

Dugan cringed at the thought of Maura and her impaired sister traveling alone and unprotected. They would be vulnerable to every kind of danger. "You cannot be serious."

"Aye, I am. Dead serious."

Chapter 14

Lieutenant Alastair Baird was furious enough to kill someone. But his preferred victim was not there. And it did not appear that she was within miles of the damned waterfall where he'd assumed she would go to hide from him.

It had become painfully clear that she'd had some ulterior motive for wandering out into these woods as they'd traveled, though he was not certain what it was. Had she met with an accomplice who was to help her elude his custody?

Baird did not know how that would be possible. He'd arrived at Ilay House without advance warning with orders from her father, and they'd left for Cromarty the following morn. There'd been no time to set up a rendezvous.

Unless the conniving little cow had managed to send out a messenger . . . Whom would she have contacted? Did she have friends in the highlands?

Could it have been those damned highlanders she'd been talking to in the taproom the night before? Maura had acted oddly upon her arrival at the inn, asking the proprietor to take her to the kitchen for an early meal. What complete and utter blatherskite. There had to have been some reason for her actions.

Baird cursed himself for his lack of vigilance. He should have assumed she would try something along the way. She had made it known she had no intention of marrying Kildary, and he should have analyzed her threat somewhat more critically. Belatedly, he realized that everything she'd said about wanting to return to Glasgow had been a ruse, an intentional misdirection. She'd planned her escape from the very start.

The lieutenant stepped away from the waterfall and the carcass of the ram that had been killed only a day or so ago, by the looks of it. He pulled absently at one of his eyebrows, pondering what had transpired there. A highlander's arrow had pierced the bloody thing . . . Had Maura encountered the animal? Had she spoken with the man who'd shot it? Was it possible that she'd made some hurried arrangement to rendezvous with the man somewhere near Fort William?

That seemed unlikely, for the highlander at the Speckled Trout appeared to have his own plans. However, Baird might have misinterpreted the man's haste to leave the inn. And if Maura had met up with that highlander, she was not going to be easy to find.

Fortunately, tracking was one of Baird's specialties.

Maura did not want to think about leaving Scotland and traveling so far away from absolutely everything she knew. In truth, she did not really want to rush away from Dugan MacMillan, now that he was not quite so accusatory.

She nestled against his braw chest and wished their circumstances were not as desperate as they were. Maura did not think she would meet any other man whose kisses had the power to shimmer through her as Dugan's did. Whose touch made her forget all propriety.

Of course, she shouldn't have allowed the kind of intimacies they'd shared . . . and yet she had done naught to stop his sensual advances. On the contrary, she had wanted more. Dugan was the one to realize how far they'd gone, and had withdrawn his hand before he'd done more than caress the skin behind her knees.

Oh good Lord. She could not go on this way. Reliving the amazing sensations that had pooled in her nether parts at his touch; wondering how much farther he would have gone had it not started raining.

"I did not know a landowner could remove an entire clan from their lands," she said, as much to distract herself from thoughts she should not be having, as to gain information.

"Ach, aye. We all have rich landlords, and most of them want their lands back."

"Why?" Maura asked.

"For their own use. Our meager rents are not enough."

Maura heard the bitterness in his voice and wondered if her father was one of those landlords. She realized with a sinking heart 'twas most likely true. Lord Aucharnie would show no more mercy toward a highland clan than he had toward his own daughters.

"You will be able to pay your rents when you find the French gold," she said.

"You are so sure I'll find it?"

Yes, she was. She felt a surprising certainty that he would. That he would somehow figure out the mystery of the map, perhaps even with her help. "The map might be no good, but there must be other rumors, and crofters who might have heard something."

"Ah, but if they knew anything about a hidden trove of gold, wouldn't they have looked for it themselves?"

Maura nodded thoughtfully. 'Twas quite clear that they would both be better off if Dugan found the trove of French gold before Argyll did, and before Baron Kildary came to claim her.

"I wonder if that old witch really knew something."

"Who?"

"The old witch I mentioned earlier," Maura said. Perhaps Dugan could interpret what the old woman had said. "Sorcha was her name. Her croft was off the bridle path north of Loch Eil and she had a massive dog as her only company. As I walked past, she beckoned me to come inside for a drink."

"Sorcha?"

"Yes." Maura looked up at him. "Why?"

He gave a slow shake of his head, but he wore a contemplative frown. "Old soothsayers blanket these mountains. Sometimes they seem . . . Well, they seem a bit magical. Or mystical. Some say they know things they could not. I know of one whose predictions came true."

"Soothsayers are known in the lowlands, as well. I never thought I believed in them. But this one . . ." Maura frowned. "The woman said some odd things . . ."

He kept his eyes focused on the trail straight ahead, and Maura sensed his preoccupation. She probably should not even mention her strange encounter with Sorcha, but the woman *had* known about Loch Camerochlan.

"I think there might be something to her riddles," Maura said.

" 'Tis just what we need—another puzzle." He sighed. "What did she say?"

"Ah, well, 'twas mostly nonsense," Maura said, deflated. "Something like 'The wind and dust will give you what you need.' "

"She said *need*?" Dugan asked.

Maura thought a moment. "No, I think the word she used was *seek*."

"Did you tell her you were on a quest? For that would imply that you sought something."

"No."

They rode quietly for a few minutes while Dugan considered the woman's words and Maura tried not to think of the wall of brawn she rested against, and the way it made her feel. " 'Tis hardly a definitive statement," he said. "Most likely 'tis only well-practiced blatherskite, designed to make you part with some of your coin."

"But wind and dust . . . It seemed so very specific to me."

Dugan shook his head. "How?"

Maura shivered. "I don't know. I suppose you are right." And yet the woman had seemed wholly magical, moving blindly in her tiny croft, with the dog that seemed to understand every word the woman spoke. "Dugan . . . she told me that I carried a prize."

"Most travelers carry a prize of sorts—something of value, whether it be money or some other possession they can barter as they travel."

"I thought she meant the map. What other prize do I have?"

"Money?"

She shrugged. "I suppose."

"Could she have seen the map?" he asked.

"No. I never took it from my bag, and even if I had, she was blind. She wouldn't have seen it."

Maura's words sent a disquieting prickle down Dugan's spine. Yet he knew Sorcha was a common enough name in the highlands, and it wouldn't surprise him to learn that a good many old women named Sorcha were blind.

'Twas entirely unlikely that she was the seer who'd foretold the disaster at Glencoe. According to the legends surrounding the massacre, she'd been old even then, and that was more than twenty years ago. No, it could not be she.

But what if this woman was as accurate as Glencoe's Sorcha?

The wind and dust will give you what you seek.

Dugan didn't believe he'd ever heard a more useless statement. If this was the kind of warning Laird MacIain had received, 'twas no wonder he had not heeded it.

"Did you ask the woman what her words meant?"

"I did, but she only answered with more riddles. Truth be told, she frightened me a little."

He laughed, glad of the distraction as he imagined the unlikely event of Maura cowering in fear. "I'm surprised to learn there is *anything* that frightens you."

She shivered and Dugan adjusted his hold on her, pulling her close. Old Sorcha really *had* frightened her.

" 'Tis no jest, Dugan," Maura said. "I think she meant something by those words. I've only got to figure them out and we'll know how to interpret the map."

"My grandfather said the clues would be known when the four pieces came together."

"Allies," Maura murmured.

"What?"

"Sorcha said something about allies coming together," she replied. "It makes sense, does it not? That the four quarters were separated, and only when four 'friends' come together will the map be complete and the clues readable."

Dugan did not see how 'twas possible for one more piece of the map to help him. He already knew where the gold was. He only had to figure out the logistics of traveling to Loch Monar and getting Maura to Braemore Keep at the same time to await Kildary.

Dugan ignored the burn in his gut at the thought of sending her off to Braemore while his men waited for Kildary to arrive with the ransom. Because it could not be helped. There was no telling how long it would take to find the treasure, and he was not about to risk eviction while he scoured the shores of Loch Monar for the gold.

"The map is no longer your concern, Maura."

"What do you mean?" she asked. "One of those parts is mine."

He hardened his heart and shook his head. "Not any longer. You are going to Braemore Keep to await your betrothed."

He felt her stiffen, and at that moment, he knew she had no intention of going to Braemore with him. She was going to try to escape him and go up to Loch Camerochlan on her own, though he did not know how she could possibly accomplish it. Her ankle still bothered her and she didn't know her way 'round the mountains. There were high passes and deep valleys where she could get lost and not see anyone for days.

Loch Camerochlan was a long way off.

"How far away is Braemore Keep?" Maura asked.

"No more than three or four days' ride."

It gave her some hope. In three days, she ought to be able to get away from him and make her way to Loch Camerochlan. He'd shown her Loch Camerochlan on the map, and she knew they'd been traveling northwest all day. At least, that's the direction they'd been going before the clouds had obscured the sun.

She had not counted on having any additional funds when she'd left Glasgow, and she knew she could get by with what she had.

"Three nights, then?"

"Four. We've tonight."

"Where will we stay tonight?"

"Look ahead."

Maura saw a thin curl of smoke rising up in the distance and she hoped it was Dugan's men, waiting for them in a warm, dry cottage. Her body was tired and sore after walking for half the night and riding most of the day with Dugan.

It occurred to her that travel in the highlands was a good deal more difficult than she'd anticipated, but she shoved that thought from her mind and concentrated on the issue at hand. Dugan might have pointed out what he thought was Loch Camerochlan, but slipping away again during the dead of night was not the least bit appealing.

Nor was the thought of stealing one of the highlanders' horses in order to stay ahead of them. Besides, she did not think they would let her get away with it.

Maura shuddered at the thought of becoming Baron Kildary's wife. The night she'd been ordered to Cromarty, she'd heard Ilay's servants whispering what they'd heard of his cruelty, but of course none of them would speak to her directly. The baron did not seem to be the kind of man who would allow Rosie to come into his household.

And that was the only way marriage to the old man would be tolerable.

They rode close enough to smell the smoke of the highlanders' fire, and the dizzying aroma of meat cooking. Maura looked 'round, but saw no croft or any other shelter nearby.

'Twas sorely disappointing but for the rabbits roasting on a spit over the small fire. While the highlanders' horses grazed nearby, the men had wrapped themselves in their heavy woolen plaids, and each one had found his own place. Conall sat smoking a pipe with sweet-smelling tobacco that mingled with the scent of the cooking meat. He blushed bashfully—and a bit charmingly—when she looked at him.

Bryce did not look up when they came into camp, but kept his full attention on carving a small figure out of wood. Young Archie sharpened the blade of his claymore while Dugan's brother tended the fire and watched to be sure the rabbits did not fall into it.

As Dugan helped Maura to dismount, she had never felt more confused. Most things in her life had been clear-cut until now. As a mere child, she'd refused to let Rosie die. She'd taken food from her father's kitchens to supplement what the Elliotts had, in order to compensate the family who'd cared so deeply and so well for her and Rosie. She'd spent two interminable years at Ilay House, twice attempting to slip away, then planning carefully and biding her time until presented with the perfect opportunity to disappear.

Maura had been so sure of herself and her plan to hike to Loch Camerochlan on her own, yet her plans had been thoroughly thwarted by the braw highlander who, even now, made her heart pound and her body tingle in anticipation of his touch.

Dear Lord. This could not continue. Whether it was convenient or not, she needed to get away from Dugan MacMillan and make her own way up to Loch Camerochlan. She only had to take her opportunity when it presented itself.

Dugan observed as Maura sat on a rock near the fire and took out blocks of cheese and bread from her traveling bag. She seemed preoccupied as she cut off pieces of both and handed them to the men.

She looked up at him. "Is this where we will stay the night?"

" 'Tis nearly sunset. We cannot go any further into the mountains after dark."

She bit her lush lower lip as she took a quick glance around. Likely she was noticing that there would be no privacy in the setting they'd chosen. Dugan wondered what else she was thinking.

About leaving, perhaps?

"Have ye ever slept upon the ground before, lass?" Lachann asked her.

She gave a slight shake of her head while Lachann shot a glance in Dugan's direction.

"Where did you think you'd sleep before . . . when you were on your own?" Lachann queried.

"I . . . I thought I'd come across some cottages. That p-perhaps their owners would allow me to stay . . . for payment, of course."

"Oh aye. There are crofters all over the highlands," Archie said. "And highlanders are—"

"Archie, go and see to the horses," Dugan commanded. He did not want anyone giving Maura additional information about the highlands. God knew she would use it to make her way to Loch Camerochlan and thwart his plan to collect the ransom.

"What, why? The horses are all right," the young man retorted.

"I want them strung together for the night."

"Aye, Laird."

Tethering the horses together was enough to put everyone on notice that the lass was not to be trusted. Dugan didn't think she would attempt to steal a horse, but he knew she could be rash and impulsive. He didn't want to risk her riding off a cliff during the night.

Full dark came quickly after dusk in the mountains. They ate their modest feast by the flickering light of the fire and Maura kept silent as she ate her share. After the meal, Dugan spread out a thick fur pelt on the ground. "You'll sleep here," he said to her.

She did not move. "Where will you be?"

"Right here next to you." And he was fairly certain he wasn't going to get any sleep at all.

Chapter 15

"**Y**ou cannot be serious."

Dugan's men slipped away to make their own beds as it was clear they sensed a confrontation coming. As well they should.

He echoed her earlier words, his tone mocking her slightly. "Oh aye. Dead serious."

She stood and crossed her arms over her chest. "I cannot sleep with you, Laird MacMillan!"

" 'Tis all I've asked you to do, Maura. Sleep."

She felt her face heat. " 'Tis all I *would* do, Laird." Which was not strictly true. It seemed his slightest touch had the power to overwhelm her better senses.

"Aye, then. Make yourself ready."

"What do you mean?"

"Turn 'round and take a wee hike into the bushes before we bed down," he said.

Maura's teeth clenched of their own volition. "I am not a child."

"Good. Then you'll know 'tis a very bad idea to attempt to leave camp during the night."

"Of course I would not leave. I am not a fool."

Of course Maura had been trying to figure a way to do just that, but she'd come to the conclusion that tomorrow night would be better. Her ankle would be in better condition then and 'twas likely she would get another look at the map before she left.

She might even figure out how to connect Sorcha's riddle with the symbols on the map. 'Twould not be amiss to find a cache of gold on her way to Rosie.

When she returned to the camp, Dugan was nowhere to be seen. Maura took it as a good sign that he'd decided against making her sleep with him. Mayhap she had as much effect on him as he had on her.

The fire had burned low and did not throw off much heat. But she lay down upon the fur and covered herself with her cloak. She'd guessed there might be nights when she'd have to sleep on the ground, but had not actually thought about the reality of doing so. She did not have a heavy plaid as the men did, though she believed her cloak would be adequate.

"You'll be warm enough here, Maura."

Dugan's voice startled her, and when he lay down beside her and pulled her into his embrace, she lay as straight and brittle as a pane of glass. She thought she might even break.

"Relax, Maura. I'm willing to share my heat."

"Y-your what?"

"I'm warm, you are not. Come close and you'll be comfortable through the night."

"Comfortable?"

"I don't suppose a lass like you ever had to share a bed with anyone. Who is your family, Maura?"

"No one. No one of note." She would not have him contacting her father if his ransom attempt with Kildary failed. She turned to her side, facing away from him, but he curved his body around hers. He was not going to wheedle that information from her just because he was big and warm.

She nearly melted with the glorious heat of him. Her body reacted to everything about his, from the way he embraced her so carefully to the scent of his skin. Maura felt a thickening and hardening behind her and knew he was becoming as aroused as she.

"You have a sire who would see his own bairn put out to die." His breath was warm in her ear, and it burned through to the tips of her breasts and her nether parts.

Somehow, she managed to speak, but her voice was just a whisper. "Which is why I must go to Loch Camerochlan for her. Rosie needs me."

"But I need you, Maura."

A shudder went through her at the intensity of his statement. *Oh Lord, Maura needed him, too.*

She started to turn in his arms, but he tightened his hold on her waist and held her still. "The ransom Kildary will pay is essential to the well-being of my clan. Because I cannot count on finding any French treasure."

Maura's breath caught and she castigated herself for her foolish yearnings. She and Dugan MacMillan were no more suited than a sheep and a wolf. " 'Tis entirely unfair, Dugan. I am not a pawn to be used whenever it suits."

"I am sorry it must be this way, Maura." And he was. He would like nothing more than to take her to Braemore Keep and . . . well, 'twas best not to think of what he'd like to do once he took her home. Especially when he knew how well she fit against him, and how fervently she would return his kisses.

"No, you're not. You're glad you have an alternative to having to search for the treasure."

Her body shuddered against him and he realized it was a quiet sob. He'd made her cry.

He gathered her close and let her weep against him until she fell asleep. And then he spent the rest of the night dozing fitfully, wondering if there wasn't some other way to achieve what he needed to do.

He did not like the thought of giving her to Kildary. He despised it. She was so young and vibrant, it seemed a sin to sentence her to a life with an ancient husband of questionable reputation who had already used up two wives before her. Dugan's stomach roiled at the thought of Kildary kissing Maura's delectable mouth, of taking her to his bed.

Gesu. She would bear the old man's child.

Dugan's head throbbed as he struggled to think of some alternative. He reminded himself of the harsh truth—that he might never find the French king's gold, even with most of the map in his possession. That small green marking might mean naught, and then he would have nothing. No chance of paying Argyll the rent he demanded.

Hell, the map's previous owner might now be at the site, digging up the landscape looking for the treasure himself.

He dozed awhile, and when morning came, he held Maura's delectable body against his own until she awoke. She seemed to realize with some disdain where she was, quickly extricating herself from his arms and stumbling away into the brush nearby.

They wasted no time at camp, eating what was left of the previous night's food and resuming their trek up into the highlands. Maura and Dugan rode together as before, though Maura kept her silence all day until they reached the walls of Caillich Castle.

He wondered who her family was, and why she would not tell him. Clearly, she was the daughter of a lowland lord who wanted an alliance with Baron Kildary. Dugan didn't know many of the lowland families, except by reputation and the fact that a good number were allied with clan Campbell.

Hence the slaughter at Glencoe. 'Twas a Duncanson who'd ordered the attack on his clan and a Campbell who'd carried it out. The soldiers had killed women and children—innocents.

There'd been days when Dugan was a much younger man that he'd thought of going raiding and slaughtering as many Campbells and Duncansons as he could find. He'd wanted to destroy their crops and scatter their animals. But, in his wisdom, his grandfather had forbidden it, warning Dugan of the repercussions such an act could cause for clan MacMillan.

Dugan would not risk the safety of his people.

But lately, it did not escape him that as a wealthy laird, he would have the power and wherewithal to avenge the deaths at Glencoe. No one would be able to touch a highland laird who actually owned his own lands.

The thought of it caused a flutter of hope, but Dugan quickly squelched it. He was far from being a wealthy laird. His clan was beginning to return to prosperity after the last uprising, and Dugan felt some satisfaction in that.

'Twas late afternoon when they arrived at Caillich Castle. The stronghold was situated on a high hill some distance from where Dugan stopped and dismounted. He could see that the huge fortress intrigued Maura, but she did not ask him anything about it. She was intent upon maintaining her silence, but for a few necessary words.

"Do you know the Earl of Caillich, Maura?"

She shook her head, then added a hesitant "No."

There was something she wasn't telling him, but he decided to let it go. He had no intention of forcing it out of her. They stopped in a small grove of trees, small enough that no army could ever hide there and surprise the castle. But there was a lot of low brush outside the cover of the trees, and Dugan knew it would be rife with game. 'Twas always good to arrive as a guest bearing gifts.

"Lachann, you and Bryce ride up to the castle and speak to the earl," Dugan said. "You know what to do."

"Aye, Dugan," Lachann replied. "You'll wait here for us in the copse?"

Dugan nodded. 'Twas only prudent to send a scout into what might be unfriendly territory. One never knew what side Caillich was on. The earl had not supported the highland uprising two years before, but neither had he aided that maggot Argyll in his effort to suppress those who fought for the restoration of King James.

It began to rain as Lachann and Bryce rode off toward the castle. Dugan helped Maura down from his horse, hoping his brother would find a friendly situation at the castle. Years ago, Caillich had condemned the actions of the Campbells at Glencoe, and the earl had been instrumental in bringing an official inquiry of the massacre to Parliament.

Dugan had always respected him for that.

He also knew there was a decent lodging house inside the walls, where he hoped to secure a room for Maura. The rain was going to continue long and hard, and he did not want her to have to try and endure it. He told himself 'twas because he could not afford for her to become ill.

And yet . . . he knew there was more to his desire to keep her safely sheltered.

He took down his bow and quiver of arrows and spoke to Archie. "Make a shelter for Lady Maura and stay with her until Conall and I return."

Archie replied with a nod.

"See that she comes to no harm."

"Aye, Laird," Archie replied with a grin.

Dugan started for the thick brush but had not gone far before he heard Maura mutter a few quiet words. "Harm, my arse."

The mist had become more than a drizzle and Maura knew that if it kept up, her cloak would not keep her dry. She shivered and hoped Lachann returned quickly with word that they were welcome to go into the castle. She doubted the earl would remember her, even though they'd met only two years before, soon after her arrival at Ilay House. She hoped to avoid him altogether.

Archie unrolled the large fur she'd slept on with Dugan the night before, and propped it up in the lowest branches of a tree. "Sit under here, Lady Maura. 'Twill keep ye dry. Uh, mostly dry."

"Shouldn't we build a fire?"

"Ach, no. 'Twould be seen from the castle. We do'na wish to make our presence known. Not yet."

His words sent a wave of disappointment through Maura. Thinking of the fire they could not build brought tears to her eyes, but she was stronger than that. A wee spot of discomfort amounted to naught in the grand scheme of things. She was making her way toward Rosie, and she could tolerate a bit of hardship in order to do so. Her journey thus far had, in fact, been easier than she'd originally imagined. And she'd gone much farther than she would have managed on foot.

She sat down on a folded length of plaid and snuggled deeply into her cloak. "Aren't you going to sit with me, Archie?"

He looked around as though there might be someone who would answer for him. "Well, I, er . . ."

"Don't be foolish, Archie. There is plenty of room beneath the fur. There's no sense in getting soaked while we wait."

Archie seemed reluctant, but he did crawl in to sit cross-legged beside her. He did not emit even half the warmth that Dugan had done the night before.

Maura did not care to think of last night, of sleeping curled into Dugan's body with his thickly muscled arm 'round her. She'd been mortified upon awakening to find one of her knees wedged between his thighs and her face pressed against his chest.

He'd been awake for Lord knew how long, waiting for her to awaken so as not to disturb her sleep. She blushed even now, thinking of the intimacy of it. And his consideration of her comfort.

And yet he was still going to ransom her and turn her over to Baron Kildary. It infuriated her.

And it hurt.

Truly, Maura understood loyalty and duty. She just wished Dugan did not insist upon using *her*. He had most of the treasure map! They could search for the gold together and when they found it, he would not have to ransom her. She would be free to go to Loch Camerochlan and take Rosie away before anyone was able to get word to her father. She and Rosie could be on a ship to Ireland so quickly Lord Aucharnie would never find them.

"I'm surprised the laird allows you to ride Glencoe with him. He's never before allowed anyone to ride his horse."

"His horse is named *Glencoe*?"

"Aye. For his home."

Maura digested that information. Everyone knew of the horrific events that had occurred in the highland village of Glencoe, and she knew that many innocent people had been slain by troops led by Robert Campbell—her mother's uncle. Worse, Campbell's orders had come from Major Duncanson, her father's younger brother.

A shudder went through her. "Was Laird Mac-Millan there? At the m-massacre?"

"Ach, aye. His father and brother were murdered by the redcoats, and his ma died in the mountains, tryin' to escape. Murder under trust, they call it."

Maura felt ill. She wrapped her arms tightly around herself under her cloak. Dear God, Dugan was the Glencoe lad Sorcha had spoken of. He *must* be. What had the old woman said about him?

Maura wracked her brain to remember, even as she swallowed back her revulsion at Archie's words. "How did Dugan come to be laird of the MacMillans?" she asked.

"Ah, weel, his ma's father was Laird MacMillan before him. Dugan and his brothers and sister, who was a wee bairn then, came to their granpa's holding at Braemore after the slaughter."

Maura tried but could not imagine the horror of the events that day at Glencoe. It had happened many years ago, so Dugan would have been a small boy at the time. 'Twas no wonder he'd bristled when Lieutenant Baird had spoken derisively to him at the Fort William inn.

And no wonder at all that he could coldly send the daughter of a lowland lord to wed yet another despicable lowland nobleman. So many of them had been involved in the Glencoe affair . . . Maura realized her predicament must provide Dugan some well-justified satisfaction.

Chapter 16

Lieutenant Baird cocked his pistol and held it to the old blind woman's head. "Was she here?" he demanded.

"I smell the rot o' death on ye," the old hag muttered.

"That would be you, old woman," Baird growled. "I'll blow your brains all the way to Ben Nevis if you do not tell me."

She had to have noticed Maura passing by. The damned dog would have barked up the same ruckus it had done when Baird and his men had come past the croft.

"Christ, woman. Just tell me what you know and I'll leave you be."

"Ye are as empty in soul as the mon ye seek to please. Ye'll no' find any favor there."

Baird swallowed. Sweat gathered between his shoulder blades and ran down the center of his back. "You know naught of it, hag."

"Ye are a twisted, self-seeking fool wi' no—"

"Last night! *Was she here?*" he demanded.

The old woman sniffed at his sleeve, like a dog seeking its next meal. "The blood of a Glencoe murderer runs through yer veins, ye damned Sassena—"

Baird fired.

The woman fell to the ground and he stepped away. He felt clammy and cold all over, and yet a certain satisfaction infused him. Aye, his father had been a young officer at Glencoe, and he'd carried out his orders perfectly. Not all the soldiers had. General Baird once spoke of the fainthearted fools who'd fired into the air rather than follow Captain Campbell's orders. Craven cowards, John Baird had called them.

Alastair looked at his pistol, then shoved it back into its holster and marched to the door. The biddy was a bloody fool. All she'd had to do was answer the question—and keep her daft remarks to herself—and she would still be alive.

The rot of death is on ye . . .

The voice gave Alastair a start. He glanced down at the body and swallowed hard. She was dead, all right.

He wiped his damp hands on his trousers, then straightened his coat and pulled open the door.

His men were on horseback, sitting in silence, waiting for him. Baird didn't bother looking at any of them, but went directly to his horse and mounted. He hoped they were not as lily-livered as some of his father's compatriots at Glencoe.

He cleared his throat. "Aye. She came this way."

She must have, else the woman would have denied it. Wouldn't she?

No one spoke as he turned and rode to the bridle path. *Why couldn't she have just answered the question? Why all that blather about souls? And Glencoe.*

"Mad old bampot," he muttered.

But, goddamn it, how could the old bat have known his father had been at Glencoe?

Dugan felt very lucky indeed. He'd brought down a ten-point stag, as well as several good-sized rabbits. 'Twas meat that would surely gain him a warm welcome up at the castle. He and Conall returned to the little grove of trees, carrying the rabbits, and found Maura sitting with Archie under a canopy made with his fur blanket.

Lachann and Bryce were already riding toward them on the path from the castle. And not a moment too soon. The fur canopy was soaked, nearly through, though Maura looked reasonably comfortable and dry underneath it. Archie was sitting with her, but he scrambled to his feet to take the string of rabbits from Conall.

No matter what news Lachann brought, Dugan had already decided he would take Maura to the castle rather than keeping her out in the rain all night. He just didn't know quite how he was going to explain her presence.

Dugan didn't think it would be wise to announce who she was, and knew there'd be no difficulty convincing her of that, for she hadn't wanted to tell him anything of her people, anyway. 'Twas hardly likely she'd tell Caillich.

The earl was not one to involve himself in the affairs of the highland lairds unless he could gain something from it. And Dugan didn't want to give the man any reason to think he might have something to gain by taking Maura from him.

No, 'twas best if he took no notice of her.

Lachann and Bryce rode into the cover of the trees but did not dismount. "The Duke of Argyll is up at the castle," Lachann said without preamble.

"Clarty bastard," Bryce muttered.

A shudder of revulsion went through Dugan. But he'd dealt with the wily brute in subsequent years and had no choice but to deal with him again. The question was—what was the duke doing at Caillich Castle?

Did he know of the gold?

"How many men?"

"Only twenty or so."

Dugan looked at Maura and noticed she'd gone pale at Lachann's words, and he wondered if she had reason to flee the duke. She could not be his daughter, for Argyll had none.

But perhaps they were related in some other way.

"Maura," he said, "you'll ride with Archie. He's your brother."

"But Laird, my sisters are—"

"Aye, Arch, I know," Dugan said. "But you've both got red hair, so they'll believe she is your sister. We're going to call her . . . Maggie . . . while we're at Caillich."

"Ah," he said. "I understand, Laird."

"Conall," Dugan said, "you and Bryce go and collect the stag and bring it to the castle. We'll ride ahead."

Archie took down the fur pelt and while he folded it, Dugan took Maura aside. "Is there aught you should tell me about the Duke of Argyll, *Lady* Maura?"

She swallowed—nervously, Dugan thought—then shook her head. "N-no. Well, of course I know who he is, but what more do you suppose I could tell you about him? The man is far above my station."

Somehow, Dugan did not think that was true. He straightened her hood over her head and thought about having the right to kiss her any time he liked. To take her in his arms and taste those sweet lips whenever he had the urge.

And damn all, he knew he would often have that urge.

He lifted her onto Archie's horse, vowing not to dwell any more on such impossibilities, on fantasies that interfered with his duty to his clan.

He watched as Archie started for the trail to the castle, then mounted his own horse and quickly caught up.

Maura felt certain Dugan knew she had some connection to the duke. But she had never met Argyll until his visit at Ilay House—dear Lord, had that been only a few days ago? She'd been introduced to Argyll at Ilay House, so he was likely to recognize her if he saw her. He would know her as the thief who'd taken the map.

For who else would have stolen it? She'd hoped that Ilay would not miss it for at least a few days, giving her a chance to get away from Lieutenant Baird at Fort William and escape into the highlands.

A shocking thought hit her. Perhaps Argyll had actually come to the highlands to search for her.

Somehow, she had to stay out of sight.

Caillich's guards allowed them to pass through the gates, and Maura was relieved to see that the outer close was a wee bustling town within the castle walls. There were shops and homes, pens with animals inside, and a very cozy-looking tavern and guesthouse with three floors. Farther on was the Lord's Tower, a massive stone building four stories high, with windows of mullioned glass on each level.

Dugan dismounted at the guesthouse and beckoned Archie to follow. "We'll take rooms here and hope I'll not be invited to stay at the keep."

Archie nodded and helped Maura down. She shrank into the hood of her cloak and followed the men inside, pleased to be out of the cold rain, and grateful to be out of sight of passersby. She did not care to attract any attention, though she took stock of her surroundings and considered how she was going to get away from the castle. And Dugan MacMillan.

Aucharnie Castle was not as large or imposing as Caillich, though there were walls surrounding her father's large bailey and barracks for his soldiers. The walls and their cannons were manned by soldiers, and no one could get past them.

Maura assumed the same was true here.

Dugan spoke to the innkeeper and arranged for some rooms while Maura warmed herself by the fire. A moment later, he picked up her bag and his own, and followed the man up the stairs to a short corridor lined with closed doors. He opened the first one and Dugan gestured for Maura to go inside. He placed her bag on the floor near the bed, and followed the innkeeper back out.

Maura was alone for only a moment before Dugan and Archie returned to the room. "Get the fire going, Arch," he said, then dropped his own pack on the floor. The one containing the maps.

He took a few items from it, and went for the door.

"Stay here, both of you."

Maura bristled at the tone of his order.

"You are responsible here, Archie. Stay with *your sister* until I return."

"Aye, Dugan."

He turned to leave, but stopped to speak sharply to Maura. "And stay out of my pack."

Dugan left. Maura waited for the room to warm, then removed her cloak and spread it out by the fire to dry. She opened her bag and took out her spare clothes and did the same with them.

"Where do you suppose Dugan went?" she asked Archie.

"To pay his respects to Lord Caillich."

"Have you been here before?"

"Oh aye." Archie sat down on the chair by the fire and leaned back in a pose of utter relaxation. "Dugan always stays in the Tower with the earl and his family. The rest of us stay here. The landlord, old Roy MacCallum, knows us well."

Maura smiled. She decided it was not going to be too difficult to get away from Archie during the night. She sat down near him to wait.

Dugan left Maura with Archie and went to the nearby room his men would share. He needed to make himself presentable before meeting Caillich and possibly Argyll.

He wondered why the duke had come so far away from his own territory. Aye, the man owned land in the highlands, but rarely did he travel to them himself. Dugan had not heard of any uprisings taking place in the highlands, and Lachann said the duke had brought a limited number of men with him.

Mayhap he had an issue he needed to negotiate with Caillich. The earl was notorious for taking no sides, but there might be a sensitive parliamentary vote coming up. Argyll might need Caillich as an ally.

There was water in the pitcher on the washstand, so Dugan pulled off his shirt and washed, then shaved with the razor and soap he'd taken from his pack. He combed his hair and tied it back, then dressed in his clean shirt and wrapped himself into his plaid. After brushing the mud from his sporran and boots, he felt satisfied that he no longer looked the part of the barbarian highlander.

He went down to the main floor of the guest-house and passed the time with Roy MacCallum, ordering a meal for his men before making his way up to Caillich's Tower on foot.

Caillich had always been cordial to the highland lairds, probably because he considered himself to be one of them, but only to a certain extent. Dugan wondered how he would be received by Argyll. Of course old maggot knew he'd raised the rent on MacMillan lands to an exorbitant rate—it only remained to be seen whether the man would mention it.

Dugan moved past guards wearing the Caillich tartan, and entered the earl's great hall, where he found a festive atmosphere. The chandeliers and wall sconces glittered with candlelight. A small troupe of fiddlers and pipers played quietly at one end of the hall while servants were busy placing trays of food and decanters of wine on the table.

Lairds MacLeod and MacRae stood talking together near the massive fireplace with Argyll and Caillich. Lady Caillich was notably absent, and Dugan wondered if it meant the earl expected some tense conversation between the lairds and Argyll. 'Twas likely true.

Dugan wore a neutral expression as he greeted the men, giving deference to none of them. He was damned if he would bow to the bastard who intended to drive his clan—his family—from their lands.

"Laird MacMillan, I understand your men brought me a stag," Caillich said.

"Aye."

"Many thanks, then. Lady Caillich is quite partial to venison. She will be doubly pleased to hear of your gift."

"What brings you down this way, Laird MacMillan?" Argyll asked pointedly. "You are far from your . . . er, *my* . . . lands."

Dugan's hands itched to draw his claymore and end it right here. "Business, Duke."

"A financial transaction, mayhap?"

"No. We traveled south to collect one of my clanswomen from Loch Nevis."

Argyll raised a brow. "Taken in a raid, then?"

"No, Duke." Dugan smiled slightly. "Visiting our kin."

Argyll liked nothing better than to depict highland clansmen as savages, doing naught but stealing from one another and engaging in bloody feuds. And yet it was clear Argyll had no regrets that his own regiment had carried out the slaughter of innocent women and children at Glencoe. Dugan was not about to play into the bloody duke's portrayal of a barbaric clansman.

"Ah. So now you are on your way back to Brae-more. How do your lands fare?" Argyll asked, smiling as though he enjoyed a private jest.

Dugan looked into the man's flat, dark eyes and wondered how the old maggot could live with himself. He was richer than the Hanoverian king of England, but was angling for even more wealth. Argyll didn't need any part of the MacMillan lands, and yet he would toss Dugan's entire clan into the sea without a second thought.

"It seems our lands are far more valuable than we ever knew."

"Of course they are, old man," Argyll said. "The price of land is always rising these days. He turned to the others and weighed his words carefully before speaking. "I understand there is good land lying fallow near some of the lochs. What have you heard of Loch Monar? Still unoccupied?"

Dugan's blood went cold.

Had Argyll reached the same conclusion Dugan had? That the French gold was hidden at Loch Monar? Was he fishing for information while avoiding showing his own hand?

"No one goes up that way these days," Laird MacLeod said. "At least, not to my knowledge."

"And Loch Nan Eun?" Argyll asked. "There is a settlement nearby, is there not?"

Dugan's thoughts scattered madly. *What of Loch Nan Eun?* Did Argyll have information about that location as well as Loch Monar? Was Dugan about to waste precious time searching for the gold in the wrong place?

They were called to their seats at the table and Dugan began to put a number of facts together, not the least of which was the possibility that the green spot he'd seen on the map meant naught. 'Twas more likely a discoloration rather than any indication of the treasure's location.

Yet Argyll suspected something about Loch Monar, else he would not have spoken of it.

Dugan engaged in conversation with the other lairds while they all avoided potentially explosive discussions about rents and enclosures. Word had spread of the outrageous rent demanded of Dugan, and no one wanted to mention it. They were all waiting to see how he was going to pay it.

Or what would happen to the MacMillan clan when he was unable to raise the money.

Dugan had expected the duke to retire shortly after the meal, but he stayed on, drinking whiskey and monopolizing the conversation with talk about Whigs and Tories and legislation that meant naught to anyone in the highlands. 'Twas almost as though Argyll could not bear the possibility that the others might make untoward remarks about him if he left them alone to speak of him.

The auld bastard was right.

Laird MacLeod was first to take his leave.

Dugan was next. He'd learned all he was going to from Argyll, and that was bad enough. The duke would soon be searching for the gold at either Loch Monar or Loch Nan Eun.

Damn all, would everyone in the highlands soon be searching for the treasure? Dugan left the Tower, swearing viciously under his breath as he made his way back to the guesthouse.

They would need to make an early start on the morrow in order to stay ahead of Argyll, for Dugan assumed the man would begin his search at Loch

Monar. He assumed the duke's reference to Loch Nan Eun was just a distraction.

The rain had let up, and Dugan hoped it would stay dry for their next few days' travel. The terrain they needed to cover was difficult and would be much easier without rain.

He was halfway to the guesthouse when he saw a lone figure slip away from the building as it kept to the shadows and rounded the corner toward the back. Judging by the length of the hooded cloak, 'twas a woman. One who was very familiar, indeed.

Chapter 17

Lieutenant Baird stood on a high promontory and tried to focus his eyes to search the terrain below. 'Twas nearly dark and he had no choice but to make camp where they stood. After leaving the old crone's cottage, they had picked up a trail that might have been Maura's. But then lost it in the rough terrain west of the old witch's croft.

He pinched the bridge of his nose and willed away the sharp pain in his forehead.

"Have ye the headache, Lieutenant?" Higgins asked.

"No," Baird snapped.

"Ah. 'Tis just that it's seemed to have bothered you all day."

Goddamn it, *aye*. For hours, he'd tried but could not get the old crone's words to leave his memory. His head pounded with every iteration. *Glencoe. Glencoe. Glencoe.*

God almighty! 'Twas impossible to think when that damned place name kept swirling 'round in his head.

Shite. What in hell did the woman know about anything? The old prune was naught but an ignorant peasant living in a filthy hovel with that ugly bear of a dog. She knew naught of politics or military responsibility. Those damned highlanders at Glencoe had needed to be taught a lesson. His father had said so, had drummed it into him, in fact.

Do your duty, lad. Obedience is all that matters.

Alastair sniffed. In spite of the parliamentary investigation into the events at Glencoe, John Baird had been richly rewarded by King William for carrying out Major Duncanson's orders. *That* was a clear demonstration of his father's worth.

And Lord Aucharnie would reward Alastair when he brought the bruised and broken corpse of his defiant daughter to him.

Alastair knew the earl wanted to be rid of her. He'd made that perfectly clear by his actions—or rather, his *in*action—toward her. For what father who cared about his daughter would allow her to wander over hills and dales without a proper escort? None. What father would sell her to an old reprobate like Baron Kildary? None. The man was reputed to have done away with his previous two wives, and now that his only son was dead, he needed an heir.

Baird winced when a particularly sharp pain pierced his skull, just above his eye. Damn it! Had the old crone bewitched him? He shuddered at the thought. "We'll camp here tonight and proceed on her trail at dawn," he said to Higgins.

"Begging your pardon, sir . . ." said Higgins. "What trail?"

"Maura Duncanson's trail, you idiot!"

"But Lieutenant—"

"Enough!" Baird bellowed, but his shouting only

made the headache worse. "Make camp down in the clearing. Keep the fire small."

"Aye, sir."

Maura would never have believed how quickly Archie could fall asleep, but after they ate the meal Dugan had ordered, the young man had made himself comfortable in the chair in her room and was soon snoring.

She took it as a sign.

That, and the fact that she had seen from her window a cistern gate in the castle's curtain wall. There was every chance she could push it open and slip away from Caillich before Dugan even knew she was gone. With luck, he would be staying the night in the luxurious Lord's Tower and wouldn't note her absence until the morrow, when she would be miles away.

Perhaps this time she would actually get away.

She packed her now dry belongings into her bag, and put on her cloak. She went to the door, but stood still for a moment, considering what she was about to do.

Dugan would be furious.

But he gave her no choice. He'd made it clear he intended to trade her to Kildary for the ransom money, and she could not allow that to occur. She thought of Sorcha's words and knew that leaving now was the most sensible thing to do. She had to get to Rosie, and Dugan MacMillan was her primary obstacle.

Maura quietly pulled open the door. No one was about, so she made her way down the steps and out a back door of the guesthouse. No one saw her.

All was quiet outside, the only light coming from the torches at the Tower's door. Maura moved rapidly through the courtyard and nearly made it to the wall.

She let out a little cry of alarm when a man stepped into her path and grabbed her arms, causing her to drop her bag.

"I should have known you would find a way to—"

"Let go of me! I'll scream!"

She opened her mouth to do just that when he yanked her into his arms and tossed her over his shoulder, forcing the breath right out of her lungs. She could barely breathe, much less scream for help.

But she kicked. She pummeled him with her feet and her fists. "Enough, Maura!" he rasped, his anger palpable.

But she did not relent and fought him with all her might, all the way back to the guesthouse. Her efforts did not slow him in the least. He entered the guesthouse and carried her up the stairs to the room where she'd left Archie.

The young man woke up with a start as they came inside, and Dugan tossed her unceremoniously onto the bed. "Laird?" he asked, standing abruptly.

"Collect your pack and take it down to the stable," Dugan said to Archie, his tone furious. "You'll spend the rest of the night with the damned horses."

"What—?"

"Do as I say. Now."

Maura had never seen Dugan so angry, especially not with young Archie, who was obviously a favorite of all the men. She pushed herself off the bed and came to her feet, as outraged as he. She put her hands upon her hips.

"You cannot sell me to Kildary!"

"Aye. I can and I will. And you will stop trying to run away from me."

"Oh no, I will no—"

"Take off your shoes."

"My—!"

"Get them off now, or I'll take them from you. The hard way." He looked so very different with his face shaved and his hair neatly tied. His shirt was clean, too.

But any positive effect was lost upon her when he crossed his arms over his burly chest and glared at her.

"I will not."

He started for her then, and Maura was dismayed to find herself backing away. "All right!" She sat down on the chair and removed her shoes.

Dugan reached down and picked them up. "Now your cloak."

She stood and unfastened it grudgingly and handed it to him.

"Take off the rest of your clothes and put them in your bag," he said. "I'll wait outside."

"I will *not*!"

"As I said before, we can do this the hard way."

"You wouldn't dare!"

"Would you care to try me, lass?"

Maura did not care for the cocky gleam in his eyes, but she especially did not like the sensual tingle that crept up her spine at the thought of him undressing her.

Seeing no choice but to do as he demanded,

she glowered at him as she unfastened the first set of ties at her throat. When she moved her fingers down to the second—the one that lay between her breasts—he gave a quick nod of approval and left the room.

The evening had been bad enough, spending time in Argyll's company. The night was going to be sheer hell. The image of Maura's delicate hands working the ties to her bodice was nearly his undoing. He'd wanted to do the unfastening himself, and feast on the bonny feminine flesh underneath.

Now that he was about to have her naked, he recognized he was the only one he trusted to guard her. Not that any of his men would fall asleep as Archie had done, but he didn't much care for the idea of Maura lying in that bed unclothed, with any of the others in the room with her.

He was the only man she would sleep with.

Dugan clenched his fists at his sides at such a ridiculous notion. What his hardening cock wanted and what he needed to do were two entirely different things. He was damned if he'd let his three thousand pounds flit away into the mist. His clan deserved better, by God.

He leaned his back against the wall and forced his attention on what he *must* do. Ransoming Maura went against every principle he believed in—except for the primary one. To ensure the safety and security of his clan. He despised the thought of turning Maura over to Kildary, but what choice did he have?

If Dugan went off to hunt for the gold, could he trust that his guards would keep Maura contained

at Braemore until Kildary's representative came
with the ransom money? She was far too resourceful and determined to sit idly, awaiting her fate.
Unless Dugan ordered her to be locked in a room
for the duration, she would surely figure a way to
escape the keep.

He bolstered his resolve by picturing his
people—his wee nephews—being driven away
from their homes by Argyll's red-coated soldiers.
The parallel between this situation and his forced
exodus from Glencoe resonated painfully in his
heart. Ach, aye. He would do what he must. Maura
was a far surer means to the money he needed than
any feckless map.

He pushed off the wall and went back into her
chamber.

He could not be too hard on Archie, for 'twas
not the lad's fault. Dugan should have tied the
woman to the bed before leaving for the Tower.

He found her lying on her side in the bed with
the blankets pulled up to her chin. Dugan looked
'round the room and saw that there were no clothes
lying about. Another glance told him that she'd
put her plain green traveling gown in the bag. Her
shoes were on the floor beside it.

"What are you going to do?" she asked.

Damned if he knew. He picked up the bag and
shoes and went to the room where his men were
just settling down for the night.

"Dugan . . . you're back?" Conall said, startled
to see him. He looked at Maura's clothes and
blushed to the roots of his hair, obviously aware
that she must now be completely undressed.

"Are you not staying at the Tower tonight?"
Lachann asked.

He put Maura's bag on the floor as far from the door as possible. "I've no interest in spending the night under the same roof with the Duke of Argyll."

The men muttered their agreement, but everyone went silent when he stepped back out of the room. "Well, where—"

"To guard my prisoner. She got past Archie and I don't trust her to stay where I put her."

Dugan ignored their raised eyebrows and went back to Maura's room and prepared to spend the night in the chair.

Maura had kept her shift on, but she might as well be naked for all that meager garment covered. When Dugan left the room, she lay still for a moment, stunned by the way he had outmaneuvered her. Then she jumped out of bed and was just about to lock the door when the infuriating man returned.

Maura gave out a little squeal of alarm when he came in, and flew back to the bed and pulled the blankets around her. "What are you doing here? I thought you—"

"Settle down, Lady Maura."

"I will not!" she retorted, her anger palpable. When she would have liked to pace the room, modesty forced her to retreat to the bed, covered by blankets. 'Twas intolerable. "What do you mean, coming back in here when I am un . . . when I am in b-bed?" Last night was bad enough, lying together fully clothed. This was a different matter altogether.

But what was she to do? Scold him? That was

such a pathetic notion, she would think it comical if she wasn't so furious.

"It is entirely inappropriate for you to stay here with me." She held the blanket to her chest. "I will not allow it."

"If I trusted you not to wander the inn to find some hapless woman's clothes to steal," he replied, picking up his bag and removing the maps, "I might be persuaded to leave you alone."

"Ooo!" She flounced down onto her back, fuming. She hadn't even thought about finding another woman's clothes to steal. "You cannot stay in here with me!"

"I beg to differ."

The room was not large, so when Dugan sat down in the chair by the fire and began to examine the maps once again, Maura could see them clearly. She could also see the flecks of gray in his blue eyes and a thin crease of concentration that formed between his brows.

She became acutely aware of her near-nakedness beneath the blankets and Dugan's close proximity. It made her breath feel tight in her chest. It was far too easy to imagine him climbing into bed with her and holding her close as he'd done the night before.

Now they were alone in the warm, snug room, and the memory of the kisses they'd shared burned like a beacon in her brain. It was infuriating that she wanted to experience them again. She should want naught to do with the hateful man.

"Go to sleep, Maura."

"I am not a child, Dugan," she snapped. "I will sleep when I am ready. And not a moment before."

She cringed at her tone, realizing at once that she *did* sound like a child. A petulant one.

She'd been too angry to realize that a far better approach would be to turn the tables on him. She could make him tremendously uncomfortable.

His eyes skated over her, and Maura realized exactly how disheveled she appeared. Her hair had come loose and was as wild a mess as ever, though perhaps that had a certain appeal. As did her state of undress in a very convenient bed. When he made a pointed return of his attention to the maps, Maura allowed the blanket to slip down so that her shoulders were left uncovered.

But he did not look up at her.

She might have felt frustrated by his inattention, but then a lock of his hair slipped out of its queue and Maura watched, fascinated as he shoved it behind his ear. His hands were large, with long, dense fingers and thick blue veins across their backs. Strong, competent hands that had held her and kept her warm all through the previous night.

She propped her head on her elbow and watched him peruse the map, unsure exactly how she was going to proceed to make him uncomfortable. "Haven't you already gone over it enough?" she asked.

He continued to ignore her, raising the map so that she could not see his face. Nor could he see hers.

Clearly, more drastic measures were needed.

The question was how far was she willing to go? And how far would he allow her to take it? He'd exerted remarkable control on the previous occasions when he'd kissed her—perhaps he did not find her quite as desirable as she found him.

She was just about to climb out of the bed and test her wiles when something about the map caught her attention. It was a light tracing on the dusty back of the map Dugan held.

Narrowing her eyes to see better, she held perfectly still and gazed at the back of the map.

There were letters etched on the parchment that formed words—in French. She leaned forward and noted that the text had been traced in something like wax, some substance that would not show up unless it was coated in dirt . . . or *dust*.

Just as old Sorcha had said.

She'd also said the Glencoe lad wouldn't discover the secret. And she was right.

They'd spread out the maps on the dusty ground and studied them repeatedly. It looked as though they'd collected the coating of dirt that was necessary to read the words. Now that Maura thought of it, she realized it was strange that the documents had been rolled with the map side out. Weren't manuscripts usually rolled with the text *in*side, to protect it?

Excitement welled up inside her. *This* was the clue they needed. *This* was the key they'd looked for!

Before saying anything to Dugan, she spelled out the words. There was *sous*. And *le gros*. Next to it was a word that began with *ro*. Beneath those words had been etched *du Lac Aveboyne*.

The words opened up more questions than they answered. Was Lac Aveboyne the location of the treasure? *Sous* meant "under." Did that mean that the treasure had been hidden under the large "ro—" at Loch Aveboyne?

Maura contained her excitement. Of course it was, else why would it be noted on the map? The rest of the clue had to be there, and if she could just get her hands on all the three pieces of the map, she knew she could figure out exactly where the gold was hidden.

Maura licked her lips and thought about what to do. There had to be a way to use this information to gain her freedom. If she shared her discovery with Dugan, would he retract his ransom demand and allow her to go free?

Perhaps, but more likely not. Until he had the treasure in his hands, Dugan would not believe someone else hadn't found the treasure before him. Which meant he would still insist on collecting the ransom from Kildary. Maura knew he was not about to risk the welfare of his clan.

But she would not risk Rosie's welfare, either.

She climbed out of bed as she considered her options.

Dugan lowered the map and his gaze raked over her. Maura felt her heart quicken in response.

She went to his chair and crouched next to him, tipping the map in order to see it better. His eyes darkened and he shifted in his chair. "What are you doing?"

Chapter 18

"Where are we now?" Maura asked. "I mean here, on the map."

Dugan held his breath. She was kneeling far too close to his widely spread legs. She was so intent upon the map, she did not even seem to notice how insufficiently clad she was.

But Dugan noticed. He took in the delicate line of her collarbones and the fullness of her breasts beneath them. They were so thinly covered, he could see their dusky peaks, and how they had pebbled in the cool air of the room.

"Here, I think," he said, somehow managing not to sound like a strangled toad. He pointed to a space west and a short stretch north of Fort William. "I believe Caillich Castle lies here in this clearing."

"I see. And this?" She touched the map, and a shiver of need shot down his spine and centered between his legs.

He pulled them together in self-defense. "Most likely Loch Cluanie."

He identified numerous other locations on the map, including Loch Camerochlan. Maura eventually asked him to point out Braemore, and Dugan indicated an area near the southwest corner of a loch just off the western coast. 'Twas the place he'd called home for twenty-five years, and he was not about to lose it now. "Here, on the banks of Loch Maree."

She touched the spot, then drew her finger south. "What about this loch? What is it called?"

"Aveboyne." He stood abruptly, anxious to put some space between them. "Why don't you return to bed, Maura. 'Tis cold in the room—"

"No colder than it was last night when we slept in the open." She came to her feet and stood close, her arms at her sides. Her hair was stunning, curling wildly about her face and down her back. Her eyes were soft and sleepy.

He could easily lift her off her feet and carry her to the bed and—

No. There was too much at stake. He could not bed the woman—she did not even know how seductive she was. Her actions were not an invitation, and he had never taken a woman who'd not been clear about her intentions.

Ach, but those breasts. Those bare, vulnerable feet. He clenched his teeth and prayed for fortitude.

"Dugan . . ." Her voice was pure seduction. And when she stood just inches from him, twirling a lock of her hair 'round her finger, he knew he was lost.

"Aye, Maura," he breathed. His hands itched to touch her, to pull her to him and feel those breasts against his chest. *Gesu*, what he wanted was to feel them in his hands. He shuddered with the intensity of his arousal.

She reached up and touched his jaw. "Am I just a burden to you?"

"Maura." He slipped one hand about her waist and drew her closer. "No, lass, you are not a burden."

"But a means to an end." She looked so sorrowful, Dugan felt shamed. How could he give her to Kildary?

He tipped his head downward, and her exquisite feminine scent surrounded him. He pulled her fully against him and reveled in the soft hills and valleys of her body. She fit so perfectly, he had to stifle a groan of pleasure. He took her lips with his, their melding creating the sensation that he'd arrived where he belonged.

She slid her hands up to his neck and when they reached his nape, removed the band of leather holding back his hair.

Dugan deepened their kiss, slipping his tongue into her mouth as one of his hands glided up her side to her breast. He cupped the full mound, then teased the nipple through the thin cotton of her chemise with his fingers.

Maura arched into his attentions, and Dugan used his other hand to unfasten the ties at her shoulders. Her shift slid down to her waist.

He kissed her neck, then her shoulders, and his arousal pressed insistently against her. He wanted to taste every inch of her, all while he was inside her.

Her arms fell to his waist and her head dropped back when he bent to lick her nipple. He swirled his tongue 'round the bonny pink tip, then sucked it fully into his mouth.

She made a little squeak when he did the same to the other, and Dugan suddenly needed more. He lifted her into his arms and carried her to the bed.

Laying her on the mattress, he quickly divested her of her chemise, leaving her entirely naked to his gaze.

She tried to cover herself, but Dugan moved her hands. "Ach, sweet Maura. You are so very beautiful. Do not hide from me."

He pulled his shirt from his kilt and came down over her, kissing that gorgeous mouth, then working his way down to her breasts, teasing each one in turn with his fingers and tongue. He moved lower, kissing her belly and moving down . . .

"**D**ugan . . . Oh! No, you cannot—"

Maura's shock turned to pleasure when he pressed his lips to the sensitive bud at the apex of her sex. She could do naught but moan and arch against his mouth. He used his fingers and tongue to drive her to some incredible peak of sensations, and when the torrent of pleasure overtook her, a cry of amazement escaped her. But Dugan did not relent. He kissed his way back to her mouth.

"Touch me, Maura."

He took her hand and guided it to the hard, hot length of him beneath his plaid, and wrapped her fingers 'round it.

Maura could barely breathe as she explored him, and she shivered when he groaned with pleasure. "Ach, aye."

She'd never felt so feminine or powerful as she did sliding her hand up and down, then across the moist tip of his manhood. She was awash in sensations, her arousal even more intense as she touched him.

Instinct drove her. She craved more of the pleasure he'd given her, and knew 'twould be even more profound when he was inside her. *When he joined his body to hers.*

"Dugan, please . . ."

He unbuckled his belt and tossed his plaid aside, and Maura reveled in the sight of his brawny chest and arms, of his flat nipples and tight abdomen. Her eyes grazed the dusting of hair that trailed down his belly to the long, thick heat of him.

He lowered his mouth to her breasts, teasing them with his tongue as he slid his hand down again to the sensitive nub between her legs. Her breath came in soft pants as he pleasured her, creating that maelstrom she craved. Her heart seemed to stop as her muscles tightened, and then he kissed her so deeply, she felt her desire peaking yet again. He spread her legs with his thigh and positioned himself right where Maura needed him most.

She felt him move against her, and her body was ready.

He raised himself over her, his arms at her sides. Poised. Ready. And yet he stopped moving. He closed his eyes and clenched his jaw.

"Dugan?"

"Ach, Maura. What am I—"

He moved off her and reached for a square of linen lying on the washstand beside the bed.

A moment later, he collapsed on the bed beside her.

Dugan felt shaken. His pulse still hammered in his ears and he felt as raw as an open wound. He might have spent himself into a convenient cloth, but he felt nowhere near satisfied. Even now he had to fight the urge to begin all over again, to revel in Maura's innocent sensuality, to plunge into her and make her his own.

But she belonged to Kildary. Thank God he'd regained his senses before breaching her forbidden territory.

Her body was warm and soft, and he pulled the blanket over them and drew her into his arms, forcing some semblance of control. That control was a tenuous thing, especially when she trailed her fingers up his chest and—

He took hold of her hand and held it fast against his overheated skin.

"Maura, we cannot."

She pressed her lips to his neck, then his chin, and his cock roared to life again. He ignored his better judgment and rolled her onto her back. He kissed her, his desire warring with his good sense. He craved her with every breath, every beat of his heart. She tasted like unrestrained need when he mated his tongue with hers. Tasted like folly. And he could not stop. Not this time.

"Dugan," she murmured between kisses.

"Hmm."

"I know where the treasure is hidden."

It didn't surprise him. "Aye, lass. And so does the Duke of Argyll. I'll have to make it to Loch Monar before him if I'm going to have it, and it might not be there, anyway."

He skimmed his hand down to her breast. And a bonny morsel of womanly flesh it was. He slid down and touched his tongue to her nipple. She took a sharp breath and melted against him. She was a singular female, and he feared he would never get his fill of her.

"Is that where you think it is? Loch Monar?" She tipped her head back and looked at him with what could only be astonishment in her eyes. "The gold isn't at Loch Monar, Dugan," she whispered.

He stopped. "No? Then where might it be, and why haven't you mentioned it before?"

"I only just discovered the key. Argyll might believe it's Loch Monar, but he's wrong."

Dugan's hand stopped moving, and the incredible sensations that had begun to grow once again dissipated. Maura closed her eyes and swallowed, fighting to compose herself.

Oh Lord, what had she done? *Become intimate with the very man who'd taken her captive and intended to turn her over to Kildary.* What kind of dolt was she? Becoming entangled with Dugan MacMillan was the worst possible thing she could have done.

But dear Lord, she wanted more. The desire to feel him inside her had not abated in the least.

It was sinfully wanton, and his lovemaking did not serve her purpose in any way. His kisses and caresses would not help her to get to Loch Camerochlan. Nor would they convince him to forgo his efforts to ransom her to Kildary.

But perhaps she could try and get him to change his mind. "If I tell you what I know, will you take me with you when you go for it?"

"Maura . . ." His tone made his thoughts clear.

Her eyes began to sting, but she would not succumb to tears. There could be no future between them, no matter how fiercely the attraction raged between them.

No matter how she might wish things could be different.

She'd known what mattered to him when she'd lain with him. It was not she. But Maura did not have to yield to his wishes. She had the upper hand.

"What is the key?" he growled.

He'd pointed out Loch Aveboyne on the map, so Maura knew where they had to go to find the gold. And so much the better if Argyll thought it was hidden at Loch Monar. It would give them more time.

"You must realize 'tis not in my best interest to tell you."

He pushed himself up onto his hands and hovered over her. "Your best interests?"

"Exactly. But I will . . . *show* you where it is."

Dugan rolled out of the bed and went for the map. Maura's jaw dropped at the sight of his powerful body. All of it, naked before her. His muscles seemed carved of granite, and Maura knew he could have crushed her at any time. He might want to crush her after he heard her demand.

He brought the map to the bed and placed it on the blanket in front of her. "Where?"

Maura sat up in the bed, holding the blanket over her bare breasts. She felt absurdly naked, considering what had just transpired between them. "What I mean is . . . I will take you there."

He seemed entirely unconscious of his nakedness as he stood before her, frowning fiercely. "No."

She bit her lip and gathered the courage she needed to stand up to him. "Yes."

Naught had changed between them. Her heart sank into an empty hole in her chest at the realization that his lovemaking had only *seemed* to link them deeply. He had not changed his plan to give her to Kildary in spite of the passion that arced between them.

"I will take you there b-because if I divulge what I know," she said, "you'll give me to Baron Kildary and go to—go to the site without me."

Maura blinked back her unwelcome tears while Dugan stood unmoving, smoldering with anger.

"I'm not going to let you lock me up at Braemore Keep, Dugan MacMillan," she said, moving onto her knees, "and then turn me over to Baron Kildary *if* he or his lackeys turn up with the ransom."

A muscle in his jaw flexed. "I don't believe you."

She shrugged, attempting to appear indifferent, but she knew she would never feel indifferent to him. She blinked away the tears that were welling in her eyes. "Be that as it may—the gold is not at Loch Monar, and the first chance I get, I'm going to go to Lo—" She stopped herself just in time. "I am going to go after the gold myself while you and Argyll waste your time at Loch Monar."

Maura knew 'twas an empty threat, for Dugan would not let her out of his sight. Not after this.

She lay down and turned over in the bed, facing away from him, pulling the blanket tightly over her shoulder. She felt cold all over, and her body trembled, for naught that she'd ever experienced could compare with the intimacy they'd shared—only to have him betray her.

He was implacable.

And she was expendable.

Maura knew 'twould be a long time before she would be able to fall asleep, but it hurt too much to talk to him any more. Besides, she needed to give him some time to decide what he was going to do.

She heard him grumble as he pulled on his clothes. He blew out the candles, then pushed the chair to the door. To guard it, presumably. As though she could leave wearing naught but her shift.

Clearly, 'twould be a cold day in hell before he cared enough about her to keep her from Kildary.

Chapter 19

Morning dawned. Maura was still asleep and every bit as alluring as Dugan had found her last night, but at least his reason had returned. So had his anger.

He got up from his chair and stretched, and made a point of avoiding looking at her. When he thought of her sweet kisses, 'twas far too easy to contemplate abandoning his ransom demand.

He picked up his maps and left her sleeping while he went into the room where his men had slept. He wanted—needed—to consult with them.

Needed to put some space between himself and Maura before his anger could dissipate.

The men were all awake, and Dugan went directly to a table that stood by the window. He cleared everything from its surface and spread out the section of the map that showed Loch Monar. "Come here, all of you."

"What is it, Dugan?" Lachann asked.

"What does this look like to you?" He pointed to Loch Monar.

" 'Tis Loch Aveboyne," Conall replied.

"No," Lachann said. " 'Tis more the shape of Loch Monar." He pointed to another blue shape.

"This is Aveboyne, north of Monar. See how much longer and narrower it is."

"Aye," Dugan replied. "Look closely at Loch Monar. Do you see any sign on this map that the gold might be hidden there?" Dugan stepped back and let the others study the document, hoping one of them would take note of the green mark.

The men shook their heads, all but Bryce. "Dugan, you do'na mean this green splotch of ink at the wee neck of land on the north shore?"

"'Tis naught but a blur of ink," Lachann said, and Dugan heard a fair degree of incredulity in his tone. "Dugan, this is just the blue of the loch, blurred away from the main part."

Conall frowned, lowering his head even closer to the map. "Mayhap not, Lachann. This is definitely a mark made in green paint, Laird."

"Well, I am fairly sure this is Loch Monar, and the Duke of Argyll asked a few pointed questions about it last night," Dugan said. "I think he's heard of the gold and he intends to look there for it."

The men were silent as they considered Dugan's words.

"Just because Argyll believes it's there doesn't mean it is, Dugan," said Lachann. "This mark . . . Well, it looks like naught to me."

Dugan rubbed the back of his neck. The green spot was hardly the beacon that should draw him to Loch Monar.

"Well then, let's find Loch Nan Eun. 'Tis another spot Argyll mentioned." Though Dugan believed 'twas just a distraction from the site Argyll really believed in.

"I see naught," Conall said.

Bryce shook his head.

"Dugan, I don't think we can put all our hopes in this spot," Lachann said, pointing to the green mark at Loch Monar.

"Nor I," said Bryce.

Dugan let out a long breath. According to Maura, the gold was located elsewhere. Could he believe her?

Could he risk following Maura into the highlands merely because she claimed she'd figured out the key to the map and knew where the gold had been hidden? Or was she leading him on in the hope that his ransom plan would fall apart if she was not at Braemore when the baron arrived?

He should have known from the moment he'd seen Lady Maura facing down that ram by the waterfall that she was a force to be reckoned with.

Dugan could not help but hope he wasn't about to make an even more serious error in judgment, worse than the enormous mistake he'd made the night before. As much as he did not like it, the lass belonged to Kildary. He'd been a fool to touch her.

A fool to want her.

But even now, he could not regret one moment that he'd spent in her bed. He wanted her still, wanted to wipe away the sheen of tears and kiss away the hurt expression in her eyes.

But he could not.

"Lachann, go to Caillich's stable and try to get a look at Argyll's baggage. See if you can determine how many men he brought with him and whether they have carts with shovels and picks."

Lachann nodded and went to follow his brother's orders. The other lads left to find Archie and hunt down some breakfast while Dugan shaved and washed and made himself ready to face Maura.

He admitted she had a very good reason to lie about discovering the key to the map. They both knew a delay in their arrival at Braemore could negate Dugan's ransom demand. If Dugan did not produce his captive when Kildary or his men arrived at his keep, he might well forfeit the ransom.

On the other hand, if she helped him find the gold, she would be free to make her way up to Loch Camerochlan and take her sister wherever she decided to go.

Dugan didn't want to give her to Kildary, but he surely did not care to think of her traveling all the way to Camerochlan alone, and then leaving Scotland for good.

Kieran and Calum would make haste in their journey to Cromarty to deliver the ransom demand, and Kildary or his men would leave immediately for Braemore. 'Twas what Dugan would do if his own bride were threatened.

But perhaps Dugan could delay Kildary at Braemore. It would take some days for the baron to travel all the way from Cromarty to the western highlands . . . By the time he arrived, Dugan might already have the French gold in his possession.

Dugan decided on a plan as he folded his plaid about his waist and fastened his belt. He would send Bryce to placate Kildary while he and the other men accompanied Maura to the location where she believed the gold was hidden. If they did not find it—well, then they would hurry back to Braemore and turn her over to Kildary.

Not that it would be easy, for Maura was certain not to cooperate.

There was no room in Maura's heart for any fondness toward Laird MacMillan, in spite of what had transpired between them in her room the night before. Perhaps *because* of what had happened. She was so embarrassed to have bared not only her body, but her soul to him.

And he'd handed it right back to her when he declared there was no change in his plan to ransom her.

She'd been right to keep her knowledge about Loch Aveboyne from him. She prayed she would be able to find the loch, for 'twas the only chance she had for getting away from Lord Kildary and on to Loch Camerochlan.

Dugan must have significant doubts about Loch Monar actually being the location of the gold, because now he'd decided to trust her. Well, not actually trust her. 'Twas clear by his cold manner this morn that he had no particular liking for his predicament. She knew his preference to send her to Braemore had not changed. Their intimate interlude meant naught.

And so it would mean naught to Maura.

She had to get her hands on the other sections of the map, though, and try to make out the rest of the words that were etched on them. Perhaps Loch Aveboyne was not actually the location. Perhaps the rest of the message indicated that the gold was miles away from Aveboyne. Or sunk in the middle of the loch.

But at least she was not doomed to become Kildary's bride. At least, not yet.

"Which way, Maura?" Dugan asked. His voice

slid through her like warm honey. But she resisted any softening toward him.

"Where is Bryce?"

"I asked you a question, woman."

She straightened her shoulders and bolstered her resolve. He would *not* intimidate her. "We travel northwest, as before."

It was early, and no one but servants were about the castle bailey. The sun had not even crested the mountain peaks to the east, but Calum, Archie, and Lachann had already saddled their horses. They took their leave and rode down to the gates rather than waiting for Dugan and Maura.

Dugan set his jaw as he took her traveling bag from her, but something caught his attention as he tossed it onto the back of his saddle. "Wait here," he commanded. "I mean it, Maura. Do not step away from this spot."

Dugan hurried away toward the chandler's shop across from the stable where a young maid—hardly more than a child—was hauling two heavy buckets, one in each hand. Maura's heart clenched when she noticed the lass's limping gait, and when she stumbled, Dugan lurched ahead to catch her before she fell.

He righted her and took the buckets from her hands. He carried them into the shop, and Maura could not help but defy his command and approach the building when she heard low voices coming from inside.

"Are you such a neep, chandler, not to see how your lass struggles?"

"And who are ye to tell me m' business?"

"I am laird of the MacMillans"—Dugan tipped

slightly forward at the waist and pointed at the chandler—"and I'll tell you what you clearly need to hear, man."

"Get out of my shop."

"Get the lass a cart so she can pull the buckets from the well rather than spilling half the water over the ground and herself." By his tone, 'twas clear Dugan would not brook any argument.

"I do'na need ye t' tell me—"

"*Aye, you do.* You'll have a more efficient shop if you provide her with the tools to perform her tasks."

An intense wave of emotion came over her as she watched the interchange between Dugan and the chandler, but Maura had no time to think about Dugan's actions when he turned to leave the shop. She gathered her wits and hurried back to where he'd left her, standing beside his horse.

Their departure was delayed yet again by Bryce's arrival. Dugan took the man aside and spoke quietly with him, then returned to Maura.

"Come on, then," he said, lifting her up to his saddle.

He mounted behind her and they followed the path his men had just taken, with Bryce alongside them.

Maura had to remind herself to breathe. The man who would hand her over to Baron Kildary without a second thought had dashed to assist a lame child-servant who was no one to him. Until now, Deirdre Elliott's husband was the only man Maura had ever seen come to Rosie's aid. And Dugan had done even more for this child he did not even know. He'd admonished the lass's master to accommodate her shortcoming.

She wanted to turn right around and kiss him.

But that would not do, not at all.

They began their day's ride as Maura considered what Dugan intended to do. It seemed he was going to follow her directions and hasten to the site where she believed the gold was hidden. In the meantime, he would send someone—Bryce—to Braemore to await Kildary. He needed someone to placate the baron if he arrived at Braemore before Dugan returned with Maura.

He wasn't willing to trust in her completely.

In spite of that, Maura could not ignore the soft warmth that came over her when she reflected on Dugan scolding the ignorant chandler for giving his crippled servant tasks she could barely perform.

It occurred to her that he would treat Rosie fairly, too—if he ever met her.

He said naught as they rode through Caillich's gates and circled 'round the walls of the castle, and Maura tried very hard to forget about the intimacies they'd shared. But that proved to be more difficult than she wished. Especially when he sat so close, his arms 'round her, his breath warm on her ear.

She had to guard her heart, for she found herself falling a little bit in love with him, and that would never do. A highland laird would never ally himself with the daughter of a lowland lord, especially a man like Lord Aucharnie. 'Twas best to keep her head and do what she must in order to get to Loch Camerochlan and Rosie.

"Exactly where are we headed?" he asked her as they caught up to his men, waiting just outside the gates.

His men exchanged puzzled glances and it was

obvious to Maura that Dugan had not told them of her stipulation—that she would take him to the gold without disclosing its location.

"We need to ride toward Loch Monar," she replied, ignoring the others.

He turned to look sharply at her. "Maura—"

" 'Tis not *there*. But that is the direction, Dugan."

Maura had not known the location of Loch Aveboyne until Dugan had pointed it out on the map, and now that she knew where it was, especially in relation to Braemore, she felt she'd be able to use the situation to her advantage, even if they didn't find the gold. While the men searched for the gold, Maura could slip away and go to Loch Camerochlan—which was somewhat farther north—without Dugan.

Chapter 20

Being so well and truly manipulated rankled. But Dugan could hardly fault Maura for turning the situation to her advantage. 'Twas what he'd have done were he in her place, and he felt a grudging respect for her strategy. Her plan was brilliant.

And since she seemed completely certain that the treasure was not hidden at Loch Monar, Dugan decided to go along with her. At least for now.

He was accustomed to being the one in charge, but he'd had to turn over his leadership to Maura—a woman whose people he did not know, and whose motivations were entirely suspect. He hoped he hadn't allowed himself to be controlled by the cravings of his cock over the cleverness of his mind.

But damned if he did not want her now, in spite of her manipulations.

The only thing Dugan knew for certain was that he had to get ahead of Argyll. Lachann had discovered the man was prepared to do some serious digging. He'd brought shovels and picks and carts, and had more than twenty men to do the work.

If Maura was not lying through her teeth, the duke's jaunt to Loch Monar would be fruitless.

Dugan did not know if Argyll had a secondary plan other than searching at Loch Nan Eun, or if he even suspected there was yet a different possible location.

It angered him to think about the bloody bastard going after a treasure that had been meant to displace men like Argyll from power. The duke had battled against King James's forces in the uprising two years before, and it was largely through Argyll's efforts that the rebellion had failed. If there was a cache of French gold hidden somewhere in the highlands, the damned Duke of Argyll should be the last person on earth to claim it. And Dugan would dearly love to be the one who kept him from it.

"Dugan, are you sure this course is wise?" Lachann asked him.

"No. I'm not sure at all," he snapped, and he felt Maura stiffen against him.

"Then why do we follow a woman whose word might well be worthless?"

Lachann might be mistrustful of beautiful women in general, but Dugan had spent the night wondering the same thing. "Do you have a better plan, Lachann?"

"You know as well as I, Lady Maura has naught to lose. If not for her tale of finding a clue only she can see—"

Dugan lost the last vestige of his patience, probably because Lachann voiced exactly his own worries. "Do you plan to wage a battle of words here, Lachann? Because I'm not exactly in the mood for it."

"No, brother," Lachann replied. "I just hope you know what you are about." He rode ahead to join the others.

Dugan turned to Maura. "Are you taking us to Loch Nan Eun?" he demanded in frustration. "Because the Duke of Argyll will be right behind us after he searches at Loch Monar."

"No," Maura said simply.

She was quiet and pensive after Lachann rode off, which suited Dugan well enough. If she wasn't going to tell him outright where they were going, he didn't mind the silence in which to think about the territory that lay ahead. It quickly became clear that their path could lead them nearly anywhere in the highlands.

"Do you think we've lost Lieutenant Baird?" Maura asked.

Gesu. Yet another damned Sassenach to worry about. "Likely not."

Dugan felt her shiver.

"He has no liking for me," she said. "There were times when . . . I thought he wanted to do me harm."

"The man was your escort," Dugan said, refusing to allow himself to feel any concern whatsoever. For all he knew, this was yet another manipulation, though where she intended it to lead, Dugan did not know. "Baird would have found disfavor had you arrived at Cromarty in any way but perfectly undamaged."

Though it occurred to Dugan that her undamaged state would not continue once she was Kildary's bride. The idea of Maura in the auld wolf's bed made him cringe. The baron would want to get her with child right away, and Dugan doubted the man would have a care for her innocent state.

He felt ill. "Most paths from Fort William lead to Caillich Castle," Dugan said.

"So he will be able to track us to Caillich?" she asked.

"Aye, 'tis likely."

"Then can we not do something clever to conceal our tracks and keep him from finding us?"

Dugan could do naught but appreciate Maura's canniness. Though he would not have minded facing the Sassenach soldier in open battle, such a clash did not serve his purpose. "Aye. I have an idea."

They rode on until they reached a shallow, rocky-bottomed burn. Instead of crossing, Dugan led his horse into the water. "We can follow the water for several miles. Which way is best, lass? Still toward Loch Monar?"

She nodded.

Dugan gestured for his men to ride ahead through the water. "'Twill be better for us all to throw Lieutenant Baird off our trail. We can afford to go a few miles out of our way if it keeps the lieutenant at bay."

Maura fought a sense of panic. She wasn't sure she actually could lead them to Loch Aveboyne, and knew that if she didn't manage to get them there fairly soon, she would have to tell Dugan about the clue on the back of the map. Then he'd have no reason to keep her with him. He could send her to Braemore with one of his men to wait for Baron Kildary while he and the others rode directly to Aveboyne without her.

It was impossible to tell distances just from looking at the map. As Maura had already seen, there were no straight lines of travel in the mountains. There were glens and high passes, and she'd noticed that they'd needed to ride far out of their way to find passages they could use in getting to Caillich. And the heavy mists . . .

But these were features that made travel just as difficult—if not more so—for Lieutenant Baird. Maura did not believe he was well traveled in the highlands. He could not possibly know the territory better than Dugan MacMillan.

At least they could get to Loch Monar without much difficulty, for Dugan knew the way. Once they arrived there, it did not appear to be a long ride north to Loch Aveboyne.

When they made camp that night, Maura needed to get her hands on the map and figure out the rest of the clue without letting Dugan or any of the men see what she was doing. She felt certain there must be at least a few more words written on the back of that map, and hoped she could bring out the rest of the wax etchings by using a light coating of dirt or ash. The only problem with her plan was that Dugan was not likely to leave her alone with the map. Ever.

She was just going to have to come up with some kind of distraction.

Ye are as empty in soul as the mon ye seek to please.

Lieutenant Baird batted at his ear to try and make the voice go away. "You are dead, hag," he muttered under his breath. "Leave me be."

But she would not. Her wisp of a voice had followed him all along the mountain trail, taunting him. Accusing him. Making his head pound.

It seemed the only thing that brought him any relief from the unrelenting headache was the promise of taking Maura Duncanson to some deserted promontory and shoving her off it, showing her what a wretched, inconsequential little worm of a female she was.

His father would never have approved of a match between them, anyway. The eleventh child of an inconsequential earl? He'd heard she did not even have a proper dowry. Not after Aucharnie had married off her six elder sisters, proper ladies, every one of them.

But Alastair intended to have his satisfaction for the way she'd rejected him and snubbed him in front of his men. And when he was through with her, she would be as humiliated and debased as was humanly possible. Then he would toss her over the cliff.

He could be the hero of this tale, really. Catching up to the poor, distraught female and valiantly attempting to save the little wench from leaping over the edge to escape marriage to Kildary . . . But alas. She'd been a few too many steps ahead of him . . .

Baird chuckled quietly. "Do you hear that, Father?" he murmured. "I did my best to save the earl's errant daughter."

Alastair heard the whisper of a reply, but he could not quite make out his father's words.

'Twas nearly nightfall when they stopped at a small copse of trees, and saw the walls of a large settlement ahead. It appeared to be a castle or town.

A good night's sleep in a proper bed after a decent meal would relieve his headache and perhaps rid him of the old witch's persistent taunts. *Damn her to hell, he'd killed her!*

He turned his attention to his surroundings. 'Twould not do for Higgins to take note of the voices that swirled 'round them. But Alastair was accustomed to them, or at least to his father's voice.

"We'll make for the town walls," he said. With any luck, he would find his wayward prey up there, and would be able to take her into his custody.

Do not be a fool, Alastair. If you take her before witnesses . . .

He heard his father's voice clearly this time and knew that the general was correct, as always, though not usually so harsh. Alastair gave a shake of his head to throw off his father's disdainful tone. The important thing was that if there were witnesses when he seized Maura Duncanson, he might not be able to play out the tempting little tableau he had planned for her.

They started up the craggy terrain toward the walls. "Speak to no one about Lady Maura," he said to his men. "Discretion is the most important thing."

"But Lieutenant, don't we need to alert the authorities—the magistrate or whoever is in charge—that we're looking for a—"

"No! No. No need to foment a scandal, Higgins. Lord Aucharnie would want this handled quietly."

"Aye, sir. I understand, sir," Higgins replied, but Baird took note of the strange look the corporal cast his way.

Baird intended to keep an eye on the man.

" 'Twould be much easier for you to travel to Braemore, lass," Dugan said, "and wait for word of our search. You would be comfortable there."

Maura turned and glared at him, raising one pale, shapely brow.

He was unruffled. "The lads and I can go to the site you tell us, and if the gold is there, we will hasten home and prevent your going with Kildary."

"And if it's not?"

Aye. There was the rub. If it was not there, she would have to become Baroness Kildary, as much as Dugan might despise the notion of it. Mayhap 'twas so distasteful because her delectable backside happened to be wedged between his thighs.

"Maura . . ." Hell, she had every reason not to trust him. Not that he felt any great obligation to trust her, either. She'd stolen his map and had tried to slip away from him. And now she refused to tell him what clue she'd seen on the map to show her where the gold was hidden.

"My answer is no. I will take you to the site, and together we can find what treasure there might be."

Dugan hadn't expected anything different, and he suppressed a grin at her audacity. She knew what was best for her, and was not about to relent. It was a quality to be respected.

Among others he'd noted. Dugan breathed deeply of her scent and remembered the taste of her, the smooth silk of her skin. He leaned slightly forward and nuzzled her neck.

"What are you doing?" she hissed, pulling away.

"Tasting you. I've thought of little else since leaving your bed last night."

"Your men—"

"Are far ahead of us. They will take no note."

"But *I* will," she said.

"Aye, lass. I am counting on it."

She stiffened. "You are going to make a spectacle of us."

"Only if you react as you did last night." The thought of it made him want to take her off the path, lay her down in the soft grass, and have his way with her.

"A gentleman would not speak of it."

"Ah, but no one said I was a gentleman, Maura. Least of all you."

He moved her hair aside and pressed his lips to her neck once again. "Do you know you have a pretty freckle here?"

"No. And do not kiss me again!"

"Are you sure that's what you want? No more kisses?"

"Of course that's what I want," she retorted. "We should never have . . . I mean, I-I . . . Oh, you make me lose track of my thoughts!"

Dugan smiled and pulled her against his chest. He let his thumbs drift up to the undersides of her breasts and caressed her there.

"Dugan!"

"You enjoyed it last night," he said. "And when I suckled your nipples."

She shivered as though remembering. But her words went counter to what her body desired. "Please limit your contact to only what is necessary, Laird."

'Twas torture holding her so close, and only made him want her more. He knew he ought to ease away, but could not find the discipline to do so.

They might actually find the French gold, and then everything would change. Dugan would have the power to negotiate fair terms for the MacMillan lands—hell, he would buy them out from under Argyll and never pay another groat for rent. Then he would buy even more livestock and improve the arable land . . .

And there would be no good reason to send Maura to Kildary. He could take her to Braemore and keep her with him.

Dugan hadn't met a woman he'd wanted to take to wife until now. He'd always known he wanted a braw lass who was steadfast and clever, one with a fire in her blood that could singe his soul. Maura aroused him like no other, and her lusty response to him when he'd taken her to bed was only part of it.

There were lairds who liked their women docile and obedient. Dugan could think of few things as dull. His own tenacious woman would stand with him before his clan, support and sustain him through good times as well as troubled.

He drew Maura close to his chest and rode on in the wake of his men. Once he had the gold in his possession, there would be no one to gainsay him. Dugan would escort Maura himself to Loch Camerochlan and collect her sister. Together they would take the wee lass to Braemore.

As the day wore on, a thick mist enveloped them and Dugan lost sight of his men. The only audible sounds were those of Glencoe's heavy breaths and the muffled sound of his hooves on the moist turf. Maura slept for a time, awakening when 'twas barely possible to see a foot ahead of them.

"It feels as though we're alone in the world," she said drowsily.

"Aye." If only it were so.

"I never saw such a thick mist at Aucharnie."

Aucharnie? Maura's body stiffened suddenly, and Dugan realized she'd divulged something she had not intended. His mind raced. He'd heard of the place . . .'Twas somewhere in the lowlands. He thought near Edinburgh.

Aye. Aucharnie Castle. Belonging to Alec Duncanson, Earl of Aucharnie, elder brother of the man who'd ordered the slaughter at Glencoe.

Dugan's blood ran cold.

"How do you know Aucharnie?" His voice sounded hoarse to his own ears.

"Dugan . . ."

"How, lass?"

She did not reply right away, but when she finally spoke, Dugan felt her shrink away from him. "I am Lord Aucharnie's daughter."

Chapter 21

He stopped them in their tracks. "You are a Duncanson?"

Maura swallowed. Archie had told her of the events at Glencoe and what was known of the officers who had ordered the slaughter. Major Duncanson was her father's brother. And Captain Robert Campbell was her mother's uncle.

Her blood could not be more tainted.

Dugan dismounted and left her there atop Glencoe. The irony of it did not escape her.

"Dugan?"

She could not jump down and follow him because she was too far off the ground. But waiting while a hideous wave of guilt washed over her was not acceptable, either.

She took up Glencoe's reins and walked the horse through the mist in the direction Dugan had gone, aware that with one misstep, she could tumble over a cliff. She would massacre Glencoe all over again.

"Dugan?"

Dear God, he might have fallen.

Maura had been dreaming while they rode, of possibilities. Of finding gold and having the freedom to choose her own destiny . . . a future that included Dugan. And Rosie, of course. She knew Dugan would not deny her sister a safe refuge at his holding.

She'd hardly been awake when she mentioned Aucharnie, otherwise she never would have spoken the name of her home. She knew what her kin had done to Dugan, to his family.

Dear God, how he must despise her.

"Dugan?" She whispered his name this time, almost afraid to face him now that he knew.

He would soon make the connection between the Duncansons and the Duke of Argyll—yet another enemy.

She came upon him all at once. He was crouched down, yanking up bits of moss from the ground between his feet. His expression was one of anger as well as disbelief. "Yet another Duncanson has a MacIain at her mercy."

"A MacIain?"

"I was born to clan MacIain. Do not pretend the name means naught to you." He tossed away the moss and stood, taking the reins of the horse from her.

"No." Maura felt shame and culpability by association. "Archie told me something of what happened at Glencoe. Dugan, I—"

"Damned MacLean mouth." His blue eyes had turned to ice, and he looked away as though he could not stand the sight of her.

"No, don't be angry. I asked him."

"About Glencoe?"

"I knew naught of it, Dugan." She reached for him. "Help me down?"

"No." His voice was harsh. " 'Tis better to keep moving."

Maura felt tears spill from her eyes as he mounted the horse behind her and used some mysterious internal compass to turn the horse in the direction they had been going. At least, she thought 'twas the same direction. For all she knew, he might shove her off a nearby cliff in retaliation for what her family had done to his.

She shuddered. She knew next to naught about the events that had occurred at Glencoe. Only that Dugan's parents and brother had been killed by soldiers who'd been billeted with his clan. That her mother's uncle had carried out the atrocious orders, given by her father's brother.

"Dugan . . . This changes naught. I—"

"Your kin slaughtered my family. And you think naught has changed?"

"I cannot tell you how sorry I am," Maura said. "I never knew such things happened." She remembered Robert Duncanson as a stiff and unyielding man, and had never liked or felt comfortable with him. But that was no excuse. If he'd been a decent Christian—

"Do you know what it means to murder under trust, Lady Maura?" He said her name as though the very sound of it on his lips was abhorrent.

Maura swallowed tightly and nodded. Murder under trust was the worst possible offense—the killing of one's host after accepting his hospitality. She felt her joints turn to jelly.

"Aye. Major Duncanson gave the orders, and Robert Campbell of Glenlyon carried them out."

"I never kn—"

He gave a harsh laugh. "Ah, right. You never knew that men like your Sassenach Lieutenant Baird merely follow orders given by bloody, fecking bastards like Major Robert Duncanson and the Earl of Stair."

"No, I do know," she said quietly. "I know they are despicable. And my father is one of the worst."

Dugan felt Maura take a deep, shuddering breath, but she said nothing more. What was there to say? That she was part of a lying, butchering clan of savages who'd slaughtered his family? Destroyed the life he had been meant to lead?

He'd vowed long ago to despise the name of Duncanson and to destroy every one of them if he ever got the chance.

He ought to pull her down from his horse and let her find her own way to . . . to wherever it was that she thought the gold was hidden. Or was that just a lie, too? A clever scheme to get him to take her to her sister? Because Monar was on a direct path toward Loch Camerochlan.

He didn't know what to believe anymore. His musings all morning about how perfect she was had been wholly mistaken. He would never take a Duncanson to wife.

Baron Kildary was welcome to her.

Dugan never spoke of the events at Glencoe to anyone. It had been the darkest, most vile day of his life, and it chilled his heart to know that Maura's kin had been part of it all.

He forced away the memory of that February morning. Twenty-five years had passed since that godforsaken day. He was a grown man now, and laird of his mother's clan, the MacMillans. He was responsible for the people there, and he would not let the damned duke's unreasonable demand end in disaster. The way Laird MacIain had done at Glencoe.

"It seems to me you owe me, Lady Maura."

She turned to look at him then, her eyes wet with tears he chose to ignore. For what did she know of it? What did she know of the kind of betrayal and gruesome loss he'd suffered?

She averted her eyes. "I know."

"The location of the gold is my price for your kin's offenses against mine."

Mayhap Dugan was right and Maura should just tell him what she'd seen on the back of the map.

But then he would send her to Braemore and turn her over to Baron Kildary, and Rosie would languish forever at Loch Camerochlan with Tillie Crane.

"I cannot tell you," she said quietly. She'd felt this kind of desolation only once before—the day Lieutenant Baird had gleefully locked her inside her chamber at Aucharnie and they'd taken Rosie away.

"Damnation, woman!"

Maura bolstered her resolve. She was not guilty for what her kin had done, and she refused to pay for their heinous offenses. At least, not entirely. "You sent Bryce to your holding to delay Baron Kildary until your return. I refuse to go there. I will take you to the gold and then go on my way to Loch Camerochlan for Rosie."

"'Tis not up to you to dictate the terms."

"But it is," Maura countered, brushing away her unwelcome tears. "I will not give you the means to be rid of me, Laird."

Old Sorcha had said the Glencoe lad would not find the map's secret, and she'd been right. The old woman had spoken of an ally, too. That the map would be of no use to Maura without an ally.

'Twas clear Dugan was her ally, whether he liked it or not.

She hoped she'd judged him correctly. True, he belonged to a breed she did not know or understand, but she did not think he would resort to violent means to elicit the clue from her. She'd seen his kindness with the crippled serving girl at Caillich, and she hoped his principles would prohibit him from treating her with brutality.

In a tense silence, they rode up a sloping hillside, and when they reached its peak, Maura looked down into a glen where the mist was not as thick as what they'd left behind. She saw Dugan's men ahead, riding toward a large, thatched cottage. It was clearly a prosperous holding, with a shed and a modest barn, although they all appeared to be abandoned. There were cattle grazing on the grasses as far as the eye could see, and a lone horse standing beside the old stone shed. Chickens were out free and pecking in the dirt.

Conall paused to look back, and when he saw Dugan's horse emerge out of the mist, he spoke to the other men. They stopped to wait.

Maura welcomed the sight of the cottage. She hoped the presence of others would help to mitigate the tension that flared between her and Dugan, and there might even be an opportunity for her to gain access to the maps again. Alone.

Exactly the way she'd expected this journey to be. Yet she'd been anything but alone. When she'd have struck off on her own after Fort William, she'd resented and feared Dugan at first. Now she believed he was a fair man who was only trying to do what he must for his clan.

The atrocity her kin had committed against his family was so profound, Maura could not blame his disgust with her for being part of their clan. If she could have changed her name and her origins, she would have done so years before.

Chapter 22

As they rode toward the cottage, Dugan knew he could rely on highlanders to offer their hospitality. He intended to take it. While Maura spent the night inside with the occupants, he would have a chance to put some much needed distance between them. Mayhap he would even leave her there.

He did not relish the thought of telling Lachann who Maura was. His brother did not trust her as it was. Once he knew she was a Duncanson . . . Dugan was not sure how he would react. With violence, perhaps.

In spite of the damage her clan had done to his family, Dugan's jaw clenched tightly at the thought of Maura coming to harm. She was as delicate as she was fierce . . .

Clearly, 'twas better to keep her name to himself, at least until he uncovered the clue she'd seen on the map.

Dugan thought about the ways he could coerce her into telling him what she'd seen and where. But all he could think of was taking her to his bed and kissing her into submission.

Gesu, what could he possibly be thinking? She was a Duncanson.

He rode ahead of the men and dismounted at the front of the cottage, leaving Maura in the saddle. Why had no one come out to see who had arrived? 'Twas unusual at the least.

He approached the cottage with Lachann at his side while the others remained on horseback, waiting.

Lachann knocked, but there was no stirring inside the house.

"Dugan," Maura called out, "the chickens are all loose."

Aye, he'd noticed.

"And the cows . . . look. They've come up to the fence to be let in. They need milking."

Dugan drew his sword and nodded to Lachann. "Open it."

Lachann pushed the door open and waited. No one appeared, but the smell of death surrounded them. Dugan stepped inside, covering his mouth and nose with his arm, and found a dead man sitting in a chair near the cold hearth. He was gray-bearded, and it looked as though he'd died in his sleep.

"Have the lads look for something to wrap him in," Dugan said. "Then they can come in and carry the poor blighter out."

Lachann turned to do his brother's bidding while Dugan remained in the cottage, looking for some indication of who the dead man was. He was prosperous, judging by the outbuildings and the furnishings in the house. The main room was large, with a sitting and cooking area as well as a separate bedroom with its own fireplace.

The man would be missed eventually, and Dugan did not want to encounter anyone who might question what the MacMillan laird was doing there in a dead man's house, so far south of his own territory. The fewer people who suspected any truth to the rumor of gold, the better.

The man had not been dead long. Dugan guessed he'd died either last night before retiring to bed, or sometime that morn, after rising.

He noticed some documents on a desk as he opened the windows to cleanse the air inside the cottage. Glancing through them quickly, he concluded that the dead man was Kennan Murray. On further exploration, Dugan found no indication that the man had family. There were no letters, no records of any wife or children. The only framed pictures were a map of the highlands, and a holy portrait of the Lord God.

As his men came into the house, Dugan went back to his horse and reached up for Maura, not sure what he was going to do with her. "The owner is dead."

A look of true sadness came over her. "Oh no."

"Probably happened last night or this morn."

Her body felt supple against his, but he ignored the jolt of sensation that surged through him at her touch. 'Twas not what he needed right now. Or ever, with this woman.

The only thing that mattered was finding a way to coerce the clue from the map out of her, or figuring out the clue himself. If she had found it, he could, too.

"He died all alone?"

A muscle in his jaw tensed. "Aye. There was no sign of anyone else belonging to the household."

"What are you going to do? With the dead man, I mean?"

"Bury him," Dugan replied.

"Without a service?"

"We can say a few words. We don't have time for anything more."

Leading his horse, he took Maura 'round to the opposite side of the door, for there was no need for her to see the dead man when his men carried him out. Not that he should care about her tender sensibilities. She was kin to some of the most bloodthirsty Scots he could imagine. He ought to allow her to witness the gruesome reality of death.

But he told her to wait there, in spite of himself.

Maura seized her chance. As soon as she was alone, she took Dugan's bag down from his saddle, and when she pulled it open, found the three quarters of the map wrapped in an oilcloth. She glanced up to be sure Dugan was not coming 'round to get her. But it seemed the men were otherwise occupied, so she worked quickly, pulling the documents from their protective wrap. She unrolled the first one and looked at its back.

Sous le gros rocher— The word starting with *ro* was illegible, so she took a handful of dirt and rubbed it against the etching. It still did not become clear. *Sous le gros rocher ro*— was all she could see.

It meant "under some kind of large rock," but what was the descriptive word? Surely there were going to be many rocks at the loch. 'Twould take forever to search under every one.

Maura felt a twinge of despair. She *had* to find the treasure for Dugan—and for herself. Mayhap there were more clues.

She rolled up the first document and carefully put it back into Dugan's bag. Taking the second piece, she opened it and looked for wax etchings on its back. She found *À la rive*—

"At the shore—" she muttered. It had to mean the shore of Loch Aveboyne, the clue she'd seen the night before.

Maura quickly determined that there were no other words on that section of parchment, so she hurried to replace it under the oil cloth in Dugan's bag, then checked the third piece. The only word on this section was *Ouest*.

Clearly, all four sections were meant to come together in order to show the way to the treasure. Maura closed Dugan's bag and swung it up onto Glencoe's back while she mentally arranged the clues until she had something that made sense.

Sous le gros rocher ro— and *à la rive ouest du Lac Aveboyne.*

She felt a mad sense of elation. Surely the missing section bore the words *L'or est,* or some other indication of what the rest of the clues were about.

Except for the beginning clue, Maura had all but one word, and she hoped that with a bit more thought, she could figure out what *ro* meant. "The gold is under a large rock of some sort," she said quietly to herself, "at the west shore of Loch Aveboyne."

This was how she was going to ameliorate the wrongs Maura's family had done to Dugan's. She would lead him directly to the treasure, and he would become a wealthy laird, beholden to no one, not even the Duke of Argyll.

And he would let her go to Loch Camerochlan for Rosie. On her own.

Maura suddenly felt shaky—all at once ecstatic but miserable. Within a day or two, she would hand over to Dugan exactly what he needed, then he would have no further use for her. From the first moment he'd seen her at the waterfall, she had been more trouble than he wanted. Certainly more than he needed.

And now that he knew who she was, Maura was certain he could not wait to be rid of her. The attraction between them . . . their kisses and all that had occurred in her bedchamber at Caillich meant naught. It couldn't—not to the likes of them.

She tied the horse to a fence post and returned to the front of the cottage where the men were carrying out the body, wrapped in canvas. Maura felt a deep sadness as she watched, pity for the poor man who had been alone at the end. She wondered if he'd had a wife or any children—and where they might be now.

She crossed her arms over her chest to ward off a sudden chill and her own pervasive sense of isolation. Soon, 'twould be just her and Rosie. There would be no one else—no one like Deirdre Elliott or Dugan MacMillan. No one to help her. No one to love her.

Only Rosie.

She walked away abruptly, fighting the horrible emptiness that threatened to swallow her whole. She had not thought past saving her sister, had not considered the life she would lead after she found Rosie and took her away.

Until now, Maura had believed Rosie's uncomplicated affections would be enough. But the life she would embark upon once she reached Loch

Camerochlan rang hollow. She'd felt the highlander's touch and knew the intensity of desire. For him. She'd learned the shape of his jaw and the rough rasp of his whiskers against her face and between her legs.

A wave of pure longing skittered down her spine. The man she would choose for herself was not about to feel the least fondness for anyone belonging to the Campbell clan. Maura's father and cousins were bad enough.

She wondered if Dugan had yet made the connection between her family and Argyll's.

Dugan kept his mind on his task as they buried Kennan Murray. He did not want to think about all the foolish notions he'd entertained about Maura before discovering her identity.

He could not comprehend how it was possible that his blood had not recognized her for the enemy that she was.

Everyone in the highlands knew the connection between the Campbells and Duncansons. As soon as he'd heard Maura's father's name, he'd known exactly who her kin was.

Dugan remembered Captain Campbell, an uncle on Lady Aucharnie's side, as clearly as if he'd stood before him only yesterday. How could Dugan forget seeing the man laughing and drinking at his father's table? He'd held Dugan's infant sister, Alexandra, on his lap and chucked the bairn under her chin, making her giggle in that sweet way she'd always had. Campbell had spent time in every croft at Glencoe. And then he'd given the order to put everyone under the age of seventy to the sword. The brutal order that had come from Robert Duncanson.

His stomach roiled.

The killings at Glencoe had been a plot hatched by a number of powerful lowland lairds—the Earl of Breadalbane, the Earl of Stair. Even the English king himself had sanctioned the massacre. 'Twas possible Maura's father had been in on the scheme to strike at the highlanders, but his involvement had not been exposed. These men acted in order to curry the favor of their king as well as to destroy the clan system of the highlands.

Instead, there had been a parliamentary investigation into the events at Glencoe on the morning of February 13, 1692. Blame had been laid at Lord Stair's feet, but the earl had received no punishment. King William had been exonerated, of course, and the Earl of Breadalbane had spent a measly few days imprisoned in Edinburgh Castle for speaking with the highland lairds—men considered to be Jacobite rebels—before the fatal events took place at Glencoe.

In Dugan's eyes, justice had never been done.

He carried his shovel to Murray's shed and searched the building for more tools they could use when they reached the site only Maura knew. He dearly hoped she was not lying.

"Laird," said Conall, "there is a small wagon back here."

They were going to need something in which to carry the gold, if they ever found it. "Leave it there, Conall. We'll take it with us when we leave in the morning."

Lachann came into the shed and took note of the tools. He put his hands on his hips. "Do you really think we'll need any of this, Dugan?"

Dugan shook his head. "I don't know, Lachann. What I *do* know is that something struck Maura last night as she was looking at the map."

"Aye. The realization that this wee journey of ours is the only way to keep us from taking her to Braemore to be ransomed by Kildary."

"I don't think so. There was something about the map. Something she saw that the rest of us have missed. I'm sure of it."

Lachann cocked one leg, and his posture, with his hands on his hips, clearly spoke of his annoyance. "I hope you're right, Dugan."

Aye, Dugan hoped he was, too.

He left the shed and went to the back of the house where he'd left Maura, and found her sitting near the fence, milking one of the cows.

"I would not have thought you knew how to do such a menial task, Lady Maura."

She glanced over her shoulder at him. "There is much you do not know about me, Laird MacMillan."

Dugan knew all he needed to know. She was a Duncanson and he had never forgotten their treachery.

"My father cast me out when he learned I'd saved Rosie. I was but fifteen then."

Dugan made no reply, but he found it incomprehensible. First, to give orders for his own bairn to be taken away to die. And then to punish the daughter who'd saved her.

Ah, but the old bastard was a Duncanson.

"Deirdre Elliott and her husband, Gordon, took me into their house, where I spent most of my time until I was eighteen. I learned quite happily to do all manner of chores while I was Deirdre's daughter."

Dugan detected a tinge of sorrow in her tone, but it vanished when she stood up with the bucket of milk in hand. She walked past him and went into Murray's house.

He unhitched Glencoe from the fence and took down his and Maura's traveling bags before turning the horse loose in the enclosure. He took the bags into the house and reached into his own for the maps.

Laying them out on the table, Dugan half watched Maura remove her cloak and tie a plain canvas apron 'round her waist.

Such a simple, homey act had the power to arouse him. Her hair was in disarray, and Dugan could almost feel the silk of it sliding through his fingers. Her pretty lips teased him and her apron hugged the curves he'd so enjoyed the night before.

But he steeled his heart against any softening of feelings toward her.

Was Lachann right? Did Maura actually know where the gold was hidden or was this just a clever ruse to get him to take her to Loch Camerochlan? Mayhap he ought to send her to Braemore now and hasten to Loch Monar before Argyll could get there. It was the logical thing to do.

And yet Dugan did not believe she was lying about the clue. He might be a deluded fool, but he doubted it. He'd learned long ago to trust his instincts.

He considered Maura's betrothal to Kildary. It seemed that Maura's father had had no use for her until now. Which indicated to Dugan that her marriage to Kildary must be of significant value to him. He'd already figured Maura had no dowry, so 'twas likely her father was in need of the funds Kildary would pay for the privilege of taking Maura to wife.

Perhaps 'twas better to thwart the marriage, rather than fulfill Lord Aucharnie's wishes. 'Twas not the bloody revenge Dugan would have preferred, but it would give him some satisfaction, knowing he'd caused difficulties for the Duncan-son lord.

He watched as Maura knelt before the grate and built a fire in silence, shutting him out.

"I've decided 'twould serve my purpose to spoil your father's wishes and prevent your marriage to Kildary."

"What?" She rested back on her heels as she turned to look at him, her green eyes narrowing. "I do not understand."

"Your father needs Kildary's funds and possibly an alliance with the baron," he said. "If I keep you from Kildary . . ." He shrugged. "Mayhap Lord Aucharnie will not be able to pay *his* rents."

Maura frowned in disbelief. And mayhap a fair dose of mistrust. "He pays no rents, Dugan. He is the earl."

"Ah, but there was a reason he bartered you to Kildary. *Money.* He needs it, and the baron has it."

"What about *your* rents, Dugan? Wh-what if we don't find the treasure?"

Aye, that was the rub. If they didn't find the gold

where Maura led them, could Dugan afford the satisfaction of blocking her father's goals by keeping Maura from Kildary?

No. The welfare of his clan had to come first.

"Was it only two days ago that you were so certain I'd find the gold?" he taunted. "Show me the clue and I'll set you free."

"Perhaps I would. If I could trust you, Laird MacMillan."

Chapter 23

Maura grabbed a basket and stalked out of the cottage, leaving Dugan to his maps. Let him try to figure out what she already knew. She had no intention of showing him the words she'd deciphered in the dust on the backs of those documents.

She did not care what he'd said about thwarting her father. He was lying. Of course he would send her with one of the men—his ill-tempered brother, no doubt—to Braemore if he discovered the clues that would lead him to the gold.

She was so angry, she could barely think.

Clue or no clue, there was no guarantee that he was going to find any treasure at Loch Aveboyne. He would be foolish not to utilize both options available to him—the ransom *and* the gold—and they both knew it.

She shooed the chickens back into their hutch and followed the birds inside. She found nests with fresh eggs and filled her basket with them, then headed toward a nearby pond to see if there were any mushrooms or wild tubers she could add to their supper.

As she'd told Dugan from the very beginning, Baron Kildary could easily ignore his ransom demand. 'Twould be no trouble for the old man to barter with yet another heartless father for the hand of some other unlucky young daughter. One fertile womb would serve as well as any other.

Maura placed her hand against her abdomen when she thought of Baron Kildary's seed growing there. She shuddered with revulsion at the thought of him planting it.

That certainly was not going to happen. No matter how events played out, she was never going to allow the old satyr to touch her. She was tired of being played like a pawn in a game of chess, and upset that Dugan would even consider turning her over to the old baron. After the intimacies they'd shared, she would have thought . . .

She raised her chin and bit her lips to keep them from trembling. Clearly, she'd been a naïve fool to think his lovemaking meant anything beyond a mere moment's pleasure.

A terrible chill came over her, and she found herself wishing for the impossible—that someone would trust her, believe in her, care for her. She felt impossibly alone.

And hurt.

She was not responsible for the actions of her kin twenty-some years ago. She did not like them any more than Dugan did, but that did not seem to matter. No, he would never forgive her for being a member of clan Campbell, and a hated Duncanson, besides.

Maura sniffed back the hollow feeling that had settled in her chest and focused on her anger.

Did she actually need Dugan MacMillan to take her to Loch Aveboyne? She had studied the torn map carefully, and taken a good look at the de-

tailed map hanging on Murray's wall, besides. She
knew what direction to take to get to Loch Monar.
If she could manage to get there alone, she believed
'twas only ten or fifteen miles farther north to Loch
Aveboyne. And when—if—she found the gold, she
could go on to Loch Camerochlan for Rosie.

The only question was whether she dared attempt to get away from Dugan again.

Maura's mind raced. She interrupted her mush-
room picking and looked back at the cottage and
the small outbuildings near it. There was a wheeled
cart stored behind the shed, and a horse that was
likely accustomed to pulling it. She might be able
to slip away on horseback during the night, when
everyone was asleep. She was not the most experienced rider, but she could probably go ten or more
miles before Dugan knew she was gone.

As dusk came over the glen, Maura looked at the
terrain to the north and tried to imagine covering
any territory at all in the dark. How could she be
sure the animal would not carry her off a cliff that
neither of them could see? She would have to make
sure she did not veer off course, and then hide from
Dugan when he and the others came after her, for
he would certainly pursue her when he discovered
her missing.

She sighed. Perhaps 'twas not the best plan.

She returned to her mushrooms, deciding she
would have to think of another.

Dugan admitted that Maura had good reason not
to trust him. First he'd planned to ransom her, now
he said he would not. He'd bullied her and made
love to her—what was she to think?

What was *he* to think?

He paced the floor of Kennan Murray's cottage, rubbing the back of his neck as he walked. The woman had stolen from him and lied to him. What man in his right mind would trust her to take him to the gold?

None.

And yet everything about her attracted him—her graceful movements, her beautiful mouth, the lusty way she kissed him . . .

He gave out a low groan as he looked out the window and watched her emerge from the chicken coop with her basket laden with eggs. Aye, she was resourceful, and she seemed so certain she knew the location of the gold. 'Twas beyond frustrating that he could not see the clue.

But at least he had figured out a plan for getting the information from her.

He was rolling up the maps and putting them away when she returned to the cottage. She did not speak to him, but went to a cupboard and began pulling out bowls and dishes. He watched with interest as she took a skillet from its hook, put some onions and mushrooms into it, and placed it on the fire.

Dugan had to force his attention away from her capable ministrations, but soon he was drawn to the aroma of the food. And the sound of her low humming.

Gesu, he could not possibly still want her, knowing who she was.

To distract himself, he went to a large wooden chest and opened its doors. Inside, he found Murray's spare clothes. Two extra lengths of plaid and a pair of trews. Also a jacket and three shirts. There did not seem to be any clothes but those belonging to Murray himself, confirming Dugan's thought that the man had lived alone.

He did not know how far they were from any neighboring cottages, but he did not think there was a village nearby. He now realized 'twas unlikely anyone would take note of Murray's absence for several days, mayhap weeks.

Maura's low humming hindered his thought process, and he found himself watching her as she peeled and chopped some potatoes she'd found in the larder, then put them with some grease into a second pan over the fire. She barely watched what she was doing, for her attention was entirely engaged by the map hanging on the wall over the cupboard.

"What are you doing?" He lunged for the framed map and pulled it from the wall. Bloody hell, had she taken a good look at it before? The last thing he needed was for her to become familiar with an accurate map. There was no telling what she would do.

She furrowed her brow and scooped the rest of the potatoes into the pan. Working as efficiently as any highland wife, she scooted 'round him and pulled a wooden stool to a high shelf and climbed onto it. Clearly annoyed with him.

'Twas a precarious perch, and Dugan did not trust the stool. *Gesu*, he did not trust *anything* anymore. He turned 'round to her and offered his hand. "I'll reach it for you. What do you need?"

"Enough plates or bowls for all of us," she said before taking his hand and stepping down.

Mayhap he ought to put his plan into action now, and take her into his arms. It seemed a natural progression from holding her hand to embracing her, to kissing those lips that so tempted him and teasing her secrets out of her.

But her demeanor was anything but inviting. She was distant and grim and she extricated her hand from his as soon as her feet touched the floor.

He felt far more disappointed than he ought, and he reminded himself just who this woman was. The only liaison that was possible between them was the one he intended to indulge in later, only to get her to reveal the clue she'd discovered on the map. Nothing more.

She took the plates from him and set them on the table, then collected enough spoons, forks, and chairs for them all.

"So . . . you are afraid to let me see Murray's map?" she asked, her tone full of irritation.

"I do not trust you to refrain from haring off on a wild chase to find the gold on your own." Dugan reached up to the top shelf and took down a full bottle of good Scotch whiskey. He had a feeling he was going to need a stiff drink before the night was over.

She glared at him. "Do you actually think I could find—find *anything* in the highlands without help?"

Her fiery glance heated his blood and Dugan could barely remember why he despised her. He only saw the woman whose touch made him crave more. Whose mouth drove him to the brink of madness; the touch of whose silky-smooth body made him as hard as the claymore in his belt.

Dugan took down an earthen mug and poured a draught of fine amber whiskey into it. He swallowed it down with a burn that did naught to assuage his hunger for her. "I believe you could do anything you put your mind to, Maura lass."

"These are not my highlands, as you well know," she said. Her hair was so inviting, with one bright curl twisting 'round her ear. Dugan remembered the taste of her skin, the feel of her tongue doing battle with his own, the wildly arousing stroke of her hand on his cock. "I would never attempt to traverse these mountains alone."

"No? Why do I find it so hard to trust you?"

"Because 'tis your nature to mistrust a Duncanson?"

Dugan muttered a quiet curse. He did not want to think about her damned clan. He took another swallow of Murray's whiskey.

She wrinkled her nose and turned her attention to beating the eggs she'd cracked into a bowl. "You might go and see if your men are ready for supper."

She spoke to him as she turned her attention to the eggs, without looking at him. 'Twas as though she were fully immersed in the task and could not spare a bit of attention for him.

Dugan left the cottage feeling more than slightly dissatisfied. He was at the very least as annoyed as she was. Mayhap even angry.

She was the Duncanson. 'Twas *her* clan that had tried to destroy *his* years before, and not only was it *her* kin who intended to evict the MacMillans, but Argyll was a rival for the treasure. As though he had any right to Jacobite gold.

Shite. What if Maura was somehow working in tandem with the old bastard? Dugan discarded that idea as soon as it crossed his mind, for he knew 'twas impossible. After all, it must have been Argyll's map she'd stolen.

But it did not make Dugan feel any better.

Maura made a simple meal just like the kind she'd helped Deirdre create numerous times in the past. It might not be the finest fare for a highland laird, but it was tasty and filling. She added the cheese she'd found in Murray's larder to the vegetables and eggs, then let it finish cooking while she sliced the last of the man's bread.

She did not understand why Dugan hadn't told his men who she was. Of course they would despise her as much as he did, and wasn't that exactly what he wanted? For everyone to know what a despicable clan she belonged to. For his men to understand how thoroughly her kin had ruined his life once before, and how she was going to do it again?

She felt outraged as well as fearful, for she did not know how they would react to the news. Mayhap their hatred for her clan ran even deeper than Dugan's.

Or they might even turn on Dugan when he told them he was not going to ransom her to Kildary.

"I did not see any ale about the place," she said to the men as they came in through the door. "But if you are partial to milk, there's a bucket full. And I believe your laird found some whiskey."

Dugan came back to the cottage, but Maura ignored him, which was not easy. With every move he made, she was aware of his powerful body. His plaid skimmed his legs at the knees and the folded wool at his shoulder emphasized the braw breadth of him. She'd felt warm and cherished in his brawny arms . . . a feeling that had turned to aching disillusionment.

Ach, she was not one to engage in idle musings, not when there was so much pressing on her mind. She could not let herself be distracted from her true purpose—to find Rosie and take her somewhere where their father would never find them.

She served Archie first, in direct contradiction to the lowly status the laird had given him for falling asleep and failing to keep her confined in the Caillich guesthouse. Then she scooped eggs onto Conall's plate, and he blushed as he always seemed to do when she came close to him. Next was Lachann, the one who disliked her even more than Dugan did. And he did not even know she was a Duncanson.

"Why do ye not tell the laird where the gold is hidden, Lady Maura?" Archie asked, perhaps to regain favor with Dugan.

"Because if I did so," Maura replied with ire, "the laird would have one of you gentlemen carry me off to Braemore and *sell* me to Baron Kildary, Archie."

" 'Tis a ransom, not a sale," Dugan retorted.

"Ach, 'tis a fine distinction!" Now she was incensed. " 'Tis *so* much better to be ransomed to a man nearly fifty years my senior than to be sold to him!"

Conall was the only one who had the grace to appear abashed at the truth of her words.

Dugan said naught, and Archie gave a wee nod and bent his head to his meal.

Lachann did not yield her point. "You have created a world of trouble for our clan, *Lady* Maura."

"You do not know the half of it, Lachann," she said, offended by his insulting tone. If he wanted to insult her, she would give him the correct reason for it. "Did the laird inform you that his life was ruined because of—"

Dugan slammed his hand on the table. "My purpose in demanding the ransom from Kildary," he roared, "had naught to do with—"

"Oh no, of course not! You took me because I was a female, alone and vulnerable—a mere hostage for you to use in whatever way you saw fit—without a thought for what was best for me!"

"Aye, and I would do it ten times over to save my clan!" Dugan bellowed.

Maura banged down the skillet and stormed out of the cottage. Fuming with anger, she ran to the barn to cool her temper. At the same time, she intended to get a look at Murray's horse before it became completely dark outside. Oh yes, she was definitely going to take the beast during the night and get a head start on Dugan and his oblivious men. She owed them naught. They could all go to the devil.

She looked about for a saddle and bridle—because of course the wagon would be too cumbersome for swift travel. And she fully intended to stay far ahead of Dugan Mac—

The barn door slammed open.

"What do you think you're doing?" Dugan demanded.

Feeling ridiculously vulnerable, Maura crossed her arms over her chest and stood fast. "Getting away from the lot of you highland tumshies and your unreasonable—"

"Unreasonable?" He advanced on her. "You

steal *our* map and you think *we* are unreasonable?"

Maura took a step back and raised her chin to glare at him. "You intend to give me to Kildary whether or not you succeed in finding the gold!"

"I will not!" he roared. She backed up against the wall and he pinned her to it with a hand on each side of her head. "I told you I will not, and I am as good as my word!"

"Your word?" she shot back. "A man who would turn over an innocent woman to an old goat like Kildary for—for money!"

"An innocent woman? You're a thief, Maura Duncanson, not to mention—"

"Oh yes. I am a Duncanson. My greatest sin." She poked Dugan in the chest. "Just to be clear, Laird MacMillan, *I* had naught to do with the events that took place at Glencoe more than twenty years ago, for I was not yet born. Besides, I am just a lowly female who would not have been consulted on my kin's despicable actions in any case!"

Tears burned at the backs of her eyes. She hated to think of him as a wee lad, fleeing that place of horror, his parents and brother murdered, likely before his eyes. It tore at her heart, yet whatever her horrible relatives had done to him, Maura could not pay for it with Rosie's well-being. 'Twould only add tragedy to the wrongs already done.

"You are hardly lowly, Maura Duncanson," he growled. Moving quickly, before she could even think, he pulled her into his arms and Maura shivered with the sheer heat of him. He made a deep, rasping sound just before he took possession of her mouth with his lips, his tongue and teeth.

He pushed her against the stone wall and held

her there as he kissed her, preventing any chance of escape—not that Maura wanted to leave. She wanted to stay there forever, where her bleak future had no sway.

She kissed him back with all the violence she felt in his body. He was solid and taut against her, and she felt the strength in his big hands and his hard muscles pulling her ever closer.

His fingers roved down her back, pulling her hips against his, and she felt his rigid arousal rubbing and pulsing against her. Desire made her knees go weak. She wanted him, wanted more than he'd given her the previous night.

Maura ripped the thong of leather from his hair and knifed her fingers through the thick mass, tugging and pulling him down to her. She savored the taste and texture of him as he ravished her mouth, demanding more.

He groaned into her mouth and pulled up her skirts, cupping her bottom in his hands, lifting her off the ground. Maura wrapped her legs 'round him, and he lowered her to the straw-strewn floor.

Chapter 24

Maura tore away the heavy woolen plaid that was draped over Dugan's shoulder while he made short work of her bodice. Suddenly, his mouth was on her breast and he was pulling her nipple into his mouth. She arched into the sensual onslaught, desperate for more—more of his mouth, more of his caresses, more of his skin.

She shoved his shirt down his arms, and he yanked it off, pulling it from his plaid and over his head.

Maura could barely see his sculpted muscles in the shadows, but she felt their strength, knew their potent shape by touch, running her hands down his arms as he tormented her breasts with his talented tongue.

He slipped one hand under her skirts, his hand coming to touch the sensitive spot at the crux of her thighs.

His touch scorched her. Maura opened for him and arched against his hand as the sensations he created caused a potent coiling within her. She felt as tight as a spring.

"Dugan," she gasped. She needed him desperately. Needed all of him.

"Aye, lass. I want you, too."

He shifted slightly, hovering over her, his mouth coming down hard upon hers. She clutched his head in her hands as his hard, hot manhood touched her where she needed it most. And then he was inside her. But only partly.

She was frantic for him, needed him to fill the void inside. She wanted him desperately.

"Easy now," he said, his voice a mere rasp. Maura felt sweat gathering at his nape. "I'll not hurt you."

He moved suddenly and she felt a sharp sensation akin to pain, but not exactly that. 'Twas more like a foreign fullness.

And she craved even more.

"Dugan . . ." She pushed against him and he plunged deeply, finally touching her where she felt the greatest need.

In her heart, and deep in her soul.

Keeping them connected, he rolled so that he was on his back and she was atop him, her hands poised upon his chest. "What . . . ?"

" 'Twill be easier on you, lass. Slide down, pet. Let me feel you clasp my cock. Ah, *Gesu*."

He slid his hand down between them and when he touched her, Maura thought she would come apart. He pressed his fingers against that sensitive nub at her crux, and her muscles suddenly clenched 'round him, causing an unspeakably exquisite sensation to ripple through her.

Maura cried out and collapsed against his chest. Dugan wrapped his arms 'round her as every inch of her body pulsed with an all-consuming pleasure. 'Twas even more overpowering than the sensations she'd felt the night before.

Dugan jerked sharply, at the same time gasping for air. He held Maura tightly against him as he moved inside her, shuddering with his own release.

Her ear against his chest, she heard the rapid beat of his heart, the great tugs of his breath. He was as undone as she.

But when she looked at him, his expression was not one of rapture.

Alastair Baird strode into the guesthouse inside the walls of Caillich Castle. The common room was sparsely furnished, but a small peat fire warmed it adequately. They saw no one about—no servants, no innkeeper.

"Do you really think Lady Maura would have stopped here, Lieutenant Baird?" Corporal Higgins asked. "There's been no sign of her."

Something caught Baird's eye—a wraithlike creature hovering over the fireplace. It stared at him with unseeing eyes, and he shuddered when it pointed its bony finger at him.

"Lieutenant?"

The damned thing disappeared.

"Are you all right, sir?" Higgins asked.

Baird rubbed his eyes. "Find the proprietor."

The corporal walked to the back of the building, leaving Baird alone. He stole a glance at the spot above the mantel again and saw naught. His eyes must have played a trick on him, for there was no wraith there now. No old woman to point and accuse—

"Lieutenant Baird," Higgins said, returning to the entry room with a man wearing Caillich plaid, "here is Mr. MacCallum."

"MacCallum, we are looking for a woman . . . a fugitive."

"Aye?" The burly, dark-haired proprietor wiped his hands on a cloth as he looked at Baird, frowning. "What's it to do wi' me?"

"Did you happen to let lodgings to a young female yesterday eve? A red-haired woman . . . ?"

The man set his cloth aside, leaned forward on his clerk's stand, and glared at his visitors in fierce highlander fashion. He shook his head. "Nay. Mine is a respectable house. I do'na make it a practice to house women alone."

Baird could not tell if he was lying, but there was something in his tone . . . "This one m-might have been in the company of a group of men . . . highlanders. Clan MacMillan."

The innkeeper rubbed a hand over his heavy beard. "MacMillans? Here? Ye jest, Lieutenant. Do ye no' know the Duke of Argyll is up at the Lord's Tower?"

Baird felt his heart trip. He did not want anyone to know he'd lost Maura Duncanson—especially not her kin! If Argyll found out and word got back to Aucharnie . . .

He refrained from nervously wiping his brow, but merely cleared his throat. "No, I did not know." How would he have known, when Argyll had been in Glasgow at Ilay House only a few days ago? Or had it been longer? A week? More? Baird pressed his fingers against his forehead and tried to remember exactly how long it had been since they'd left Glasgow.

Since he'd left that witch dead on the floor of her croft outside Fort William.

"Aye," said MacCallum. "Yer duke is here conferring with Laird Caillich."

Alastair could not think, not when the icy grip of bony fingers spread across his neck. He swatted them away, but not before he heard the voice. *Ye bear the stink of death upon ye.*

"Damnation," he blurted. He refused to be cowed by a figment of his imagination. There was no ghost, no old woman pointing accusing fingers at him. No wraith to choke him, to confuse him.

He caught the proprietor looking at him askance and quickly lowered his hand from the back of his neck.

"How long will the duke be staying at Caillich?" Baird demanded somewhat more forcefully than necessary.

MacCallum leaned forward onto his forearm, and when he spoke, sarcasm drenched his words. "Oddly enough, *Lieutenant*, I am no' privy to the duke's plans."

"Well then." Baird straightened his coat and shrugged off the weird sensations that were now crawling up his spine. Perhaps when he found Maura Duncanson and disposed of her, these unnerving sensations would disappear. Aye, that was it. He only needed to rid himself of Lady Maura, and all would be well again. "Have you any rooms to let?"

The highlander grinned, baring his teeth. "Nay, Lieutenant. I have nary a one. Beggin' yer pardon, o' course."

The cold hand returned to the back of Baird's neck. Again, he slapped his hand against it but found naught. "I don't believe you, MacCallum."

"Ach, aye. I can see how ye might think I'd keep my rooms from ye just to keep ye from finding yer comfort tonight."

"Well, then are you?" Baird asked, feeling entirely unsettled. He continued rubbing the back of his neck to dispel the cold, clammy feel of the hand that would not leave him be.

The proprietor crossed his arms over his chest and watched him. "Weel now—"

"Lieutenant . . ." Higgins touched his arm. "Mayhap we should go elsewhere."

Baird shook off Higgins's hand. "Where do you suggest, Higgins? Are there so many other rooms to let here at Caillich?" Even to his own ears, he sounded more than slightly panicked. He lowered his hands and took a deep, if unsteady, breath.

Alastair, always the one to lose your composure.

He felt weak. His father never admonished him. *Never.*

"Never mind. We'll go." He would not stay and listen to . . . No. It could not be his father's voice. And that gruesome wraith over the fireplace? It had merely been a trick of the shadows.

Baird turned and stalked out of the guesthouse. MacCallum was overtly antagonistic and would not have told him if Maura Duncanson had gone right up to him and identified herself as Lord Aucharnie's daughter.

"Lieutenant," said Higgins, "I'm sure we can bunk in with Lord Caillich's men."

"Oh, you are sure, Higgins?" Alastair asked irritably.

"Reasonably sure, sir."

"Then why don't you just go to the barracks and see what you can find."

All Baird wanted was a good night's sleep. He'd been plagued by those headaches and more than a few horrible nightmares since Fort William, but he felt certain 'twas only because they'd been sleeping on the hard ground, in the damp air. Once he spent the night in a proper bed—and dealt with the wench who was the cause of all his troubles—all would be well.

And his eyes would stop seeing things that were not there.

Dugan could not remember a time in his life when he'd felt so utterly rattled. He had never deflowered a maiden, nor had the act ever wrung from him the degree of pleasure he'd experienced with Maura.

A Duncanson.

He wanted to gather her into his arms and carry her inside to Murray's bed and spend the night with her there, exploring all manner of sensual pleasures with her.

"Let me up, MacMillan," Maura said.

Dugan moved aside. He could barely see her in the shadows. *Gesu*, he'd taken a virgin on the floor of a barn. He ought to be whipped. "Are you . . ." He rubbed his hand across his mouth. "*Gesu*, Maura, are you all right?"

She began to right her clothes—clothes he'd practically ripped from her. "Yes."

He could still taste her sweet skin, feel the silk of it beneath his lips. And he wanted more.

He rose from the floor. "Let me help you."

"I can manage."

But he took her hands and pulled her to her feet. When she kept her head down and started working on the fastenings of her bodice, Dugan moved her hands aside and did them himself. He ought to apologize, but could not bring himself to say the words.

She was ominously quiet.

Dugan tipped his head down and captured her lips. She gasped, but melted against him when he pulled her close. He was not sorry at all for taking possession of her. His only regret was the appalling setting in which she'd experienced her first love-making.

"I will not apologize, Maura, for I fully intend to let you ravish me again," he whispered against her mouth.

"*Me*? Ravish you?"

He laughed. "Oh aye."

"Dugan MacMillan, you are the most vexing man in all—"

She started to pull away, but Dugan held her fast. He took her mouth again, intent upon wiping the irritation from her voice, from her mind. He did not want to argue.

Chapter 25

Maura's heart pounded madly.

She stood at the door of the barn, with Dugan right behind her, snaking his arm 'round her waist. Pulling her against him, as though he had not just made love to her again.

And she had allowed it, knowing how he despised her name.

"You'll sleep beside me tonight, Maura," he whispered in her ear.

Oh God. Maura wanted to. But she wanted more than this night and knew she could not have it. Lachann and the others were counting on Dugan to pay their rents, and they all knew how nebulous the promise of gold was.

She felt raw and helpless against him. "Dugan—"

"Hush, lass. Go into the cottage and eat," he said. "I'll join you soon."

Join her? In Murray's bedchamber?

Lachann already thought badly of her, and Dugan had not even told his brother that she was one of the hated Duncansons. She left the barn and started for the cottage, unsure how she was going to face the others after what she'd done. She was unsure how she could face *herself*.

She wondered if Dugan's opinion of her had changed, now that he'd bedded her. Had anything else changed? She was still a Duncanson, and her own uncle might have been the one who'd killed Dugan's family.

It made her feel queasy. She'd never cared for Robert Campbell, and now she knew it was for good reason. Any man who would murder families—innocent women and children—was not worth the leather that soled his boots.

She stepped inside the cottage where Lachann and Calum had already wrapped themselves in their heavy plaids and were sleeping on the floor near the fireplace. Archie had fallen asleep sitting up with his head on the table, next to the empty bottle of whiskey.

Now she understood why they seemed dead to the world and was glad she did not have to worry about facing them tonight.

The cottage was nearly as dark inside as it was out, so Maura lit a lamp and brought it to the table. She touched Archie's shoulder and he roused himself just enough for him to belch before bidding her good night. Then he followed the example of the others and, without another word, found a comfortable place to lie down.

Maura prepared another meal with the unused ingredients, and just as she took it from the fire, Dugan returned.

He glanced 'round the darkened room, then spoke quietly to her. "Were they all asleep when you came in?"

She held up the whiskey bottle that had been at least half full when she'd left the cottage. "Yes.

Archie fell asleep in his plate. I woke him and sent him to bed."

Maura felt self-conscious as Dugan observed her scooping out two servings of food onto plates for them. She set down the pan and went to wipe her hands on her apron, but realized she'd lost it somewhere.

The barn. Her face heated and she did not know quite what to say. The intimacies they'd shared were meant for a husband and wife—and she and Dugan were anything but.

" 'Tis not much—"

"Aye, 'tis a grand feast. And unexpected," Dugan whispered. "You need not serve us, Maura."

On the contrary, Maura felt there was a great deal she ought to do for his clan to make amends for the actions of her own.

Dugan had made her no promises. He'd seduced her so easily, her own wantonness made her feel ashamed. Yet she could not help but want what he'd said just before she'd left him—to lie with him all through the night.

For their time together was limited.

Maura sat down across from Dugan, but before she could pick up her spoon, he laid his hand over hers. "You are beautiful, lass."

She shivered with pleasure. "There's no need to flatter me, Dugan," she whispered.

" 'Tis not flattery when it's the truth."

Maura's breath caught in her throat. His eyes were so blue in the flickering light of the candle. And sincere. 'Twould be so easy to fall in love with the man, but even after all they'd shared, she still could not trust that he wouldn't give her over to

Kildary. How could he make that promise when the welfare of his clan might depend upon the ransom?

The only thing Maura could do was follow the course she'd set the previous night when she discovered the French words waxed into the backs of the maps. Take him to Loch Aveboyne. And if there was no gold to be found . . .

Maura prayed that she could figure out the missing clue and the treasure would be there.

They ate in silence, and when they were through, Maura stacked the plates and bowls on one end of the table. She began to gather the forks and spoons, but Dugan lifted her into his arms. "Bring the lamp," he whispered, moving quietly so as not to awaken the others. "I want to see you when I make love to you this time."

It was still dark when Dugan left Maura sleeping in Kennan Murray's modest bedchamber. His mood was somber in spite of the satisfaction he'd experienced during the night, whether he was inside her or just lying next to her. Holding her naked body close to his was a sensation as near to heaven as he could imagine.

He'd been so occupied with her lush body and the delights he'd experienced through the night that he'd forgotten his true purpose in seducing her. Dugan had learned naught about their destination or the clues she'd discovered.

He jabbed his fingers through his hair. Plans be damned, he wanted her in his bed. He wanted to feel her silky hair trailing across his chest as she pressed kisses to his most sensitive places.

He groaned at the memory of her sensual caresses. He could not imagine tiring of the soft sounds she made when he pulsed inside her and brought her to her peak.

Gesu. Dugan forced his attention to what he must do.

He pulled his hair back into its queue and lit a candle at the table. Lachann, Conall, and Archie were still sleeping soundly when he retrieved Murray's framed map from beneath the chest near the bedroom. He opened up his traveling pack and took out the old maps again, laying them on the table alongside Murray's framed map.

Dugan figured out the location of Murray's cottage on the man's map and determined that they were about two days' ride from Loch Monar. 'Twas likely the Duke of Argyll was already headed there, and making good time. Dugan wanted to stay as far away from the duke and his men as possible. He did not want their paths to cross at all.

Of course it had occurred to him that Maura might be lying. 'Twas a constant worry. How could she admit that Loch Monar was the location of the treasure? Such an admission would ruin her ploy of having to lead him personally to yet a different secret location.

But he did not sense a lie in her. Her expressions were wholly transparent, as much as she attempted to keep her feelings hidden. She'd seen *something* on those pieces of map—and she knew better than to tell him what it was.

Dugan sat back and crossed his arms over his chest. He did not want to give her to Kildary. 'Twas more than the idea of spoiling her father's plans.

He hated the thought of abandoning her to the

old baron. Hated knowing that soon, whether or not they found the treasure, they would part ways.

He despised the thought of leaving her to fend for herself, as it seemed she'd had to do for all of her life.

Dugan removed Murray's map from its frame and rolled it up, then put it and the others into his pack. He might not know what to do about Maura, but at least he had an accurate map to show him where they were.

"Laird?" Conall asked as he rose from his place on the floor near the fire.

"Aye, Conall. Good morn." Though Dugan thought 'twas anything but good. His irresponsibility during the previous night grated on him. He'd shown less discipline than a rutting youth, binding himself to Maura when those bonds would soon be severed.

Conall pinched his eyes closed and rubbed his head, swaying slightly.

"You look as though you took one dram too many," Dugan remarked.

"More like five, but 'twas a fine baurley-bree, Dugan," he said, his words slightly slurred. "Sorry we did'na leave any for you."

"You'd have been a sight better off if you had," Dugan replied, though he was glad they'd all been so inebriated they had not taken note of his activities last night with Maura. He did not need a discussion on the wisdom of his actions at the moment, not when he was questioning them himself.

Lachann sat up next, rubbing his head. "What's all the shouting for?"

Dugan closed his pack and allowed Lachann's

eyes to adjust. 'Twas going to be a long day, by the looks of them.

The sun's rays streamed into the eastern windows as Dugan crossed the room to sit down at Murray's desk. He took pen and paper from a drawer and uncapped the ink bottle.

"What're you doing, Dugan?" Conall asked, lying back down.

"Writing a note to whoever finds this cottage empty and wonders what happened to Murray. 'Tis only right."

Dugan dipped the quill into the ink and wrote a simple paragraph about the man's demise for anyone who came along looking for him. He wrote the date and mentioned where they had buried the man. Then he signed it.

He looked over at his men. "We leave as soon as you can haul your sorry arses up off the floor."

Maura managed to escape the cottage without exchanging a word with Dugan's men, and went down to the pond to bathe. The water was brisk and it washed away the sweet warmth of Dugan's body.

And yet she knew he was anything but sweet. Oh, he'd taken care with her, being certain not to cause her any discomfort. He'd brought her pleasure time and again as they twined themselves so intimately under the blankets in Kennan Murray's bed. But they both knew his mission had not changed. This would soon end. Even now, Baron Kildary might be making his way across the highlands to Braemore.

She swallowed a laugh of despair at the thought

that their paths could easily cross while they journeyed toward Loch Aveboyne. Cromarty was east, Braemore to the west, and the path she and Dugan followed was directly in the middle. *Oh God*.

Maura could not bring herself to think about it. Not now.

She sat down on an old stump and pulled on her stockings and shoes, then her gown. Naught had gone as she'd planned since the night she escaped her escort at Fort William. Maura did not know if she would be able to find the French treasure, nor had she made any progress in getting away to Loch Camerochlan. Perhaps worst of all . . . she had given her innocence and most of her heart to a man who would send her to Cromarty in exchange for three thousand pounds.

At least she was not cheap.

She bent at the waist and laid her head down on her lap.

She'd been so damned foolish to give away her heart to a man who would never share his own—at least, not with her. She was still merely a pawn in the contest between Dugan and Argyll.

As alone as she'd ever been.

Maura wiped her tears on her skirts and took a long, shaky breath before returning to the cottage. The deep connection she'd felt with Dugan was illusory, and she needed to remember that.

Dugan's men were out saddling the horses when she got back, and the three looked as rough as Maura felt. Dugan came out of the barn leading the horse-drawn wagon. When he looked up and saw her, his gaze was indifferent, leaving a hollow sensation in the center of her chest.

And she'd thought she'd prepared herself.

"Do you ride, Maura?" he asked.

She took a deep breath. "Some."

"Good. 'Twill be better. Archie . . ."

"Aye, Laird."

"You'll drive the cart and Maura will ride your horse."

Dugan took Maura's arm. "Are you ready to leave?"

"I'll just get my bag—"

"I already put it in the wagon."

"Oh, then . . . Yes. I'm ready."

He lifted her onto the horse and Maura attempted to settle herself in the saddle, though it did not come naturally to her. 'Twas a man's saddle.

And she was . . . tender.

"Can you do it, Maura?"

Heat flooded her face and she knew she'd turned as red as a tomato. He was asking if she could manage to ride after giving him her virginity. After making love with him over and over during the night.

"Of course." She was not going to admit to any frailty. How could she when his manner was so distant? "I'm ready."

Chapter 26

When they arrived at Angus MacDonnall's holding some miles south of Loch Mullardoch, Dugan doubted Maura could have ridden any farther. She seemed to be in significant discomfort, but there was naught he could do for her.

Other than staying away from her last night, and 'twas too late for that. He chastised himself yet again for his actions. He'd known better, and yet . . .

Laird MacDonnall came out of his keep, a stone tower that was half the size of Dugan's home, and greeted him. They were old friends, having trained together many years before in the western isles with the MacDonalds. Dugan dismounted and they clasped hands. "MacMillan, what brings ye to m' lands? I hav'na laid eyes on ye fer a good two years! No' since Perth. Are ye healed, then?"

"Aye, Angus. Hale and healthy."

"Aye, I can see that."

"We are just passing through. And begging for a spare bed if you have one." Dugan glanced toward Maura, who was visibly wilting.

"Aye, of course." He slapped Dugan's back. "So, ye've taken a wife, have ye?"

"No, MacDonnall." His throat suddenly closed up, too dry to swallow. "No wife. This is . . . a kinswoman in need of a good night's rest."

"Unmarried, is she?"

"Aye," Dugan replied hesitantly.

"Rhona!" MacDonnall shouted. "Edeen!"

The two serving women hurried out of the keep to answer their laird's summons.

"Take the young lady inside and heat water for a bath," MacDonnall ordered the servants. "And tell Catriona we'll feast tonight."

The men dismounted as Dugan lifted Maura down. "Go with MacDonnall's servants," he said quietly. "They'll see you're taken care of."

As brash as she usually was, Maura was quiet and withdrawn now, and Dugan felt a pang of guilt. He quickly dismissed it as he turned her over to the MacDonnall servants. He and Maura had acted upon a mutual attraction. Mayhap he ought to have exercised better discipline, but what was done . . . was done.

MacDonnall put a brotherly arm about Dugan's shoulders as Maura disappeared into the keep, her step considerably slower than was usual for her. "Ye'll sup here with me this eve," MacDonnall said, "and ye'll rest easy among the MacDonnalls tonight, Dugan."

Dugan could see that the idea of a night with the MacDonnalls suited his men well, for there were several young maids from the cottages nearby who'd come close to get a look at the newcomers. One in particular had her eye on his brother, and she was plain enough that Lachann wouldn't suspect treachery in her every move. He wished him good luck with the lass.

Dugan collected his traveling pack and went inside with Angus. He'd been there only once before, and the place looked different. Not as clean or orderly. "You're keeping dogs inside now?"

"Ach, aye. After Meg died, I . . ." He shrugged.

"My sympathies, Angus," Dugan said. "I did not know you'd lost your wife."

MacDonnall nodded. "Aye, 'twas soon after I saw ye last. She was taken by a fever. But I find m'self in the mood for a new wife, of late."

Maura sank into a tub of hot water and said a prayer of thanks. Her muscles were tired and her nether parts were more than a wee bit sore. She hoped never to have to ride horseback again.

Except she knew the morrow would bring more of the same. She hoped it would take only one more day to reach Loch Aveboyne, but knew that highland distances as depicted on a map could be deceptive. It might take longer.

She would not dwell upon that possibility now, not while she could bask in the hot comfort of the bath. She would not even think about Dugan and his indifference toward her all day or the hint of concern she'd sensed from him when he lifted her down from her mount. Chivalry was in his blood— likely toward *any* female in distress.

Hadn't he felled the ram at the waterfall before he'd even met her?

Maura sighed and sank down deeper into the water. She just wanted—needed—to get this journey over and done so that she could make her way to the loch where Tilda Crane was keeping Rosie.

She hoped they would find the treasure, and

quickly. That was the only way Dugan would ever free her to go search for Rosie and take her away.

Maura felt a pang in the pit of her stomach at the thought of leaving him. Though their night of intimacy had seemed to have little effect upon him, to Maura it had been profound.

And yet she had always known that the only future she would have was the one she created for herself. Somehow, she and Rosie had managed to get on without any nurture or support from their parents and siblings. 'Twas only because of the kindness of the Elliotts that they'd endured.

Maura had no choice but to endure again.

It was not going to be easy once she reached Camerochlan and Rosie, but she'd never believed it would be. She recognized that she was as alone now as she'd been the day she met Dugan, when he'd killed the ram for her. She knew she could not meekly submit to his plans for her.

A vague idea began to take shape in her mind. What if she led them past Loch Aveboyne—locating it for her own benefit—but then slipped away from Dugan and returned to the loch to search for the gold herself?

Ach, 'twas impossible.

She had already attempted to get away, and had not been successful. And there was the matter of what she would do with the gold. If there was a significant amount of it, she would need something in which to carry it. A wagon. Drawn by a horse.

One of the maids came into the room. "I've brought ye some soap and a gown for the evening."

"Thank you—Rhona, is it?"

"Aye, ma'am." The girl went to the fireplace and added a brick of peat to the fire.

"Laird MacDonnall requested that ye be made ready to sup with him . . . at his right hand, ma'am."

Maura opened her eyes. She wondered if it meant the laird had decided to show her special favor. And whether she might be able to use the man's partiality in order to escape.

Because the fact remained . . . She was unlikely to be able to escape Dugan, and if there was no gold at Aveboyne, he was surely not going to allow her to leave him and give up the ransom from Kildary.

The MacDonnall had brought in musicians to entertain them during the meal. He'd had the old rushes swept out of the great hall and new ones, fragrant ones, laid. The dogs had been chased out, and the savory scent of roasting fowl was in the air. Even the laird himself wore a clean shirt and plaid, with an ornamental doeskin sporran about his waist. He'd combed his hair and pulled it into a neat queue at his nape.

Now that Dugan took note, MacDonnall was not half bad-looking. He was only a year or so older than Dugan, and though a wee bit shorter than the MacMillan brothers, MacDonnall was no weakling. Dugan knew he was an apt archer and an even better swordsman. The man had the means to care for and protect his clan. And the good luck not to be obliged in any way to the Duke of Argyll.

"Take a draught o' my best whiskey, Dugan, while we wait."

"Wait?"

"Fer the lady. I've invited yer kinswoman to sup with us."

MacDonnall poured some of the clear amber

liquid into a delicate glass and handed it to Dugan, who had the distinct feeling he ought not to drink it and cloud his thoughts.

As he had done the night before.

MacDonnall turned toward the curved stone stairs as Maura descended. "Ach, look at 'er," he said. "She will do nicely."

Dugan frowned at MacDonnall, then turned toward the stairs. God's eyes, but she was beautiful.

"I had the lasses take whatever they needed from Meg's belongings since she's had no need of 'em these past two years."

Maura's hair had been arranged artfully, and some white stones—pearls?—were strewn about her curls and dangling from her ears. The brocade and lace gown was one Dugan had not seen before, so it must have belonged to MacDonnall's late wife. The thing suited Maura to perfection.

'Twas the blue of a darkening sky, with a low bodice that displayed the assets he'd so enjoyed the night before. The gown fitted tightly to the waist, then flared out, draping her legs modestly, and yet so seductively Dugan had to fight the arousal that hit him like a punch to his gut.

Worse was the glorious smile she bestowed on MacDonnall.

"My bonny lady!" Angus approached her and took her hand, bowing over it in a manner Dugan knew was far more formal than he ever would have done had he known she was a Duncanson.

"Good evening, Laird," she said. "Thank you for inviting me to join you." She gave a cursory glance in Dugan's direction and murmured, "Laird MacMillan," as though he was not the man whose cock had made her whimper with pleasure all through the night.

MacDonnall called for the meal to be served, then took Maura's hand and led her to the table. He seated her, then sat down beside her, clearly as pleased as a pig in clover to be the recipient of her brilliant smile.

"Dugan tells me you are a kinswoman," he said.

"Well no, not exactly—"

"Maura came from Fort William," Dugan interjected. Damn all, he did not need everyone in the highlands to know he was escorting a Duncanson through their territories. MacDonnall was liable to toss them out onto their arses if he knew.

"Ah. Clan Cameron. Or clan—"

"Close enough," Dugan quipped as he tossed back the rest of his whiskey.

Fortunately, MacDonnall found it far more entertaining to blather all about his own exploits rather than question Maura or Dugan about their travels. Dugan did not care to lie to his old friend about Maura and the ransom. He especially did not want to discuss the possibility of gold hidden somewhere in the highlands. But the man's overly engaging manner with Maura grated on his nerves.

And if MacDonnall did not raise his eyes from the abundance of bonny flesh displayed above Maura's neckline, Dugan was going to be compelled to put his fist down his old friend's throat.

Dugan sat back in his chair and forced himself to be calm. Maura could spend a festive evening in the relative safety of MacDonnall's hall, wearing the clothing of his dead wife, for she would be back in the saddle on the morrow. Leading Dugan to the treasure that was going to get him out from under Argyll's—aye, *her cousin's*—thumb.

Angus poured yet another glass of wine for Maura and she laughed at one of his inane jests. "Ah, Laird MacDonnall! You are so very clever."

Dugan felt himself frowning fiercely, for he'd never enjoyed watching a man make an arse of himself for a woman. He stood up. " 'Tis time Maura retired. We'll take our leave at dawn on the morrow, MacDonnall."

"Aw, 'tis early yet, Dugan," MacDonnall said while keeping his eyes trained on Maura. "And I'd hoped to convince ye t' stay another day. Or two."

" 'Tis not possible. Regrettably," Dugan added between clenched teeth. He extended his hand to Maura. "I'll escort you to your chamber."

She rose—without taking his hand—and turned to MacDonnall, who stood at the same time. "Thank you for a splendid evening, Laird. Will I see you in the morn?"

"Ye may count on it, dear lady." MacDonnall took her hand and planted a solid kiss upon it.

It felt to Dugan as though he needed to haul her away from MacDonnall. Against her will. He had no idea what the man's appeal could possibly be.

He took a candle and lit their way up the staircase.

"Which room?"

"Up again, one more flight," she replied.

They walked in silence down a narrow passageway to yet another staircase. Dugan followed her up the next set of stairs, and when they reached the top, he saw that the staircase ended at the door to a large solar. The water from Maura's bath had been cleared away and the empty tub stood just behind a screen next to the fireplace.

The bed was large and inviting, but Dugan had no intention of making use of it. He'd made that mistake once, and was not going to repeat it.

Much as he might want to do so.

"I don't understand your sour mood, Laird. What has gotten you into such a temper?" Maura asked. She walked into the solar and sat down at the dressing table. "I thought you would enjoy an evening with your old friend."

"You mean the man who is looking to marry himself another wife?"

"Oh? Is he?"

She began to remove the gems from her hair. "I found him charming."

"As charming as a hedgehog." Dugan watched intently as she slipped her delicate fingers into her fiery curls and drew out the pins that held the pearls.

"Oh, not at all. He has a way with words, and seems to understand how to truly appreciate a woman."

"Aye, by looking down her bodice!"

She laughed, and the sole freckle near her eye crinkled. The urge to kiss it was nearly insurmountable. But he managed. He stood against the wall with his arms crossed over his chest. Why he did not just remove himself from her chamber and find his own bed . . .

"Hardly, Dugan," she said. "He was a complete gentleman, and I am half tempted to—"

"You have other plans, Lady Maura."

"They are not my plans, Laird." She looked at his reflection in the glass, scowling. "I have not had any say over my own actions in more than two years."

He would not feel guilty for it. "You'll not be staying here with MacDonnall."

"Of course not," she said with a catch in her voice. "I am your prisoner, Laird."

Dugan felt the whisper of a curse pass his lips. "Maura, you—"

"What? I am not your prisoner?" she taunted. "That is lovely to know, Dugan. Mayhap I will just—"

"You will continue to travel with us on the morrow. Just as we planned."

"We?"

Dugan said naught.

"Never mind," she said as she stood and came to him. "Help me with these. I don't wish to call the maids."

She presented her back to him as though she'd not just accused him of holding her against her will.

Aye, he was. And he was not ashamed of it. A laird did what was necessary to protect his clan. They both understood his duty.

"I don't know what MacDougall's wife would have wanted with such an elaborate gown," he groused. "We've no need of these ornate—"

"Hush, Dugan," she chided. "You are only being disagreeable."

"Oh, aye?"

He finished with the fastenings and turned her 'round to face him, keeping hold of her arms. "Why would I want to be disagreeable with one of my oldest friends?"

"Mayhap you can tell me, Dugan," she said.

The gown gaped in front, giving him an enticing view—or would have if he bothered to lower his eyes. Which he would not. He was a well-trained warrior with far more discipline than he'd displayed the previous night.

But her cheeks were flushed an enthralling pink and her eyes sparkled with green fire. He trapped her hands behind her back and lowered his mouth to hers.

Maura was drowning. Dugan's sensual onslaught was all-consuming and overpowering. He was taking her to that place where she could not think, where she could not even reason. All she could do was feel—his mouth, his tongue, his hard body against hers.

He released her hands and she felt her gown slip off her shoulders and down to her feet. Without breaking their kiss, he lifted her into his arms and carried her to the bed. Laying her down, he came over her, nipping her neck with his teeth while his hands freed her breasts from her shift.

He bent over her and sucked the tips of her breasts into his mouth, the exquisite sensation shooting right to her womb. Maura reached for him and laced her fingers through his hair as he pleasured her.

"You will never share a bed with MacDonnall."

His words shocked Maura back to reality. Her emotions threatened to choke her. She did not want to share a bed with the MacDonnall or any other man. She only wanted Dugan MacMillan, and he was a blockheaded fool if he did not realize it.

"Do you think not, MacMillan?" She rolled out

from under him and straddled him when he lay flat on his back.

"He is not for you, Maura."

She balanced herself on both hands resting upon his chest. He drew her down for his kiss.

"I suppose only *you* are," she retorted, blinking back tears.

"You know I am," he said. He took her mouth, and as he battled with her tongue, slid his hand under her shift and touched her intimately.

Maura broke the kiss as she blinked away tears. "Oh yes. You and Baron Kildary!"

Dugan froze. He was nearly mindless with the need to sink into Maura's tantalizing body, but her words chilled him to the bone. He lay perfectly still for a moment, then extricated himself from her bed, from her body.

He strode to the door and pulled it open, but not before noticing that she'd rolled to her side and faced away from him. Her shoulders trembled, and Dugan knew she wept.

"*Shite*," he muttered as he left the solar and closed the door behind him.

Why did it have to be her? Why was Maura Duncanson the one who stirred his blood in a way no other woman had ever done? Why did she have to be a Duncanson?

Chapter 27

Corporal Higgins brought Baird's horse to him, saddled and ready to go. Then he stood and faced him squarely. "Lieutenant Baird, sir?"

"What is it, Corporal?"

"Sir, the men and I . . . We believe 'twould be best for us to return to Aucharnie for more men."

"No." Goddamn it, Alastair had no interest in dealing with a mutiny, not after the hideous night he'd spent.

That damned dead witch had found him in the barracks and touched him again and again, laying her icy fingers upon him and keeping him from being able to find any decent rest during the night.

The witch had finally left him, but then the other voice came . . . the hateful voice. The berating voice that whispered contradictory, despicable words in Alastair's ears, calculated, he was sure, to make him doubt himself and his mission.

Now his head pounded again. He would prove them wrong—his father, Aucharnie, Ramsay . . . and even Higgins, wrong. He *could* find Maura Duncanson, no matter what they might believe.

Baird sneered with derision. "I am not about to

go back to Aucharnie and Ramsay and tell them I lost the little wench."

"Lieutenant, you seem . . . *unwell* these past couple of days. Mayhap—"

"I am perfectly fine!" Baird snapped. When he found himself picking at his eyebrow, he slapped his hand down to his side. "Never better."

As soon as he finished off little Maura Duncanson, the old hag that refused to leave him alone would also be vanquished. And his father would cease his prattling. For—oh yes—he knew 'twas General Baird who'd come to torment him during the night. The old man just could not—

"But, sir—"

"This conversation is over, Corporal Higgins."

"Begging your pardon, sir . . . it is not." Higgins was eyeing him strangely. Warily. "The men and I seriously think you ought to consider returning to Aucharnie for assistance."

Baird felt his control slipping, but he stood fast. He could not let his father see him lose command. He felt a burning in his throat and a twitch in his eye. No one defied him! *No one!*

"This is insubordination, Higgins." He started to draw his sword, but Higgins moved quickly and disarmed him.

"Lieutenant, I have no wish to defy you," he said. "But we have made no progress in finding any trail whatsoever for Lady Maura. We cannot even be sure she travels this way."

"That MacCallum bastard certainly saw her."

"No, sir, he did not."

"He said he—" Baird brushed away those damned cold fingers once again and tried to remember whether 'twas MacCallum who had said

Maura was here . . . or whether it had been the
hag's words, meant to confuse him. "Can you not
see—"

"Lieutenant, all will be well if we return to
Aucharnie," Higgins said, his tone infuriatingly
deferential. But Alastair knew he was not sincere.
Not in the least. "We can muster more men and—"

"You can stuff that pitiful tone, Higgins. 'Twill
garner you no favor."

"Sir, I am not trying to garner favor. I would
just like to go back and get some help. 'Tis a wide
territory, and the earl's daughter could be anywhere . . ."

Baird was finished listening. He mounted his
horse and reached down for his sword. Higgins
handed it to him, and Baird had to fight a fierce
urge to cut the insolent man down. "You and the
others are hereby ordered to return to Aucharnie
for more men. I will remain here in this vicinity—
because I am quite certain the wench is here—and
will meet you upon your return."

"But sir—"

"You have your orders."

"Sir . . ."

"What? Do you want them in writing?" Baird
mocked.

Higgins gave a quick nod. "Aye. I would appreciate that, sir."

Dugan spent the night in MacDonnall's hall, but
did not get much sleep. How could he, when his
mind was full of Maura Duncanson and his body
taut with need of her?

How could the fates have brought her to him and taken her away all at once?

At least his men would be well rested and ready for the morrow's travels, for it seemed they'd found sufficient amusements—and beds—in the village near the keep.

He was glad at least *they* had found some comfort.

He took the staircase past Maura's solar to the roof of the keep and leaned against the battlements as the sun made its way through the murky eastern sky. Their journey that day was going to be a wet one, but if they kept a good pace, they would reach Loch Monar well before dark.

Dugan wondered if Argyll had already reached the loch—his mistaken destination. Even if he left Caillich Castle after Dugan had gone, he figured the duke would likely reach Monar before nightfall. Dugan's group had stopped early the night before last, when they'd stayed at Murray's, while Argyll was likely to have ridden longer and harder.

When sounds of the household stirring became obvious, Dugan started back toward the stairs. But the sight of riders coming toward MacDonnall's keep from the north caught his attention and gave him pause. He could not make them out, yet he could see that there were more than a dozen men in the company.

He hastened down the stairs and found MacDonnall standing bleary-eyed in the great hall, having just risen from his bed. "You've got company about to arrive."

"Wha'?" He straightened and became alert.

"Rouse your men," Dugan said. "There are

riders—mayhap twenty of them—coming from the north."

MacDonnall muttered a curse as he tightened his belt and stepped out of the keep. Dugan heard the alarm sounding as he climbed up to Maura's solar.

She sat on the edge of the bed wearing only her shift, looking rumpled and sleepy, and entirely delectable.

He took her traveling gown from the chair and brought it to her. "Maura, get dressed. There are intruders riding in, and you might need to take shelter somewhere."

"Dugan?"

"Aye, Maura."

"If . . ." She looked at him for a moment, then gave a quick shake of her head. "Never mind."

Dugan could not take his eyes from her—the steady pulse in her neck, the delicate lines of her collarbones, the fullness of her lips. As danger approached, he could think of naught but keeping her safe.

The intensity of this protective urge shook him, but there was no time to ponder it now.

He returned to the great hall and went outside where his brother and the others had gathered along with MacDonnall's men. All were fully armed and ready for battle.

MacDonnall started giving orders to his men. "Rory, go with Connor and ride out to the crags and see if you can tell who it is. Niall, I want you and a few others to gather the women and children." He turned to Dugan. "Laird MacMillan, will ye come with me. The rest of ye, mount yer horses. We prepare for battle until we know who it is and what they want."

Dugan signaled to his men to follow MacDonnall's orders, and returned to the keep with Angus. "Where do you keep the women, Angus?"

" 'Tis safest here in my hall." MacDonnall collected his spyglass, and the two men climbed up to the roof. Angus went directly to the northern end of the battlements and peered through the glass at the riders.

He handed the glass to Dugan. "Have a look."

Maura heard the men going up to the roof and grabbed her shawl as she followed them. She reached the top of the keep and stood back to watch as Dugan and the MacDonnall gazed out over the battlements, and wondered if the newcomers posed a threat.

The wind tousled Dugan's hair and rippled his deep red plaid about his knees, and Maura's heart thudded in her chest at the sight of him. He would fight hard and fierce for MacDonnall, just as he would to prevent his clan from being evicted from their own lands.

She shuddered with the awareness of what that meant for her.

Dugan leaned against the stone battlement and raised the glass to his eye. "They're highlanders."

"Aye," MacDonnall replied.

"At least two dozen of them," Dugan said. "Wearing . . . Is that the MacKay standard?"

MacDonnall took the glass from Dugan and looked out again. "I think you're right. I have no quibble with MacKay."

"But we'll remain battle-ready, in case something untoward is afoot." Dugan turned to go for the stairs and stopped when he saw her.

"Good morn to ye, lass," MacDonnall said, walking past him. "We've a wee situation here."

"Yes," Maura said. "I see."

She had given Dugan the opportunity to contradict her last night. But he had left her, rather than deny that she belonged to Baron Kildary.

"Go down to the great hall with the rest of the women," Dugan said, ushering her to the staircase behind MacDonnall. "The women and children will be gathering there. Stay there and you will be safe."

"Who are the MacKays?" she asked.

" 'Tis a clan whose lands are well north of here. Up beyond Loch Camerochlan. I do not know why they'd have come so far south."

Maura's heart clenched in her chest. "Camerochlan?" Mayhap they would know something of her sister!

Dugan took hold of her arm, preventing her from flying down the stairs and out the door of the keep. "Maura. Consider this a dangerous situation until I say otherwise. I know what you are thinking, but you are not to come out of the hall until I give you leave."

Maura took a shuddering breath. "They might know something of Rosie!"

"Aye. And they might see fit to cut your throat with nary a by-your-leave."

Dugan did not enjoy having to put the fear of God into Maura, but he knew how rash she could be. She was impulsive and reckless, and so outra-

geously alluring, he was hard-pressed to keep from
pulling her into his arms and raining kisses on
every inch of her body and making her promise to
take care. For him. For his peace of mind.

But he followed her down the stairs and stayed
to watch for a moment as Maura joined the women
and children in the hall. Without a pause, she took
a screeching bairn from its mother so the woman
could tend to her frightened younger children. She
spoke quietly to the woman, who calmed visibly
at her words. She moved among the others who
had gathered for safety, turning chaos into order
by assigning tasks and gathering children together
for games.

She was as capable as any great laird's wife,
staying calm, keeping her dignity, and reassuring
everyone that all would be well. Dugan gritted his
teeth at the injustice of fate and went outside.

A light drizzle had begun by the time Dugan
joined the rest of the men. MacDonnall had lined
them up into a tight formation while they waited
for the return of his scouts. He quickly led them out
and away from the village to face the visitors, far
from the women and children. Dugan rode to the
front beside MacDonnall, his sword at the ready.

Two MacKay riders approached and shouted a
greeting.

"We come on behalf of Laird Robert MacKay.
In peace." The two men were unarmed, but for the
sgian dubh in their hose. The small knives were
more ceremonial than lethal, and would do them
no good against MacDonnall's army.

But Dugan did not relax. Not yet.

"What is Laird MacKay's business here?" Mac-
Donnall called back.

"Our journey is only for our laird to speak of. He wishes to confer with you."

MacDonnall hesitated for an instant. "Yer laird is welcome to join me in my keep."

"And his brother as well, Laird?"

"Aye. He may bring one other. The rest of you stay where you are."

The MacKay messengers gave a nod, then turned and rode back to the phalanx of highlanders wearing the MacKay plaid.

"No need for us to sit out here in the mizzle," MacDonnall said to Dugan. He rode back to the keep and dismounted. "We can send the women back to their homes."

Dugan agreed. He sensed no threat from the MacKays.

They cleared the hall, but Maura remained when Robert MacKay and his brother, Struan, arrived.

The formalities were observed, and when they had sat down to a table laid with ale and bread, the MacKay came to the point of his visit. "We are looking for a place called Kinlochleven. My brother believes we should have reached it by now."

The hair on the back of Dugan's neck stood up. He could think of no good reason for a northwestern laird to travel all the way to Kinlochleven, unless he was looking for something and someone in particular.

Hector Mackenzie and his piece of the map.

"Have ye kin there?" MacDonnall asked.

"No kin, MacDonnall, but a quest that is too private to speak of."

"Aye, then. I'll respect that."

"Kinlochleven is still a long way off, MacKay,"

Dugan said. "You still have several days more travel."

The MacKay frowned and scrubbed one hand across his beard. "Then we are headed aright? We'll come upon it if we keep up our present course?"

"I'll draw a map for you," Dugan said, though he knew a map would do him no good. Because Mackenzie had already sold his piece of the damned map. Dugan could not help but wonder if the MacKay possessed the fourth quarter of it.

The man's quest added an urgency to Dugan's. Perhaps the MacKay laird had started with more information than what Dugan's grandfather had told him. If he had additional information . . . Mayhap he would turn up in the exact place where Maura was leading them.

"You are from the north country, Laird MacKay?" Maura asked.

"Aye," the two men replied in unison.

"Do you know of Loch Camerochlan, then?"

"Ach, aye. 'Tis not far from our own lands," MacKay said. He frowned and shook his head. "How do ye know Camerochlan? 'Tis a wee, out-of-the-way place."

"I know someone there. A woman named Tilda Crane."

The MacKay brothers looked at each other, then at Maura. "Then we've bad news for ye, lass," said the laird. "Tilda Crane died but a few weeks ago."

"What!" Maura jumped up from her chair. "Died? How?"

"She drowned."

Chapter 28

Maura's brain froze inside her skull. *Drowned? Tilda Crane was dead?*

She came to her feet in a rush. "What of the child, the crippled girl in her care?"

The two MacKays shook their heads. "We do'na know of any child, lass."

"But you must! Tilda Crane was her nurse," Maura cried. "Who is taking care of Rosie now?"

"Rosie?" The MacKay laird's expression was one of puzzlement.

"Lass, we do not typically spend any time at Loch Camerochlan," Struan said, "but only happened to pass through on our way south."

" 'Tis the only reason we heard of the woman's death, for drownings are not common."

Maura made a dash for the staircase. She ignored the voices calling to her, so desperate was she to be on her way to find Rosie. If Tilda was gone, then who was taking care of her sister? Was she still at the loch?

She ran up to the solar and shoved her few belongings into her traveling bag, only to be whirled 'round by a pair of strong hands.

"What are you doing?" he growled.

"What does it look like, Dugan?" she demanded, shoving her hair back behind her ear.

"You are acting rashly. Just because—"

"My sister—my *helpless* sister—has been left to fend for herself, and you think I should remain calm? You do not understand, Dugan. Rosie is . . ." She swallowed back her tears. "She is all I have."

"Maura, I'm only saying—"

"Saying what? That she is all right on her own? She is not, Dugan! She needs care, and as despicable as Tilda Crane might have been—at least she took care of my sister."

"Maura . . ."

"Who has been caring for Rosie since the Crane woman's death? Do you think anyone at the loch would take in my poor crippled Rosie?"

"Aye, lass. I do," he said gently, and Maura felt tears roll down her cheeks. " 'Tis what highlanders do."

"I must get to her."

"Aye, you will. I'll take you there."

She gave a bitter laugh. "Will that be before or after you turn me over to Baron Kildary?"

He muttered a low curse and Maura knew his answer.

She turned away to fasten the ties on her bag.

"Maura, all this time, we've been traveling in the direction of Loch Camerochlan."

"So?"

"Unless you've been misleading us, the treasure is on our way there. Give me the clues."

Despair shuddered through her. "Give you the clues?"

"Aye." He crossed his arms over his chest and waited, implacable.

Maura stood frozen in place. She knew Dugan was just as dedicated to his clan as she was to Rosie. But neither of them could count on the gold being where the clues indicated. If they did not find it at Loch Aveboyne—

She had to get away. "We're wasting time." She went for the door.

"Maura—"

She turned to face him. "If I give you the clues, will you let me go on my own to Loch Camerochlan?" she demanded.

He remained silent.

Dugan wanted nothing more than to promise Maura he would take her to Loch Camerochlan himself.

But 'twould be an empty promise. If they did not find the treasure at the place where she led them, he had to make use of the only other method he had to acquire the funds he needed.

The ransom.

It went against everything in him to turn her over to Kildary, but he hoped and prayed it would not come to that. He remembered a few unsavory bits of gossip about the man and if any of them were true . . .

Gesu.

The MacKays were already outside mounting their horses and starting to ride away when Dugan reached the hall. Maura was taking her leave of Angus MacDonnall, clearly anxious to get started.

"Lass, I could see the MacKays' news was not good."

"No, Laird, 'twas not. I must be away immediately."

MacDonnall looked over her head at Dugan. "I regret yer visit must be cut so short," MacDonnall said. Then he winked. "We were only beginning to know each other."

Dugan bristled at his old friend's blatantly flirtatious gesture. "She's coming with me, MacDonnall."

"Your kinswoman appears to have a mind and a purpose of her own, MacMillan."

Aye, that she did. And if she were more reasonable, she would have shown him the clues she'd seen on the map long before now. 'Twas entirely possible Dugan would have known a better route to the site, and his need to make haste was all the more important now that the MacKays were on their way to Kinlochleven. Though they would be days behind him once they reached Hector Mackenzie's village, Dugan could not afford to waste any time at all.

Maura started out the door, but MacDonnall stopped her, taking her by the shoulders. He planted a kiss on each of her cheeks.

Dugan felt his face heat and his teeth clench as he watched Angus's display of affection. One more minute of it and he would have to—

MacDonnall released her. "Fare thee well for now, then, lass. And good luck to ye."

"Thank you, Laird."

"Mayhap I will come and pay you a visit at Braemore Keep. 'Tis a long time since I was up in MacMillan territory." He gave Dugan a sly glance. "How will that suit ye, Dugan?"

Dugan mumbled a disparaging remark but did not mention how unlikely it was that Maura Duncanson would ever set foot onto MacMillan lands. 'Twould require explanations Dugan had no intention of giving.

They walked outside where Dugan saw that the misty rain had not abated. "Ride ahead," he ordered his men. "We'll be right behind you." He turned to Maura. "Maura, you'll drive the wagon."

She bit her lip and looked up dubiously at the high bench.

"Allow me," MacDonnall said, assisting her to climb up to it.

"MacDonnall, have you an extra length of wool to spare?" Dugan asked.

"Of course—the servants will see to it," the laird replied, sending one of the lads into the keep with Dugan's request.

"Dugan, we are wasting time," Maura said.

"Only another minute more."

He could see that her anxiety was far from abating, and she shot a frustrated glance in Dugan's direction. He ignored it and waited for a servant to return with the cloth he'd requested. She might not thank him for it now, but he knew she would appreciate it later.

" 'Tis plain t' see ye're upset," MacDonnall said, holding her hand and lingering over it. "I pray yer travels take ye to happier news."

Her chin began to tremble and Dugan saw tears fill her eyes. He turned away.

"You are very kind, Laird," she said to MacDonnall.

One of the servants came out of the hall with a

long, heavy length of MacDonnall plaid and gave it to Dugan.

He climbed up to Maura, pleased as hell to put an end to Maura's tête-à-tête with Angus and to get on the road again. "This will help to keep the rain off you," he said as he wrapped the cloth 'round her head and shoulders. "I don't want you to become ill."

"No, of course not," she said with a catch in her voice.

She took the reins in hand and Dugan jumped down from the wagon. "Here are my gloves," he said, handing her the worn leather.

Maura pulled on the gloves, but her hands were nowhere near large enough to keep them from falling off.

"Wait," he told her.

"I think mayhap the lass ought to ride your horse, Dugan," said MacDonnall, "and you drive the wagon."

"Not today," Dugan retorted as he pulled two lengths of thin leather from his pack. MacDonnall knew naught . . . he had no idea how uncomfortable Maura had been after a day on horseback—or why. He was loath to cause her any more pain.

He returned to her. "Give me your hands."

She reached down to him and he savored the moment of contact as he tied a band of leather 'round each of her wrists to keep the gloves securely in place.

"Thank you." The tears she'd been holding back spilled down her face and she wiped them away with her gloved hand.

"You can do this?" he asked. Her tears would remain forever on those gloves.

She sniffed. "Yes. Of course."

"That's the brake," he said, "next to your left foot."

"I won't need a brake, Dugan. I have no intention of stopping."

The slow pace made Maura frantic. She had no idea how long it would take to get to Loch Camerochlan, but she needed to get there as quickly as possible. *Dear Lord, Rosie was on her own.*

The thought of how her fragile sister fared without her nurse gave her a chill.

Mayhap she should have pleaded her case before Laird MacDonnall. He might have helped her . . .

She nearly laughed through her tears. The MacDonnall did not know she was a Duncanson, and was unlikely to take kindly to that information. He did not know Dugan was after the French treasure, and Maura did not want to consider what Laird MacDonnall might do if he knew they had what they needed to find the site.

"Slow down, Maura."

"But Dugan—"

"You risk breaking a wheel at this pace."

"Then let's rid ourselves of the wagon," she cried. "I can ride with you as I've done before!"

The exasperating man shook his head. "With the extra weight, Glencoe would have to go even slower. Besides, we'll need the wagon. For the gold."

Maura swallowed back her tears. She had driven a conveyance like this only once before, with Deirdre Elliott's husband, and they had gone even slower, though they'd had a clear path.

She had to follow Dugan's instructions or risk delaying their progress even further. But her worries did not subside.

"Dugan, I've heard that highlanders are superstitious," she said.

"No more than anyone," he replied.

"Do you think the people at Camerochlan will consider my sister bad luck?"

"Why would they?"

"Because she is different!" Maura cried. Hadn't she explained Rosie's difficulties to him before? "She can speak only a few words . . . and her spine is crooked, which makes it difficult for her to walk."

"Maura—"

"And the Crane woman drowned! Won't that be construed badly?"

Dugan shook his head. "Highlanders are a hospitable lot, Maura. They are more likely to give Rosie shelter than shun her."

"If you are just saying that to—"

"Maura, have you yet encountered an unfriendly highlander?"

"I—"

"Or been shown anything but hospitality since leaving Fort William?"

"Only from the MacMillan laird, who still plans to give me to that horrid Kildary, without a care!"

It hurt her deeply. In spite of the moments of exquisite tenderness between them, Dugan still did not deny that the baron owned her. Not even in the heat of passion. Or now, when he knew Rosie's peril.

Maura did not know what to do. If she could get away from the MacMillans, she would do so immediately. But she was not in possession of the map, and she knew only the general direction of Loch Camerochlan. She'd always felt she'd be able to find her way there, but Dugan wasn't about to let her go free. She had no choice but to take him to Loch Aveboyne and show him the clues.

She prayed no one had already gone there searching for the treasure and taken it.

Dugan did not like seeing Maura in pain, and what she was suffering physically on that hard bench was only a small part of her anguish. She had risked everything to get away from Lieutenant Baird, only to fall directly into Dugan's scheme to collect the money he needed from Baron Kildary.

'Twas hardly an honorable thing to do, but he could never forget his responsibility to his clan.

"Dugan, please let me go," she said. "If you promise to set me free, I'll give you the clues."

"You would go all the way to Loch Camerochlan alone?"

"What difference will it make to you? You'll have your gold and I'll have my sister."

But it *did* make a difference. The idea of Maura traveling alone through the wild northern highlands made his blood turn cold. Oh aye, highlanders were hospitable people, but Dugan had not forgotten the highwaymen who'd accosted her when she was barely out of Fort William. And he knew there were plenty more of those lurking about these cliffs and crags.

"This is the route to Loch Camerochlan, Maura," he said. "We continue as before."

Maura's silence as she drove the wagon through

the glen was like a wall between them. He understood her worry about Rosie, but the lass had been without her caretaker for some time, according to the MacKays. Either she'd survived with the help of others at Camerochlan, or she'd already perished. Another few days' delay would make no difference.

"Where do we go once we reach Loch Monar?" Dugan asked.

"North," she said, keeping her eyes straight ahead.

Dugan considered the possibility that she would lead them all the way to Loch Camerochlan and bypass the site of the treasure altogether.

"Pull up, Maura," he said. "Let's have a look at the map."

"I know where I'm going, Dugan."

"That may be," he said without giving voice to his concerns. "Did you know the Duke of Argyll is likely to be at Loch Monar, already searching for the treasure?"

"Argyll?" She looked at him then. "But . . . wasn't he at Caillich Castle?"

"Aye, he was. But 'tis more than likely he has gotten ahead of us."

"How?"

"He would not have stopped early to spend the night in a dead crofter's cottage, nor did he take half a day to deal with MacKays." Dugan did not add that the speed Argyll and his men could achieve was likely far greater than the pace Dugan's group could make. He did not think she would appreciate being told that she slowed them down.

"And when Argyll doesn't find the gold there?" she asked. "What will he do then?"

"Pull up, Maura, and put on the brake."

She hesitated, but finally did so. Dugan dismounted and walked 'round to the back of the wagon. He took Murray's map from his pack, then climbed up to sit next to Maura. He opened and spread out the map across both their laps.

She smelled as sweet and feminine as she had last night in the MacDonnall solar, when he'd feasted upon her mouth and held her glorious breasts in his hands. He could almost hear her sighs of pleasure.

Dugan swallowed thickly and reminded himself that she was not his. She would never be his. No Duncanson would ever wear the MacMillan plaid.

"See if you can find a different route to . . . to our destination . . . without having to go near Loch Monar."

Maura took the map in hand, absently licking her lips. She might not have thought anything of the gesture, but Dugan felt it all the way to his groin.

A wisp of her hair brushed her cheek and Dugan restrained the urge to touch it, to twine it 'round his finger, and caress her silky skin. 'Twould be so easy to give in to the desire to kiss her, to mold her body to his and pursue the pleasures he knew they could find together. Dugan wanted to ignore who she was and find a way to keep her from Kildary, whether or not they found the gold.

Gesu. What was he thinking?

"Just show me the clues, Maura. 'Tis possible I know a shorter way to get to the site and we can cut some time from this quest."

"And then?" She looked at him with doubt and distrust.

"And then I'll take you to Loch Camerochlan. That is . . . if you're not planning to mislead me."

She returned her gaze to the map.

"You know you will be in far better circumstances if there is gold in your purse when you reach Loch Camerochlan," he said.

"Then you agree you will n-not give me to Baron Kildary?"

The hopeful expression in her eyes was his undoing.

Chapter 29

Maura thought she'd wept her last tear during the night in the solar at MacDonnall's keep. But Dugan's silence wounded her. He was going to achieve what he needed, no matter what happened at Loch Aveboyne.

And she was going to lose.

Lose him. Lose Rosie.

"What if there is no gold at the site?" she asked.

"We'll find it."

Once she'd felt certain of it. But now . . .

The clues were there on the pieces of the map, but incomplete. It would take days for them to search the entire west shore of the loch—days she did not have.

"Dugan—"

"You cannot travel all the way up through the highlands on your own, Maura. 'Tis madness even to think it."

She wiped away a stray tear on a corner of the extra plaid Dugan had requested from MacDonnall, glad she had more than just her cloak to cover her, for it had been raining most of the day. Her tears were hardly obvious in these conditions.

She sighed in despair, wishing she could believe

they would find the gold. She wished she could trust that Dugan would take her to Loch Camerochlan whether they found the treasure or not.

"Braemore is here?" She pointed to a location on the shore of Loch Maree.

"Aye."

She looked to the east and found Cromarty, then traced a line from Kildary's home to Braemore. She had difficulty swallowing her panic when she saw how close his route to Braemore would bring him to Loch Monar. And Aveboyne.

Dugan noticed what she was doing and muttered a low curse.

Dugan's decision had been made days ago, he just hadn't been able to face it. There was no honor in sacrificing Maura, even for the security of his clan. He could not give her to Kildary, even if he didn't locate the treasure. He would find some other way.

He had not wanted to consider going to war, but mayhap that was the answer. For there was no guarantee that Argyll would not come back again next year for even more outrageous rents. 'Twas time the old maggot and the other landlords were taught a lesson.

If there was no gold to be found, Dugan decided he would go to his MacDonald relations in the west and enlist their warriors to his cause. Hell, every highland laird would likely come to his aid, for most of them had lands at risk from greedy landowners.

"I've never wanted to give you to Kildary, Maura."

Her chin started to quiver and she looked at him as though she could not possibly believe him.

Dugan did not blame her. He'd given her no reassurances at all. He'd made her a hostage in hopes of trading her for Kildary's gold, and then taken her virtue while he gave her no promises.

How could he, when the livelihood of his clan was at stake?

Her eyes filled with tears. "Dugan—are you saying . . ."

She took hold of his hand and squeezed it tightly, hopefully.

He prayed there would be gold at—at wherever it was she was taking him. "I will not trade you to Kildary, Maura. I vow it."

"Even if there is no gold at the site?"

He clenched his jaw and nodded. "Aye."

She wiped her eyes with MacDonnall's plaid. "We c-could veer west." She touched Loch Monar on Murray's map, and 'twas clear that she was debating the wisdom of telling him what she knew. "Then we travel north again."

Ah. She still did not trust him, but Dugan felt reassured. For if she'd planned to go directly to Loch Camerochlan, she would not lead them in a westerly direction. "If we go far enough west," he said, "Argyll won't even know we're passing through."

Maura looked directly at him, her eyes serious, her expression tense, worried. "That would be best, of course."

"Aye, it would," Dugan said. Maura was Argyll's kinswoman. He would not take kindly to the news that she was traveling with a highland lord. Not with his map. "Argyll is a complication we do not need."

"Dugan . . . ?" she asked softly, putting her hand on his knee.

His brain ceased working. "Aye, lass." He could have her undressed and beneath him in less than a minute.

"If I show you the clues I found, will you let me go? Let me leave now for Loch Camerochlan? Please, Dugan. I need to get to my sister right away. And now you have an extra horse that I could—"

"Maura." Dugan rubbed his hand over his whiskered chin, in an attempt to rein in his lust and restore some sanity. He did not want to think about her sister now.

"I'll take you to Camerochlan myself. After we search for the gold."

She looked away, her throat moving heavily as she swallowed. "We'll travel north awhile longer, then west." Her voice was none too steady, reflecting exactly the way Dugan felt.

The rain suited Lieutenant Baird's purposes perfectly. It muffled the sound of his horse as it cantered through the highland glen, so when he came upon the girl, there would be no warning sounds before he was upon her. She was up here somewhere close by.

Where else would she have gone? The little wretch had decided to defy her father and refuse Baron Kildary, and her escape into the wild highlands was the only option she had. She thought no one would find her.

Ye are a mean, self-seeking fool!

"No, I am not!" he roared into the rain. He whipped his head 'round to try and see the witch that tormented him, but he saw naught but clouds of rain.

"Daft old hag," he muttered. He knew she would quit harrying him as soon as he found Maura Duncanson. He could barely wait for her harassment to end.

Ye'll never find her, ye pathetic weakling. No' even yer own father can bear to keep you near . . . Sending ye off to Aucharnie where there's no future—

"You are wrong, witch!" he screamed, then stopped himself. He fought for control.

'Twas only the wind, though he trembled at the eerie sounds and looked 'round frantically again for signs of the wraith that so tormented him.

He saw no horrible, finger-pointing specter this time, but its absence was no comfort. The damned voice would not let him be.

He gritted his teeth and kept on riding, hard and fast. He could catch up to Maura Duncanson, because there was no other direction she could have gone, even if she had joined those damned highlanders. He would prove the old witch wrong. He would show his father that he was ready to be transferred to a post that mattered. Somewhere far from Aucharnie. Somewhere like Caillich.

Alastair wondered if Maura would go with the MacMillans all the way to their—

He slammed his fist on his thigh. "Damnation!" he shouted as he pulled his horse to a halt. He was on the wrong track! Why hadn't he thought of it before?

Because that damned witch had been plaguing him ever since he'd stopped at her filthy little hovel outside Fort William.

But he realized it now. Maura would not have bothered with highlanders. She'd have gone to find her idiot sister!

Baird laughed aloud. Before Maura had been sent away to Glasgow, her little crippled sibling had been banished somewhere into the north country. He'd heard the place mentioned more than once, had even seen it on a map . . . But what was it? Some loch at the arse end of nowhere. He recalled 'twas far to the northwest, well north of Inverness.

Christ, he could have shortened his journey and perhaps even arrived at Maura's destination ahead of her by traveling directly to Inverness and then going north from there.

No matter. Now that he knew where she was headed, he could adjust his own direction. He decided to skirt 'round to the east side of Loch Monar, for that would shorten his journey considerably.

Let that idiot Higgins and the others return to Aucharnie Castle in disgrace. They were likely to receive a reprimand, while Alastair would return home with the foolish wench's body, for he intended to intercept her before she arrived at the place where her sister had been sent. 'Twould be a fine resolution for the earl and his wife. Lord Aucharnie would be so grateful for his lieutenant's dedication to duty that he would give him a commendation.

"And my father did not send me to Aucharnie to be rid of me, you old hag!" he roared into the wind and rain. The damned witch had to have heard that.

Alastair grinned when he considered how his father would receive such good news. General Baird was going to be exceedingly proud of his only son.

Yer soul is empty, Alastair Baird.

"No!" Alastair hunkered down in his saddle even as he swatted at the voice in his ear. "Hell and damnation, I thought I was rid of you! Begone, old woman!"

Ye smell the rot o' death now, do ye not, Alastair? The hag cackled. *'Tis yer own.*

He swallowed, reminding himself he was deep in the highlands with no one near. No one.

Ye can'na stop one puny female, can ye?

"*Get you gone!*" he bellowed.

'Twas only rain and the wind. That old witch had planted the seeds of disquiet in him, making him hear her absurd words, causing him to jump at shadows and see glimmers of things that were not there. Of course he could stop the Duncanson female. He was going to find her and put an end to her.

He shivered under his layers of wool. He only had to do the deed and the old witch would leave him be. They both knew what had to be done.

"**S**he does'na complain, Laird," Archie said.

Dugan had told Maura to ride on ahead while he conferred with his men. They were headed toward a high ridge where they would have a vantage point from which to view the land before them.

"And she's doing far better with the wagon than I'd have thought," Conall added.

Even Lachann grumbled his agreement.

Dugan wondered how they would react if they knew who she was, and that he'd decided to forgo the ransom. He wasn't worried about Archie and

Conall, but Lachann? He was liable to toss her onto the back of his horse and take her to Braemore himself.

The day was miserable for traveling, but the men were right. Maura did not complain, not when speed was of the essence.

"Considering Argyll's questions about Loch Monar when I saw him at Caillich," Dugan said, "I believe that's where he intends to look for the treasure."

"Damned maggot," Lachann said sharply.

Dugan nodded.

"Dugan, are you sure—"

"Maura says the gold is not at Loch Monar. We're going to head northwest to avoid the loch and the duke, if he is already there."

"Then where will we go?" Conall asked. "Has Maura said—"

"No." Dugan avoided looking at his brother. He'd promised not to give her to Baron Kildary, but she still did not trust him.

When they found the treasure, he would give her a share of it. Her own cause was no less just than his—her dedication to her sister was admirable. Besides, he had delayed her more than was justifiable. Rosie Duncanson did not deserve to be left adrift at Loch Camerochlan, a dreary, isolated world unto itself, cut off from the one person who cared for her.

Maura did not deserve the hand she'd been dealt, either. She seemed nothing like her Duncanson kin—

"What if the gold is not where she says it is?" Lachann asked.

"She is not lying about the clues."

"Mayhap not, but what if the rumors of gold are merely that—rumors?"

Dugan glanced up ahead. "Oh *Gesu*!"

"What—?"

Lachann had barely spoken when Maura's horse reared with fright and took off at a gallop. It jerked so violently that Maura was thrown from her seat to the floor of the wagon, and the traces ripped from her hands. She just barely managed to grab hold of the edge of the wagon to keep from being tossed off.

Dugan did not stop to think what had caused the horse to spook or what he was going to do. He dug his heels into his gelding, lowered his body as though racing for a prize, and galloped after her.

Good Christ, she could be thrown off the high ridge where the horse was headed before he got to her! The grass was wet and the wagon careened wildly.

Dugan's own horse's rapid gait was unsteady, but he pushed him on, never relenting.

"Dugan!" Maura screamed and Dugan felt his heart pounding in his throat.

He sent off a silent prayer as she tore ahead of him toward the precipice. Dugan galloped on through the rain, gaining on her only by inches. "Come on, Glencoe. Faster," he murmured almost as a prayer as he flew toward her.

Should he shout for her to jump? God, no—the fall would kill her at that speed. But she would not survive a fall down the cliff, either.

His horse pumped its legs harder and faster, and Dugan saw that Maura was trying to reach for the traces . . . trying to regain control of the crazed animal. He wanted to tell her to just hold on, but did not know if he would reach her in time. Worse, he didn't know how he was going to save her once he *did* reach her.

Her extra plaid flew off her shoulders and onto the wet ground somewhere behind him. Dugan kept both eyes on her as she crawled slowly toward the bench and grabbed it. If he'd thought her audacious before, he did not know a word to describe this. Dauntless? Foolhardy? Incredible?

She showed more courage than most men he knew.

"Almost there, Maura!" He had very little time before the wagon pitched over the edge.

The wagon careened wildly, tossing Maura to the side. Dugan did not have to hear the thump to know she'd bumped her head. And this time, she did not get up right away.

His heart was in his throat, but he would not falter. He gained on her, mayhap because her horse was tiring. Dugan did not care what the reason— all that mattered was that he catch her in time.

In spite of her injury, she inched her way forward to make a grab for the traces. They bounced out of reach and she pitched forward when the wagon flew over a dip in the ground.

Dugan came up beside the wagon. Keeping one eye on the edge of the cliff that loomed much too close for comfort, he rode up beside her.

"Hold on, Maura!" he shouted.

Dugan matched his horse's pace to that of Maura's. Keeping steady, he reached over for the harness and the traces that were dragging from it. Glencoe pulled away, reluctant to get too close, but Dugan forced him over.

At last, he managed to get hold of the harness. He gave it a steady, firm pull as he reached for the traces, finally slowing the horse and gradually bringing it to a halt.

They stopped no more than twenty feet from the edge of the cliff. Dugan turned the animal and wagon 'round to face the opposite direction and saw Lachann, Conall, and Archie racing toward him. They slowed when they saw he had matters in hand, but Dugan quickly jumped down from his horse and went to the wagon.

Maura was crouched in the wagon bed, still holding onto the seat in front of her. Her face was devoid of color and the pulse in her neck beat rapidly. A small trickle of blood trailed down her forehead from her scalp.

Dugan climbed in and dabbed the blood away, pulling her into his arms. "*Gesu*, Maura. You could have been killed!"

She said naught, likely because she was trembling too hard to speak.

"Laird? Is she . . . ?" Conall asked, coming up beside them.

Dugan released her just enough to look at her head. "Let me see how bad it is."

'Twas a small cut, likely caused by the edge of the bench when she was thrust into it, but he knew that small injuries like this one could cause large problems.

"You're riding with me from here on."

Maura did not think she'd ever been so frightened in her life. She'd done many impulsive—and mayhap even a few foolhardy things—but hanging on to a runaway wagon was the worst yet. Not that her predicament had been her own fault. She did not know what she could have done differently. She'd lost control the second the adder had slithered in front of the horse.

"D'ye know what scairt yer horse, Maura?" Archie asked.

"A snake," she replied. "An adder."

Maura took a deep, unsteady breath. She had seen naught after that, naught but the sky when she fell to the floor of the wagon. And then Dugan, with his plaid whipping about his knees and his hair flying wildly behind him as he raced ahead to get her horse under control. It was only because of Dugan that she still lived.

"Ye did well, Maura," Lachann said, his first kind words to her, ever, "not to panic . . ."

Oh, but she *had* panicked. She'd been so frantic to get some kind of control, to do something—*anything* to keep from careening over the edge of the cliff just ahead—she hadn't even noticed when she bumped her head.

She shuddered once again at the thought of how this episode might have ended. With her at the bottom of the cliff, and Rosie with no one to take care of her.

Dugan helped her down from the wagon, but she was too dizzy to stand. She staggered, and Dugan pulled her into his arms to steady her. She could feel his heart thudding rapidly against his chest. So he'd been frightened, too.

Ah. Because if she'd gone over the cliff, the clues would have died with her.

"Lachann," Dugan said, "ride ahead and make sure we stay clear of Loch Monar."

"Aye, Dugan."

"Archie, tie your horse to the wagon. I want you to drive it until we stop tonight. Conall, you go with Lachann."

Dugan's men did as he bade them.

Maura grasped Dugan's sleeve. "If I'd gone over . . . There would be no one to see to Rosie." The thought of leaving Rosie forever on her own shook Maura almost as much as the accident. How could her sister possibly survive? How had she managed until now?

"*Gesu*, Maura. You think of your sister now? When you nearly lost your own life?"

Tears gathered in her eyes. "She needs me."

Dugan shook his head. "You can barely stand."

He gave Maura a boost onto his horse, then mounted behind her. He took a moment to adjust her between his thighs and then they were off.

"Loch Monar should be a few miles past that ridge," Dugan said, pointing to the right.

Maura did not care where it was, or Loch Aveboyne, either. Not while she was still trembling and fighting nausea. Her head was pounding and her dizziness did not abate. Her only comfort at the moment was the hard warm wall of Dugan's chest at her back and his strong arms 'round her.

They stayed well west of the ridge, and 'twas a relief that they saw no sign of Argyll or any of the duke's men. He would recognize her, and of course he must have deduced it was she who had taken his map.

Maura's heart was torn. Dugan had saved her life. He'd said he would take her to Loch Camerochlan. She ought to show him the clues she'd found on the backs of the maps.

But she was so very tired and her thoughts were muddled. She wished she could lie down.

"Only a short while longer, Maura."

"Mmm." She closed her eyes and let Dugan's heat and strength envelop her.

"Do not go to sleep, Maura."

"But I'm so tired."

"Lass, 'tis the bump on your head making you tired. You must stay awake."

Chapter 30

"**B**ut I—"

"Talk to me about Rosie," Dugan said, but his voice sounded very far away. "Tell me what you remember when you think of your sister."

"Her pretty eyes," Maura said. "They're green, but so very sparkly. And she always smiles when she sees me."

Dugan could not imagine prettier eyes than Maura's, or a more beautiful smile. She snuggled deeper within Dugan's arms and he felt her drifting off again.

"What else?" he asked. He needed to keep her awake so that she did not slip away from him. He could not imagine losing her now, not when he'd just come so very close to it.

"Wee Rosie keeps Deirdre's bairns amused so that Deirdre can do her chores. Dugan, what if something . . . wh-what if something happened to Rosie, too?"

"Do not borrow trouble, lass," he said. "We'll get to her. Soon."

"Why? You hate Duncansons. Why would you help us?"

"Because I find that not all Duncansons are the same."

"No?"

"You would never blindly obey orders, would you?" he asked.

"Umm. I have enough trouble with orders I can see."

He chuckled against her back. "Who is Deirdre? Another sister?"

"Ach, no. My other sisters are so very grand they will have naught to do with Rosie. Or me."

"How many of them are there?"

"Six. All older, and each one more beautiful than the next."

'Twas impossible to believe any of them could possibly be lovelier than Maura.

"And four brothers."

"There are twelve of you?"

"Mmm."

Dugan bristled at the idea of brothers who did not take care of their sisters. He would no sooner leave Alexandra to fend for herself than he would leave a newborn bairn to die. "Your brothers do not stand up to your fath—"

She laughed, then groaned and put her hand to her head. "My siblings are good, obedient sons and daughters of the Earl of Aucharnie. They do as they are told. They've all made good marriages. My father takes pride in them."

"Your father is a fool."

"You know 'tis my father who is keen for me to wed Kildary."

"Aye. I know."

"Dugan . . ."

"Hmm."

"Will you really take me to Loch Camerochlan?"

"I said I would."

Alastair Baird rode over a high pass and came to a crag that towered above a long, sparkling loch and noticed some movement down near the shore. He stopped to watch for a few minutes, but . . .

He rubbed his eyes. Were they playing tricks on him again?

He shuddered almost uncontrollably. Would this damnable wet never cease? He'd thought the weather would work in his favor, but all it had done was make him cold and miserable.

He'd assumed Maura would head due north toward the place her sibling had been taken. But now he wasn't so sure that was where Maura would go.

He looked to the loch below, but all the activity was too far away to see exactly what was going on. He saw no colorful plaids, so they would not be highlanders. Their scarlet coats indicated they must be His Majesty's troops.

He watched the scene below for a few minutes and decided it was real. There were no witches or wraiths screeching at him now. His father's disapproving words were nowhere near.

If he had more time, he would ride down to determine exactly what was going on down there. But he had his mission, and it did not include investigating the activities of any other battalion.

It was far more important to prove wrong his father's disparaging words and capture Maura Duncanson.

He had made good time on his ride northward, and it was only when it became nearly dark that he realized he was hungry. He had neglected to bring any provisions but for some dried meat when he'd ridden away from Higgins and the others. Fortunately, he did have his pistol and could do some hunting.

Do not count upon it, Alastair. You're a poor shot. Always were.

"Stop berating me, Father!" he shouted angrily. "I could have shot those peasants at Glencoe as well as you!"

A deep, scolding chuckle arose from the shadows that lurked in the gloaming just out of sight. Alastair shuddered.

He took out his pistol and loaded it, ready to shoot the man who so taunted him.

You should not have sent your men back without you. How will you survive out here alone?

"Are you there?" Baird demanded. He looked 'round but saw no one. "F-Father . . . ?"

That laugh again. Alastair covered his ears, but still he could not shut out the voice.

You are weak-minded, boy.

"No!"

You could not get one puny female to Cromarty without mishap.

"You do not know her, Father! She is a bane to all who know her!"

You are the bane, Alastair.

"No! Enough! I won't listen to you. Or to that dead hag, either!"

See how far you can go alone, boy.

"I can do it! I've done everything I was ordered to do!" Baird shouted. "I went to that pit where you sent me—Aucharnie Castle. Six years, Father! I've been at Aucharnie six years without promotion. The earl barely acknowledges me! And Ramsay—"

Baird paused to think. "Is that what you expected when you sent me up there? To be ignored? To be out of your way?"

Alastair slid off his horse. There was no reply to his questions, and he stood still for a moment listening to the silence. It should have been a blessed lack of sound, for the auld witch had been tormenting him for days. And his father—

He gave a brief shake of his head. What in hell was he doing, shouting to the hills? He must be mad.

Dread filled him. He was completely alone now, in the wild highlands with very few provisions. He had no map, and wasn't quite sure where Maura Duncanson's sister had been taken. How could he even ask for directions if he did not know exactly where he was going? How was he going to—

He heard voices again, along with the sound of horses and bridles jingling in the mist.

He dropped his pistol to the ground and bent at the waist, covering his head with his hands. 'Twas altogether too much—the phantom voices, that damned wraith, his father—

"You there!"

Baird looked up. Then he straightened up and saluted the captain who glared down at him. The man rode at the head of a long file of uniformed men. A grizzled old nobleman in thick furs wearing a trim white beard sat mounted beside him. "Yes, sir! Lieutenant Alastair Baird at your service, sir."

"What are you doing here, Lieutenant?" the captain asked. "Where are your men?"

Baird felt at a sudden loss. Naught had gone right since Fort William, and now this. Suddenly, his plans to beat Maura to the place where her sister was being held seemed ill-conceived. "Sir, my . . . my mission is my own concern."

"Baron?" the captain asked, glancing to the old man beside him. "What are your orders, my lord?"

Baird quickly bent over and picked up his pistol. He gathered his horse's reins in hand.

The baron looked eerily like Baird's father, with his pointed white beard and dark, judgmental eyes. In a few more years, the general's beard would be completely white and he would look exactly like him.

It had been six years since Alastair had seen his father. That was just before the general had ordered his son to repair to that useless holding at Aucharnie.

To be rid of you!

God, no. Not the voice again. Alastair blinked his eyes and tried to make sense of all this. But 'twas all too confusing.

Only because you're an oddity, Alastair.

"What's wrong with you, man?" the captain demanded.

Alastair tightened his grip on the pistol. He ought to shoot him now. *Shoot the bastard between his eyes!*

The white-bearded baron spoke. "Do you know Laird MacMillan?" he demanded.

Alastair frowned. His hand shook. "Mac-MacMillan?"

"Aye. Laird Dugan MacMillan of Braemore,"

the baron said with an ugly sneer. "He has my property, and I've come to get it."

Dugan had spent far too much of the day's ride alternating between trying to keep Maura awake, and reliving the moments when she had been at the mercy of the runaway horse and wagon. He had come so damnably close to losing her.

And yet she was not his to lose.

He lowered Maura down to the ground and turned her over to Conall and Archie, for he was in desperate need of some distance. He did not want to think about the siblings who ought to have taken better care of their youngest sisters, or the father who'd abandoned his imperfect youngest and arranged a contemptible marriage for the next.

He didn't want to think about the day he would leave her to fend for herself at Camerochlan.

"We'll camp here," he said. "Lachann, come with me."

"Laird?" Conall asked. " 'Tis early still."

Dugan looked toward the setting sun. Aye, they might be able to ride a few more miles, but he didn't want to push Maura any more today. Besides, there was something he wanted to do before they went any farther. "Make a shelter for Lady Maura against the rain and try to keep her awake awhile longer. We'll be back soon."

He turned his horse and went back the way they'd come, with Lachann riding abreast of him. "Where to, Dugan?"

"Back to Loch Monar. I want to see what Argyll is doing."

"And whether Maura lied to you?"

"She didn't lie," he growled. She'd mentioned allies . . . Dugan knew *she* was the ally spoken of by the Frenchman who had given his grandfather their piece of the map.

And she was nothing like any Duncanson he could have imagined. He found it difficult to think of her as part of that despicable family, and everything she'd said about them rang true. She was nothing like them.

He pictured her walking through MacDonnall's great hall that morning, walking among the women and children who had gathered there for protection, and knew she'd conducted herself as would the wife of any great highland laird. She'd given appropriate orders and kept the women and children calm in the face of a possible threat. She had not panicked then, or even when Murray's horse had startled and run off.

Dugan recognized he had put her in an untenable position. She had good reason not to trust him. She did not believe he wouldn't give her to Kildary . . . and Dugan had to admit that until a short while ago, he hadn't been sure of it himself.

He decided not to mention his decision even to Lachann, not yet.

They rode to an outcropping that overlooked Loch Monar, then left their horses and walked to the lip of the ledge that towered over the loch. When they saw activity below, they dropped to a crouch and watched.

There were at least two dozen men below, many of them wearing Argyll's regimental red coats. Lachann spoke quietly to Dugan. "If Lady Maura is telling the truth, then the old bastard brought his soldiers to dig around the wrong location."

"Aye," Dugan replied.

A regular campaign camp had been set up, with torches illuminating the northwest end of the loch—exactly where Dugan had seen the green marking. A cook fire burned nearby, and the smell of their rations wafted up to them.

"Looks like they plan on digging up every inch of ground at this end of the loch," Lachann said.

"Aye, but look. They've concentrated their efforts on the spot where I saw the green mark on the map."

"So they have."

"And they've found naught," Dugan said. "Argyll must be working from memory."

"Lady Maura . . ." Lachann frowned in thought.

"Aye?"

" 'Twas Argyll's part of the map she stole?"

Dugan nodded.

His brother paused for a moment. "Mayhap she's not entirely untrustworthy."

'Twas a huge admission for Lachann, and Dugan decided not to spoil it by telling him how she came to have access to the duke's map.

They watched as Argyll's men came up empty time and again while digging around the vicinity of the green spot, and Dugan knew he'd been right to trust Maura. She had not lied to him.

"What do you think Argyll will do when he doesn't find the gold?" Lachann asked.

'Twas the same question Maura had asked.

The green marking had not been obvious—most of Dugan's men had not seen it. But Argyll had, and he'd followed it here. What if the clue Maura had seen was equally obscure? Mayhap Argyll had seen that one as well. He would set out for Maura's

site as soon as he'd exhausted his possibilities at
Loch Monar.

Dugan did not want to mix Maura up in this
mess any more than he already had. He needed
her to give him the clue, and once they found the
treasure, he would personally escort her to Loch
Camerochlan.

He wasn't going to think about the alternative.
Not until it was absolutely necessary.

"Is that Argyll?" Lachann asked.

Dugan smiled. "Aye. Let's ride down and see if
we can cause the man some more grief."

"Dugan, are you sure that's wise?"

"Not certain at all. But 'twill be gratifying to
witness the maggot's plans going awry." Seeing
Argyll squirm would go a long way to making his
day complete.

Archie and Conall made a meal with some of the
provisions Laird MacDonnall sent with them, but
Maura had no appetite. She was far too worried
about Rosie to eat.

How had Tilda Crane drowned? Had Rosie
been at risk, too? Had they been in a boat on
the lake? Or had some other accident occurred?
Maura could not imagine what had happened. If
Tilda had drowned a few weeks ago, it still would
have been wintery weather in the highlands. What
would Tilda have been doing in a boat?

Ach, Maura could not torture herself with
thoughts of what might have happened. Rosie *had*
to be all right. Maura had to believe—as Dugan
had said—that the highlanders of Loch Camerochlan
would not leave her on her own to perish. They

would take care of her. The idea of anything else was too painful to contemplate.

Maura could not afford any more delay. Not here, and not at Loch Aveboyne, which must be at least one more day's ride from where they were. She was going to give Dugan the clues she had and . . .

He would not want her to go. He'd said he would take her to Rosie, but not until after they found the gold. And then there would be yet another delay when he went to pay his rent to Argyll. Anything could happen to Rosie in the meantime. She'd been left alone long enough!

Maura knew better than to try and leave the highlanders. Mayhap 'twas time to trust Dugan's word. He'd said he would not give her to Kildary, but what about Lachann and the others? What if there was no gold at Loch Aveboyne?

Conall spread out a fur under the wagon that had nearly taken Maura to her death, and bade her to take it for her bed. But now that they had stopped, she was too restless to lie down.

The rain had let up, so she sat on a wide, flat rock and watched the sun set, her thoughts racing. She did not know what Dugan would do if he was unable to find the treasure at Loch Aveboyne. And he might not, for the clues Maura had discovered were incomplete.

She wracked her brain trying to figure out the missing words, but had had no luck. She feared 'twould not become clear until they reached Loch Aveboyne and they started digging under the large rocks they found on the western shore. And even then, Maura might not figure it out.

If they didn't find gold, what would Dugan do about the rents he owed Argyll? He could not let his clan be tossed off their lands. No laird would allow it without a fight. And yet he'd given her his word.

Maura's stomach clenched. The MacMillans would have to go to war against Argyll if Dugan found no way to pay the money the duke demanded.

She lowered her head into her hands, biting back a cry when she touched the bump she'd sustained during the earlier mishap. Dear Lord, she did not want him to go to war. She'd seen with her own eyes what a fierce warrior he was. But anything could happen during a battle.

The thought of losing him to a Campbell sword was too much to bear.

Only a week ago, she'd thought 'twould be enough to take Rosie from Tilda Crane and go away somewhere far from her father's reach. Now the idea of running away and never seeing Dugan again, never tasting his kiss, never feeling the chafe of his whiskers against her skin, or the low rasp of his voice in her ear, was unbearable.

But she was a Duncanson. Every time he looked at her, he would be reminded of the crimes her kin had committed against his family. He would never take her as his wife.

Maura sniffed back a new spate of tears. His wife? The only marriage Dugan had ever considered for her was the one she might be forced to make with Baron Kildary. He'd told her he would take her to Loch Camerochlan himself, and he knew what she planned to do once she found Rosie.

Archie came up behind her. "You should eat something, Maura."

"Thank you, Archie, but I'm not hungry," she replied.

Archie sat down beside her. "Will ye no' tell the laird where the treasure is? Ye know yer clues might have been lost today. If . . ."

"If I'd gone over the cliff." Guilt gnawed at her. She could not risk the possibility that Dugan would be unable to find the treasure if something happened to her.

"Maura . . . I know ye think ye must keep the clues to yerself to prevent Dugan givin' ye to the auld baron," Archie said. "But though he's a fierce warrior, he's a wee sook and would never do that to ye. I think he loves ye."

Chapter 31

"You are far afield, Your Grace," Dugan said. "Stirling Castle must not be to your liking these days." 'Twas common knowledge that the duke kept his mistress there.

Of course Argyll's men had seen Dugan coming from a long way off, and had sent guards with pistols to escort him to the duke.

Argyll looked up his long, pointed nose at him. "Laird MacMillan. I'd have thought you'd be at your own pile of rocks by now."

"No need to rush home, Your Grace."

"You seem to have a good deal of leisure time, MacMillan, when you ought to be seeing about raising funds to pay your rents."

"Ah, but when the opportunity to grovel before my landlord presents itself, I take it, of course. Besides, I have some time before the payment must be made," Dugan said with a grin of confidence that was likely premature. He didn't have the French gold yet. But he could see about delaying Argyll from looking elsewhere for it.

"I might prefer to purchase my lands, Duke."

Argyll barked out a laugh.

"I am quite serious."

"You could not afford to pay—"

"What would it take? To buy my lands from you? Name your price."

"Why, you insolent—"

"I am dead serious."

"Ten thousand pounds!" Argyll bellowed, and the soldiers nearby turned to see what was amiss.

"Oh aye. I thought you would choose a bonny, round number," Dugan said. 'Twas all such a gamble, and Dugan knew his cockiness could kick him in the arse. "Six thousand."

"You are mad."

"Mayhap. What say you?"

"Eight."

"Make it seven and have your solicitor draw up the papers."

"This is sheer idiocy."

"Then I'll have mine do it. Are we agreed?" Dugan asked. He extended his hand.

"Oh yes, we are agreed," Argyll said with a mocking sneer. "Bring your rents—or the price of purchase—to me at Inverness on the appointed date. Or I will have you evicted within the week."

Dugan felt oddly calm. Men like Argyll always won. But not this time. He felt it in his bones.

"Your men are hard at work. Digging, I see . . ."

Argyll grabbed Dugan by the arm and ushered him farther from the site of all the digging. " 'Tis none of your concern."

"Whose land is this, anyway, Your Grace?"

"MacMil—"

"Is it Laird Grant's? Er, no, I believe this is Chisholm territory," Dugan said. "If I remember right, King Jamie's French troops were given leave to make camp here during the rising of the clans two years ago."

Dugan had the satisfaction of noticing a flush of color bloom on the duke's cheeks. He'd succeeded quite nicely in riling the wee bastard.

"You mean the *rebel* uprising." Argyll spat on the ground.

"Call it what you will, Duke."

"Take your man and go, MacMillan," he said. "You've no business here. And I . . ." Argyll clamped his jaws tight.

"And you . . . ?"

"Just go!"

It grew dark, and still Dugan did not return from wherever he'd gone. Maura's restlessness did not abate, but her earlier fatigue returned. She had been asleep under the wagon for some time when she felt Dugan slide onto the fur bed and under the dry plaid next to her. He slipped his arm about her waist and pulled her into the curve of his body.

"Dugan?"

"Aye."

"What happened?" She turned to face him. "Where were you?"

"Conferring with your cousin."

"My— Who?"

"Argyll. We found him digging at Loch Monar." He sounded pleased.

"Did you . . . You mean you talked with him?"

"Oh aye. I believe he won't be a problem for us, at least for a few days."

She turned to look at him in the darkness, but

she could barely make out the shape of his face. It did not matter, because she would always know his scent and the impression of his body against hers.

"How is the bump on your head, my bonny Maura?" he whispered.

"Sore."

"And the headache?" His hand wandered the length of her back, slipping below her waist and pressing her pelvis against his. He was fully aroused.

As was she.

"Better." Ah yes, her head felt much better now that he was there beside her. His touch sent shivers of pleasure through her, and when he touched his lips to hers, she ignited.

He sensed her arousal. He kissed her with a slow heat that sizzled through her, inflaming every part of her body.

He slid down and rained kisses on her throat while he opened her bodice, then pressed his mouth against her breast. "Ah, Maura . . . I want you, lass."

Yes, he wanted her, but Archie was wrong. He did not love her—he would never love a Duncanson.

His lips and tongue pleasured the tips of her breasts, bringing them to hard, sensitive peaks. "Ach, sweet Maura . . ."

She reached for him, slipped her hand beneath his plaid, and found him ready. He made a low sound at the back of his throat when she encircled his hard length in her hand and stroked him.

He moved up to her lips and took possession of her mouth, turning her onto her back and sliding her skirts up so that they were body to body, his naked hardness against her bare, welcoming softness.

He was hers for now, and Maura wanted him in the most elemental way possible. She wanted to feel that same completeness she'd experienced when they'd made love before—she was breathless with the need to belong. With him . . . Only with him. "Now, Dugan. I want you inside me."

"Ah, Maura. You are not too tender?"

"No. Now, Dugan!"

"Aye, sweet."

He kissed her mouth again, and all at once, she felt him slide into her.

'Twas a wondrous feeling, and when he rolled to his back, keeping her on top of him, she nearly wept with the pure pleasure of it.

"Move, my Maura. Any way you like."

"I could stay this way forever." If only reality did not have to intrude. If she could have been a MacDonald or a Frasier . . .

She settled into the feel of him, then lifted her bottom slightly, shuddering with pleasure when she slid back down the length of him. She angled her body just so . . .

"I'm not sure I'm doing this right . . . I've not experience to guide—"

"Ach, Maura—if you did it any more right, I'd be dead."

Maura found the rhythm that suited her, and by the quiet rumblings he made, she knew it pleased him well. She kissed his mouth and nipped at his ear and his neck. Pleasure built inside her, her womb stretching, tightening, frantically reaching . . .

Her muscles contracted 'round him and pulled energy from every inch of her body until it culminated where they were joined. Dugan shuddered and surged into her, and their shared pleasure made her feel complete. They remained joined together, weightless and breathless in a place where her name meant naught.

She did not know how long she stayed there, lying atop him, joined so intimately, but he made no move to shift their positions, and soon they slept.

When Maura woke, Dugan was gone. She left the furry bed she'd shared with him through the night, and while she performed her morning ablutions, considered her plan.

His traveling pack was still under the wagon, so she opened it and removed the three sections of the map. Then she walked to the place where the men stood saddling their horses and preparing to leave.

She heard Lachann's voice. "All I'm asking, Dugan, is whether you'll be able to turn the woman over to Kildary when the time comes."

Dugan did not reply, but reached under Glencoe and tightened his girth. Then he lowered the stirrup.

Maura's knees went weak and her step faltered. He did not deny that he would turn her over to the baron. He made no statement whatsoever to Lachann. Her sense that she and Dugan belonged together was based on naught but her own wishful thinking. She was not a MacDonald or a Frasier. She would always bear the taint of her Duncanson blood.

Oh God. Should she do this? Was she about to lose the only bit of leverage she had?

Rosie needed her, so she had to risk it. 'Twas the only way Dugan was going to let her go.

"What if Maura's clues lead us to naught," Lachann asked, "just like the one Argyll followed? You know 'tis possible there will be no gold."

"I don't think so, Lachann," he said. "She is our ally. The one Grandfather said we would need."

Maura shivered. 'Twas what the old witch had said, too. That she would need an ally.

She observed her brawny laird as he spoke so confidently to his brother, and hoped he was right.

She stepped into their midst. Dugan had made his promise to her, and she would trust him. "I have something I'd like to show you," she said.

With the pieces of the map in hand, she went to the large oak tree near camp and knelt on the ground. Dugan followed, and crouched beside her. He watched her expectantly.

She unrolled the first map and turned it over with the drawing side down. She heard Lachann behind her, his sharp intake of breath.

"Ach, is that it?" Archie cried. "On the *back* of the map?"

Maura nodded and unrolled the second quarter, then the third. She put all three together, then sat back and looked at Dugan.

"The words are French," he said.

"Yes. *Sous le gros rocher . . .*" Maura said. "It means 'under the large rock.'"

"Under the large rock?" There was no mistaking the disdain in Lachann's voice. "*That* will surely help."

"What's this?" Dugan pointed to the word she had not been able to make out.

Maura shook her head. "I'm not sure."

He touched the wax words—the clues that he had not seen until now. "This says Aveboyne."

"Loch Aveboyne. And *a la rive ouest*. What I can tell is that it's under a large rock of some sort on the western shore of Loch Aveboyne."

Dugan looked 'round at his men. "Aveboyne. We can be there in just a few hours."

"I'm ready, Dugan," Archie said. Conall had already mounted his horse. Lachann stood looking skeptically at her.

She could not blame him. There were likely to be many large rocks at the loch.

"Archie, drive the wagon again." Dugan picked up the maps and rolled them together as Archie jumped onto the wagon and started off behind Conall. "Lachann, go with the others. Maura, you're with me."

"Dugan . . ." She swallowed. "You have what you need. 'Tis past time I made my way to Loch Camerochlan."

Dugan took Maura by the shoulders. "I told you I would take you to your sister."

"But not—"

"Maura, you saw the map. Loch Aveboyne is on our route to Loch Camerochlan. We would have gone past it first even if the clues had not pointed there."

"But the highlands are so . . ."

He could see turmoil in her eyes. "Maura, you trusted me with the clues. Will you not trust me to get you to Rosie?"

"What if you don't find the gold?"

He pulled her close. Inexplicably, his encounter

with Argyll had made him optimistic, perhaps unrealistically so. Mayhap the thought of being free of the duke had turned him daft. "We *will* find it."

He kissed her deeply, recalling the heart-stopping intimacies they'd shared the night before, and determined to share many more.

Everything she'd done was for the purpose of rescuing her sister from the Crane woman. She could not possibly be less like her Duncanson kin.

"The best way to get to Camerochlan is through the Aveboyne glen. It's just a stop on our way to your sister, Maura. You must trust me."

Chapter 32

"*You!* You know of Lady Maura?" Baron Kildary demanded.

Alastair Baird had let slip that he was Maura Duncanson's escort. And that she'd run away from him.

"You incompetent idiot!"

The day was cool but Baird began to sweat. Why had he spoken of her? Jesus God. 'Twas because he had not slept well with so many strangers about—even though they were soldiers just like he. He'd been so unnerved by them . . . and his father had not left him alone. At least the old hag had not spoken even once all night long.

He should be grateful for that.

"M-my lord, I—"

"You lost my bride to that bastard MacMillan," Kildary sneered, and Baird's eyes locked on to the old man's pointed white beard. "You are the one who's costing me another three thousand pounds to wed the wench!"

"Lady Maura is not a usual sort of p-person, my lord," Alastair said. He wiped his brow with the back of his hand. "She has . . . powers . . ." *Try not to be any more of a fool, Alastair.*

"What do you say, man?" Kildary demanded. "The woman is a witch?"

Alastair swallowed and somehow managed not to scream at his father . . . er, Lord Kildary. He rubbed his eyes and focused on the man before him. "She is a wily—"

"Ach, enough blather," Kildary said. " 'Tis your fault that I've been dragged out here to this raw country to ransom my own bride!"

The soldiers all stood by, watching—some laughing behind their hands—at Alastair's humiliation. He remembered now . . . 'twas exactly like the harsh chastisements his father gave when he was a lad. And later, after his scolding, the servants would jeer and repeat the general's words.

His father's pointed white beard bobbed as the man spewed his disdain, and Alastair wished for his pistol. He wished 'twas loaded and primed, and in his hand. He could shoot the old bastard dead right now and show the others he was not so incompetent. He was a man of some significant ability, not to mention good sense.

He was well past due for a promotion, by God!

The old man did not wait for any response from Alastair, but whirled away and mounted his horse. "Let's move, Captain. I have no time for fools."

Aye, you are a fool, Alastair. Not even your mother could abide you.

"Shut up," he muttered to the baron's back. His eyes blinked furiously, a habit he'd never been able to control. "What do you know of my mother?"

Dugan had been right. It had only taken a few hours to reach Loch Aveboyne. When he and

Maura arrived at the western shore, the men had already taken the shovels and ax out of the wagon and were rolling the largest rocks off the ground where they'd stood for years.

Maura hoped they would soon find the one that had been in place a mere two years.

'Twas a nebulous task. How deep should they dig before giving up on any one site? Which of the rocks was large enough to hide a treasure underneath? Which one would yield the prize Dugan needed so desperately?

They dismounted, and Dugan took out the maps once again. "Maura, will you study this again, and try to make sense of the word that's missing?"

"Dugan—"

"I know. You want to go to Loch Camerochlan right away. But a few hours' delay won't make any difference."

Maura's stomach was tied in knots with worry. She desperately hoped Dugan was right, and someone had taken her sister in, but she knew 'twould be a hardship. Rosie could not work . . .

She forced her thoughts toward the clues on the pieces of map, carrying them away from the water's edge. She unrolled them and studied the words etched in wax, but could not put an end to her anxiety. She was afraid to let herself feel as confident as Dugan did about the treasure.

What if he did not find it? Would he go to war with Argyll?

The thought of it made her feel ill.

The men removed their shirts and began to dig, but Maura had eyes only for Dugan, the man who would lead his clan into battle against Argyll's army if he did not find the treasure. His decision not to give her to Kildary left him no choice.

Maura tried rubbing dust on the clues again, but the word starting with *ro* did not become any clearer. She eventually gave up trying to see it, or guessing what it might be, and joined the men in their search.

It was a rocky terrain at the water's edge, and some of the rocks resembled small boulders. By dusk, the men had overturned a dozen of them, but had found no sign of any treasure.

"We'll continue by firelight," Dugan said.

"Christ, Dugan," Lachann said, leaning on his shovel, "when will you accept that—"

"Just keep digging, Lachann," Dugan said. "'Tis here. I know it."

'Twas the strangest sensation—the surety Dugan felt about the treasure and this location. As soon as he'd realized Maura was the ally he needed, he was certain he'd find the gold under one of these bloody rocks.

And he'd decided that though she might carry the Duncanson name, she was hardly a representative of that contemptible clan.

Her heart was loyal, and her soul pure. Dugan wanted her in his house, in his bed—

"Riders coming!" Conall called.

Dugan immediately looked for Maura. "Maura!" he shouted. "Take Glencoe and hide in the trees away from the loch."

Maura took Glencoe's reins and hurried away from the loch and into a stand of trees some distance from the shoreline.

"Toss your shovels into the wagon," Dugan said in a deadly quiet tone, "and shove these rocks back into place before they get here." They'd already covered most of their tracks from their digging for they didn't want anyone to come along and take note of what had taken place there.

They pulled on their shirts and brought their horses to the water, making it appear as though they'd just stopped to drink.

But shite. 'Twas just what he did not need—highlanders . . . or worse, Sassenach treasure seekers.

A company of red-coated soldiers approached at a steady pace, coming closer with every second that passed. There were at least a dozen of them, and likely more at the rear.

"Swords ready," he said, although he was nowhere near certain the four of them could handle twelve trained soldiers.

At least Maura was safely away.

"Dugan . . ." His brother spoke without moving.

"Aye?"

"Beside the officer at the head of the phalanx."

"Aye. I see him," Dugan responded. "An old man in a dark cloak. White beard."

"Could it be Kildary?" Conall asked.

"Aye," Dugan replied. "I think that's exactly who it is." What other wealthy Sassenach lord would be riding on a direct route from Cromarty to Braemore?

"Dugan, he's come to pay the ransom!" Conall whispered.

"Do ye think we can take his gold from him?" Archie asked with the rashness of youth.

Dugan shrugged. "I doubt it, Arch. We are outnumbered."

"We've been outnumbered before," Archie said with bravado.

The riders came closer and Dugan recognized Lieutenant Baird among them. The man looked ill at ease, as well he should. He was the one who'd lost Maura. Dugan shuddered to think what could have happened to her had Dugan not pursued her from the inn at Fort William and found her.

He wanted to give her his protection—always.

" 'Tis the lieutenant from Fort William, is it not, Dugan?" Conall asked. "The bald one."

"Aye," Dugan replied. "But he comes from the east, so he did not follow us here."

"Do you think he found us by chance?"

"His direction is not from that of Caillich Castle . . . Somehow, he crossed paths with Kildary."

"Dugan," Lachann said. "We can put an end to this idiocy now. The woman has entertained you long enough. Give her to Kildary and we can be done with it."

Dugan's temper flared and he fisted his hands at his sides. "No. And there will be hell to pay if you say one word of her to Kildary, Lachann."

Dugan stalked away from his brother. Whatever happened, he knew now that he might well make an arse of himself over this woman, worse than Angus MacDonnall would ever do. But Maura was his woman. And no man—not even his brother—was going to interfere with the bond between them.

As the soldiers picked up their pace, Dugan knew he had to think quickly. 'Twould not be easy to untangle the situation he'd brought upon himself. He needed time to search for the gold, and by God, he was going to figure a way to get it.

"Archie, get into the wagon and stay low," Dugan said. "And load your pistol. You'll know when 'tis time to fire."

When the riders arrived, he was ready for them.

"There's a good twenty men, Dugan," Conall said under his breath. "We'll never be able to take the three thousand pounds off Kildary with those odds."

The soldiers came to a stop.

Baird dismounted all in a rush and approached Dugan, turning to address Kildary as he stumbled through the rocky sand. His voice sounded more than a little wild, and the Sassenach captain appeared discomfited by the lieutenant's breach of protocol.

"That's him! MacMillan!" Baird called to Kildary. He pulled off his hat and wiped his brow, his eyes blinking rapidly. "Where is she?" he shouted at Dugan.

"Return to your mount, Lieutenant!" the captain ordered.

"I'll handle this," the white-bearded old man said as he dropped to the ground and came to stand in front of Dugan. "What have you done with my bride?"

"You are Kildary?"

"Of course I am Kildary! Where is the woman?"

Maura heard Dugan say, "She is at Braemore. We sent her ahead with some of my men to wait for your arrival."

"He lies!" Baird shouted.

"Search the woods!" ordered the officer who'd ridden beside Kildary.

Maura left Glencoe where he was and took off running. It was not yet dark, but she could see nowhere to hide. She kept going as fast as she could, but when she tripped and fell, she quickly found herself surrounded by men on horseback.

"That's far enough, Lady Maura." An officer jumped down from his horse and confronted her. "I will take you to Baron Kildary."

"No! Please!"

He grabbed her by the arms and pulled her up to her feet, then held on to her, pushing her roughly back to the loch where Dugan waited with Conall and Lachann. The soldiers who remained at the water's side stood with their pistols trained on the highlanders.

She desperately hoped Dugan would not do anything rash. She could not bear it if he was killed.

"Put her on one of the horses," Kildary said.

"No!" Maura cried.

Dugan stood perfectly still, her fierce highland warrior with his jaw clenched tightly, powerless against the men who had their firearms aimed at him. His own sword remained in its belt, his bow and arrows in the back of the wagon. But where was Archie? Maura could not see him anywhere.

She screamed when one of the soldiers lifted her up, and tried kicking and pummeling to get him to drop her. But her efforts against him were for naught. He tossed her facedown across one of their horses, and the impact knocked the wind out of her so she could no longer scream. One of the soldiers mounted behind her and tied her hands together.

Maura could barely breathe, and tears of pain

and frustration filled her eyes. A deep, dark despair filled her heart. She did not know what they would do to Dugan.

"Kill them," Kildary said, his voice cold as ice.

"Dear God. Just like Glencoe," Maura groaned. 'Twas an inhumane order, given by a callous excuse for a man.

They rode off, and a few moments later the sound of gunshots rang out.

Chapter 33

Archie took the first shot from where he'd lain hidden inside the wagon, twenty paces away. He gut-shot one of Kildary's soldiers.

The rest of the soldiers dropped to the ground, giving Dugan and his men the chance to draw their swords and mount their attack while Archie reloaded.

The odds were in Dugan's favor, for there were only seven Sassenach soldiers remaining. He took the two on the left, while Lachann and Conall split up the next four. Archie picked off the seventh with deadly accuracy.

Archie always had been the MacMillans' best shot, and Dugan was thankful he'd ordered the lad into the wagon before Kildary and his party had gotten close enough to take notice of him.

Dugan fought with passion, his sword serving him well, but Archie's shots served him even better, disrupting every attack the Sassenach soldiers attempted. While the redcoats ducked and looked for cover every time a shot was fired, Dugan and his men were confident Archie's shots would not go astray.

Dugan took one shallow slash to his upper arm,

but 'twas hardly more than a scratch, and gave him the necessary sting of anger to finish off his two Sassenach soldiers and join forces with Conall and Lachann to lay waste to their opponents.

When it was done, he already had a plan in mind.

"We're going after Maura," he said. "Lachann, are you with me?"

Lachann looked his brother dead in the eye, and Dugan hoped he finally saw that Maura was more than just a bit of entertainment for him. "Aye. We'll get her back."

"Let's go, then!"

They flew onto their horses and tore off in the direction Kildary and his men had gone, catching sight of them through the trees, but staying far enough behind to keep out of sight. As darkness fell, it was more difficult to follow, but Kildary's company eventually stopped to make camp. 'Twas clear they believed they had naught to worry about.

The soldiers stopped in a rocky, wooded terrain and pulled Maura off the horse, none too gently. Kildary ordered her hands to be kept tied behind her, and one of the soldiers sat her down in the damp grass while they set up camp.

Maura felt numb, except for her shoulders, and they screamed in agony from being held so far from their natural position. Worse, the sound of those gunshots at Loch Aveboyne still rang in her ears and her heart ached with the knowledge that Kildary's men had killed Dugan. Tears of pain and despair ran down her face.

If only she'd given Dugan the clues earlier, everything might have been different. They might have made it to Loch Aveboyne sooner if he'd known where he needed to go.

Now he'd been killed, and on the orders of the man who was to be her husband.

Maura swallowed her tears and hardened her heart. She would *never* wed Baron Kildary. Because the first chance she got, she was going to shove a dagger into his cold, black heart.

The man was just as horrible as she'd expected, and certainly no better than her own kin who had carried out the slaughter of Dugan's innocent clan at Glencoe.

Maura took stock of her surroundings and tried to think of a plan in case she managed to free herself. She counted less than a dozen men at the camp site, and Lieutenant Baird was one of them. He looked at her with such malice her skin ought to have melted with just a glance.

Beneath his malice was something else, a menacing wildness Maura had seen only hints of before. His dark eyes seemed like dull, black pits of blame, and as he stared at her, he swatted at his ear as though swiping at a fly, while muttering some kind of nonsense to himself.

She realized he was mad. A sickening chill ran through her, and Maura had a clear sensation that he was going to try to kill her. It brought a new urgency to her need to escape, but she did not know how. If only her hands were not secured behind her!

She felt the rocky ground for something to use as a weapon—or something sharp to cut away at the bindings 'round her wrists. Baird growled incoherently at her and stomped away, and Maura felt she could breathe, if only for a moment.

And then her hands alit on a sharp-edged rock. She put it to use immediately, frantically sawing at the ropes that bound her wrists.

As she worked to free herself, she kept her eye on Baird, who stopped in the midst of the other soldiers who were at work making a fire, taking out provisions, and laying down bedrolls. The lieutenant stood there as though unsure of what he was about. Then he reached into one of the packs—

Maura could not see what he took out before her attention was deflected by Baron Kildary, who came to stand before her. Maura averted her eyes from the despicable old man. "Stop your sniveling, you willful quine."

"I would wipe my face if my hands were free," she snapped.

He slapped her, knocking her over. Maura tasted blood.

"Have you any idea how much trouble you put me to?"

Maura clamped her jaws together. There wasn't a retort in the world that mattered, now that Dugan was dead. Now that there was no possibility to get to Loch Camerochlan and rescue Rosie.

For once she killed the baron, she had no hope of survival. Either his soldiers would kill her or they would take her to Cromarty to be tried and hanged.

"Ach, I'm of a mind to send you back to your father."

Maura licked the blood from her lip as she watched Kildary stalk away from her. He came up against Lieutenant Baird, who stood in his path and did not move aside for him. Maura saw that he held a pistol in one hand.

"Get out of my way, you useless dolt!" Kildary snarled. "This is your fault!"

Baird raised the pistol and aimed it at Kildary's chest.

"Idiot! Put that down!"

The captain of Kildary's company suddenly took note of Baird's threat and drew his sword. He lunged at Baird and ran him through with his blade, but he was too late. The gun went off with a deafening blast.

Kildary staggered and fell to the ground, with Lieutenant Baird on top of him.

Dugan reached the encampment just as Kildary knocked Maura down. He lurched ahead, ready to rush the bastard when Conall held him back, pointing to Baird, who stood behind Kildary, his gun loaded and cocked.

"He's going to shoot him, Dugan."

"Or Maura." Dugan drew his sword and sprang from his hiding place and went for Maura. The shot rang out before he reached her, and suddenly the Sassenach camp came alive. The men seemed to believe they were under attack, and all drew their swords, looking for an enemy.

They found Dugan and his men.

The Sassenach captain pulled his sword from Baird's body and went for Maura, but Dugan yanked him 'round to face him. "Leave her be, you bloody bastard!"

The captain thrust his sword toward Dugan's chest, but Dugan blocked it, then parried with him as the rest of his men battled the other soldiers all 'round them.

Yet another blade came at Dugan, but he ducked and dodged it, then turned and dealt a killing blow to the captain. He wasted no time in doing the same to his second assailant.

He heard Maura scream just as his brother gave a shout to call Dugan's attention to her plight. One of the soldiers had grabbed her and was dragging her away from the camp.

Another swordsman prevented Dugan from going at once to Maura's aid, but he overpowered and slew the man without delay. He took off running.

Maura had never felt so helpless. She tried to dig her heels into the hard ground to keep Kildary's soldier from being able to drag her any farther from camp, but he was far too strong for her to resist.

"Stop!" she cried.

"Shut yer trap, wench!"

"When Laird MacMillan comes after you—"

"Laird MacMillan is as good as dead," he grumbled, but before he could finish saying the words, Dugan came at them with a roar that could frighten the very devil. The soldier dropped Maura to the ground and drew his sword. But he was too late. Dugan allowed the man two or three lunges, dodging easily before he dealt the killing jab.

The soldier fell to the ground and Dugan came to her.

"You're alive!" she cried.

"Aye," he said. He took out his dirk and cut the rope that bound her hands and she nearly cried out as the blood came rushing back into her arms and hands. "You didn't think a few Sassenach soldiers could keep me from you, Maura."

"I w-was so . . ." She took a sobbing breath as she grabbed hold of his arm. "They didn't slaughter you . . . l-like at Glencoe!"

He pulled her into his arms. "I'll never be so unprepared again, lass. Are you all right?"

"Dugan—"

"Stay here," he said. He started to turn away, but drew her tight against him and kissed her, long and hard. "Hide until I come for you."

Maura's knees felt wobbly, and she was bruised and battered all over. But she hid behind a tree where she could observe the battle taking place in the camp.

Her heart was in her throat as she watched, even though the highlanders seemed to have the advantage. When Dugan returned to the thick of the fighting, her warrior laird and his men finished off the last few soldiers.

Maura sank to the ground, hardly able to grasp all that had happened. She began to shiver, feeling as though she would never feel warm again.

Dugan sought Maura in the woods outside camp and found her crumpled on the ground not nearly far enough away. Now that the danger was passed, he grinned wryly to himself and knelt down to gather her into his arms. "Will you never learn to follow an order, Maura mine?"

"I-I h-hid, just as y-you told me," she said through chattering teeth.

He drew his plaid 'round her and held her close to warm her and stop her from shaking. "Ach, aye. Ten feet from the battle."

"Mmm." She cuddled closer, pressing her nose to his chest. It felt as though her shivering was beginning to subside.

"You're free now." Dugan said the words, but they were far from satisfactory. There was a great deal more he wanted to say.

Maura lifted her head and gazed up at him. "Everything could have been so different, Dugan. You didn't find the gold at Aveboyne. You could have taken Kildary's money in exchange for me."

"No. I couldn't, Maura," Dugan replied as his lungs expanded with an emotion he only just recognized. "I love you, lass."

Dugan realized he was holding his breath when she tightened her grip on his shirt. "Oh, Dugan! I love you so much! But I-I was afraid you could never . . . I mean, I'm a Dun—"

"The past doesn't matter any longer." He kissed the palm of her hand. "I want you at my side, Maura, always. I want you for my wife."

She sniffed her tears away and, with an exquisite tenderness that tugged at Dugan's heart, cupped his jaw in her hand. "Oh yes, Dugan MacMillan! I will be your wife!"

He rose to his feet and pulled Maura up after him, then lifted her into his arms. He wanted to get her away from the carnage of battle. "Let's leave this place."

"I c-can walk," she said.

He doubted it, but that was his intrepid Maura, never admitting to any weakness. "There's no need, sweet. I'll take you to my horse and we'll ride Glencoe to our own camp."

While Lachann and the lads searched the Sassenach camp for Kildary's ransom money, Dugan and Maura rode back to Loch Aveboyne. He felt relieved to know he would soon have enough money to pay Argyll, though 'twould not be enough to buy the land.

It did not matter. The MacMillans would be spared from eviction, at least. And Maura—his life, his love—was safe.

Dugan and his men stripped down and washed off the blood and sweat of battle in the loch, then quickly made their beds and settled down to sleep.

But sleep evaded Maura. She lay cradled in Dugan's arms, her body aching, her lip stinging where Kildary had split it, and her head throbbing. But at least she was warm again.

She was glad to be alive, glad to be lying in the arms of the man she loved with her whole heart and soul.

She kissed him lightly. "You are the Glencoe lad, just as Sorcha told me."

"*What?*" He pulled back to look at her in the faint starlight.

"The old witch I spoke of," she said quietly. "She told me the Glencoe lad had become a fierce warrior."

He lay quietly beside her for a moment. "There was an old soothsayer called Sorcha at Glencoe," he said. "Laird MacIain did not heed her warnings."

"He likely did not understand them," Maura

said. "She spoke in riddles to me. Only now do I have any grasp of what she was telling me."

"Aye?"

"Yes. That I would need an ally to find the treasure."

"My grandfather told me the same thing."

"He did?" Maura asked.

Dugan nodded slightly. "And yet . . ."

"No gold," Maura said, and Dugan hugged her close.

"If only we could make out that one word on the map," she said.

"We have time now, Maura," Dugan said. "I'm going to send Lachann to Inverness with Kildary's gold. He can pay Argyll while we go to Loch Camerochlan for Rosie."

Maura took a deep, shuddering breath and Dugan pulled her into the curve of his body. How she loved this man who would delay his return home to help her rescue her sister.

"What is it, love?"

"I'm afraid of what I'll find there. What if Rosie—"

"Someone has taken her in," he said.

"How can you be so sure? My own father didn't want her when she was born. He never even looked at her after he decided her spine was crooked. She *was* too small," Maura recalled. She'd hidden in the tower room where her mother had given birth, watching the proceedings, listening to his father berate the midwife for allowing the bairn to be born too soon.

"'Tis no excuse. Your father ought to be whipped."

His gruff words warmed her. "My father never

saw Rosie's perfect little fingers or her rosebud lips . . ." Maura remembered her mother's screams as she labored to birth her youngest child, remembered looking at wee Rosie, covered with wax and blood, lying abandoned in the well-used cradle. "Her lips were gray . . . not rosy red as they should have—"

She stopped abruptly as a thought struck her. "Rosy."

"Rosie?" Dugan repeated.

Maura sat up, wincing at her many aches and pains. "Her lips were shaped like a tiny gray rose, but they should have been red. Rose red. Rouge. *Rouge*, Dugan! That's the word that's missing from the clues!"

"Rouge?"

"Yes! That's where the treasure will be—under a large *red* rock!"

Dugan pushed up onto an elbow and looked up at her. "I saw one—a great rusty red boulder," he said. "At the tree line where you ran into the woods to evade Kildary."

"That is where you must dig, Dugan. If there's any gold to be found, it'll be there."

Maura settled down into Dugan's arms again, but hardly slept all night. She was anxious for dawn, eager to see if she was right.

Dugan knew his confidence had not been misplaced. Once he'd realized Maura was his ally, he'd been certain he would find the treasure. His luck could not possibly be all bad.

'Twas time the fates ruled in the favor of his clan, and not the bloody Duke of Argyll.

When morning came, Dugan kissed Maura awake. " 'Tis time, love."

"Dugan—"

"We'll find it."

Joined by Lachann, Archie, and Conall, Dugan walked down to the water's edge, then they turned and looked back at the line of trees.

Dugan held back the rush of excitement that ran through him when he saw it, a great red rock that was barely visible from the loch. "There it is," he said. "*Rouge*. Just past those trees."

'Twas huge. While Maura paced nervously at the water's edge, the men dug 'round the massive rock to loosen it. Finally, with all four of them pushing, they tipped it over and discovered what they had been chasing for what seemed like eternity.

A metal chest, far larger than Dugan had expected.

"Are you going to open it, Dugan?" Archie asked.

He knelt on the ground beside it. Using the ax, he dug away the earth at its front and reached down to the latch. He held his breath as he pulled it open.

"Jesus, Mary, and Joseph," Lachann muttered in a low voice. "Maura was right."

Dugan slipped his hand into the cache of cool, brilliant gold coins, and only then did the magnitude of his discovery strike him. "There must be thousands of pounds here."

"Aye. Ten, at least," Conall said.

Lachann slapped Conall's back. "Thirty if there's ten!"

With this kind of wealth, Dugan's clan would never have to grovel again. He could buy their land

and more cattle than anyone in the highlands possessed. When he married Maura they would raise their family without fear of further exploitation by Argyll or anyone else.

Suddenly, Maura was beside him, kneeling in the dirt. "Oh Dugan! You found the treasure!"

"Aye, lass," he said, his heart full at the sight of her. "And I found a chest of gold, too."

Chapter 34

Loch Camerochlan. Early May 1717.

"**W**e're looking for a small, red-haired child," Dugan said to the first man they came upon when they reached the village at the edge of Loch Camerochlan. He kept his arm about Maura's shoulders, giving his love and support, for he knew how worried she was. "The lass was brought here a couple of years ago with a woman by the name of Tilda Crane."

"Ach, aye!" the old fisherman said. "Terrible thing, that woman drownin' as she did. But 'twas her own fault, goin' out alone in Cathal MacLeod's curragh."

"Where is she?" Maura asked. Questions about Tilda Crane could wait. "The child, I mean."

"Ye'll find her up at MacMurrough's cottage." He pointed to a tidy little house on the hillside west of the loch. "Geordie MacMurrough and his wife took her in after . . ." The man shrugged.

Maura wasted no time, but sprinted up the path toward the cottage. She heard Dugan thanking the fisherman and following after her.

Dugan had not delayed their quest to find Rosie,

sending his brother with their solicitor to meet the Duke of Argyll at Inverness and hold him to the bargain they'd made at Loch Monar. Lachann would pay him for the MacMillan lands, and never again be subject to the duke's whims. With the treasure in his possession, Dugan had the financial power to meet the wily old man on any terms.

Maura reached the MacMurrough cottage, out of breath and anxious, and was greeted by the sight of her small sister sitting on the ground outside the house, with two other children playing nearby.

Rosie turned her head and looked at Maura as she approached. Her sister looked well enough, but too small for her age, her back still bent, crippling her. But her face was as bonny as ever, her smile revealing her sunny temperament.

"Rosie?" Maura said quietly, hardly able to believe that she was here. Finally.

Rosie's smile faded and she looked blankly at Maura. But only for a moment.

Suddenly, the bright smile reappeared on her face. "Morra!" she cried, and raised her arms toward her sister.

Maura dropped down to her knees and took Rosie into her arms. "Yes, my wee one," she said. "We've come to take you home."

Dugan spoke to the MacMurroughs while Maura lavished her affection on her sister.

For the first time in Maura's life, all was right in her world.

Epilogue

Braemore Keep. Late July 1717.

Maura covered her hair with a length of plaid to keep the dust from it as she swept out a large room near the bedchamber she shared with her husband. With carpenters and masons working on improvements to Dugan's tower at all hours of the day, the place was impossible to keep clean, even with all the servants Dugan kept.

She worked her way to the window where she could gaze down at the rich MacMillan fields to the west, and the loch beyond. 'Twas a beautiful holding, and now that Dugan owned every acre of it—much to the consternation of the Duke of Argyll, who could not bring himself to turn down Dugan's payment in gold—he'd begun to make significant improvements. Maura could see hundreds of cattle grazing on the hillsides, and her heart clenched tightly at the sight of Archie MacLean lifting her wee sister into the special chair he'd constructed for her inside a small wheeled wagon.

Dugan had chosen a big shepherd dog to watch over Rosie, and the diligent canine had taken to his task completely, much to Rosie's delight. Even now, the dog, Davey, was circling 'round and barking at Archie to take care with his fragile mistress.

Rosie laughed with true glee when Archie lifted the handle of the wagon and pulled her down the lane and out of sight with Davey running alongside them. Maura did not think Rosie's life had ever been quite so full.

Nor had her own.

"What are you doing up here, love?" Dugan asked. Maura turned and smiled at him as he came to her and took her into his arms. "'Tis a fine day full of glorious sunshine and we should be outside in it. Let the servants do this work."

He was warm and sweaty from his exertions on the practice fields. Though he was now the wealthiest of highland lairds, he would never take his clan's safety or security for granted. Maura knew he had witnessed with his own eyes exactly how easy it was to lose everything.

But he was a generous man. He'd enriched his entire clan with his treasure, and was doing all that he could to enhance the grazing land and the arable acres.

"I'll come out," Maura replied, "just as soon as I finish sweeping out this room. I've chosen it—"

"Why must it be you who does the cleaning? Hmm?" He pulled the cloth from her head, letting her hair fall free. He slid his fingers through it, causing delightful shivers to skitter down her back.

"Because this room is special, my dear laird."

"'Tis just a bedchamber." He bent to kiss her. "Have I told you today how very much I love you?"

Maura smiled through the kiss and pulled his plaid from his shoulder. She began to untie the laces of his shirt. "Yes, but that was hours ago.

'Tis always a pleasure to hear the words from my much-loved husband."

"Ah, Maura lass, you are my life." He nipped a few light kisses on her ear and down her throat. " 'Tis complete only because of you."

" 'Tis about to become even a bit more complete, Dugan."

"Aye?" His kisses did not stop as he lifted her into his arms and carried her away to their bed-chamber.

"*Ach, aye,*" she said, imitating his highland brogue, "when our firstborn joins us come the winter."

Dugan stopped walking and gazed down at her. His throat moved as he swallowed thickly. "Our firstborn?"

Maura nodded. "In February, according to our midwife."

Dugan grinned. "You've made me the happiest man alive, my sweet Maura."

He kicked the door shut behind him, and Laird MacMillan and his lady wife did not make it out of doors to enjoy the glorious sunshine until much later. They were far too busy enjoying each other.

Author's Note

The Earl of Aucharnie is a fictional character, and so is his relationship—and Maura's—to Major Robert Duncanson and Captain Robert Campbell.

However, a terrible massacre actually did take place at Glencoe, Scotland, on the morning of February 13, 1692, on the orders of a Major Robert Duncanson, who wrote that the royalist soldiers were to "put all to the sword under seventy." It was called murder under trust because the soldiers had been fed and sheltered by the clan in their own small homes for about two weeks prior to the incident.

Scottish history books and the Internet are full of information and details about the events that took place at Glencoe in February 1692. My source was primarily a book called *Glencoe*, by John Prebble, first published in 1966, with many reprints.

The gold that is rumored to be hidden somewhere in the highlands did not actually come to Scotland from France until after 1746. The gold was supposed to have assisted Prince Charlie in his escape from Scotland after the battle of Culloden, but its location is still unknown.

If you happen to visit Scotland, don't try to find

Aveboyne, Loch Camerochlan, Braemore, or Loch Monar, because they are all locations that sprang from my imagination as I was writing this tale. But if you do find the French gold, well, let's just say I would be very interested in talking to you!

Don't miss any of the sensual, sexy, delectable
novels in the world of
New York Times bestselling author

STEPHANIE LAURENS

Captain Jack's Woman
978-0-380-79455-3

Don't miss the story that informed and inspired
the Bastion Club novels.

The Lady Chosen
978-0-06-000206-0

Tristan Wemyss, Earl of Trentham, never expected he'd
need to wed within a year or forfeit his inheritance.

A Gentleman's Honor
978-0-06-000207-7

Anthony Blake, Viscount Torrington, is a target
for every matchmaking mama in London.

A Lady of His Own
978-0-06-059330-8

Charles St. Austell returns home to claim his title as earl
and to settle quickly on a suitable wife.

A Fine Passion
978-0-06-059331-5

Lady Clarice Altwood is the antithesis of the wooly-
headed young ladies Jack, Baron Warnefleet, has
rejected as not for him.

At Avon Books, we know your passion for romance—once you finish one of our novels, you find yourself wanting more.

May we tempt you with . . .

- **Excerpts** from our upcoming releases.

- Entertaining **extras**, including authors' personal photo albums and book lists.

- Behind-the-scenes **scoop** on your favorite characters and series.

- **Sweepstakes** for the chance to win free books, romantic getaways, and other fun prizes.

- Writing **tips** from our authors and editors.

- **Blog** with our authors and find out why they love to write romance.

- **Exclusive content** that's not contained within the pages of our novels.

Join us at
www.avonbooks.com

AVON

An Imprint of HarperCollins*Publishers*
www.avonromance.com

*G*ive in to your Impulses!

These unforgettable stories only take a second to buy and give you hours of reading pleasure!

Go to *www.AvonImpulse.com* and see what we have to offer.

Available wherever e-books are sold.

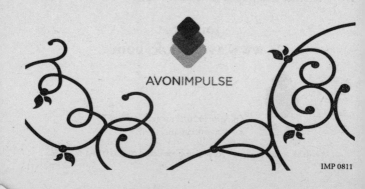

AVONIMPULSE